BLACK WATER

Through the Canvas: Book One

NINIE HAMMON

STERLING & STONE

BLACK WATER

Chapter One

HADN'T TAKEN T.J. Hamilton long to find it in the back of the storage shed, wrapped in a tattered rag quilt the mice had gotten into and eaten big hunks out of. He had kept up with it for more than half a century because … He didn't know why, had never before today questioned why. He'd just kept it, that's all.

Now, he pushed his West Virginia University ball cap back, cocked his head to the right and shook it slowly, staring at what he had just leaned against the wall. It was illuminated by the light streaming through the phlegm of dirt on the garage door windows, and the bright orange sunset splattered across grumbling storm clouds granted it an eerie, rosy glow — not that it needed an otherworldly shine to make it creepy. It was plenty spooky enough all by itself.

A sense of unreality washed over T.J. and he felt more confused, more *dumbfounded* than he'd ever been in all his — what? Going-on-seventy years? Sixty-nine, no, sixty-eight. He always had to concentrate to recall how old he was because age was such a meaningless number he'd never bothered to keep track of. The suggestion of a smile pulled at the corners of his lips. Shoot, he probably looked like his grandmother'd looked when she used to come visitin' from Nashville when he was a little boy, in *Before.*

T.J.'s childhood was split in two like an axe stroke right down the middle, with before Mama fell and hit her head lined up on one side and everything that come after on the other.

Last time he'd seen his granny, her ebony skin'd been wrinkled up like a raisin, but she'd been all plump and round and T.J. couldn't have managed 145 pounds if he took three runnin' jumps at the scales. At six feet tall, that was *skinny.* In the last few years, his belt had got where it wouldn't keep his pants up, and he wasn't gonna wear 'em halfway down his butt with his underwear showin'! So he'd bought himself a pair of suspenders, bright red ones. He had a habit of hooking his thumbs in them when he was considerin', trying to figure something out. He had his thumbs hooked in his suspenders now, but wasn't nothing to figure out here. It was what it was.

And what it was was a painting. Looking at it here, seein' it unwrapped for the first time since Mama'd hid it in the chicken house two days before she knotted an extension cord around her neck and hung herself from a barn rafter, turned his knees to bags of water. It stole his breath, the reality of it leapin' out at him as crisp and clear as it'd been when the paint was still wet almost six decades ago. And he felt terror crawling on hairy black legs up the back of his throat like he hadn't felt since them days, wakin' up every morning in After.

Oh, he'd known fear in all the many years since then, been scared lots of times. Didn't seem like he'd had more'n half a dozen solid bowel movements the whole time he was in Vietnam. But that was life scared. It was real. Natural. Not like this. Wasn't nothing natural 'bout this and maybe wasn't nothing real about it neither. Maybe he was just imaginin', maybe—

The back porch steps creaked and then the screen door

squawked, but T.J. didn't go back into the kitchen right away. He couldn't drag his eyes away from the painting. It couldn't be. Could. *NOT.* Be. But it was, and he couldn't stop staring at it. Which was the point, of course. That right there told him everything he needed to know.

Dobbs had poured himself a cup of coffee and was sittin' at the kitchen table when T.J. came in from the garage. He had the reel off his fishing pole laid out in front of him, must have been tryin' yet again to fix it so the line wouldn't jam. Dobbs cocked his head to the right and then shook it the same way T.J. had shook his a few minutes earlier, staring at the impossible painting in the garage. Yeah, they'd taken up each other's mannerisms after all these years. But that was the only way the two of them looked alike. Raymond Dobson was a barrel-chested man, had two or three chins marching down his neck into the t-shirt he wore beneath overalls that bulged out around his belly. T.J.'s wooly hair, the pale gray of a winter sky right before it snows, was cropped short. Dobbs's shock of white hair was as unruly now as it'd been sixty years ago when it was pale blond and his mother'd tried to stick it down with Vitalis. After he'd told her one day he wished he was black like T.J. so his hair'd be kinky and stay put, she'd washed his mouth out with soap, and after that he and T.J.'d had to sneak off into the woods to play together.

"Somebody moved into the Watford House," T.J. said and immediately wanted to bite off the end of his tongue. What'd he say a thing like that for? The words had popped out and he wasn't ready to talk about it, hadn't got his own head around it yet.

"Who?"

Dobbs didn't look up, was only half listening. He lifted his coffee cup and took a drink, his mind focused on the gnarl of fishing line stuck inside that reel.

"Not nobody local, not nobody I ever seen before." But he had seen her before. That was the thing, wasn't it. The whole thing. He *had* seen her before. "A moving truck, one of them with the little-kid drawing on the side that says 'Two Guys and a Truck' was parked out front a week ago Tuesday, but all I seen was four guys who didn't look nothin' like that drawing hauling furniture into the house. So I been watchin', trying to catch sight of the new tenant."

He was stalling.

"I seen her for the first time two days ago, carrying empty boxes out onto the porch." He paused, tried to throw the next words away. "She looked … kinda familiar, though, but I couldn't place her."

Dobbs stopped what he was doing and made a big show of looking out the window and up at the sky.

"I don't see anything yet." In mock seriousness, he searched a stormy sky darkening toward evening. "But it'll start raining frogs any minute now." He glanced at T.J., a grin deepening the creases in the folds of his big cheeks. "You not remembering a face, that's one of the final signs of the Second Coming."

Then he went back to work on the reel, not looking at T.J.

"Oh, I finally did figure out where I seen her before."

"Where was that?"

There it was then. Beyond that question lay two different worlds. In one of them, T.J. could go on with life like it'd been all these years, could take that canvas out of the garage into the backyard, pour gasoline on it and burn it, like he'd seen his mama do with canvases time and time again. Or throw it into the lake. He still had time. He could—

"Remember when we was kids—"

Dobbs pinched his finger in the mechanism and dropped the reel on the table in disgust.

"I remember we could go fishing without having to spend all day untangling the danged line! Those cane poles and plastic corks, they worked fine. Why'd I ever let you talk me into buying this thing?"

He picked the reel back up and began to pull on the line again.

"Remember…" T.J. took a deep breath. "Remember how Mama … used to paint."

Dobbs froze in place as still as a tombstone.

They hadn't never talked about it. Never mentioned it, not one time in all the years they'd known each other. When it was over, when that time was done, they acted like it had never happened, and both of them honored an unspoken agreement never to speak of it.

"Yeah." His voice sounded airless and haunted. "Of course, I remember. Why would you ask me a question like that?"

"It's just that … well, the woman at the Watford place, she was on the porch … *painting.*"

"Painting what?"

"What do you think?" T.J. snapped. "The porch railing? Her toenails? A hippopotamus sittin' in a mud hole in the middle of the front yard?"

T.J. spun away from Dobbs, went to the cabinet, got a mug from it and set it down on the counter in front of the coffee pot. "She was paintin' a picture, that's what."

"What kind of picture?"

T.J. reached for the pot, then stopped, afraid that if he tried to pour a cup, his hands would shake.

"No, it ain't that."

"She was painting a table with a fruit bowl or flowers on it, and behind the table there was a window." Awe and wonder and more than that colored Dobbs's words. "There was, wasn't there?"

"No, I'm just sayin' she was painting was why I noticed her." That wasn't why, though. He'd have noticed her if she'd been on the porch plantin' daisies. But he'd got Dobbs started and the big man was rolling downhill, gaining speed the farther he went.

"But there was nothing in the window. It was blank. Not blank as in nothing special — you could see out of it and there was a yard or a tree or a pond — but blank as in empty, no image at all?"

Oh, how T.J. wished he hadn't said nothing. How he wished he'd minded his own business and then he wouldn't have had to try to keep his mouth shut about it to Dobbs.

Dobbs wouldn't let it go, of course.

"T.J., you think what she was painting is…?" Dobbs stopped, like he'd just realized how preposterous such a suggestion was. "After all these…? That was … what? Forty-five years ago? No, fifty. Sixty! She was painting—?"

"I never said that!"

T.J. hadn't meant to shout, but the words exploded out of him. When he spoke again, it was so soft he had trouble hearing it his own self. "Her paintin', that put me in mind of … that's all. This ain't about what she was painting, about the picture."

"Then what is it about?"

T.J. let out a breath of surrender. He was in too deep now, wasn't no way out but to tell Dobbs the whole story. And who did he think he was foolin' anyway? He was always gonna tell Dobbs all about it.

If T.J.'d done what he'd ought to have done — walked on by, payin' that woman no mind — he wouldn't have had to go diggin' around in the dust of that shed looking for what he hadn't laid eyes on in more than half a century. But he hadn't done that. When he'd seen the woman on the porch with her easel all set up, a pallet in her hand — well, that sight alone … he never seen somebody paintin' a picture that it didn't make his heart stutter a couple of beats. It was her *face* that'd stopped him, though. T.J.'s memory for faces was legendary. The two previous times he'd seen her, she'd looked familiar, but he'd let it go. This time, though, she was standing still, concentrating, and he'd got a good look. When he did, he instantly acknowledged two contradictory certainties. He had never met the woman standing on that porch. And he *knew* her.

He had to get a closer look at her, so he leaned over and unhooked the leash from Sparky's collar.

"Go make a new friend," he said quietly, and Sparky took off. He was the most social little mutt in all of Kavanaugh County. Soon's he seen somebody on the sidewalk coming toward him he'd start tuggin' at the leash, wantin' to get closer so he could jump up and down and they'd make over him like they hadn't never in their lives seen an animal adorable as he was.

The little dog scampered across the grass that needed mowing and up the porch steps. And, of course, she done what everybody else always done soon's they seen Sparky.

"Ooooh!" Women all made that same squeaky sound. "That's the cutest little dog!"

And Sparky was cute, alright! Not one doubt about that. He looked like a stuffed animal, fur two inches deep that was so soft and fluffy it didn't even feel real. Apricot colored, that's what the breeder'd called it. His ears was red, though, Irish Setter red. His face was lighter and he had a white patch of fur on his chest right where he'd have had an S if he'd been Superman. All four of his feet was white, too, like he was wearing booties. And danged if it didn't look all the time like he was *smiling*, that Golden Retriever smile that melted the hearts of anybody, anywhere, any age, who'd ever in their lives let themselves fall in love with a dog.

The woman's face had lit up soon as Sparks got near her. T.J. followed along behind and the world got less and less stable under his feet the closer he got. Her hair was striking, long black curls with such a lustrous shine that movement sent silvery highlights sparkling across the surface. Even in the bright sunlight, her hair had the shimmering quality of moonlight on a midnight sky. Her eyes were hazel, multicolored dark green like the surface of a still pond reflecting the trees and grass on the shore. Even thin as she was — not skinny, boney like he was but on her way there — you could tell she'd round out nicely once she got some meat on her bones. Her face was pretty, not what you'd call strikingly beautiful. But probably wouldn't take much woman's magic with makeup and such to turn her into a show-stopper.

She set the pallet on a little tray thing on the side of the easel and got down on her knees in front of Sparky.

Of course, Sparky was all over her, licking her hands and her face, any piece of bare skin he could find, wiggling and squirming in delight, his tail wagging so fast you couldn't hardly see nothing but a blur.

The woman looked up at T.J. and he noted the dark circles under them green eyes, the hollow cheeks, pale skin, looked like a junkie 'cept wasn't no track marks on her arms. Sick, maybe. No, she wasn't sick. That wasn't it. This here was a woman life had kicked square in the gut and she hadn't yet managed to suck in another lungful of air.

"What kind of dog is he?"

"A golden doodle, half poodle, half golden retriever. Only he's a mini, weighs twenty pounds. It looks like forty 'cause his fur's so thick, but he won't get no bigger."

"What's his name?"

She was rubbing Sparky in that special spot right behind his ears, and his eyes liked to roll back into his head from pleasure. This was somebody who knew her way around a dog.

"Sparky the Wonder Dog." He was poised to answer the inevitable question. How he and Dobbs had gone to pick out a female, but this little guy'd followed T.J. around like he was on one end of an invisible string and the dog was on the other. So T.J.'d figured the dog had picked *him*. The thing was, though, all the dog names he was considerin' was girls' names, so Dobbs had joked…

She didn't ask, though. She merely buried her face in the

soft fur on the top of his head and made little cooing sounds that almost sounded like she was crying.

T.J. held out his hand. "My name's Thomas Jefferson Alexander Hamilton."

Then he started his rap, the one he used whenever he met anybody new. It rolled out effortless and smooth after decades of practice and it usually put folks at ease. "Now what kind of mama names a cute chocolate-drop newborn Thomas Jefferson Alexander Hamilton, dooming the poor little thing to a lifetime of funny looks and not enough space to sign the back of his driver's license?" A one-beat pause. "They call me T.J."

"Nice to meet you, T.J." She reached up and shook his hand and that's when it happened. She tossed her long hair to the side for an instant and there it was. On her neck, under her right ear. Three small moles arranged in a perfect triangle. T.J. never expected to see that again, on anybody. But it was real, wasn't no denying it. She kept talking, rubbing on Sparky, introducing her own self, but T.J. didn't hear what she said clearly, couldn't because of the buzzin' in his head like lunatic chainsaws. His heart stopped beating, went dead as an anvil, then it started up again frantic as a woodpecker trying to peck its way out of his chest. If he'd been a white man, he'd have turned the color of a new gym sock. Black as he was, though, his face likely resembled ashes in ice.

The woman happened to glance up from Sparky then.

"Is something wrong?"

Shoot, maybe he did look like a gym sock.

"Oh, no, I'm … ain't nothing wrong. I…" His voice had the breathless quality of a man who'd just watched a water moccasin glide out of the shoreline reeds right where he was about to put his foot. Scrambling for something — anything — to say, he blurted out, "That painting … my mama was an artist." He could hear himself babbling but couldn't seem to stem the tide. "Mama had paint splatters on her all the time looked like M&Ms."

The woman got to her feet as he kept yapping. Sparky was not at all done with her attention, though, so he stood on his hind legs, put his front paws on her leg and gave her his pitiful look, and she melted in a puddle like everybody always done, leaned over and went back to petting him. Gave T.J. a chance to grab hold of himself and shut his mouth. When she looked at him again, he managed to sound mostly sane and reasonable.

"My mama's pictures was…" Little kids with big eyes and big ears and toothless grins. Innocent. Harmless. That's how it had started, anyway, how it had been in Before. He pointed to the still-wet painting. "What is *that?*"

"It's a kidney." She eyed the shapes on the canvas that resembled the inside of a fish when you gutted it. "Actually, it's a kidney with a tumor." She pointed to a blob in the upper right corner. "Cancer. I'm an illustrator for medical textbooks."

A shattering crash of thunder roared so suddenly Sparky jumped and yelped. The woman looked out beyond T.J. at sky that had turned dark and threatening without either of them noticing. A gust of cold, rain-smelling air sent the empty soft drink can by her foot scurrying noisily across the porch and she began to gather up her art supplies.

"You'd better get Sparky home before he gets soaked."

She leaned over and patted the top of his head.

"Goodbye, cute little dog." Finality rang in those words with the solemnity of funeral bells.

When T.J. finished telling the story to Dobbs, the other man sat very still, staring down at the table for what seemed like a long time but wasn't likely more'n a minute. Then he lifted his eyes and T.J. looked into the familiar faded-denim blue, waiting.

"So if it wasn't what she was painting, what was it about

that woman that put you in mind of your mama? What's the rest of it?"

"You don't want to know."

"No, I expect I don't. But tell me anyway."

"I'll show you."

Dobbs got slowly to his feet and the two men stood together silent. Theirs wasn't regular silence, though. It was the silence of men who knew each other so well wasn't no need to mess up communication with talk.

Dobbs finally spoke.

"It's starting again, isn't it, T.J.?"

T.J. didn't say nothing.

They filed without speaking into the garage. It had gotten dark and the storm that'd been threatening when T.J. left the Watford House had finally struck. The streetlight on the pole at the corner of the block shone through the windows with a rain-shrouded glow. Thunder cracked loud and a bright strobe of lightening torched the night sky and burned the details of the garage interior into their retinas. When the flash was gone, there was still plenty of light to see the painting leaned up against the far wall. To see the small table and bowl of fruit at the bottom of the canvas in front of the totally out-of-proportion window that completely filled the rest of the frame.

To see the face in the window.

Dobbs took an involuntary step back from it once he got a good look.

It was a woman's face, a white woman, lying on her back. Her hollow eyes were closed but the rain squirming in silver worms down the garage windowpanes made it look like she was crying. Her lips seemed purple against her pale skin. Blood streamed from the gory bullet wound in her right temple.

"I didn't know you had one," Dobbs said, awe in his quiet voice. "I thought your mama burned them as soon as…"

"It's the only one left." T.J. couldn't seem to breathe in

enough air to form more than a handful of words at a time. "She painted it a couple of days before she died."

The image of his mother when he found her, dangling lifeless from a barn rafter, flashed brighter than the lightning and was gone.

"What's this painting got to do with the woman you met this afternoon?" Dobbs knew. T.J. could tell by the way he asked the question that he knew.

T.J. looked with wonder and fear and other emotions that didn't have no names at the face in the painting, at the perfect triangle of moles beneath the woman's right ear.

"It's *her.* Not no doubt about it. This is a portrait of the woman who's renting the Watford House. Said her name was Jessie Cunningham."

Chapter Two

She'd told him her *real name,* just blurted out, *"Jessie Cunningham."* That old man with the adorable dog, she'd told him who she was!

Jessie stood for a moment in the doorway of the room downstairs that she had turned into an art studio. She'd had lots of rooms to pick from in this huge house. They really ought to check out the suitability of the places where they parked her before she showed up with her suitcase and furniture. But they didn't, of course. That first place, the one in Albuquerque, had been a duplex. She supposed this house demonstrated that she'd moved up in the world since then.

She carried her paints to the shelves that some carpenter years ago had painstakingly set into the walls on both sides of the room. In a house like this one, the room had obviously been *the library.* One set of shelves framed the big window that looked north. Good light for painting, north light. It was a shame, really, that the first time she'd had good light and a place to spread out her art supplies, she wouldn't be using it.

She was more surprised really than alarmed by her slip of the tongue earlier. Or was it a slip of the tongue? Was it something more profound, some need to connect on a deeper level as *who she really was* with another human being? Now. At the end.

Naaaaaw, there was nothing deep about it. She'd just been distracted and let her name slip, that was all. She hadn't practiced the new name enough yet. Bailey Donahue.

That's why she'd insisted on Bailey as her "permanent" first name after that time in Omaha when the bank clerk called out Connie Bradshaw and she'd sat there like a bump on a pickle. The woman had noticed and it had been *awk-ward* even after Jessie hauled out the excuse that she'd just gotten married.

It was too hard to answer to a new first name, too hard to make it automatic. All the different last names were hard enough and she hadn't managed to get either one of them right this afternoon.

The name with which she had begun life was Jessica Nicole Bailey. When she was in high school, she'd played sports. If there was a ball bouncing somewhere, Jessie was catching it, hitting it or spiking it. The name on the back of her basketball/softball/volleyball jerseys was, of course, Bailey. And the cool kids called each other by those uniform names — "Hey, Bailey, we got algebra homework tonight?" You know, to put the peons in the stands in their places, impress upon them the pecking order, with jocks at the top and everybody else an also-ran.

Since she'd answered to the first name 'Bailey' for four years, she could remember it now. It wasn't as totally foreign as Connie or Amanda or … what was the one in Peoria? Alexis. Seriously? Who could remember to answer to a name like *Alexis?*

Though her parents had never been married, never as far as Jessie could determine, or spent more than that one night together, her mother'd changed her last name, taken her father's. No, not father. What did the kids call it now?

Sperm donor? No, that term was way out of vogue, too. It had enjoyed a brief time in the sun back when there was some sense of outrage still that shiftless do-nothings went around fathering children to see who could collect the most notches in his masculinity belt. There was no sense of outrage now, though, no moral implications of any kind. That was just the way it was. Men got you knocked up and bailed, might even get two or three girls knocked up at the same time. Now they called that particular strata of low-life "Baby Daddies."

The world had not yet turned completely wrong side out when her mother was young, though, and as soon as she discovered she was pregnant, Nora Monroe became Nora Bailey. That was the name she'd printed proudly on the birth certificate — Jessica Nicole *Bailey* — for the little girl Nora made a stab at mothering before she threw up her hands in defeat and let the state place the two-year-old in foster care, in "a good home."

Right. Copy that. A good home.

The animal shelters that would only release strays to "a good home" likely did a better job of enforcing that requirement than Child Protective Services had done for her. Rescue puppies had a better shot at growing up in a loving family environment than she'd been given.

She thought of the old man's dog. Such an adorable dog.

She stopped breathing for a moment.

Maybe Bethany had a dog.

Maybe.

Jessie tried to picture her as a little girl with a dog, with the dog she'd seen today, the cute, friendly little thing, Sparky the Wonder Dog, whose fur was so soft he felt like a stuffed toy. She could picture the dog with a child, but it was a generic child, could have been anybody. She couldn't picture Bethany as a little girl with a dog because the child was frozen in her memory as a toddler, only barely able to walk more than a

15

couple of steps without falling on her backside. Now Bethany was about to turn three.

Jessie had missed her second birthday. *But she wouldn't miss her third.*

She'd been there for the first one, though. She and Aaron had both been there.

A BABY in a highchair sits banging a spoon on the metal tray.

Whap. Whap. Whap.

"Can we let her blow out the candle?" Jessie asks, holding the small chocolate cake with a lone candle burning in the center.

"What if she reaches for the flame?"

Aaron is always practical. Always protective.

"Right. We can sing her the song and blow it out for her."

Aaron takes up the refrain in a deep baritone. "Happy Birthday to you. Happy birthday to you."

The baby in the highchair bangs the spoon happily on the metal tray as an accompaniment to the words.

"Happy birthday deeeeeearrr Beth-a-ny." Then they try to harmonize the last "happy birthday to you." But their harmony is way off, he is flat and she is sharp and it sounds awful.

Bethany doesn't mind a bit.

Aaron blows on a little horn with streamers and Jessie puffs air into the paper roll-out thing that extends toward Bethany's nose. She grabs for it but it retracts before she can catch it.

"Make a wish, honey," Aaron says to the little girl.

Whap. Whap. Whap,

"Make a wish for her," Jessie says.

Looking at him now, his brown hair in eyes that are the color of robins' eggs, Jessie thinks Aaron has never looked more handsome, and she feels that thing in the bottom of her belly. That little fluttering. She wonders if she will always feel that when she looks at Aaron.

"Okay, I wish ... I wish to become her official candle-blower-outer, whose job it will be to blow out the candles on every one of her birthday

16

cakes until she gets married, which she never will because I don't intend to let her date."

He sucks in a big breath of air, puffing out his cheeks, then blows, snuffing the candle flame, sending up a little trail of black smoke in its dying breath.

Aaron quickly pulls the candle out of the circle of candy that kept it in place in the center of the cake so Bethany can't grab the hot wax on the top of it. Then he takes the cake from Jessie and places it in the center of the metal tray on the highchair. At first Bethany just looks at it. Then she drops the spoon she'd been banging on the tray and reaches out a tiny index finger and touches the icing. When she returns the finger to her mouth, her little eyebrows shoot up in delight, and Jessie and Aaron both laugh.

They laugh even harder when she reaches out with both hands and grabs handfuls of the icing and cake, shoving them into her mouth, smearing the chocolate icing all over her face.

Aaron grabs his phone and begins filming her as she destroys the cake and slathers her face with icing.

Watching her, watching Aaron move around to get different angles of the carnage, Jessie is willing to admit that this is not likely a unique event as first birthdays go, that hundreds of thousands of toddlers buried their hands up to the elbows in their cakes every day, likely had to be hosed down to get them clean. But at the same time, she is certain that no child has ever looked more adorable with chocolate cake in her hair than Bethany. And no father has ever looked more smitten than Aaron. The little girl had had her daddy twisted around her little finger since the nurse handed her to him in the delivery room and she wound her little fingers around his. What's he going to be like when she turns sixteen?

The thought of Bethany at sixteen, looking like a female version of Aaron, fills her head and her eyes suddenly well with tears.

"She's growing up so fast," she says.

Aaron sets his phone down and puts his arm around her shoulders and the two of them stand an adoring audience to the disemboweling of a chocolate cake.

"I wish I could keep her just like she is forever," Jessie says.

IN A BLACK-HUMOR, cruel-joke kind of way, Jessie got her wish. Though Bethany had grown, had changed, had become a little girl instead of a toddler, she was frozen in Jessie's memory at fifteen months old, holding out her arms to Jessie, crying when Aaron handed her to Jessie's sister, María. Jessie had not seen the child since.

And Bethany was about to turn three. Three years old. Jessie was sure there'd be a party. Aaron's family would make over her, shower her with presents. And they'd let her blow out the three candles on her birthday cake. Aaron had wished that *he* would always be there to blow out Bethany's birthday candles. *His* wish had not been granted.

Well, Jessie wasn't going to miss her birthday. Not again. She would never again miss Bethany's birthday. She realized then that her cheeks were wet, though she knew she hadn't cried. Couldn't possibly have cried. She was cried out, had poured out every single tear in her whole body and now she was as dry as chalk dust.

She stepped over to the counter, pulled open the drawer and picked up the Smith & Wesson revolver. It looked smaller than it had when she'd purchased it in Hendersonville. But it was big enough to do the job. Had it felt cold that day in the store? She couldn't remember. But it felt cold now as she passed it back and forth from one hand to the other.

It felt as cold as death.

"WHAT ARE you going to do about it?" Dobbs asked.

The words seemed overloud in the empty garage, almost like they was echoing off the walls, repeating. But the echoing was only going on inside T.J.'s head.

"I don't know. I ain't decided yet."

"Not making a decision *is* a decision."

The wind slapped the branches of the sycamore tree against the side of the garage. There was a crack of thunder so loud and close it sounded like lightning had struck something right out in the front yard. Sparky whimpered and T.J. could feel the warmth of him cowering against his leg.

"It's alright, Sparks. Ain't no loud noise gonna hurt you."

The dog had been scared of storms ever since he was a pup, but T.J. resisted the urge to reach down and pick him up and coddle him. That'd just make it worse. And besides, there was scary things in life for a fact. And even dogs had to figure out how to go on living in spite of 'em.

Another clap of thunder rumbled in the sky and though T.J. didn't see the lightning strike that made it, the streetlight went out, plunging the garage into darkness.

T.J. was glad of the sudden veil of darkness that hid his face from Dobbs. But then, Dobbs didn't need to read his face to know what he was thinking.

He fumbled around in the dark on the work bench until his hand fell on the flashlight. He slipped the switch and a bilious, dim ray of light stuck out like a half power lightsaber into the darkness. Of course, you never thought to change the batteries in a flashlight until you needed it. He shook it once and the light was brighter. He turned and shined the beam on the face of the dead woman in the painting.

"All these years, you never said anything about having one of your mama's paintings." He could hear the awe in Dobbs's voice. "Why'd you keep it?"

"I dunno." But he *did* know. His mama'd painted it two days before she killed herself. It'd been the last one. He hadn't thought about it in close to half a century. Everything about that time was scorched around the edges. Any time he thought about After, his mind filled with the image of her dangling limp, her head twisted to the side at an unnatural angle, and his whole being pulled back from that sight like his soul had touched a hot stove. Jerking away was involuntary. "This is all I had. She burned all the others."

His mother painted — *was compelled to paint* — images she didn't understand. People she didn't know. Places she hadn't never seen in an entire lifetime spent in one little hollow in the West Virginia mountains. After that first time, she hid them paintings, the ones she created with the paintbrushes flyin' over the canvas and her head thrown back, her eyes closed. But often, he found her collapsed on the floor in front of an easel that held a canvas with the paint still wet on some awful scene, dead bodies, mangled corpses. He'd describe them to a wide-eyed Dobbs as they sat with their feet danglin' in the creek down from Dobbs's house.

He'd told Dobbs about a severed-hand painting and Dobbs had come runnin' breathless to their secret place in the woods the next day, babblin' the story he'd heard his father tell about how Ulysses Everett had got his hand chopped off helping Henry Tucker cut wood. Most of the paintings only haunted his mother, though. For days after she painted 'em, she was … strange. She'd cock her head the way you do when you hear something, only wasn't no noise he could hear. Or her nose'd wrinkle up like she smelled something foul. Then, in a few days, maybe a week after she painted it, she'd take the painting out to the backyard and burn it soon's Pa left that morning for the mill. She had to burn 'em, of course. If Pa knew she'd been paintin' 'em … but he didn't have no idea what was going on in his home with his wife and three sons, was falling-down drunk every night after work soon as he got to the bottle of cheap whiskey or moonshine he kept in the cabinet.

T.J. spoke into the darkness, words tacked onto the thought that had been chasing around in his mind ever since he seen the woman on the porch of the Watford House that afternoon.

"*Can* I do anything about it?" He was surprised at how

ragged his voice sounded. "You and me done had this conversation once, you remember?"

Dobbs stopped breathing. "I remember." His voice sounded near as ragged as T.J.'s. Then it dropped to a whisper. "I was scared spitless."

Chapter Three

RAYMOND DOBSON WAS SCARED NOW, too, though the ragged edges of his fear didn't cut deep, swathed as it still was in a generous slathering of denial. Even so, grown-man scared was worse than little-kid scared and little-kid scared had been bad enough.

DOBBS LOOKS up anxiously at the break in the trees. T.J. is late and Dobbs can't stay long. When he left the house, his mama'd called after him, "Don't you be late for supper again, Ray-Ray." He hates it when his mama calls him Ray-Ray even worse than he hates it when the other kids call him Ray-mun. When he grows up, he's gonna be Dobbs, the name T.J. gave him. Just Dobbs.

He hears a scuffle on the rocks and T.J. appears out of the woods. One look at his face and Dobbs knows they're not going to go to the pond and skip rocks across the water, or strip down naked and use the grapevine to swing out and drop. They're not going to do anything fun. Not after whatever has happened to T.J.; Dobbs has seen that look before.

"What's wrong?" But he knows the answer before he asks the question. Ever since T.J.'s mama fell off that ladder and hit her head, T.J.

has worn that scared, confused look almost all the time. Dobbs would have done just about anything to make it go away.

"You … best come see." T.J. turns around and slips back through the trees. Dobbs doesn't want to go with him. Oh, how he doesn't want to go! T.J. has shown him what his mama paints in the shed out back of their house, paints there even in the dark sometimes … with both hands, at least, that's what T.J. says and there's no reason not to believe him. T.J. never lies. Still … with both hands?

But he goes along because he can't not go. T.J. Hamilton is the best friend he has ever had, the only real one. The kids his mama makes him play with because their mamas go to church with her, or the ones in Charleston, when they drag him there to see the fancy school his older brother attends, the one they're packing him off to for high school. They're all white, but they're only pretending to be his friend. When the grownups aren't around, they tease him, call him fat and stupid. Even with the grownups in the room, they call him PDB. If one of the adults asks what the letters stand for, the kids reply innocently that they don't stand for anything, just letters put together that rhyme and sound funny, that's all. But what PDB stands for is Pillsbury Dough Boy.

T.J. has never been like that. What Dobbs knows that his mother and father would never believe is that T.J. is a finer human being than any of the white people he has ever known. T.J. is kind and … and good. And brave. Very brave. Everybody knows what T.J.'s father does to his mama, they've seen her, what he does to T.J. too, sometimes, though he always says he fell down or he ran into a door. But T.J. isn't cowed by his father. And — for reasons Dobbs is too young to understand — he even more admires the fact that T.J. isn't eaten up with a rabid desire for revenge, either.

When they come out of the woods behind the shed, T.J. fishes in his pocket for the key to the padlock on the door. His mama tells his daddy that she keeps it locked because all her art supplies are stored in there and they're expensive and she doesn't want anybody to steal them. And the family wouldn't survive without the money she brings in from selling her caricatures to tourists down at the dock. But that's not the real reason she keeps it locked. It's so T.J.'s daddy doesn't see the paintings she produces there.

His mama has taken his little brothers, Luke and Jacob, to Vacation Bible School at Highview Baptist Church in town and T.J. sneaked the key out of the bottom of the quilt box his grandmother gave her that Dobbs thinks looks like a coffin.

T.J. opens the door and there's a painting still on the easel, not yet hidden under the piece of canvas tarp in the chicken house. The paint glistens in the fall of light from the open doorway, so it's still wet. Dobbs has to come all the way into the room so the light isn't glaring on the shiny paint before he can see the image on the canvas.

He blinks when he sees it.

There's a man lying on his back with lumber piled on top of him and … his guts are hanging out, squashed out of him.

Dobbs turns and bolts out of the room, runs across the meadow behind the shed and into the woods. Runs and runs and runs until he is out of breath and has to stop, put his hands on his knees and gasp for air. It's only then that he sees T.J. has come with him.

"I'm sorry, T.J., I just—"

"I know. Me neither. I seen it and I puked up my breakfast."

That's another thing Dobbs loves about T.J. He never pretends he's not weak, never acts like he is tougher than he really is, and doesn't even know that not pretending to be strong is what makes him so.

The two boys collapse, panting, in the soft, fragrant needles beneath a big juniper pine.

"You know where that is." It's a statement, not a question, but Dobbs nods anyway. It's the lumber mill where T.J.'s daddy works.

"Do you know who it is?"

Dobbs shakes his head.

"That's Lloyd Green, Robby's daddy. Did you see the others, in the background?"

Dobbs shakes his head again.

"There was other men, too, got crushed. A stack of lumber must have tipped over on top of them."

The boys sit together in silence.

"Do you think…?" T.J. stops, then starts over. "Should we … tell somebody? Tell Robby, maybe?"

T.J. has never suggested such a thing before. After the picture of the dead white child that Dobbs never saw because T.J.'s father destroyed it, T.J.'s mother has painted other pictures of what T.J. calls "what hasn't happened yet." They were all dead people. But they were strangers, people Dobbs and T.J. didn't know. This time is different.

Dobbs looks at his friend as an unreasoning terror rises up in his chest that so grips him he can't speak. To tell somebody, to get involved in what was going on, to insert themselves into … It was bad enough being a spectator, but if they told and then it happened anyway…?

"We can't." He pauses, then rushes on, "Your daddy would…"

That's just an excuse, though. Dobbs doesn't fear T.J.'s daddy. He's a black man and Dobbs is a white kid. He wouldn't dare. He isn't even afraid for T.J. and his mama and the littles. He should be, but in his own cowardice they're not his primary concern. He, Raymond Dobson, doesn't dare defy this magic. Something … something unthinkable will happen to him if he crosses whatever force it is that is able to see through the canvas into the days stacked up out there on the other side of it. That is able to make things happen there in that future place.

"T.J. … if your mama painted it, it wouldn't do any good to try to change it. You know that. If she painted it … then it is. We can't change what's … supposed to be. It's … destiny." It's a big word he's never used before, but it's the right word. "We can't change destiny."

T.J. WATCHED Dobbs look out into nowhere, seeing nothing, a thousand-yard stare. He spoke without turning back toward T.J.

"We were kids. We were scared. *I* was scared. Just because two little boys decide that there's no changing destiny, that doesn't make it so."

As happened so often, Dobbs had spoken T.J.'s thoughts,

had tacked words onto the question that had been prowling around in T.J.'s mind since the moment he looked at the picture, confirmed for himself what he already knew. This was a painting of Jessie Cunningham ... dead.

"So you're saying you think it's possible to stop it?"

"I'm saying we have to find out."

The streetlight flickered back on briefly and then went out again.

"What am I supposed to do?"

"You're the cop, not me. But it seems pretty obvious to me that—" T.J. knew Dobbs was pointing to the bullet hole painted in excruciating detail in the picture leaned against the wall. "That's a self-inflicted wound. You're not trying to prevent a murder. She shot herself in the head."

"So you want me to go knocking on her door and ... and *what?* Tell her I know she's planning on killing herself? I know because my mama painted a picture of it half a century ago ... but I don't think it's a good idea, maybe she ought to give it more consideration."

The irritation drained out of him when Dobbs didn't answer. "People kill themselves for a reason. They's a lot of roads in that woman's life that led her to this point. When a body has come to the end of themselves, when they don't see no way out short of dying, it likely ain't no easy thing to talk them out of it."

"You've got to try."

"Why? Why do I got to try? I ain't involved in this. I didn't paint no picture of a dead woman. My mama did and she's been dead herself for half a century. I don't see I got no obligation to stick my nose in somebody else's business."

"Yeah, you do, T.J." Dobbs spoke in his reasonable, made-for-radio voice. "Your mama never did anything about the things she painted. All those years, all those paintings. It ate her up. You know as well as I do that's why she hung herself after the fire. Now, you have a chance to change that. Your mama's last painting … don't you think you owe it to her memory to try to stop what she painted on that canvas from becoming reality, a real dead woman? Don't you think you have to *try*?"

T.J. didn't have an answer.

Chapter Four

JESSIE SAT at the kitchen table in the light of a flickering candle, wondering how she had come to this. Oh, not how she had come to be here, ready to end her life, cash in her chips and call game over. She *knew* how she got there!

But how had she come to the gun part?

She'd considered other means, of course. She'd briefly considered hanging herself, but she wasn't up to that. It seemed a little too iffy. What if it didn't work? What if all she did was drop off a chair without breaking her neck, so she dangled there, choking slowly to death? No, not hanging, absolutely not hanging.

Slicing her wrists? Not a chance. That would *hurt!*

How about carbon monoxide? An appealing alternative, perhaps, but this house didn't have a garage. No, it had to be a gun. It was the most fitting choice. It made a statement Jessie wanted to make, expressed an emotion too huge and ugly for a wimpy passing.

She'd wanted music as an accompaniment, too. Though she wasn't a fan of country music, it had seemed fitting. Appropriate. Some crying-in-your-beer song about trains and dogs and unfaithful sweethearts. That was what she wanted to hear when she put the barrel of the revolver to her temple and pulled the trigger. She had searched the radio dial and found the right station. Then the electricity went out and the world filled back up with silence.

A gunshot wound was an ugly, messy way to die. That's why most women opted to summon a reaper dressed in white chiffon and lace, a reaper who soothed you to the other side — not that Jessie believed for an instant there was another side — with pills that allowed you to drift off and never wake up.

Plop, plop, fizz, fizz, oh, what a relief it is.

Peaceful.

Jessica Cunningham wasn't looking for peaceful. She wanted *violence!* She wanted somebody to have to clean her blood and brains off a wall after it'd soaked into the wallpaper so the image of it was always there, forever after, no matter what you did. When she exited the world — no more sunrises or Christmas mornings — there should be some vile sound to mark her passing.

Oh, sure, that was anger talking. Or fear. And she shouldn't be listening to the voices of either anger or fear now, at the end. She should be listening to the voice of the Essential Jessie. And the Essential Jessie, sitting here in the very back row of herself, only wanted it to be over. Just wanted her world to end. And she wanted it to end on her terms. Blood and gore and the roar of a gunshot. Too much in this life was quiet and timid. She had no intention of leaving it with any less a sendoff than a *bang* that made those who heard it uneasy, wondering … an explosive force that would embody all her pent-up emotion, vent all her confined fury, scream out her anguish and defiance to a world that wouldn't hear it. Had never heard it. Couldn't hear it. She would only be crying out in rage at silence, as she had been doing every day for a year and a half. Eighteen months, one week and two days to be exact.

But that was how it had to be. For Bethany to live, to have a normal, happy, *safe* life, Jessie could have no part in it.

Oh, but it'll all be over soon, they'd said. She'd get her life and baby back ... soon. Soon. Soon.

When Jessie got to the end of hoping it would soon end, she'd begun to spiral downward, faster and faster. She could almost hear her descent, the rushing sound of water carrying hope and love and wonder and joy out of the world, rushing with it in a roaring rumble to the open maw of a giant drain where all light ended and all darkness began. Jessie had fallen into that darkness. She didn't know you could *feel* darkness as well as see it. Darkness was cold. Not so cold it burned your touch, but a kind of chill that passed slowly through your skin and organs until it settled in your bones, in the very marrow of your being. And then it began to freeze there.

As that darkness settled into her being, Jessie came to the inescapable conclusion that if she couldn't be a part of Bethany's life, she didn't want to have one of her own.

She looked at the clock on the stove that said 5:15. But that wasn't right. It wasn't 5:15. The clock had stopped when the storm knocked out the electricity. All the clocks in the house were wrong and that seemed fitting somehow, the recording of time in the universe turned off as she prepared to step out of time into infinity.

A mosquito that had been buzzing around her face landed on her forehead above her right eye and she swatted it. Bugs were getting into the house through a hole in the backdoor screen ... but that was not *her* problem. Nothing in this world was her problem anymore.

She picked up the revolver again and looked at it, grateful that cleaning up the mess she'd be leaving behind wasn't her problem, either.

Which begged the essential question, of course ... whose would it be? Who was going to find her body? Who would miss her? She didn't know a soul in Shadow Rock. And not only who would find her body, but *when?* Would she lie here on the floor until…?

Nope, couldn't think about that now. It didn't matter. That was for after and she wasn't going to be here for after.

She looked carefully at the revolver in her hand. It was hard to see the details in the flickering candlelight and she wished she'd paid more attention to what the man in the gun store had said about it after he'd stopped trying to talk her out of buying it.

"Ma'am, the Smith & Wesson Model 63 revolver is useless for self-protection. It's a .22."

When she'd looked blank, he'd continued. "Say somebody comes after you, you could shoot the guy three times before he grabbed the pistol out of your hand and beat you to death with it. Then he'd walk away and die from blood loss two hours later. But you'd still be dead."

Apparently, you had to hit some vital organ with a small pistol. She'd figured the brain was a vital organ.

And all the talk about how to *re*load that Jessie didn't listen to at all because she only needed one pre-shot. Still, she did have to know how to get that lone round in front of the firing pin.

She turned the gun over, examining it. The barrel was short, only about three inches, with a big, hunking sight on the end of it she wouldn't be using. She fit her finger inside the trigger guard and looked at her own hand with the gun in it. It looked like somebody else's hand entirely. She lifted the revolver and put the end of the barrel to her right temple. It felt cold. Then she glanced at her watch. She still had time, a little time. She had gone into labor with Bethany at exactly 8:31 p.m.

She and Aaron had been watching a special showing of *Napoleon Dynamite* on FOX. It was the part where Napoleon and his brother go to the bus station to meet his brother's girlfriend. Jessie's explosion of laughter at the sight of LaShonda stepping off that bus had started it.

At that moment, she'd felt a pang, a tightening around her whole belly, like she was wearing spandex that had suddenly gotten a size smaller. That was the moment when her life with Bethany had begun. Though the actual birth wasn't until six grueling days later, after her labor started and stopped and started again. After they went to the hospital and were sent back home — twice. After she dilated halfway and then stopped. After they gave her Pitocin, which slammed her into active labor — zero to sixty in seconds, followed by ten more agonizing hours. Aaron never left her side, wiped her brow, held her hand, panted through every contraction with her.

Jessie had always in her heart of hearts considered June 19 Bethany's real "birthday," not June 25. She had missed the whole event last year, had sat on the floor in the bathroom of that stupid tri-level condo in Peoria, not daring to move away from the toilet because her grief hurt so bad, was such a dagger in her belly, that she had vomited up everything in her stomach, and then dry-heaved for hour after hour. At some point, she had staggered, *crawled* to the kitchen, and forced down a beer. Then another. After that, it had been drink and vomit. Drink and vomit. June 25, Bethany's actual birthday, had passed by in a blur. And when she had come to on June 26, her skull splitting open from a gigantic fissure in the middle of her forehead, she had actually sighed in relief. She had made it through. She had survived. And *soon...*

Jessie wouldn't go through that again. She was done. She would not miss another of Bethany's birthdays because she would be dead before the third anniversary of the arrival of the bright light, the comet that lit up the whole sky and showered sparkling embers over every day, so brilliant Jessie surely must have wandered a world shrouded by clouds the previous twenty-seven years.

The comet was still lighting the world. But Jessie would no longer watch it streak across the sky. Not after tonight.

She sat very still, even held her breath, waiting. Surely, there'd be some emotion now. She'd cry, sob, scream, wail, throw things. Howl at the moon. *Something!* She was about to *die*, for crying out loud, she ought to feel *something*. She'd expected that here at the end, the final few steps before the abyss, a grand surge of emotion would well up in her chest as tall and powerful as a tsunami about to hit the beach.

She waited.

Nothing.

Then she realized that "nothing" was all the emotion she had left. She had cried herself to sleep every night after … had screamed and … she'd done it all, maxed out all her emotional capital. Broke the bank. Now she had nothing left but a big empty vault with a couple of pennies lying on the floor. She'd spent it all. She was emotionally bankrupt.

Soon.

That word once had promised a reunion with her daughter. Now, the word promised an end to longing for it.

The knock on Jessie's door was so startling she almost pulled the trigger. And she wasn't ready, hadn't quite screwed herself up to the actual thing, the doing of it. Who in the world could possibly be at the door in the middle of the night in a storm? *In the dark?* The electricity was off all up and down the street.

She tried ignoring the knock, but it only became more insistent. After the third *bang, bang, bang,* she gave up, set the gun down on the table and headed to the door. As she did, it occurred to her she ought to be frightened, at least concerned. She didn't know a soul in town. Wasn't likely Avon calling. Or some little girl in a brown uniform hawking thin mints or snickerdoodles.

She heard in her head the voice of one of the parade of foster mothers. "You find out who it is before you open the door, missy. It could be *anybody* on the other side. A serial killer, maybe. An axe murderer."

Jessie stifled a laugh. Parental programming was stickier than gum on your shoe. She was sitting at her kitchen table with a loaded pistol, ready to blow her own brains out, and she ought to make sure there wasn't a killer on her front porch?

She peeked through the curtains on the window in the door and couldn't quite get the image she saw to fit into reality. There was an old man standing on her porch in a black rain slicker carrying a Coleman lantern.

It was *him*, the old guy who had been at the house earlier. The man with the cute dog. When he saw her peek through the curtains, he called out.

"I need to talk to you. Let me in."

She was flabbergasted.

"What do you want?"

"I done said — I want to talk to you. Now, you gonna let an old man who's wet all the way to the bone stand out here on your porch and catch pneumonia?"

"What are you doing here?"

"You gonna let a little wet dog sit out here shivering?"

He pointed down but she couldn't see the dog at his feet.

"Tell her you want to come in out of the rain, Sparky," he said to the dog.

The dog barked.

Seriously? This was nuts.

"Go away. Whatever it is you want can wait. Come back tomorrow."

"I ain't going nowhere, and if I's to wait to come back tomorrow, wouldn't do neither one of us no good. It'd be too late."

What did he mean by that?

"Now let me in. You think I'd come traipsing out here in

the rain with my dog if what I wanted to tell you wasn't," he paused for a beat, "a matter of life and death?"

The way he said that, in a kind of knowing way, sent chills down her spine.

He couldn't possibly know…

"I promise I won't take five minutes of your time. You got something to do that's so important you ain't got a spare five minutes for an old man and a wet dog?"

Fine. Let him in. That was probably the only way to get rid of him.

She released the deadbolt, stepped back from the door and pulled it open. The old man opened the screen door in a protesting squeal and the dog hopped into the house like he lived here. He jumped up and put his wet paws on her leg, his tail a wagging blur, begging for attention. He was wearing a hooded yellow raincoat snapped under his belly that appeared to have kept him reasonably dry. She leaned over, pushed the hood back and patted his head, marveling at how he looked like he was smiling. The dog was an irresistibly adorable little animal and that was obviously the point. Clearly, the old man got a lot of mileage out of how cute he was.

Stepping inside behind the dog, the man stood dripping water off the slicker onto the puddles on the hardwood floor. What had he said his name was? Something long and odd and historical. Signers of the Constitution or something like that. But he went by initials. T.J., that was it.

T.J. set the lantern down on the coffee table and turned the knob on it, sending out bright yellow light to chase shadows into the corners. Jessie had time to think that she must look like an under-a-bridge derelict, hadn't combed her hair all day, when it occurred to her that it didn't matter. She was going to look a whole lot worse after she blew the brains under the hair out onto the wall.

The man reached down, unsnapped the dog's raincoat and slipped it over his head. The dog did one of those full-body shakes that sent splatters of water from his legs, feet and tail off in every direction, then trotted over to the couch, hopped up on it and began to roll around on his back, like he was trying to dry off, staining the threadbare blue upholstery.

When the man started unsnapping his own raincoat, she called a halt.

"Whoa there, you don't need to take your coat off. You're not going to be here that long. Five minutes — remember?"

The old man ignored her. He took his raincoat off, used the back of his hand to swipe excess water off it onto the growing puddle on the floor, then turned and hung the raincoat on the hook behind the door

How did he know there was a hook there to hang a coat on?

He must have caught the look.

"My mama worked here when I was a kid, cleaning house for the Whittakers. She fell off a ladder in the kitchen…" He stopped. "I'll get to that part later. Right now, I'll settle for a soft drink since there ain't no electricity to run the coffeemaker. But no ice. I got teeth so sensitive the least little bit of cold will send me off—"

"*Coffee? Soft drink?* What happened to only five minutes?"

He headed toward the kitchen and she moved quickly to block his path.

"No," she said, too loud. She didn't want to have to explain why there was a loaded gun on her kitchen table. But she didn't owe him an explanation. This was her house and that was her gun and it was her life she was about to end. None of this was any of his business.

"I don't have any soft drinks and even if I did … what are you doing here?"

"Yes, I'd love to have a seat. Thanks for asking."

He went over to the couch and sat down beside the dog, idly rubbing the animal behind the ears.

Jessie stood motionless, stunned.

"What do you want?"

"I only want to help you, that's all."

"I don't need any help. Do I look to you like I need help? All I need, all I want is for you to tell me whatever it is you have to say and then leave."

He looked at her for a long moment, like he was measuring what he was going to say or trying to decide how she was going to take it.

"What I come to tell you is easy, don't take but three words to say it." He paused. "Don't do it!"

Her knees suddenly felt rubbery, unstable.

"Don't do what?" she asked, the words husky because the wind had been knocked out of her.

"You know what. Don't take that gun that's probably lying on the kitchen table right now and put it to your head … your right temple, actually, and pull the trigger. Don't do it!"

She sat down heavily in the wingback chair across from where he and the dog were seated on the couch. There was a great roaring sound in her ears.

"How do you … what makes you think … I don't know what you're talking about."

"Look, why don't we skip the you arguin' with me part and get right to the point."

He stood and turned toward the kitchen. "The gun's in there on the table, ain't it? And if I hadn't shown up when I did, you likely would have done used it."

She would have stood to block his path but she couldn't manage to make her legs work.

He left the room, left the dog on the couch, his wet paws soaking the cushion. Left her sitting … was her mouth actually hanging open?

The old man returned a few seconds later carrying the revolver. He held it as relaxed as if it were an extension of his hand, certainly more comfortable with the weapon than she was.

"Little thing like this won't make much of a hole in your skull, that's for sure, but it'll definitely get the job done." He sat down beside his dog again, moving the gun idly from one hand to the other.

She wanted to speak, but words wouldn't form. All she could manage was a croaked, "How…?" before she ran out of air and couldn't finish.

"How do I know you's plannin' to kill yourself?"

She could have sworn a small smile tried to sneak out onto his mouth from the corners.

"Sweetie Pie, if you think you're surprised that I know you're 'bout to try to commit suicide, you ain't got no idea how surprised you gone be when you find out *how* I know."

Then the shadow of a smile disappeared. He set the gun down on the coffee table between them.

"I didn't just come here to tell you somethin'. I got something you need to see."

He stood, went back to the front door, opened it and the screen, reached out and picked up something that was leaning against the outside wall beside the screen. When he pulled it into the house, she saw that it was flat and square, wrapped in the plastic from a couple of garbage bags. It was a picture, or maybe only a frame, a painting.

"Take a look at this here, and when you're over the shock, we'll talk about it."

The old man pulled the plastic bags off the canvas and held it out into the light from the lantern.

For a moment, the image didn't register. The light from the flickering candles she'd set out earlier sent shadows, faux butterflies to twirl and dance across the edges of the canvas that weren't illuminated by the fierce, yellow glow of the lantern. They gave the image the sensation of movement, as if the surface of the canvas were alive.

Then the fractured pieces of dark and light and shadow became an image. When it did, Jessie sucked air in through her teeth, suddenly so nauseous she was afraid she was about to chuck up the small piece of an apple that had been her supper into the puddle of water on the hardwood floor.

The painting was a portrait of *her*. Of her *dead*, with a bloody bullet hole in her skull.

The likeness was stunning, so perfect it might have been one of those digital photographs made to look like a painting. Except you could see the paint itself. In places around the edges it had begun to peel off. You could see the texture of the brush strokes on the surface of the canvas. Her eyes devoured the painting, trying to look at every detail as a separate entity and see the whole of the thing at the same time.

The moles!

The trio of moles!

Chapter Five

THE "MAGIC TRIANGLE." That's what that frat boy in her History 101 class at Tulane University had called the trio of moles on Jessie's neck, said she'd been marked by elves, moderately original as pickup lines go.

Jessie reached up now and touched them, though she hadn't willed her hand to move.

Then her hand began to move — again, without her bidding – up to her forehead, and the spinning of planet Earth ground to a halt. It stopped revolving around the sun. Time sucked in a gasp and stopped breathing altogether.

The mosquito'd gotten her after all.

She could feel the itchy bump.

She could *see* the bump, too. There was a small pink dot, not merely a single brushstroke but shaded to give it depth, above the right eyebrow of the dead woman in the portrait.

Staggering to her feet, Jessie pinballed off an end table and a wall and barely made it to the bathroom in time to vomit noisily into the toilet. She wretched until her stomach was empty, which didn't take long, then dry-heaved until tears ran down her cheeks and dripped off her chin. When the reflexive heaving was over, she stood up shakily, got a whiff of the foul-smelling vomit in the toilet and quickly flushed it down before it made her nauseous again. Then she turned on the tap and ran cold water into the sink. She splashed it on her face and that helped to steady her. Gratefully, the flickering candle sitting on the back of the toilet didn't offer enough light for her to get a good look at the face that peered back at her out of the gloom in the mirror over the sink. She took the hand towel from the rack and wiped her face, scrubbed it hard, as if she could somehow wipe the mosquito bite off her forehead. But it wasn't the bite on her face she wanted to get rid of. It was the one on the painting.

She finally shut off the water and walked unsteadily back into the living room, carefully avoiding looking directly at the painting that was now leaned up against a chair by the door, in shadow there, with candlelight butterflies flitting across its glossy surface. The old man was seated where he'd been when she left the room, the pistol resting comfortably in his right hand. The dog was curled up on the couch beside him, sound asleep.

"Where did you get that painting?" Her voice sounded hollow and foreign in her own ears. She felt like a string on a guitar that was pulled so tight you couldn't tell if the sound it was making was music or crying.

"Out of the shed behind my house. I went in there and dug it out after I seen you here on the porch this afternoon."

What was a portrait of her doing in a shed…?

"Why was … how did…?" Her thoughts were so fractured she couldn't seem to piece them together well enough to form a complete sentence. Finally, she gasped, "Who painted it?"

"My mama."

His mother.

The other pieces of thought in her brain banged into the back of those words when they stopped dead in their tracks.

His *mother?* What was he — sixty-five, seventy years old? If his mother had painted it, then the portrait must have been—

"Exactly fifty-seven years old. That's what you's calculating in your head, how old it is. My mama painted it when I was eleven and I'll turn sixty-nine come August."

"Are you telling me…?" There were more words, but they dangled off the end of the thought and she couldn't manage to grab hold of them.

How…? It was too preposterous. It couldn't … She tried again. "Are you telling me that your mother painted this portrait more than *half a century ago?*"

"Yes ma'am, that's what I'm tellin' you."

He might as well have told her Mount Rushmore was a naturally-occurring rock formation and Mother Teresa sidejobbed as a pole dancer.

"My mama was an artist, you see." He was speaking fast, the way you do when you might not have enough time to say all you have to say. "She started out sketchin' faces and such with the stub of a pencil on grocery sacks while she waited by the dock — the old one, it ain't there no more — for the boats to bring in fresh fish. After somebody give her a dollar for one of 'em, and a dollar back then was like five hundred dollars today, my daddy used part of the money to buy her canvases and paints. If she could get a whole dollar for a pencil drawin' on a grocery sack, what could she get for a color picture, a painting! So she set up on the street corner every Saturday in front of Adams Drug Store. And she'd paint random faces. Caricatures. We didn't call 'em that, but that's what they was. Little girls with exaggerated big eyes and pouty red lips or freckled-faced little boys with big ears and cowlicks. The folks who walked by looked at 'em, could see how good she done and every now and then she'd sell one. And then one day, this couple of tourists asked would she paint a picture of *their* little boy. After that, they was always a line formed soon's she got there of a morning."

In spite of herself, Jessie was drawn into the old man's story.

"What she earned paintin' was what kept food on our table. My daddy drunk up every dime he made at the mill and woulda used her money, too, but he didn't have no idea how much she made so she could hide most of it from him. Life woulda gone on like that and she never woulda painted that picture…" He gestured toward the painting but Jessie didn't turn her head, couldn't look at it anymore. "And you and me wouldn't be here in this house fifty-seven years later having this conversation. But one day she was up on a ladder chasing cobwebs — right there in that kitchen." He pointed to the room where Jessie'd been sitting at the table, holding a gun with a barrel that felt cold on the skin of her temple. "She was a maid when she could get the work, and that day she was helpin' Mrs. Whittaker get ready for a Fourth of July party. Mrs. Whittaker heard a thump and run into the kitchen and found mama on the floor and the ladder turned over. She musta fell off, hit her head. They brought her home unconscious. She lay in the bed, still as death and we was sure she wasn't never gonna wake up. Then one day, she opened her eyes. They popped open and she come back to us. But she was … *different.*"

He stopped to take a breath and that was Jessie's chance to interrupt him, to shut him up and make him leave. But she didn't.

"She started paintin' pictures so different from what she done before … got up in the middle of the night and painted in the toolshed by the light of the moon…" He spoke the next words so softly she must have misunderstood, because she thought he said, "Or with no light at all."

He continued in an urgent voice, the words coming fast, "The pictures was as detailed as some fancy portrait — lightyears beyond the little line sketches she done before. They was all paintings with people in 'em, but nothing like a portrait of the queen of England sitting on a throne. The people in Mama's paintings was all dead. Not died-in-their-sleep dead, neither. Messy dead. And the paintings all had windows in them. In the beginning, when she first started painting 'em, the windows was blank, didn't show nothing at all, but then one day there was a little girl in one of them. She'd been strangled."

He paused, looked at her with such a direct stare she had to avert her own eyes.

"Except that particular little girl was very much alive. Becky Adams, that was her name. She wasn't dead ... *yet*."

He let the word hang out there in the air between them like a dead fish on a stick, and Jessie tried to reach out and grab hold of the concept, but her mind backed up from it, refused to engage.

Suddenly, the lights in the room came back on. The sudden bright blinded them and they both blinked like moles let out on a sunny day.

The picture leaned up against the chair was even more horrifying in the light from lamps and the ceiling fixture than it had been shrouded in shadow, dreamlike, illuminated only by candles and the lantern.

It snapped then — the insanity of the whole scene slammed into Jessie with the force of a wrecking ball. That was it. Jessie was done. The last thing she needed, on the last day she intended to occupy space on the planet, was a crazy old man in her living room prattling on about a picture his *mother* had painted ... or he'd painted ... or Bozo the Clown had painted...

She stood, drew herself up as tall as she could and was surprised and impressed that her voice didn't shake when she spoke.

"You need to leave now."

"No ma'am, I ain't going nowhere long's..."

She took two steps to the fireplace and picked up her cell-phone off the mantle. With her fingers poised over the keyboard, she said, "I don't even have to dial all three numbers: nine one one. It's a one-stroke key on my phone. Unless you leave — *right now* — I'm punching that key."

"You don't want to do—"

"You don't have any idea what I want or don't want!" she shouted, not meaning to but when she saw the effect it had on him, she was glad she had. "You don't know anything about me. I didn't invite you into my life, you barged in like you owned the place." Her mind flittered to the raincoat hook behind the door. "Well, you better barge right out again before the police show up and drag you out."

The old man didn't look angry. He looked sad. Without a word he stood and the little sound-asleep dog beside him sprang instantly to life.

"And put the gun back down on the table." He might not even have realized he'd picked it up again while he was talking. No, he knew he had it. He meant to keep it.

"If I's to leave this gun here, you'd use it—"

"—to shoot rats in my basement. Or a bald eagle perched on the clothesline in the backyard. Or for any other thing I happen to want to shoot." It felt good to be angry. Anger was hot, and for a moment it warmed the coldness of her bones. "That is *my* gun. I bought it legally. I have the license to prove it. The gun belongs to me and if you walk out of here with it, that's stealing. Given how much I paid for the stupid little thing, stealing it is bound to be a felony."

The old man hesitated.

"I said, *put the gun down.*" There was such force and determination in her words she sounded like a detective in a cop show. "Unless you have somebody to feed your dog while you're in jail, I suggest—"

"Alright. We best go, Sparks. Let this nice lady blow her brains all over the flowered wallpaper in the kitchen."

He went to the hook behind the door and donned his raincoat. He snapped Sparky's raincoat on him, picked up the lantern off the coffee table, turned the tab all the way until the yellow glow went out, leaving behind a red afterglow as the wick cooled.

"And take that … that *thing* with you!" She pointed to the painting, which had become as repulsive to her as a tarantula spider.

He looked at her for a moment.

"You just said your own self it's against the law to steal, to take somethin' that belongs to somebody else. This here painting ain't mine. It's yours. I only been keepin' it for you all these years. You can do whatever you want with it, but my part in all this is over."

She started to argue with him, but she didn't want to engage him at all. She just wanted him gone.

He turned toward her and she steeled herself for some parting shot. But his voice was kind and gentle.

"I'll see somebody comes by here *early* tomorrow. So you won't have to…"

What? Lie here dead until the neighbors smell the stink? It was almost like he knew she'd been thinking about that.

"I'm glad I got to meet you." The old man searched her face. "I was so hoping it was possible to … but I guess it ain't." He stopped again. "I'm sorry."

Then he turned and walked out, letting the screen door bang shut behind him.

❦

THE BRUNT of the storm had spent itself and was blowing out over Whispering Mountain Lake. Here, it was only sprinkling and a piece of the full moon peeked out from behind scurrying tatters of clouds.

T.J. sloshed through the water pooled in depressions in the old sidewalk, with Sparky bounding along beside him, hopping the puddles. Now that the storm had passed, the dog's high spirits had returned. They said dogs were much more sensitive than people about such things and Sparky's vibrant personality was always subdued until he was sure the discontented rumble of faraway thunder wasn't coming his way.

Dobbs had parked his Jeep in the driveway of the Watford House. T.J. opened the back door and let Sparky leap up into the seat, where his allover shake sent only a little water flying in all directions. Then T.J. got into the front seat beside Dobbs.

The two of them sat together in silence. T.J. felt spent, used up. It was that hour of the night when all bad things were possible, when the bogeyman came out of the closet and brought all his nasty friends. That hour when death seemed as near as the darkness, as cold as the moonlight and as certain as the coming dawn. He didn't know if he'd ever felt quite as helpless as he did right now.

Dobbs said nothing, just sat behind the wheel, watching the wipers clear the last of the sprinkling rain off the windshield. He pulled his watch out of his pocket, the one on a chain attached to a belt loop on his pants, and looked at it, not that he wanted to know what time it was. It was just something he did — he'd pull the watch out, a gold-plated watch with ornate carvings on the front and back and a flip catch that released the cover so you could see the stylized Roman numerals on the face beneath the glass. His Uncle Hurl had given it to him when he was sixteen — T.J.'d heard the story a dozen times, the impression it'd made on Dobbs when he seen the gnarled, liver-spotted old hand lay the watch in the palm of the young unblemished one. It didn't keep time, was like to tell you it was midnight when the sun was coming up, hadn't worked when his uncle had given it to him all those years ago. But he'd pull it out anyway and look at it the way another man might smooth his mustache or slick his hair back from his forehead.

"She wouldn't listen, would she?"

T.J. shook his head. "But I left the picture with her. I wouldn't take it back when she tried to give it to me. And sitting there looking at a picture of your own self dead, how you gone look, that'd have to have an effect on somebody, wouldn't it?"

He hated the hope he could hear in his own voice because he knew it wasn't real hope but some sad cousin of desperation.

"Yeah, you'd think so." Dobbs was humoring him.

"I bet she's sittin' in there right now, staring at that painting. Looking at it with the lights on. I bet she—"

A loud *bang* ripped open the night. T.J. slumped back against the seat and put his head in his hands.

COMING off the Highlands Festival weekend was worse than coming off a ten-day drunk, not that Kavanaugh County Sheriff Brice McGreggor had ever been drunk for ten consecutive days. But he had policed drunks, crazies and teenagers on eight consecutive Highlands Festival weekends and he was here to testify that nothing short of an Ebola outbreak could possibly be worse.

Except maybe the Fourth of July hot on its heels, which this year was shaping up to be the Mother of all Fourth of July celebrations. The holiday, coupled with the grand opening of the Nautilus, the floating casino in the lake, would create a perfect storm of revelry it would take his department a month to recover from.

He looked at the pile of paperwork on his desk and decided he'd been wrong. The policing of the Highland Festival wasn't as bad as clearing up the paperwork afterward. Traffic reports formed the biggest pile — DUIs and driving while impaired by some as-yet-undetermined substance, reckless driving, speeding, followed close behind creating a public disturbance, drunk and disorderly conduct and the Grand Kahuna of them all — underage drinking.

The sheriff picked up one of the underage drinking reports and shook his head. He flat out could not tell anymore. On his first day as a rent-a-cop security guard at the Mall of America in Minneapolis a decade ago, he'd "busted" two fifteen-year-olds trying to buy beer at a liquor store. They'd been easy to spot. Now, twelve-year-olds could pass for twenty — the girls, anyway. Wouldn't want to be a young man in today's world, trying to swim through the shark-filled waters of jailbait girls who looked way more like seasoned hookers than sophomores in high school.

Thank God for small favors, though. He didn't envy the state's Department of Fish and Wildlife Water Patrol, whose officers had to deal with all the same issues, but with the added wrinkle that their jurisdiction was twenty-five thousand acres of water and more than six hundred miles of winding shoreline.

There was a polite rap at his partially closed door before Deputy Raleigh Fletcher opened it and leaned in just far enough to announce, "The unit that was dispatched to the possible 'shots fired' on Sycamore Street — Stephens just radioed in, said it appears to be a suicide at the Watford House."

Deputy Fletcher was the second in command every law enforcement officer dreamed of. Raleigh Davenport Fletcher was tall and blue-eyed, with piano key teeth — even had a cleft in his chin. He looked like the square-jawed good guy in a superhero cartoon. And he came from money. Old money. Charleston money, which meant that on special occasions his family would still haul out the silver that'd been hidden in the pigsty so the Yankee soldiers wouldn't find it. And for all that, Fletch played everything strictly by the book, was a straight arrow, worked hard and always gave the credit to other officers.

He was everything a sheriff could want from a deputy. He had only one drawback. There were politically correct ways to put it now, Brice was sure, but truth was truth: Fletch was as dumb as a box of doorknobs, cursed with incurable stupid. Sheriff McGreggor suspected that Fletch'd been promoted through one special education class after another all the way through school by the force of his family's influence, which likely landed him a slot in the police academy. He'd blossomed there, though. Oh, *not* academically — but he took to the hierarchy of law enforcement as naturally as a dog to a fire hydrant, was fearless in combat training, absolutely obedient and morally upright in the kind of intensely pure way only the very innocent or the very dumb could be. Working as a deputy sheriff in nowhere Kavanaugh County, West Virginia, should have been a knothole in the family tree, but they were just glad he had a job.

Give Fletch a clear task to do, break it down into reasonable steps, and he would run through brick walls to accomplish it. He was probably incapable of filling out an incident report, but he would cheerfully have followed Sheriff McGreggor down the barrel of a howitzer.

The sheriff pushed back from his desk, got to his feet and started for the door, his six-foot, five-inch frame moving with the economy of motion and latent agility of a former athlete. Which he wasn't, unless diving into foxholes in Kosovo was considered an Olympic sport. Still, he possessed a big-man's grace when other men his size were clumsy.

He smiled at Fletch, grateful for any interruption to take him away from the administrative work on his desk — even one as grisly as a suicide. The Watford House. He didn't know who lived there now.

"Who called it in?" he asked as he lifted his hat off the hook by the door, hoping the rain had let up.

Fletcher looked at the clipboard in his hand.

"A mister…" The sheriff watched him sound out the syllables. "Ray-mond Dob-son and…"

"And T.J. Hamilton," the sheriff finished for him and his smile broadened.

～

AFTER THEY HEARD THE GUNSHOT, Dobbs called 911 while T.J. walked slowly across the sodden lawn back to the house and up the steps to the porch. He knocked loud, called out her name again and again. No one answered. The front door had been unlocked — he'd walked out of it only a few minutes before — so he could have stepped inside, could have gone to her. But he didn't, just stood vigil by the front door. Didn't go in.

Which was testimony to how his whole world had been upended by a chance conversation with a woman on this porch only a few hours before. Except that wasn't when it started, of course. It'd started sixty years ago.

His decision to stay on the porch had nothing to do with the grisly nature of what he'd find if he went inside. T.J. Hamilton was a man well-acquainted with death. He'd seen it, in all its various forms — with its varying degrees of insult to the human body. There were an inexhaustible number of ways to die — and T.J. had been present for more than a representative sample. Hand grenades in Vietnam. These days, Marines dealt with more sophisticated things called IEDs, improvised explosive devices, but a hand grenade did the same kind of damage and sometimes it offered a couple of seconds' warning. You saw it roll across the ground toward you, watched your best friend jump on it to save the rest of the squad.

He'd spent ten years as a soldier, a decade of his life in the jungles of Vietnam, and in other off-the-books places where his mission wasn't acknowledged and he didn't exist. Shoot, he hadn't been out of high school a year when he'd gone boots down with the rest of the 9th Marine Expeditionary Brigade, wading ashore on China Beach north of Da Nang. Every day of those ten years had been the longest day of his life. Until the next one.

Add to that another two years in — what was the sexy term they used now? Black Ops — and when he showed up among the Hoosiers at Purdue University, he was the oldest student in his class. Purdue. That's where he'd met the only woman he ever loved. Three years later, armed with a Bachelor's Degree in Criminal Justice and a new bride, he graduated first in his class from the Chicago Police Academy and spent the next thirty years with the Chicago Police.

All told, life had set T.J. Hamilton down in a front row seat at a command performance of man's inhumanity to man for four decades. As often as not, though, man's stupidity and indifference caused just as much carnage. It had become clear to him the day he watched the snow melt around the unrecognizable bodies of nine children laid out in a row after a drunk driver slammed into a school bus that stupidity and indifference killed more people than vicious intent. And them folks was just as dead.

So why *did* T.J. stand outside on the porch, uselessly calling out the name of a woman he knew was dead? Still unwilling to pick at that scab, he only allowed himself to understand a little of it, to see that a more elemental horror than anything he'd experienced in the years since had been set free in his soul when he looked at the painting he had kept for decades when he should have destroyed it, burned it like all the others.

It was a horror that had drawn first breath more than half a century ago and T.J. flat out did *not* want to go there again.

So he simply waited for emergency responders to arrive. Let them look at what he could not. It was their job, not his anymore. He was a bystander, a spectator, a non-combatant.

As he stood there on the porch waiting, he felt such a

tangled mix of emotions it was impossible to pull any one of them free. Except relief. He recognized that sensation as it washed over him. Yeah, relief. He had finally, *finally* heard the other shoe fall. The final shoe. What had begun when his mother fell off a ladder when he was eight years old had ended here where it started, this night, beyond that door. It was finally over.

He and Dobbs were shunted quickly to the side as soon as the paramedics arrived and then the sheriff. They gave a short statement, said they happened to be driving past when they heard a gunshot coming from the Watford House. T.J.'d met the new tenant that afternoon, knew she was a woman living alone, so they'd stopped to check on her. When she didn't come to the door, they'd dialed 911 and stayed until the authorities arrived. After that, they stood on the far edge of the porch, waiting for the body to be wheeled away.

But instead of the controlled order of removing a body, there was frenzied activity. Voices calling out. Running feet. Then the gurney they thought would bear a sealed black bag burst out the door of the house bearing a woman to be whisked away in an ambulance.

Jessie Cunningham wasn't dead. Correction: *Bailey Donahue* wasn't dead.

Sheriff Brice McGreggor had approached them then. T.J. only knew the sheriff to speak to, not well, but what he had seen of him, he liked. He didn't showboat, kept his head down and did his job. And he was a fellow Marine. There was that. T.J. had fought in the jungle; Brice in the desert. Semper Fi.

The sheriff carried a driver's license in his hand. He watched the taillights of the ambulance disappear around the corner, lights flashing, siren waling, an odd look on his face. Then he brought his attention back to T.J. and Dobbs.

"I've seen a lot of suicide attempts in my time," he said, shaking his head, "but I've never seen one where the victim painted a picture of how she was going to look dead."

T.J. kept his composure. Dobbs choked, but made it sound like he'd got struck by a sudden coughing fit.

Gratefully, the sheriff didn't explain, just held out a driver's license.

"Says here the woman's name is Bailey Nicole Donahue. That's not the name she gave you this afternoon, is it? You said she told you it was Cunningham, Something Cunningham, didn't you, T.J.?"

And for a reason he couldn't quite put his finger on, T.J. did a quick bob and weave. With his best imitation of Sparky's pitiful look, he said, "Now, Sheriff McGreggor, for all I know she mighta told me her name was Betty Boop. My hearing's not what it used to be."

The sheriff barked a laugh.

"Don't give me some 'poor old man' rap. Your hearing is better than mine and we both know it. Your eyesight's probably better, too."

"Gotta have cheaters to read with," T.J. put in.

"Cheaters then, but not hearing aids. Why do you suppose she told you one name when her driver's license says another?"

T.J. went with his original gut response.

"I wouldn't make this more than it is if I's you, Brice. It's no big mystery. I'm sure I heard her wrong. See, I'd just gotten a good look at what she was painting and I was kinda in shock, expecting trees and flowers and butterflies and such — not cancerous tumors. You seen what she paints?"

The sheriff nodded, then commented that "*all the art*" he'd seen in her house had been disconcerting and let it go. Clearly, he'd seen the portrait T.J.'s mother had painted. A blind cave fish would have noticed that painting. But he said nothing about it and T.J. was more than willing to let that particular sleeping dog lie.

Chapter Six

THIS WAS NUTS.

Brice McGreggor stood looking down at the still form on the bed.

It was crazy.

This was the third time he'd been here, standing like a cherry on top of a sundae, doing nothing. Wasn't anything to do. The doctors said there was almost no chance the woman who'd put a gun to her temple and pulled the trigger would ever wake up, said they couldn't even take the bullet out of her brain because doing so would most definitely kill her.

She was going to lie there like this, day after day. Seeing nothing. Knowing nothing.

So why did he keep coming back here day after day to watch her waste away?

That wasn't nuts. No, that was *sick*.

And the reason might be worse than sick.

To be totally, brutally honest, Brice McGreggor would have to admit that the fact that she'd never open her eyes, never look up at him, was part of the attraction.

No, that wasn't sick. That was pathetic.

He studied her, glossy black hair spread out on the

pillow, a face doll-like in its perfection, unmoving. The small bandage on her right temple was little more than a Band-Aid. The bullet hole made by a Smith & Wesson Model 63 firing a .22 caliber slug wasn't very big. Of course, she probably didn't know, or care, what size the hole would be. Most people unfamiliar with guns think they'll all blow a hole in you big enough to drive a road grader through. If she'd used a .44 or .357 Magnum, she would have done considerably more damage than a delicate little opening in her temple. There would have been no temple or much of a face left, in fact, and her brains would have blown out an even bigger hole in the back of her head and splattered on the wall.

Who was she, other than a name on a driver's license: Bailey Donahue? Not the name she'd given T.J. when she met him the afternoon she shot herself. He could tell T.J. was covering for her and he couldn't figure out why. The woman had been in town for less than a week — how could he possibly have met her and the two of them gotten so chummy that T.J. was willing to lie to the police about her?

Correction. He hadn't lied. He just hadn't told the whole truth. A subtle difference, but one that didn't escape a former Chicago Police Department detective like T.J. Hamilton. He was hiding something. Brice wanted very much to know what it was, but there was no reasonable, professional reason for him to go digging around in this. Clearly, no crime had been committed. And figuring out what had driven her to the point of desperation that dying was preferable to living — or why T.J. had covered up the name discrepancy — was an exercise in futility. To what end? This case was closed. And he had plenty more that weren't closed that needed his attention.

Still, he stood there, looking down at her.

He almost felt like he knew her, though he'd never seen her smile, didn't even know what color her eyes were. And would never find out. That thought brought the loop full circle and he was forced to admit that was part of the motivation for returning here day after day.

She was Sleeping Beauty, with no prince to kiss her and wake her up. Which made her *safe*. Brice could not *care* about a woman. Any woman. Period. He couldn't do that to himself and he certainly wouldn't do it to anybody else. Brice Creighton Drummond McGreggor — his mother had been determined not to let her baby boy forget his roots — would spend the rest of his life, however brief, a loner. And no, he wasn't gay. It wouldn't have mattered if he had been. The same rules applied either way.

A nurse dressed in a smock spotted with — was that Shrek and Donkey? — stepped into the room and was startled to see Brice standing there beside the bed, his hat in his hand.

"Sheriff…?"

Act like you have a reason to be here!

No convenient deception leapt to mind, however, so he had to go with the truth.

"I was just checking on her," he said, as if that were a perfectly normal, indeed a professional, explanation. "We're still trying to track down her family, but no luck so far."

That part, at least, was true. It was like she'd sprung up with the dandelions after a spring rain. Poof, there she was. The address on her driver's license was … odd. It listed the Watford House's street and number. The expiration date was 2015, so the license was brand new, which meant her previous license had obviously expired as she was about to move, so she'd put down the address of where she was moving *to*, not where she was moving *from*. Convenient timing, that. No previous address to check out. He'd run her name through a routine NCIC (National Crime Information Center) check and she came out spotless. Not so much as a speeding ticket.

There were other places he could check, other ways to back draft her life … but what for? He'd wandered through her house after the ambulance rushed her to the hospital. It had all the intimacy and personality of a room at Motel 6, where Tom Bodett always left the light on for you. Not a single photograph — family, friend, selfie. Nothing. There was only furniture enough for a handful of rooms, a bed, nightstands, dresser, kitchen table and chairs, couch and a meager assortment of other furniture, antiques he suspected had been here when she moved in. The Watford House had half a dozen bedrooms — no, more than that, but he hadn't been counting — a parlor, library/study, family room, sunroom, den. It was huge. Why did a woman living alone need a house that big?

But to some extent, he'd figured out that minor mystery when he checked the rental listings and discovered that the description hadn't made it clear the place was enormous, that it had once been the home of almost a dozen borders. Joe Phillips, the real estate agent, wasn't above doing a bit of a shell game to get some unsuspecting tenant to sign a lease sight unseen. It was hard to find a tenant to rent a house like the Watford House in a town with lots of other houses just like it!

And then, of course, there was the worthy-of-an-Agatha-Christie-novel mystery he had discovered moments after he entered her house. Why had she painted a self-portrait of herself dead? Her art studio was full of organ illustrations — kidneys and hearts and other internal organs he couldn't identify. None of them bore even the slightest resemblance to the stunning portrait leaned up against a chair in her living room.

What possible reason could she have had to do a thing like that?

"Maybe that's why she did it," the nurse offered as she hooked another bag of whatever to the line snaking down into the needle in her arm. "Maybe that's why she tried to kill herself — because she was alone in the world."

Then the nurse finished and paused for a moment on the opposite side of the bed. They both looked down at *Bailey Donahue* like she was a body in a coffin laid out for viewing.

That creeped Brice out and he stepped away from the bed wordlessly and preceded the nurse out of the room and into the hall.

"The doctors think she'll ever wake up?" Brice asked, knowing she couldn't give him private medical information, and he'd already talked to the doctor who had admitted her anyway. But maybe things had changed.

The nurse in the Shrek smock shook her head.

"Not likely. Anything's possible, I guess, but the safe money is on she's going to be like that for the rest of her life ... which won't be long."

Brice knew that a person in a PVD, persistent vegetative state, had a limited life expectancy before vital organs began to shut down. He turned in place and strode down the hallway to the elevator.

LIGHTS THROUGH A THIN SLIT. Each one spinning, and all of them spinning around each other. Around and around.

Her eyes weren't open but she could still see the lights through her eyelids.

Voices. Somebody was speaking but her mind wouldn't translate the random sounds into words.

A woman. Then a man. Then the woman again.

They were standing near her, but it sounded like their voices were coming from a long way off, down one of those long hallways in dreams where there's a door at the end and you're running for it but you never get any nearer. You run and run, past other closed doors, but the one at the end remains the same distance away.

And then she was getting nearer the door. The hallway was dark, but the door at the end was open a little and a sliver of light stabbed out into the darkness. And as she got closer, it got brighter and brighter in the hallway.

The voices were in the light. They were coming from the light behind that almost-closed door.

Then she stopped running, the lights and voices faded. The hallway darkened.

When she heard voices again, it was like turning the volume up on a television. They started out soft, then got louder and louder until she could tell that the people speaking were right beside her.

Jessie opened her eyes and looked up. People she didn't know were looking down at her so she closed her eyes again.

"Miss Donahue." A man's voice. "Miss Donahue, can you hear me?" He asked the question with the authority of one accustomed to people responding when he spoke.

Jessie wished whoever Miss Donahue was would answer him so he'd shut up. She was dizzy and she was getting nauseated, felt like she was about to throw up. But the nausea passed as quickly as it had come, a wave receding off the beach.

"She's coming around."

"Amazing."

"No telling how far back she'll come."

The voices receded, the bright lights behind her eyes darkened and there was cool, quiet nothingness again.

"Miss Donahue!"

"What?" Jessie tried to say, but her mouth wouldn't work and there was some kind of plastic thing in her nose and down the back of her throat.

She opened her eyes and the world was vague, blurred around the edges like watercolors, smeared images. Then they resolved, became substance, became people.

"Miss Donahue, can you hear me?"

The man who spoke the words had dark hair and black eyebrows and his forehead was not flat but rounded, like the brain behind it was so big it was bulging out. He had a hook nose and a mustache the same color as his hair. It was thick. Jessie thought of Pancho Villa.

"Miss Donahue, I'm Dr. George Bennett. Can you understand what I'm saying?"

She tried to reach up and pull the plastic thing out of her nose so she could talk, but found she couldn't move her arms.

The world was getting more solid now, resolving into a room and people and voices. She moved her head and the pain that shot through her skull was so excruciating she could not have cried out even if she had a voice. Even if she'd had that thing out of her nose so she could make sound. The pain blurred the world, blurred the room, muted the voices and gratefully they faded away and were gone.

It was quiet and dark when she opened her eyes. All she could see was a white rectangular shape with strips of white metal around it. She blinked.

A ceiling tile, with three brown spots on it, water spots, shaped so they looked like the face on a stick figure.

The ceiling resolved out of blur and she could see pieces of plastic tubing and could hear an annoying beep, beep, beeping sound like those machines that measured heartbeats with little dotted lines so you could see the valleys and then the mountains and then the valleys again until they suddenly stopped forming and the dots stretched out horizontally on a valley floor and the beep, beep, beep sound became a solid beeeeeeeeeeep.

That meant you were dead.

The beeping continued.

Reality began to form around her. She could feel ... a bed. She was lying on a bed, which explained the view of ceiling tiles. She moved her head on the ... *pillow* ... and a thudding throb of pain coursed through her skull.

A babble of sound became a voice and words. A face appeared above her.

It was a woman. She was young, with blonde hair that she

had pulled back from her face. She had on a colorful smock of some kind, decorated with … were those Winnie the Pooh characters?

"Hello, Bailey," the woman said, in the tentative tone you used to address a person you weren't sure spoke English.

Bailey?

"It's good to see you awake."

Awake. She had been asleep and now she was waking up. Waking up *where?*

She had annoying plastic tubes stuck up both nostrils and when she reached to swipe them away, her arms wouldn't move. That brought the world into sharper focus. Why couldn't she move her arms? She struggled to lift her right hand. Was she … paralyzed?

"Bailey, how do you feel?" the woman asked. Clearly, the woman was talking to her. The woman searched her face as if the answer to the how-do-you-feel question lay there and she could read it without benefit of a reply.

"My head hurts," Jessie said. The woman's face brightened in surprise and something resembling alarm. Maybe she really did think Jessie couldn't speak English. "And I'm thirsty, my mouth's dry." She turned her head slightly to take in more than the woman looming over her and pain lumbered through her head again, a behemoth with big feet, and her world quaked with each step.

The woman picked up something Jessie couldn't see and brought it to her mouth. A microphone with a thick cord. No, some kind of remote control. "Page Dr. Bennett," the woman said into the microphone. "Stat."

This was a hospital.

Jessie was lying on a bed in a hospital. She had … she didn't know why she was here. Thoughts were hard to find. Words were harder. Something had happened and she was injured somehow. A wreck, maybe. Where was Aaron?

Sudden fear pumped adrenaline into her veins and everything became instantly clearer and brighter.

"Bethany? Is Bethany alright? Where's Bethany?"

"Everything's fine. Just stay calm."

Oh, how Jessie *hated* it when people told her to stay calm.

"I want Bethany. Where is she?" Jessie was shouting now and she didn't know how her voice had gone from hoarse and raw to usable, but it had and she was using it.

The woman reached up and fiddled with something on the plastic tubing Jessie could see out the corner of her eye and the world instantly blurred. No sharp edges. Everything wrapped in cotton. The room grew dark and Jessie couldn't find the strength to say anything else. But that didn't matter because she didn't know what she wanted to say, anyway.

Chapter Seven

THE NEXT TIME Jessie came back to the world, she kept her eyes shut, pretended to be asleep, afraid if the nurses knew she was awake, they'd turn that little dial on her IV line and zap her back to LaLa Land.

She lay in the bed, listening to hospital noises, trying to piece together what had happened. Given the pain movement planted between her ears — not the saber stab of agony that was a ghost in her mind, but a thudding, pounding presence — made it clear something was wrong with her head.

Duh.

She tried to remember how she got the head injury.

Her thoughts didn't feel right in her mind, things that ought to make sense didn't. It didn't seem to her like she had lost any thoughts, any memories. But then if she had, how would she know? She believed everything was still there, only not arranged in the order it had been before. She could find a thought if she looked for it, but she had to dig. All sixty-four of the crayons in the giant economy box had been dumped out on the floor, mixed up. Coloring a picture required digging around through the pile, searching for the shade you needed.

Understanding dawned on her slowly, not some dramatic memory, but little memories tiptoeing into her mind as silent as mice in house shoes. Fear for Bethany and Aaron faded away and was replaced by a bleak sadness that hurt way more than the injury to her head. She didn't have to worry that they had been in some kind of accident with her and even now lay in an adjacent hospital room fighting for their lives.

She knew what had happened to Aaron, and was profoundly grateful that the quality of her remembering apparatus made it impossible to process those images, made it easier for her to dodge away from that place, that time, duck, so the agony of it missed her, flew over her head so close it ruffled her hair.

And she knew why Bethany was not here with her.

She remembered a kitchen in a house somewhere, a gun … and an old man with a painting of her with a hole in her head, but she must have dreamed that part.

The soft swish-swish of nurse's shoes came closer, and other footsteps, too. She could hear conversation. They were talking about her and she didn't like being discussed as if she were a tuna in the fish market.

She opened her eyes and found four people surrounding her bed. The two from before — the doctor who looked like Pancho Villa had told her his name but she couldn't remember it. And the Eeyore nurse, only today her smock featured characters from *The Little Mermaid*. Did she work in pediatrics? Or did she wear idiotic cartoon figures because she thought they would soothe and reassure the adults she treated?

They were not reassuring. They were annoying. Any minute, she might look up and Barney the Purple Dinosaur would be standing in the doorway.

"Where's Barney?" she asked, hadn't meant to say the words aloud but they popped out.

The four people exchanged looks. Dr. Villa and Eeyore had been joined by a woman so thin she would need to be outlined in magic marker to keep from disappearing when she turned sideways. A doctor, obviously, a stethoscope dangling around her neck being the badge of doctor-dom. That and the white lab coat she wore instead of a Disney movie poster.

"Who's Barney?" Dr. Villa asked.

She caught herself before she answered. A woman with a head injury inquiring about purple dinosaurs was likely a one-way ticket to the funny farm.

"Nobody. I was still half asleep, must have been dreaming."

The four seemed more than a little surprised that she was carrying on a coherent conversation. Good thing she hadn't dropped the purple dinosaur bomb on them.

After they introduced themselves and she promptly forgot their names — not brain injury, she never had been able to remember names, and she couldn't keep up with a pair of sunglasses for more than three days either, even before...

Before she shot herself in the head.

The thought process untangled itself from the jumbled pile.

That's what happened. That's why her head hurt. She had shot herself in the head...

And survived.

"How do you feel, Miss Donahue?"

She almost asked who Miss Donahue was but caught herself. Again, just in time.

"Please, call me—" She dug through the pile of crayons frantically, trying to find the name. "Bailey." She was *Bailey.* Not Jessie, Bailey. The trick was to think of herself as Bailey Donahue, *become* Bailey Donahue. And she knew the trick. Oh my, yes, she knew the trick. "And I feel ... okay. My head hurts and—" She pulled at the restraints binding her wrists to the bed railings. "The cause of death written on my toe tag is going to be 'terminal nose itch' if you don't untie me so I can scratch it."

The level of their surprise at her little speech was evident on their shocked faces. And displayed in the sideways glances they gave each other. Did they think she was blind as well as brain-fried, that she couldn't see the "knowing looks" that passed among them? Clearly, they were accustomed to dealing with patients with only a handful of firing synapses and were astonished she was able to put more than a couple of words together, let alone make a funny about her itching nose.

By mutual unspoken agreement, they began to interrogate her, or so it felt, asking her questions about what year it was and who was president and how many fingers they were holding up. They noted things on their metal-bound legal pads at her responses, passing looks back and forth that seemed to be more and more approving as the process continued. After she accomplished the miraculous feat of multiplying five times seven and identifying the largest city in England, followed by a stunning performance explaining the difference between the two objects they held up to her, a car key and a paper clip, they seemed to reach another unspoken agreement, closed their metal legal pads and smiled at her benignly.

"Miss Donahue—"

"Bailey," she corrected.

"Very well, Bailey," said the new doctor whose name she'd already forgotten. "You do know why you're here, don't you?"

"Gunshot wound to the head." Somehow it made her queasy to say, *I shot myself in the head.* She had, though. She had wanted to die and tried to kill herself. She knew why that was, but right now she could not bear to pull those knife-slicing thoughts out of the pile. That could wait. The pile wasn't going anywhere.

"*Self-inflicted* gunshot wound to the head," Eeyore corrected.

"Busted. I tried to kill myself. If you need me to admit it, there it is."

Her thinking had become oiled with reason enough for her to grasp that she needed to convince these people that it had been some kind of mistake, she hadn't meant to do it. If they knew the truth, they might be unwilling to let her leave to finish the job she'd obviously botched. And finish the job she would!

"I was depressed … lonely…" She'd tell them she'd been drunk or on drugs but surely they had blood tests that would dispute that. "I threw myself a massive pity party and was the only guest. I was an idiot."

They didn't buy all she was selling, but they were willing to go along with her as if they did.

"It's good to know you feel that way about it," Dr. Villa of the bulging forehead said.

She almost demanded they take off the restraints … since she "felt that way about it," but bit her tongue.

"If you think you're up to it, we need to talk to you about your condition."

"What 'condition'?"

There was an awkward pause, as if they hadn't sufficiently worked it out in advance who was going to say what and nobody wanted to go first. She primed the pump.

"Why am I not dead?"

Another pregnant pause.

"Because the round that should have killed you … didn't. You are a very, very fortunate young lady."

Well, see, that depended on your perspective. It was all about perspective.

He took a deep breath and launched into an anatomy lesson. Frontal lobe. Occipital lobe. Parietal lobe. Temporal lobe.

Finally, she waved her hands for him to stop.

"I couldn't understand all that even if I didn't have a very recent hole in my head. Could you please drop the rub-a-dub-dub words!" Before they had a chance to ask, she explained.

"The old man who lived next door to me when I was a kid refused to talk with anyone who used words with more syllables in them than rub-a-dub-dub. Just tell me, simple. Small words. Straight out."

No Name Doctor straightened, cast sideways looks at the others, and said, "The bullet you shot into your brain should have killed you…"

"But you took it out, so—"

"No, we didn't take it out."

"Didn't take it out? You mean … it's *still in there?*"

Bailey didn't hear any of the rest of what Drs. No Name and Villa said because she was trying to process the preposterous concept that *there was a bullet in her brain.* She tuned back in, though, in time to hear the words, "… kill you instantly."

"I'm sorry, could you repeat that?"

"I said we couldn't remove the bullet because to do so would almost certainly have been fatal," Dr. No Name said.

"Okay, I get that, but what's the 'kill you instantly' part?"

"The bullet in your brain is a foreign object. As long as it remains where it is…" She let that sentence dangle. Bailey wished she could recall her name. You should know the name of someone you were yearning to punch in the face. "But there is no guarantee it will remain *in place,* and movement in a particular direction would kill you instantly."

"What would cause the bullet to move?"

Another exchange of looks.

"Just about anything…" Dr. Villa said.

Jessie — *Bailey! She was Bailey!* — must have looked as stunned as she felt.

"…or nothing at all. Really, there is absolutely no way to predict what will happen. You might live another seventy years with that bullet in your brain and suffer no ill effects whatsoever. After all, it should have killed you to begin with. Since it didn't, perhaps it never will."

No Name Doctor took the hand-off. It was clear to Bailey

that the woman liked being the bearer of such dire tidings. She was enjoying herself. A power thing.

"Or it could shift and cause all manner of … damage."

"Define 'damage.'"

"Blindness. Deafness. Paralysis."

"So you're saying I could go blind, or deaf or be paralyzed … or die if I — what? Get hit in the head with a baseball bat?"

"Or bump your head getting into your car."

The rest grayed out. Ugly thoughts on customized Harleys chased each other around and around in her head. She wanted to be dead. Not blind or deaf or unable to move. Dead.

"You need to rest now, Miss Donahue," said Pancho Villa.

The Little Mermaid nurse reached up toward the plastic tubing above Bailey's head. Bailey realized instantly what she intended to do.

"No, don't. Please, I don't want to sleep. Don't knock me out."

But even as she spoke the last words she felt the mellowing of reality, the gauzy quality of the air, the release of some spring somewhere inside that kept her tight. When it went limp, so did Bailey.

The foursome filed out as Bailey began to blur out. As she nodded off, she looked up and spoke to the white ceiling tile that had become her new best friend. "Guess I better get a bigger shower cap."

Bailey came instantly awake. No gradual passage through ever-brightening levels of consciousness until she finally broke the surface with sparkling bubbles into reality.

She was insensate and then she was wide awake and acutely aware. One beat and then two.

The room was dark. Night had folded wings of shadow around the hospital while she lay in drug-induced slumber and the hush of soft voices made her feel like her ears were stopped up, like she had gone up in an airplane or down in an elevator and her ears had clogged.

She reached for the call button. Except she couldn't reach anything. Her arms were still bound to the metal sides of the bed with what looked like the ties from a fleece bathrobe.

How was she supposed to call the nurse if she needed help when they had her tied to the bed? She didn't need help, she needed information, but had no way to summon anyone to get it.

One of the questions the idiot foursome had asked her when they were measuring the level of her lunacy was "What year is this?" She had told them correctly, 2015.

They hadn't asked what month. If they had, it would have brought the thought — the bright red, candy-apple red crayon — out of the pile. It had to be June. Had to be. HAD TO BE. She hadn't been out *that* long.

But what day in June?

She didn't want to call out for help, ever mindful that if Eeyore or Grumpy/Sneezy/Doc judged her *overwrought*, they could flip the switch on her plastic tubing and send her sailing off into LaLa Land on the Good Ship IV Drip.

She had to know.

A nurse glided softly past her door on shoes that must have had soles of cotton candy.

"Nurse!" she called out, trying to produce only sufficient volume to be heard and not enough to elicit alarm.

Nothing. The nurse hadn't heard—

The nurse appeared in her doorway.

"Do you need something?"

Yeah, I need for you to untie my arms and let me reach up and pick my own nose. I need you to put the idiot call button within reach so if I really did need help, say I chanced to be choking or fell out of bed on my head, you could help me.

"What's today?"

"Wednesday."

She tried to sift through all the crayons, looking for the one that told her when she had sat down at the kitchen table with the gun. But it was too much trouble.

"The date? What's the date?"

"June 24."

Bailey had been straining upward as best she could, trussed up in somebody's old bathrobe, but now she sank back on the pillow and stared up at her dear friend the ceiling tile.

"Do you need anything else?"

"No," she whispered.

The nurse left and Bailey began resolutely digging through her crayons, trying to put it together accurately. She shot herself. She didn't like thinking of it that way. Somehow that seemed so ... barbaric.

Concentrate.

She'd shot herself on June 19 because she couldn't bear to miss another one of Bethany's birthdays, better to be dead than absent. June 19 had been when it began, of course, when Napoleon Dynamite's wimpy brother's buxom girlfriend stepped off the bus.

But Bethany wasn't actually *born* until June 25, six days later.

June 25. Tomorrow.

Bethany's birthday, her real *birth*-day, the day she left her mother's body and breathed and cried and lit up every dark, shadowed corner of Bailey's existence — was tomorrow.

What time—?

Her eyes fell on the big round, industrial-size clock that hung above the door.

It was five minutes to twelve. Couldn't be noon, had to be midnight on June 24. In five minutes, Bailey would live through another of her child's birthdays — absent. Excluded. Exiled.

No, not again.

No!

75

She'd tried! She'd done everything she could. She had tried to *die*, but woke up here instead, still breathing, with a bullet—

A bullet in her brain.

If the bullet moves, it could kill you instantly.

If the bullet moves...

Bailey strained upwards on the bathrobe ties, yanked with all her strength, but they held fast.

Any little thing. A bump on the head. Anything.

Bailey lifted her head up off the pillow and banged it back down with all her strength. Waves of pain, nauseating, undulating ripples spread out from somewhere in the middle of her head and crashed with brutal fury on the insides of her skull.

It hurt so bad she couldn't get her breath for a moment.

Then she gasped.

It didn't work.

Gritting her teeth against the agony, she lifted her head and banged it back down violently, again and again and again until the pain grayed out the world and darkness came clawing at her from the corners and she had to stop or pass out.

She blinked back tears, fighting the nausea, turned toward the clock. Two minutes.

She had two minutes to make it happen. Two minutes to leave this world as she had intended to do when she pulled the trigger of the gun and launched a bullet into her brain. She whipped her head from side to side on the pillow, lifted it up and banged it back down again and again, and then the agony-filled world downshifted through shades of gray to black.

Darkness.

Bailey blinked. Opened her eyes. Her friend the ceiling tile was waiting for her, still smiling. Slowly, reluctantly, she turned her eyes to the clock. Eleven minutes after twelve. June 25. Bethany's birthday.

A party and cake and streamers and ice cream and presents and happy birthday and blowing out the candles and...

Bailey began to cry softly, total defeat sitting in somber disquiet on her shoulders. The hot tears slid slowly down the sides of her head and pooled in her ears.

Chapter Eight

T.J. HEARD the horn on Dobbs's truck, the one he drove when he wasn't in his Jeep.

Beep-beep.

Seriously?

The beep-beep sounded like a tricycle horn. The sound was so effeminate T.J. had trouble associating it with the big rig with the double-wide cab and the oversized tires and the whatever else Dobbs found to put on the vehicle.

The man had a thing for anything with wheels, which T.J. saw as nothing more than conveyances to haul you from point A to point B. Dobbs, on the other hand, could get misty-eyed over a 1965 Mustang. He had always loved cars. As a kid, he'd spent hours playing with the Matchbox collection he had accumulated through birthdays and Christmases until he had a whole herd of 'em. No, herd wasn't likely the collective noun for cars. Well, it wasn't gaggle or … fleet, it was fleet. Dobbs had a fleet of—

Beep beep.

The horn sounded irritated and insistent. No, it wasn't the horn that was irritated. It was T.J. How was it that he always 'lowed himself to get talked into things like this? He flat out, one hundred percent did *not* want to go to the hospital to visit Jessie Cunningham … or Bailey Donahue … or whoever in the Sam Hill she really was.

T.J. hadn't heard her wrong that afternoon on her porch when Sparky'd licked her face while T.J.'d stood dumbstruck, staring at the triangle of moles on her neck. Wasn't no way she'd said "Bailey Donahue" and then later he'd decided what she'd really said was "Jessie Cunningham." Either she'd given T.J. a phony name or the name on her driver's license was bogus.

And danged if Dobbs didn't grab hold of that as one of the reasons they needed to pay her a visit today!

More mystery to unravel, he'd said, as if the painting itself weren't mystery enough. What Dobbs failed to see was that them visiting her wasn't gonna solve no mysteries. Or accomplish anything else that mattered. Dobbs hadn't been there to see the look on her face and hear the rage in her voice when she'd thrown T.J. out of her house. Dobbs had no real appreciation for how angry she probably still was with T.J., so it was easy for him to say they ought to go pay her a visit, try to get to know her, try to be her friends — since she sure as Jackson didn't know anybody else in town. Then they could try to edge her back from the black abyss of oblivion.

T.J. thought Dobbs was full of it.

Sliding into the truck cab beside the big man, T.J. glanced at the Krispy Kreme doughnut box in the floorboard.

Dobbs saw his glance.

"Don't start. If I needed somebody to grouse at me about my cholesterol, I could find somebody a whole lot better looking than you are to do it."

"This is dumb."

"No, it's not."

"And pointless. We go there. She throws us out. She goes home. Bang, game over for good this time. What part of that scenario ain't dumb?"

"It's not dumb because it *isn't* destiny." Dobbs had glommed onto that interpretation of reality and would *not* let it go. Like maybe he'd always wanted to believe they could have changed things years ago, or felt guilty that they hadn't tried. "We proved it isn't inevitable, engraved in granite. What your mama painted doesn't *have to* come true."

"We didn't prove nothing of the kind. We didn't keep this woman from putting a hole in her head just like Mama painted, did we? We didn't keep her from killing herself, neither. We only put it off a little while. If she's determined, ain't nobody—"

"We got to try, T.J. You know we do."

He didn't know any such thing, but he shook his head and said nothing. There was no changing Dobbs's mind when he'd plotted a course and set sail on it. He was a battleship … no, an aircraft carrier … sailing resolutely forward, full steam ahead. Turning an aircraft carrier wasn't no easy thing at all.

But it was still dumb.

~

A BRIGHT SHAFT of sunlight shined into Bailey's eyes, blinding her. But even more blinding than the sun poised to attack outside the drawn curtains was the relentless cheeriness of the nurse.

Short, roughly the size and shape of a vending machine, the woman chirped like the first robin of spring as she waddled over to the window, yanked back the room-darkening draperies, pulled up the shades, and began to crank the head of Bailey's bed up into a sitting position.

"Ready for a normal breakfast, are we?" she asked. "A day of regular diet and a couple of strolls down the hallway to the end and back and you'll be ready for discharge tomorrow."

"Go away and leave me alone." Bailey squeezed her eyes shut against the glare. "I'm not hungry."

"But we have to eat to get our strength back."

"If *eating* is what makes *us* strong, you must be ready to bench press a Buick."

Bailey was instantly sorry she'd said that. She had never been capable of cruelty. Had the bullet in her brain changed that? Did she get a pass now because she had a hole in her head? No, it hadn't and no, she didn't.

The woman blew by the insult, though, either didn't hear it, didn't understand it or didn't care. She set the tray down on the tray holder that stretched out across the bed and began to untie the restraints that held Bailey's arms affixed to the side rails.

Bailey flexed one arm and then the other, then reached up and ruthlessly scrubbed an imaginary itch on her nose.

She looked at the breakfast tray. The plate held some lumpy yellow substance that was either a scrambled egg or toenail fungus, two overcooked link sausages it took no imagination whatsoever to envision emanating from the south side of a dog going north and two slices of what was either wheat toast or buttered particle board. A reasonable facsimile of a blueberry muffin sat beside the napkin and plastic cutlery.

She held up the fork. "You sure I'm not going to try to off myself with this?"

"I'm going to sit right here and keep you company while you eat," the woman burbled. "And here," she indicated a piece of paper and a pencil, "is your satisfaction survey."

"You're joking." Bailey picked up the pencil and drew a giant frowny-face on the survey and held it up for the woman to see before dropping it face-down on the tray and reaching for a glass of water, grateful she could drink it all by herself — like a big girl.

There was a timid knock on the door. Bailey and the woman spoke together with the perfect unison of a Greek chorus.

"Go away!"

"Come in!"

The door opened slowly and in walked an old man who looked familiar. Bailey ought to know who he was, but the memory was one of the scattered crayons.

She tried to concentrate, but that kind of mental effort was tiring and she really didn't care enough to dig around for — he had a dog, an adorable little dog!

He'd stopped and talked to her when she was painting outside on the front porch that day — the day she had jammed full of tasks and activities to occupy her mind and time until she was ready to…

There was more, though. What was it?

He had come to her house that night, too! She'd been sitting at the table in the kitchen with the gun and he'd knocked on her door and…

That part faded into gray fog, not a misplaced crayon — *gone*. Retrograde amnesia. The doctor said most people with traumatic brain injuries couldn't remember what happened right before they suffered the injury.

Though she couldn't remember the images from the man's visit, she could remember the emotions. She'd been mad at him, furious. She'd wanted him to leave, get out of her house, and he wouldn't go.

Even absent the why, she felt the same anger now.

What was he … what were *they* doing here?

Behind him was a mountain of a man dressed in bib overalls, with broad shoulders, an equally broad belly and a head of unruly white hair.

"Good morning, Miss Bailey," the black man said, clearly as uncomfortable to be here as she was to have him. "This here's Raymond Dobson. Me 'n him's been friends our whole lives, ain't we, Dobbs?"

"We sure have," the big man said, forced affability making it look like he'd learned how to smile from a manual. "Since we were knee-high to grasshoppers."

"We just come by to check on you," the skinny man said.

"To see how you're doing."

"Dobbs here was gonna bring you flowers from the gift shop in the lobby but they couldn't make change. He always carries a hundred-dollar bill in his wallet. Mad money. He'd stuff it down in his shoe, but if he did, wouldn't nobody take it when he tried to spend it."

The old man was babbling like a magpie!

Before she had a chance to speak, the door opened and a nurse backed into the room, hauling behind her a piece of medical equipment, with knobs and buttons, and leads sprouting from the top like Medusa's head of snakes.

The chirpy nurse asked what she was doing in here. The pushy nurse said this was Room 319, wasn't it, and she'd been instructed to perform some unpronounceable medical procedure/test on its occupant.

The chirpy nurse informed the intruder that this was Room 319, alright, but the patient was not scheduled for any kind of medical procedure. She took two steps and began to shove the machine back out the door. Pushy nurse stood her ground and they began to play reverse tug of war, pushing the machine one way and then back the other. Bailey watched, mildly amused until a doctor — you could tell by the stethoscope around his neck — put an end to the fracas by ordering both nurses out of the room and into the hallway where you could hear the dressing-down they were getting through the closed door.

It wasn't until then that Bailey became aware that the two men were still there, shoved aside by the war of the titans. She was not amused by that. Not even a little bit. A homeless memory bobbed to the surface of her mind and floated there alone. A painting of a face. It had something to do with the old man, and all the emotion surrounding it was *rage*.

"What are you doing here?" She set down the water glass, dropped the pencil from her left hand and used both hands to make shooing gestures. "No, don't answer that. I don't want to know why you're here. I just want you to leave. Now!"

The old man surprised her by agreeing instantly, apologetically, then totally flummoxed her by asking politely, "If you ain't gonna eat that blueberry muffin," he indicated the only piece of identifiable food on the tray, "I sure would like to have it."

The other man looked as surprised as Bailey was. Holding onto her temper by a thread, she growled through clenched teeth, "Take it. You can have everything on the whole tray if you want it. Just go!"

The man hopped forward, carefully wrapped the napkin around the muffin, and held it in front of him like he was carrying a Ming vase. He scurried out of the room without a backward glance and the bigger man lumbered after him.

They were both already gone when the memory bloomed in bright color in her mind, a painting done in exquisite detail. A portrait of *her face* ... with a bullet hole in her temple. And a mosquito bite above her right eyebrow.

THE INCREDULITY in Dobbs's voice was thick enough to pave a street.

"A *blueberry muffin!* What was *that* about? I would have given you one of the Krispy Kreme doughnuts if I'd known you were only moments away from starving to death."

T.J. pushed past him and headed for the sign that said "Stairs" above a door across the hall. He shoved open the door, went out into the stairwell and stood looking down at what he held in his right hand.

Then he began to pace back and forth, so rattled he was unable to stand still.

Dobbs followed him out the door, totally mystified.

"You were willing to be bull-goose rude to get that muffin

— are you going to eat it or just walk around holding it in your hand?"

T.J. noticed he still had the muffin and shoved it at Dobbs.

"You eat it." When Dobbs wouldn't take it, he dropped it on the floor and continued his pacing circuit of the small space, his mind so full of thoughts and feelings and images he couldn't seem to grab hold of any one of them to think or feel or see.

"T.J. … what in tarnation—?"

"This!"

T.J. stopped in front of Dobbs and held out the napkin he'd wrapped around the muffin. On top of the napkin was a piece of paper he'd picked up with it, covered in blueberry muffin crumbs. Dobbs took it, shook off the crumbs and examined it.

On one side was some kind of "satisfaction survey." There was a frowny-face drawn across the front.

On the other side was a pencil sketch.

"Didn't you see her?" T.J. asked. Dobbs looked blank. "While the nurses were playing king of the mountain, Bailey was drawing on this piece of paper."

"She drew this? Looks like … what? A Cracker Jack box?"

"That's not a Cracker Jack box." He paused, spoke the rest in a soft voice because the wind had been so totally knocked out of him he didn't have enough air to say the words any louder. "Don't you see — it's a window! An *empty* window."

Dobbs didn't physically back away from him because there was nowhere to go in such a small space. But with every possible syllable of body language, he was shouting "No!" and scrambling to put distance between himself and what T.J. had just said.

"Whoa there, Bessie! Let's back this wagon up to the barn and start loading it all over again." Dobbs's voice came out a bit high and reedy. Nobody else would have picked up on a sound change that subtle, but to T.J. it was as obvious as a cigarette butt on a birthday cake. "This is a *rectangle*. Okay, a box. But a window? Come on, T.J. And those marks down at the bottom, those could be any—"

"That's a table ... that line is a tabletop, can't you see?" Dobbs said nothing. "And that circle there, it's a bowl, the beginning of a bowl, anyway, a bowl of fruit. And behind all that is the window."

"The rectangle."

"The window!" T.J. began to pace restlessly back and forth on the stairway landing again, too agitated in body and spirit to hold still. "How? *Why?* I don't get it."

"I don't see that there's anything to get. You're running waaaay out past your headlights here, T.J. The woman in the bed drew a sketch—"

"While those nurses were arguing."

"Yeah, okay, she drew it while—"

"While she *was watching* those nurses argue."

"We were all three watching the argument."

"We weren't all three drawing a picture with one hand and holding a glass of water in the other — while we were looking at something else entirely."

He had Dobbs's attention now.

"I watched her. She never took her eyes off them nurses, but she still picked up the pencil and started drawing on the back of that piece of paper. Never once looked down at it."

"Oh, now *there's* a conundrum to mystify the ancients. Totally unheard of in all of human history for somebody to *doodle*. That day I spent half an hour on hold waiting to yell at the guy at the DMV for *losing* my truck title — I looked down at the notepad I'd written the phone number on and saw I'd covered it up with shapes, marked out the number with a bunch of ugly black swirls that looked like tornadoes. Everybody doodles."

"You're not listening, Dobbs." But T.J. wasn't irritated. He was past any emotion as simple and clarifying as irritation. "She was drawing a picture without looking at it ... *with her left hand.*"

"And that's significant because…?"

"If you's gonna blow your brains out, chances are you'd hold the gun in your dominant hand. Don't ya think?"

"The bullet hole was in her right temple so—"

"She's right-handed."

Dobbs was beginning to get it. "I never heard of anybody who could do a thing like that."

"Yes, you have." T.J.'s voice was soft and even he could hear how haunted it sounded. "Mama could. She could paint with both hands *at the same time.*"

Chapter Nine

T.J. SITS *in the golden shaft of afternoon sunlight streaming through the window of his room. He pushes a car across the rough boards of the floor. Back and forth. Back and forth. The toy car belongs to Dobbs, who told him to take it home with him tonight and play with it. Dobbs is like that. He has way more of everything than T.J. and he is always generous, always wanting to help his friend.*

Like he wanted to help this afternoon as they sat on the riverbank, dabbling their toes in the cold creek water.

Dobbs knew T.J. was upset and T.J. knew he had to tell Dobbs about it. Had to tell somebody and who else was there, who else did he want to confide in but his best friend?

But he hadn't known where to start.

"She's different," he said simply.

"Your mama?"

"Since she woke up after she hit her head, she's different."

Dobbs knew that T.J.'s mama had fallen off a ladder in the kitchen of the Whittakers' house and hit her head on the hardwood floor. She was knocked unconscious and she didn't wake up. Mr. Whittaker had actually lifted her up and took her into the living room and laid her down on their red velvet sofa, the one with brocade cushions they'd bought in Charleston that were the same color.

He probably wouldn't have laid her down on the sofa if her head had been bleedin', but it wasn't. She had a goose egg that kept getting bigger and bigger on the right side of her head, where they speculated maybe she'd connected with the kitchen table when she fell. But they finally decided it was just the floor done it.

They'd even called a white doctor to come see to her! Of course, T.J. didn't hear about any of this until later, when they brought her home in Mr. Whittaker's car, carried her carefully into the house and laid her on her bed with the mattress filled with corn husks. He'd heard Mr. Whittaker tell his father that they "did everything we could" and that the white doctor had said there wasn't no treatment, they just had to wait for her to wake up.

His daddy had asked when that'd be and Mr. Whittaker said the doctor didn't know how long she'd be unconscious. It sounded to T.J. like Mr. Whittaker wanted to say more and maybe he had said more as Pa walked beside him out to his car, but T.J. hadn't heard that part. He'd set himself down beside his mother's bed and wouldn't leave it. For once, his father hadn't been a monster in a human being suit, and had not forced him to go to school the next day.

After that, it was Saturday and he could stay home to look after his mother. The neighbor ladies came and went, but T.J. never left her side unless they shooed him out for "privacy," they said. But his mother never moved. Never opened her eyes. Never said a thing.

On Sunday, he'd sneaked away briefly to meet Dobbs in the woods, to tell him what was going on. The two had been forbidden to play together by Dobbs's mother, so they had to go where wasn't nobody looking, which wasn't hard since there was woods everywhere.

T.J.'s mama hadn't cared. She had invited Dobbs inside and fed him her fresh gingersnap cookies and laughed when he showed her how he could cross his eyes and stick out his tongue and look like a lizard. Dobbs thought T.J.'s mother was wonderful. And he had enough sense to make himself scarce anytime T.J.'s father was around.

T.J. didn't go to school on Monday, either. By then, he could hear whispered conversations about his mama "slipping away" and he could *see it. Her eyes were sunken, her lips parched and split. She hadn't had nothing to eat or drink since Thursday. Even a boy of eight knew you couldn't live long if you didn't eat or drink nothing.*

When wasn't nobody in the room, he took her hand and squeezed it and begged her to wake up. He cried and pleaded with her, but her eyes remained closed, her breathing gettin' more and more shallow every day.

He had been outside, going to the privy when he heard the shout from inside. It terrified him at first. The sudden fear in his belly hurt worse than if he'd been stabbed there. She was dead! He had left and she had died while he was gone.

But the cry had come from one of the women sittin' with his mother and she didn't sound sorrowful.

When he raced into his mother's bedroom, she turned her black eyes toward him and smiled. Just a little smile but it was enough.

It had taken more'n a week for his mother to get back on her feet again. She was all trembly from lying there not moving for so long, or so the other grownups said. But T.J. saw it was more than that. He watched her closely, studied her, knew every crease, line and plane on her face and there was somethin' there he had not seen before. He didn't know what it was, but she had awakened "different," not the same person she'd been before she fell.

It was going on two weeks after the accident that he came home from school and discovered she'd set up her easel in the shed and was in there, paintin'. She never painted at home. What was there to paint 'cept the grinning faces of the tourists' children down at the dock and marina?

And if she wanted to paint at home, why in the shed? There wasn't no windows in the shed. No light. Unless you took a lantern in with you, the only light was from the open doorway, and in the late afternoon like it was, with the sun already gone down behind the mountain, there wasn't hardly enough light in there to see the rake and the hoe, let alone a canvas.

When he found her in the shed standing in front of the easel painting furiously, he spoke to her. But she ignored him. He spoke again and stepped around to the side of the easel so he could see her face.

Then he knew why it didn't matter that there was no light in the shed to paint by. Mama was paintin' with her eyes shut. She had her head tilted back, eyes closed like she was sleepin' as brushes hurried across the canvas.

Brushes she held in both hands!

How could anybody paint a picture with both hands? It was like watching Mr. Beddingfield play the banjo. T.J. had always marveled at that, watching the old man's hands, wondering how he could do two entirely different things at once, his left moving around, holding down one set of strings and then another, while his right fingered different strings on the other end. Mama was doing somethin' like that. Her right hand painted the top of the picture, puttin' in the frame around a window, while her left hand filled in a table and the beginnings of a bowl of fruit on the bottom. He had watched in stupefied fascination. And fear. He was terrified and he didn't know why. All he knew was that there was some-thing profoundly wrong *about what his mother was doing. Wrong with his mother.*

She suddenly dropped both paintbrushes in the dirt at her feet and stepped back from the canvas. Then she tilted her chin back down and opened her eyes. She looked surprised, then stunned and then, like T.J., she looked scared. She stared at the paintbrushes on the ground, at the paint smears on her fingers, as if to confirm that she had, indeed, been paintin', but it was clear from the look on her face she didn't have no idea what she had painted until she opened her eyes and seen the canvas.

T.J. didn't tell Dobbs about that. He didn't tell nobody. His mother realized he was standing next to her and she told him not to talk about the picture, like the picture was bad somehow, though it was only a simple picture with a table, a bowl of fruit and a window behind it. You couldn't see nothing out the window, though. It was blank. Empty.

She had taken a cloth then and smeared the still-wet paints until there was nothing on the canvas but splotches of color. Later that day, when the smeared colors had dried, his mother had used white paint to cover the smear so the canvas was blank like it'd been before.

He understood why she might want to use a canvas more than once, though she couldn't do that when she painted the caricatures of children at the dock, took the dollar bills and the change — she charged a dollar and fifty cents — from the tourists and stuffed it down into the pocket of her smock. Every one of them pictures was painted on a brand new canvas.

"I ain't gonna never do nothin' like that again!" his mama'd told him, more like she was making a promise to herself than to him.

T.J. had pushed the image of his mother painting that day out of his head.

Until it happened again.

He saw the shed door ajar and found her as before, gawked at her while she slapped paint onto the canvas in a fury that produced an incredibly detailed picture, much more skillful than the first. But it was the same scene. A still-life of fruit on a table. And a window in the background. But the window was huge in this picture. Much, much bigger. All out of proportion to the table and bowl of fruit, it took up almost the whole canvas. Just like before, the window was blank.

He had sneaked away, didn't disturb her. Didn't want her to know he'd seen her do what she had swore she wasn't never gonna do again.

The third time she done it he didn't see her actually painting but went into the shed and saw a canvas with wet white paint sittin' on the easel. Two days after that, he met Dobbs in the woods to tell him about his mama being "different."

Dobbs tries to be positive about it. He always tries to look on the bright side of things. He doesn't see no harm in what she's doin', even if it is a little odd.

T.J. can't seem to convey to his friend the strangeness of it all, the otherworldly quality of his mother standing there with her head thrown back, swipin' paintbrushes in a frenzy over the canvas, completing an entire picture in minutes.

And so he goes home, packing one of the Matchbox cars from Dobbs's collection. It is a Ford Mustang, bright red, with miniature doors that actually open on both sides. It is Dobbs's favorite — well, they're all Dobbs's favorites. But he shoved it into T.J.'s hand and told him to take it home to play with overnight.

T.J. knows Dobbs is as mystified as he is by Mama's behavior, even if he tries to put a good face on it. He gave T.J. the car to try to take his mind off things, to make it better somehow. It's a simple gesture, but so heartfelt T.J. took the car in silence, saying nothing because he had a lump in his throat.

So now T.J. sits, runnin' the car back and forth across the floor in front of the window in the beam of sunlight that will disappear in a few minutes when the sun passes behind Big Bear Mountain.

The sudden, high-pitched, wailing shriek that rips open the late afternoon silence so startles T.J. that the car leaps out of his hand and flies across the room.

He does not remember leaving the house, crossing the yard to the shed or throwing open the door. He is simply sitting with the red Mustang with the doors that actually open in his hand and then he is standing in the doorway of the shed and he has no sense of the passage of time in between.

In the shaft of sunlight illuminating the dark shed interior, he can see his mother in the dirt in front of her easel. She's lyin' on her back, screaming, as if fighting some invisible monster, writhing back and forth, cryin' "nooooooo!" Her hands at her neck. It's like she is caught in the grip of some horrific nightmare and he steps forward instinctively, puts his hand on her shoulder and shakes it.

"Mama…?"

Her eyes pop open. Too wide, looking from side to side, clearly terrified and looking for some horrible thing that is the source of her terror.

Then she focuses on T.J.'s face. Her own face begins to lose the contortion of terror, begins to relax, transform into a confused, disoriented look.

"T.J.?" she says and reaches up to touch his face.

"Mama, what's wrong?"

She seems to remember then, and she looks up at the painting on the easel. She instantly sits up and scoots on her butt away from the image as fast as she can, frantically, until her back collides with the wall of the shed, then she keeps diggin' her heels into the dirt to shove herself away, digs holes in the dirt, trying to move. All the time with her eyes fixed in wide-eyed horror on the canvas on the easel.

T.J. follows her gaze, turns to look for the first time at the painting.

He cries out. Makes some kind of sound that is foreign to him, like it'd come out of somebody else's throat.

It is a portrait, as detailed as the ones he seen the one time he went with Dobbs into the library in town, paintings of LeRoy Ackerman, the president of Ackerman Coal, who had donated the money for the library, and other white men T.J. didn't know. But the object of the portrait is not staring forward, all serious, features dignified and solemn.

It is a little girl, not a man. A little white girl with short, curly blonde hair. Perhaps he knows her, but her face is so contorted her features are hard to make out. And her skin is an odd color, purple, her lips pale. On her neck are ugly marks, dents in the skin. Her eyes are open, starin', bloodshot so there is no white at all around the blue centers. There is a small trail of blood inchin' out between her lips and oozing down her cheek in a pink dribble.

T.J. has never seen a dead person before, unless you count the body of his grandfather in his coffin at the church the day he was laid to rest. But he doesn't need to have seen a corpse to know that this little girl is dead.

T.J. TOOK the piece of paper with the survey on one side and the window on the other back from Dobbs and was amazed that his hands were not shaking. They should have been. His whole body felt like it was vibrating, thrumming like a bow string after the arrow is released.

"You remember that red Mustang you used to have?"

Dobbs looked at him like he had lost his mind.

"I never had a red Mustang."

"The toy one, the Matchbox car. You remember — the one with the doors that actually opened."

T.J. was surprised when Dobbs continued to look blank. He'd have bet his pension Dobbs remembered every one of them cars in that box.

"If you say so, T.J., I guess I had a red one. What are you getting at?"

"That's the one you gave to me to take home and play with the day Mama painted the picture of the little dead white girl."

Dobbs remembered that part well enough. Neither of them would ever forget the event that shaped the next three years of their childhoods.

T.J. looked down at the drawing on the piece of paper in his hand. It was a window. *It was.* He didn't want to believe that, didn't even want to think it, but he had grown up, was no longer the little boy pushin' the red Mustang back and forth in a shaft of afternoon sunlight. And the man that little boy had become had learned along the way that ignorin' an awful reality didn't make it go away.

"I remember your mama saying how … you can't un-know the truth." Dobbs's voice was quiet. "Once you see it, once you know what it is, you are forever responsible for what you do about it."

It was like Dobbs had read his mind. It had often been like that over the years, like where one's thoughts stopped the other's began.

"T.J. … why are you so convinced this … these pencil lines are a window and that the drawing somehow connects to your mother who also painted windows?"

"*Started out* paintin' windows, empty ones. But they didn't *stay* empty."

"What does one thing have to do with the other? Why would the woman in that hospital bed draw a window?"

"Why did my mama draw 'em? I asked myself that a thousand times during them years. Asked you, asked the stars, asked God. Why was this happenin' to my mama? What was the *force* that compelled her to draw when she didn't want to, to draw things she didn't want to? What was the force that opened up a … window into the future so she could paint what she seen there?"

"The woman in that bed was born half a century after your mother died. What possible connection could there be? Why her?"

"Why *anybody?*"

He sighed, and all the energy and emotion drained out of him and he felt very old and tired.

"We done had this conversation, Dobbs." And this time Dobbs didn't look blank. This time he only nodded. He remembered.

"We've had it more than once."

As the two of them had watched the events that unfolded in Possum Run Hollow for the next three years, they'd asked themselves and each other for an explanation of what was happening over and over again. And why. And they'd never gotten a satisfactory answer to either question.

The force, the energy that had swept out of the frail little woman named Eulalie Hamilton and transformed canvas after canvas was as inexplicable as it was powerful. It had been so powerful, in fact, that it had finally consumed her, burned her out. The power had killed her.

But not before she painted one last portrait. The picture of a young woman with a bullet hole in the side of her head who wasn't even born when she painted the picture.

T.J. looked down at the lines on a piece of paper in his hand. In truth, they could have been a Cracker Jack box. But they weren't. The lines formed a window. He couldn't explain why he knew or how he knew but he was as certain of that as of sunrise on Easter Sunday morning.

There was no reason it should be so. No explanation that came anywhere near it. But the cold, hard reality was that his mother had painted "what hadn't happened yet" for a horror-filled three years of his childhood. And if what he held in his hand was indeed a sketch of a window, drawn unconsciously by the woman lying in the hospital bed not thirty feet away, then maybe she was slidin' relentlessly down the same slope. Whatever it was that had swept his little mother away into the rapids, and eventually into her own death, could very well be lappin' at the feet of a young woman whose name was Bailey Donahue. Or Jessie Cunningham. One or the other. Or maybe somethin' else entirely.

Chapter Ten

Bailey was going home.

Goody.

The doctor had given the go-ahead last night when he'd made his rounds, telling her all manner of things she should do, shouldn't do, could and could not do. Bailey hadn't listened to any of them.

Of course, that'd been after the shrink had made his third and farewell appearance, peering at her over the top of his wire-rimmed glasses in a look calculated to seem studious and astute that was wooden-nickel phony. He was no more a real shrink than she was Bigfoot. Oh, he might have the credentials, might even — though she doubted it — have graduated from the school from which they were issued. But he was either monumentally incompetent or lazy. She opted for Door #1. What real psychiatrist asks a suicidal patient if she still wants to die and then buys the answer that she's had a sudden and miraculous change of heart? Seriously?

She wasn't a particularly convincing liar. Though her life for the past few years had honed skills in that department she hadn't realized she possessed, she still wasn't very good at it. Any mildly proficient psychiatrist would have seen that her story about why she'd wanted to die — about how her lover had dumped her for someone else and she had no family, no friends, and suicide had seemed the *only* alternative — had more holes in it than a wino's raincoat. This dude had smiled angelically, looking like a beneficent Friar Tuck with his bald head and soap ring of hair beneath and handing her a basketful of platitudes about life and hope and the 'practice of daily gratitude.' He had actually *said* that!

She wouldn't have been surprised if he'd patted her on the head when he left. He probably would have, but somebody must have told him she had a bullet in her brain beneath her black curls and he didn't want to be the one who dislodged it and dispatched her to the fate that had put it there in the first place.

He'd checked the box on some idiot form that said she was mentally healthy enough to be discharged. She could go home.

But not to the little white frame house on the corner with the big live oak tree in the yard with one limb that stuck out straight from the trunk, low enough so you could reach it if you put one of the chairs off the patio under it, and once you were on that limb, the whole rest of the tree was yours, to climb up to the heights and look out over your small corner of the world.

That was the closest thing to "home" Bailey'd ever known because it was there that she'd befriended a frightened little Puerto Rican orphan named María who had become the little sister she'd never had, bound to her by shared loss that knit them together closer than any DNA, flesh-and-blood bond.

But that home hadn't been Bailey's first. She had come there from somewhere else. A brick house with weeds for a yard and so many children that the foster parents couldn't keep their names straight. Not that they tried. "Hey, you!" accompanied by grabbing an ear or a hank of hair was sufficient to get their message across. It was a simple message: I'm bigger than you are and this is my house. The father had knocked the boys around when he got mad — punched them in the stomach so it wouldn't leave a mark, and fondled some of the girls in ways that made Bailey's skin crawl. Bailey wasn't there long enough to attract his notice, though. Apparently, some injury he had inflicted on the boys had left a mark after all and a teacher reported it, and Child Protective Services workers had descended on the place like crows on roadkill.

Before that had been the place where the mother stayed drunk all day and the older girls did all the work. And before that had been … nowhere. The place in her mind containing the memories of where she'd been before the alcoholic mother — and what had happened to her in that place — was as empty as an old shoebox. At first, she'd filled the shoebox with imaginary stuff — that she had been the only child of adoring parents who lived in a house with a lawn and a tire swing and a princess bed and her mother read her stories and sang her to sleep every night. Even as she was doing it, she knew the "memories" she was putting into the box weren't real. She only did it because the empty box was frightening, invited curiosity and inspection, became an itch she wanted to scratch and she knew that eventually she would pick at it and pick at it until the scab came off and the box would fill up with reality too hideous to look at, too monstrous to countenance. Later, when she was older, she'd acknowledged to herself that the box was full of fantasy. And that was fine as long as she kept the lid on it.

She had met Aaron at a coffee shop where she waited tables, a second job to pay for the night classes that would earn her a teaching certificate. She had never aspired to be an art teacher, but neither had she aspired to eating Ramen noodles three meals a day and that was her future on the income from freelance artwork.

She admitted to him later, one rainy Sunday when they lay together in bed in her tiny studio apartment listening to fat raindrops splat against the windowpanes, that she had spilled his coffee on purpose so she could spend time with him, helping him clean the stain off his obviously pricey suit jacket. He had laughed then, that wonderful rumbling laugh of his, and told her the jacket he'd feigned such concern over was made of some super whiz-bang, state-of-the-art stain resistant fabric you could dump a truckload of road tar on and it'd wash right out. And that he had a dozen more in his closet like it.

She'd had no idea at the time that Aaron Cunningham was *the* Aaron Cunningham, of the Newport Cunninghams, who'd described themselves as wealthy — 'rich' was gauche — and had Aaron's life all plotted out, as they had orchestrated the lives of his two older brothers before him. Add water and stir. Marrying Jessie — a *penniless artist*, for heaven's sake! — was not in their playbook and they never forgave him. If they could have flipped a magic switch to make their daughter-in-law vanish in a puff of smoke, they'd have crawled over two miles of rusty can lids to get to the switch.

When Bethany was born, they loved the child, of course they did, they were grandparents after all and that's what grandparents did. But tainted as she was by Jessie's twenty-three unpedigreed chromosomes, the child would never be "in the club" with Aaron's nieces and nephews.

She didn't care. She had Aaron and the two of them made their own home, the first real home Jessie'd ever known. They'd shared it briefly with María before she went off to business college, and then welcomed Bethany into it, a for-real family.

And then it was gone. All of it. It had vanished without even the little sparkle of a soap bubble and the word *home* meant nothing anymore.

"Don't call it a home!" she'd wanted to shout at the doctor last night. But she hadn't, aware as she was that the doctor had the authority to keep her tied to a bed, that if he suspected she didn't have all four wheels on the road he could have her committed even over the objections of Dr. Halfwit, the bungling psychiatrist. So she'd smiled, nodded like a good little bobblehead doll.

She had gotten out of bed this morning, dressed in the gray t-shirt and jeans — freshly washed — she'd been wearing when…. They were so loose she could have pulled them on without unzipping them. Shooting yourself in the head was an effective, though extreme, weight-loss strategy. Don't try this at home.

When the nurse brought her final discharge papers, she'd been agreeable and pleasant, said she'd "stop by the business office sometime next week" to iron out any issues with her insurance coverage, smiling until her gums felt dry. All so she could go — not home, *house*. And there'd better not be any insurance issues because she most definitely would *not* be back with an ironing board next week. She planned to return to the Watford House and settle in, relax, sort out the crayons still spilled on the floor, and begin again to plan her own death. There was no urgency now, not anymore. She could take her time and *do it right this time* so she wouldn't wake up later in a hospital bed, becoming close personal friends with a ceiling tile. The next time she exited this life she would step out of it and bang the door shut behind her. Lock it with a dead bolt and a chain. The next time she left this world, she wouldn't come back.

She smiled at that thought, and when she looked up, a tall, red-haired man in a brown uniform was standing in the doorway of her room, smiling back at her.

"Looking forward to going home?" he asked.

She ground her teeth. "Who wouldn't look forward to getting out of this place?"

"Well, your chariot has arrived." He crossed the room in long strides and extended his hand. "I'm Sheriff Brice

McGreggor. You came here in an ambulance, so I figured you probably needed a ride home."

The sheriff was a big man, at least six-five, broad shouldered and handsome in a rugged, lumberjack sort of way. His hair was dark red, wine colored, almost burgundy. She looked into his eyes expecting blue but found brown instead, light brown, the color of the caramel squares that were her favorite candy. And his face and hands wore an overlay of freckles so close together there seemed hardly any space in between.

"So the police here provide a hospital shuttle service?"

He chuckled. It was a relaxed, friendly sound.

"No, you can call a cab if you want. But Shadow Rock only has one taxi service and it only has two cabs. Those stay pretty busy shuttling tourists back and forth from the airport. Trust me, my cruiser is a much more reliable conveyance."

BRICE MCGREGGOR STOOD in the doorway, studying the young woman sitting on the side of the hospital bed. Not for the first time, of course. But this time, her eyes were open and when he crossed the room he saw that they were an amazing shade of green, a multi-hued dark hazel.

He'd wanted to dash to the hospital as soon as he'd learned she was awake, that *she had come back*. It upset him more than he was willing to admit that he felt that way, and he most certainly didn't give in to the urge. There were a host of reasons why not, most of which he didn't want to pick at. She wasn't Sleeping Beauty, after all. She was awake. Aware. And thus in the no-fly zone into which he had placed all women. Somehow, crazy as it was, he was disappointed about that. He felt … lonely? He didn't have a perfect sleeping doll to visit who wouldn't expect a reciprocal response he could not give.

The first time he'd come to her hospital room, he hadn't gone in, merely looked at her from the door. Looked from her to the picture of a painting on his cellphone, the picture he'd taken of the piece of art that'd been leaning up against the side of a chair in her living room when he'd responded to T.J.'s 911 call. From one to the other. The painting. The face. They were the same. From the doorway, he couldn't tell if she did, indeed, have a perfect triangle of moles under her right ear, but he didn't doubt that it was so. Everything else about the painting had been as accurate as a digital photograph.

He'd mentioned to T.J. Hamilton that night how strange he thought it was that a suicidal woman would paint a self-portrait of how she would look dead. But that had been before he really examined the painting in her living room. Before sunlight and a magnifying glass had revealed what lamplight the night before had concealed.

The frame, cracked dry wood. Dusty on the edges where a hasty cleaning had failed to remove the years of grime. The paint itself, so old it had peeled off in places, leaving bare canvas beneath. Old canvas, so fragile he feared to touch it, afraid it might disintegrate under the slightest pressure.

The woman who lay in a hospital bed with a bullet in her brain could not possibly have painted the portrait that captured the image of her own dead face. She *might* have been an artist sufficiently talented to pull it off — though every other painting in the house suggested she was a skilled technician at best, with an ability level equal to the task of rendering a gallbladder realistic enough to be useful to a medical student. Nothing there suggested she was capable of the magic of the death portrait. It was perfectly detailed to be sure. But it was much more than that. It was *art*! It conveyed an emotional wallop that was a product of much more than the sum of its parts. It was stunning. And if the art teacher at Kavanaugh County High School — whom he'd consulted as the only art "expert" to which he had access — was correct, it was also at least thirty years old. More likely closer to fifty.

He'd stood on the front steps of the high school after Ted

Byerly's assessment, studying the painting in the bright summer sunshine, trying to cram facts into his head that refused to fit without dangling in tangles out both ears. This was unmistakably, unquestioningly a portrait of the woman who at that time was lying unconscious and unresponsive in a bed at Kavanaugh County Regional Hospital. But just as unmistakable was the reality that it had been painted more than a quarter of a century before she was born.

Then she woke up. With a bullet in her brain.

He thought of the Tar Baby in the Uncle Remus story. Touch it and you stuck to it. The more places you touched it, the more bound to it you became.

Bailey Donahue had become Brice's Tar Baby. He'd reached out to her as she lay unconscious and been captured by Sleeping Beauty and her mysterious portrait. Okay, he was mixing his fairy tales here, but the metaphor still held. The fact that she knew the bullet in her brain could kill her at any time forged another connection — stuck him to her in yet another, even more profound way. He knew what it felt like to live every minute of every day with a guillotine hanging over your head. He understood as few people in the world understood, what it was like to wake up every morning wondering if today was going to be the day, the day his life was over. Instant death was a much less terrifying prospect than what he had faced every day since he'd put the final piece in place and saw the horrifying completed puzzle.

The woman sitting on the edge of the bed didn't view death as a bad thing, of course. She was here, after all, because she had done her dead level best — no pun intended — to end her life, and had been thwarted in the attempt. She would welcome death. At least in the frame of mind she'd been in when she put a revolver to her temple and pulled the trigger. But her frame of mind could change. Might already have changed, in fact. Even if it hadn't, there was still hope.

She saw him, and he turned up the juice as best he could

on his "disarming, unthreatening smile."

It was a calculated thing, though he was not by nature a calculating man. He had learned over the years that the best officers used whatever gifts they'd been given in whatever way would help them get the job done. He knew he could seem stern and unyielding at times and so he had learned to display a kinder, gentler version of himself. He was not *pretending* to be charming, merely being intentional about it.

That he was so affable and well-liked was, after all, what had gotten him elected in a county where competition for the sheriff's job was fierce. Those on the outside looking in saw it as a cush position. Police a small population of mostly law-abiding locals. Be a hard-ass keeping the peace and an ambassador for the chamber of commerce with the tourists who returned year after year to spend their money on paddle boats, rented bicycles, mopeds and jet skis, sailboats, tour guides, historic site admission fees, and the basics of food, gasoline and tourist crapola that kept the county solvent. Without them, Shadow Rock would have collapsed into the same financial ruin that had struck down every other small town in West Virginia when the coal mines closed.

But the affability was just one side of a man much more multifaceted than the less discerning of his constituents would have believed. Oh, when the manure connected with the air conditioning and some situation started to slide south, it was definitely Brice McGreggor you wanted in the foxhole beside you. More than that, though, he was a man who would know instantly when the slide began. He was uncannily intuitive about people and behavior. Perhaps because of his own constant sense of impending doom, his innate understanding of others was dialed up. If he thought a guy was bluffing, well then, the guy was bluffing. Even if he wasn't, McGreggor could handle it, with force, swift and brutal, or with the strength of his words and character. He'd calmed down and disarmed more broken-bottle-wielding drunks in almost a decade in law enforcement than most men in his position did in a thirty-year career.

Right now, he wanted to put this young woman at ease. She was a conundrum, a mystery that had been wallowing around in his mind ever since he'd walked into the living room of the Watford House more than a week ago and heard the paramedics call out that the "suicide" was still alive.

The "suicide" who had painted a picture of herself as she would look dead. Except she hadn't painted that picture. Couldn't have. And if she hadn't, who had?

He tried to make small talk with her as he walked beside the wheelchair the nurse insisted she ride in out to the portico where he had left his cruiser, with the engine running so the air conditioning would have the interior cooled to something less than a gazillion degrees.

How long had she been in town? Making the question casual, of course, not like the cop grilling the suspect in the featureless room with the two-way mirror, the empty table and two straight-backed chairs depicted in every idiot cop show on television.

Where had she come from and why had she moved here? Those were the questions next in his lineup, but she had so tensed at the first one that he switched tactics smoothly in midstream and gave her his humorous monologue about the weather in Kavanaugh County affected as it was by the lake, and how its changeability had provided days like Monday of this week, where it had been foggy, misty, then rain, then bright sunshine, then thunderstorms in the afternoon that surely had raised the water level on the lake half a foot in their deluge and laid down an inch-thick blanket of hail on the far side of the county.

Talking. Watching. Reading her. And what he read confirmed for him what he already knew. She was not at all who she appeared to be, who she wanted the world to think she was.

And if he couldn't figure her out, couldn't unravel her mystery, there was no way he could keep her alive. He knew that it was impossible to prevent a determined suicide. But in his view, the key word in that sentence wasn't "impossible." It was "determined." In that word, there was hope.

He got into the cruiser behind the wheel, but didn't put the car in gear.

"How about we get the elephant out of the front seat so it's not so crowded up here. That head injury," he indicated the bandage on the side of her face, "is a self-inflicted wound. You tried to kill yourself."

He left it there, hanging, waiting to see where she would take the ball once she picked it up and started dribbling it.

"How about we get the *real* elephant out of the way." She turned eyes on him that he could see now had golden streaks in the center of the dark hazel. The eyes were sunken in dark craters in her thin face. "Tell me, Miss ... Donahue..." She hesitated, only a fraction of a second. Most people wouldn't have picked up on it but Brice McGreggor wasn't most people. The name was, as he had suspected, bogus. "Are you planning on trying to finish what you started?"

"Okay. We'll start with that elephant. Are you?"

Now, she studied him. The intensity of the eyes would have been disconcerting to a man not accustomed to probing looks.

"Oh no, officer, I'd never do anything like that again. I've learned my lesson. I'm grateful to be alive. I don't want to die anymore." She paused. "You believe any of that?"

"Not a word."

"The doctors bought it. If they hadn't, I'd be locked up in a rubber room in Saint Somebody's Home for the Bewildered, making some other ceiling tile my new best friend."

He didn't get the last reference, but let it go.

"So why are you being straight with me? I could get you locked up in a rubber room as easily as they could."

She cocked her head to the side. "I'm not sure, exactly. You don't strike me as a man who plays games. You could put me away for … I don't know, however long is legal in West Virginia. And I'd just make nice with the doctors there and eventually they'd have to release me. Then maybe you'd show up again to give me a ride home and we could have this whole conversation all over again and — what's the point?"

"Meaning nobody can stop you. If you want to kill yourself, you'll do it. Sooner, later, eventually, you'll do it. End of story."

"Yeah, pretty much. Game over."

"And do you intend to kill yourself?"

She shifted her gaze away from his face and into a thousand-yard stare out the front window.

"Yes, I do."

"That's what I figured."

She cut her eyes back to him. He could tell he puzzled her. Good.

"And you're not going to ask me why? Why would a young, healthy — well, except for a bullet in the brain, there is that — but still a woman with a 'bright future' and 'everything to live for' want to die?"

"Would you tell me if I did?"

"No."

He shrugged. "Figured that, too."

Something approaching a smile skittered across her lips, a suggestion, then it was gone.

"Buckle up. Seatbelts save lives."

She rolled her eyes.

"You want to listen to that dad-gum buzzer? They tested it on lab rats, you know, found the sound that made them turn on their own kind and eat each other alive."

She buckled her seatbelt and he pulled out from under the hospital portico and drove away.

Chapter Eleven

W<small>HEN</small> B<small>AILEY HAD ARRIVED</small> in Shadow Rock, driving the nondescript four-year-old Honda that'd been provided to her, registration bearing the same name as her driver's license — Bailey Nicole Donahue, *Donahue!* — she had not been interested enough in her surroundings to care about anything except following the directions of the British-accent GPS voice to what had already become, in her mind, the end of the line.

Riding along with the sheriff to a destination he didn't need a GPS to find, she could look around, and when she did she had to admit that the little town had charm. In fact, with its gift shops, ceramics shops, dress shops, candle-and-aromatherapy shops, and tourist do-dad shops in every shape and size sandwiched between ice cream parlors on every corner, the little town was *relentlessly charming*.

"Is this place for real?" she finally asked. "It looks like something out of a model-train catalogue."

"Thomas the Tank Engine, actually." He stopped at a green light and waved on a package-bearing pedestrian in the crosswalk. "These aren't real people. It's all make-believe. Sir Top'm Hat has an office right down from the pretend post office and the faux courthouse."

She smiled, a real smile that felt uncomfortable on her face.

He glanced at her. "I can introduce you, if you'd like to meet him. We're homies."

"You're from here, then? Kavanaugh County?"

"Born in Big Mac Hollow." She looked skeptically at him and he crossed his heart and held up two fingers. "Not making it up. It was named after my family a hundred years before some dude in a white suit flipped his first burger. You don't have to invent strange place names in the West Virginia mountains and Big Mac is tucked so deep in them the sun only shows up about three times a week."

"Lived here your whole life?"

"I didn't say that. I was born here, almost three centuries after the first settlers built cabins on this side of the lake, and a dock stretching out into the water so boats carrying supplies would have a place to tie up and offload." His grin was self-effacing and a bit sheepish. "I'm a history buff, love digging into the old records in the courthouse, finding out the stories of the people who built the town and settled in the mountains around it. I could have been a tour guide — safer line of work but the pay sucks. I'd be glad to give you the ten-cent tour if you like and won't charge you but a quarter."

"Shoot." Then she winced. "Unfortunate word choice."

"I'll give you the Reader's Digest Condensed version."

Then he told her the story of a sleepy little coal town on the edge of a lake with water so clear you could see the bottom until it got so deep the light faded. The town was called Shadow Rock because legend had it that there was a rock — though nobody seemed to know quite where — that early settlers used to tell time by the position of the mountain's shadow on its round surface.

"It's one of those stories that if it's not true, it should be."

He returned to a description of the lake.

"Scuba divers come here to practice. There's not much to

see down there, but you *can* see. We're the warm-up for excursions to Florida and the Bahamas, where there are colorful reefs and weird-looking plants and fish."

He said Shadow Rock was saved from the fate of the other West Virginia coal towns after the mines closed by a visit Andrew Carnegie made in the late 1800s, after he had already amassed a fortune in the steel industry. A friend brought him to a little out-of-the-way place within driving distance from his home in Pittsburgh where the fishing was spectacular and where deer, pheasant, elk — even wild boar — were plentiful in the deep woods blanketing the mountains.

"Carnegie fell in love with Kavanaugh County. He was a Scot, too, you know. The lake was named after Whispering Mountain, which has its own folklore dating back to pre-Civil-War times, but Carnegie called it Loch Cairn Brae. A lot of locals still call it that."

"What does Cairn Brae mean?"

"Loch is Gaelic for lake, of course, and cairn is Gaelic for pile of rocks, or monument. Brae is a village on the island of Mainland in Shetland, Scotland where the Carnegie clan has its roots. There's a pile of rocks on the lakeshore where the original dock was built that's supposed to be the cairn, or the monument Irish and Scottish immigrant miners erected in tribute to Andrew Carnegie a hundred and fifty years ago." He paused, then continued in a stage whisper, "If you ask me, that rock pile is a little too convenient as a tourist stop to be authentic. But it's never a good idea to question the chamber of commerce's version of history."

Of course, the mansions were definitely authentic, he said, not built to entertain the tourists but as summer homes for the uber-rich friends of Andrew Carnegie.

"There are about two dozen of those summer 'cottages' still standing. A few are privately owned, and the others have been turned into museums — decked out in the finery of the early 1900s. Some of them have mannequins dressed in high-necked gowns or top hats and tails to represent the folks who frolicked on the lakeside, but four of them actually have guides dressed in period garb, conducting tours of the obscenely ornate mansions, or of the central dining hall where the rich gathered for communal meals, cooked by the finest chefs money could buy, and entertained by a full orchestra every night."

He smiled.

"That dining hall has been turned into a food court where the tourists can get hamburgers or subway sandwiches during the day, or come to dinner at night and listen to jazz bands, bluegrass or country-western musicians — talented performers from Nashville who sing backup for the stars in the recording studios."

"So Kavanaugh County is home to you." She heard the wistfulness in her voice at the word "home," but didn't think the sheriff picked up on it.

"Yes, but I spent a considerable amount of my life in a scary, unknowable place West Virginians call 'Away From Here.' It's where the wild things are, past the line on maps that says, 'Beyond Here Be Dragons.'"

"What did you do in that strange land?"

"The military. Marines. I wasn't famous, though. Didn't haul home a trunk full of medals like T.J. did."

T.J. Where had she heard—?

He saw her confused look. "T.J. Hamilton. He's the man who was driving by your house, heard the gunshot and dialed 911. He saved your life."

A hole opened up in the universe and Bailey tumbled off into it, out of the sunshine of the make-believe town, out of the presence of the too-good-to-be-true sheriff, down into the dark depths where the real wild things were.

The old man in the wet raincoat and the little dog that had curled up on her sofa, soaking the cushions.

Don't do it! Don't take that gun that's probably lying on the kitchen table right now and put it to your head ... your right temple, actually, and pull the trigger. Don't do it!

The sheriff didn't see her face, was looking left and checking traffic before he pulled out onto another too-quaint-for-words street.

"He said he met you that afternoon, was walking Sparky —" The man's face lit up. "Now there is one cute pup. You might not remember T.J. but there's no possible way to forget that dog. He's like the town mascot, the—"

He saw her face then and stopped babbling.

"What's wrong?"

"Nothing's wrong."

"I thought we agreed we weren't going to play games with each other."

"We never agreed to any such thing."

"Yes, we did. It was an unspoken agreement, but those are the most binding kind. What did I say that upset you?"

She kept her mouth resolutely shut.

"Sparky? If you're upset by Sparky, you're the only person for a hundred miles in every direction who is."

She looked away from him, watching Oz float by outside her window.

"T.J. Something happened with T.J. What was it?"

Nothing.

"Would you rather I asked him, since you're not inclined to talk about it?"

"Yes, ask him. Ask that old man what possible reason he could have to—"

She caught herself in time. Did she really want to get into a discussion with the sheriff about that painting? Worse, still, if the sheriff talked to him, the old man might remember that she'd told him her name was Jessie Cunningham. Her retrograde amnesia had not erased that memory.

"To stick his nose in where it doesn't belong. I didn't ask him to save my life. If I hadn't wanted to die, chances are I

wouldn't have put a gun to my head and pulled the trigger."
She paused, scrambling for a way to change the subject. "And
speaking of pulling the trigger, where *is* my gun? Did you
take it?"

"I did. It was a firearm used in a shooting. I confiscated
it."

"What did you do with it?"

"Well, seeing as how the shooting wasn't a crime, I can't
legally hold onto it. But I think I'll keep it all the same."

They turned a corner and Bailey recognized the house at
the end of the block, the one the real estate agent had proudly
pronounced was the "historic Watford House." Though it was
big and drafty and very old, it was not one of the Carnegie
posse's original homes, just a wannabe. As soon as she'd gotten
a good look at it, she'd understood that "historic" was real-
estate-speak for "should have been bulldozed twenty years
ago."

When the sheriff turned into her driveway, Bailey turned
to face him.

"It's my gun. I bought it legally. I paid for it. It belongs
to me."

There was an echo to those words that distracted her.
She'd said them that night, told the old man—

"I want it back, but if you're bound and determined to
keep it, be my guest. I know the doctors must have told you
about my … problem." She tapped her temple gently. "I could
sneeze getting out of this car and drop over dead. You know
that, don't you?"

He nodded.

"Given the availability of ropes, knives and other methods
of self-destruction — coupled with a bullet already in my
brain, do you really think keeping my gun away from me will
change anything?"

"No, I guess not." But he didn't offer to give her back the
gun, merely got out of the car and walked around to her side

and opened her door. When she got out, he stood there. Didn't offer to walk her to the door.

Well, it wasn't like he was a prom date.

He held out his hand, though, and when he took hers he held it firmly in a hand that was uncharacteristically soft.

"It was good to meet you, Ms. Cunningham, and I wish it could have been under other circumstances. You know that if you ever need anything, anything at all…"

"Thank you." She pulled her hand free. "It was good to meet you, too."

She walked up the steps, inserted the antique skeleton key into the door lock and stepped inside, resisting the urge to look back at him through the crack in the curtains beside the door.

She heard his car door close, heard the car crunch out of the gravel driveway. She let out a sigh of relief then, though she couldn't have articulated what she'd been so tense about. She took two steps away from the door before it hit her.

The force of the realization literally staggered her and she sat down heavily on the arm of the sofa.

He had called her *Ms. Cunningham!* How had he…? The old man! Again! What grievous transgression had she committed against the universe that'd sentenced her to a meddling old fool—?

The sheriff had called her Ms. Cunningham a*nd she hadn't corrected him.*

He'd used her real name. No, not her real name. Her real name wasn't Ms. Cunningham. It was *Mrs.* Cunningham. Mrs. Aaron Webster Cunningham. Webster had been his mother's family name — of the Fox Grove Websters, of course. He'd teased her when Bethany was born, said he wanted that to be her middle name, too.

He'd mentioned it that night on the way to the airport.

. . .

IT'S RAINING, a cold winter rain. Pouring. They have barely come to a complete stop at the stop sign at the end of their block when Jessie turns to Aaron.

"I miss Bethany," she says.

He laughs.

"I'm not joking! I miss her. A whole week. That's too long!"

"We'll survive." He glances away from the road. "We'll be ... busy." And he gives her the look that always sets free flocks of delicious butterflies inside her.

Not this time, though. Instead of butterflies in her belly, she feels her gut yank into a knot. She wouldn't be rocking Bethany to sleep tonight, cuddled up in her yellow Minion blanket, sucking on the corner of it! She had rocked the child to sleep every night since she was born, wrapped snug in that blanket. But tonight—

"Aaron," she sounds bereft but she can't help it, "I'm not sure—"

"Sure we need a vacation? Are you serious? Working ten- and twelve-hour days on the Madison account for a month without a day off ... that does not a happy husband make."

"But—"

He reaches his hand across the seat and takes hers.

"Honey, we need this, we need you-and-me time. It's been too long. I miss you!"

"But Bethany—"

"Will be fine. Your sister has been itching to get her hands on that baby ever since we brought her home from the hospital. She will spoil her rotten, you know she will, give her anything she wants."

He stops and his smile broadens. "Remember how horrified María was when I had her convinced we were going to name the baby 'Webster'?"

Jessie has to smile at that. It's true, her little sister had been so upset she literally cried in relief when Aaron admitted he'd been joking. María had fallen head-over-heels in love with Bethany the first time she held the baby in her arms. She had been almost as omnipresent as Aaron during Jessie's labor, would have been there every second if not for school. And she had cut all her morning classes and spent the whole day of Bethany's birth in the waiting room — pacing back and forth. There was no one short of Jessie herself who would take better, more tender, attentive care of Bethany than María would.

She lets out a sigh. "Okay, you're right."

Thunder rumbles as the rain that had been a light drizzle ratchets up to a downpour.

"Sunny Caribbean, here we come!"

Jessie loves Aaron's smile. And if she lets herself, and doesn't dwell on how much she's going to miss Bethany, she can get excited about spending alone time with the gorgeous dimpled man beside her whose slightest touch could make those butterflies in her belly take flight and flutter so fast they were a blur of color.

The downpour turns into a monsoon. Raindrops thunder like a thousand harried hooves on the roof of the car. The windshield wipers have trouble keeping the windshield clear and traffic is reduced to a crawl. They spot the girl when they come to a stop at the corner of Juniper Street and Lakewood. A lone young woman is standing in the pouring rain beside the bus stop sign — only a sign with a three-foot square awning. No bus shelter. Obviously homeless, clutching her every worldly possession in her arms, she is a pitiful, dismal sight.

There are no businesses nearby where she can take shelter, no trees or roof overhangs. The bus stop post stands lone sentinel next to the curb and the drenched woman huddles beside it trying to squeeze her whole body up under the meager protection of the awning above.

"There's a bus shelter at the Crocker Street stop," Aaron says. "We're going right by it. Roll your window down and tell her we'll give her a ride."

It was an act of simple kindness, so like Aaron. It was sick and sad and ironic that it was his generosity that had cost Aaron his life and Jessie her husband and child.

Chapter Twelve

THE SILENCE in the room throbbed full and heavy. Bailey sat in the too-quiet house in the dark. Just sat, like some toy discarded by a child because the battery was dead.

She was sitting on the couch facing the window that looked out over the front yard, but she hadn't noticed sundown, hadn't noticed the lengthening shadows that slid out from the dark pools where they lived under trees and bushes, and spread out across the yard.

She ought to get up and turn on the lamp.

Why?

Well, because it was dark and ... light was better than dark, somehow.

She started over.

She ought to get up off the couch and turn on the lamp, because...

Alright, she knew why. But there was a much larger question than why she didn't turn on the lamp.

Why *anything?*

An image formed. They did that sometimes now, popped into her mind and she didn't know where they'd come from. Crazy images. In this one, she is clinging to a piece of something, a board or pole or mast — yes, the mast of a ship — in a body of water that stretches out for as far as she can see in every direction. The water is still. The sky is cloudless, so much the same color as the water it's hard to see the stitching of horizon, sky and water seamed together.

She is alone. The only survivor of some mighty shipwreck. Or maybe she is the lone survivor of some cataclysmic end of the world, and maybe she alone lived through Armageddon.

Her reward for survival is life.

Her punishment for survival is life.

She'd never had any trouble articulating the whys of her life. And when her world had come crashing down around her, she had clung to the only why left: Bethany. Bethany was why she got up every morning to face another day. Bethany was why she was willing to endure the loneliness of a total outcast, the emptiness of every day, every hour. Bethany was why!

And when realization had seeped into her being like groundwater into the foundation of a house, that *soon* was an illusion, a mirage, a fantasy. She would never see Bethany again, she had no why. No reason to keep on living.

But her decision to die had given her a new why, a new purpose. She got up in the morning, went about the day's tasks, made preparations, propelled by the purpose of exiting existence before Bethany's third birthday.

Now, even that purpose was gone.

She did not want to go on living.

But right now, she lacked the resolve to get on with planning her death.

She got up, turned on the lamp and started toward her bedroom. She would take a hot shower, feel the water punishing the skin of her face. She would...

Bailey raised her hand and there was a paintbrush in it.

When did she go into her studio and get a paintbrush? And what for?

There was wet paint on it. Blue paint.

She turned toward the door to the studio and saw that it was standing open. She kept it shut because the curtainless windows admitted so much sunlight the heat defied the air conditioner. Her thoughts had been muddy since she woke up in the hospital, the new best bud of a stick-figure water spot on a ceiling tile, but there had been no real holes in her *thought processes*, nothing like…

She walked into the studio and flipped on the light. There was a canvas on the easel. The paint on it was still wet. It was not a dissected section of lung tissue, an enlarged spleen or a canker sore. What was painted on it looked like an illustration from *Oil Painting for Dummies*. A table. Checkered tablecloth. A bowl of fruit — an apple, an orange and banana. All out of proportion, childlike in the lack of depth perception.

Behind the table was a window. The window was ridiculously too large for the room, took up almost the whole canvas. The window looked out on … nothing. It was empty. Blank.

Bailey's heart kicked into a gallop, causing echoes of pain in her head with every heartbeat.

The painting she'd found leaned up against the arm of the couch when she came home from the hospital, the one she'd shoved under the china cabinet so she wouldn't have to look at it until she felt up to destroying it. Smashing it or cutting the canvas to ribbons or burning it — yes, burning it! — that painting had had a table and bowl of fruit, too, all dwarfed by a giant window.

But there was a face in the window. Her face, with a bullet hole in her temple. Bailey began to tremble so violently she dropped the paintbrush on the floor, splattering blue paint on the rag rug.

∼

When Bailey heard the knock at the front door, she was certain she'd find the sheriff on the other side. He hadn't said as much, but she would have been surprised if he hadn't shown up sometime today "to check on her."

And maybe to give her back the handgun he had illegally confiscated. If she had him pegged right, and she wasn't usually wrong about such things, he was a man who couldn't abide shadings of right and wrong, gray spaces wide and deep between what was legal and what wasn't. For a man like that, keeping her gun might have been allowed by his conscience for a little while. But she was certain there was a finite limit on that time and it was probably over.

She opened the door. On the other side of the screen was the old man, T.J. Hamilton, his large friend whose name was Hobbs or something like that, and of course, the adorable dog whose name was Sparky the Wonder Dog.

"You have *got* to be kidding me." She was so totally flabbergasted, those were the only words she could force out between her lips. "You … *again*. What part of 'leave me alone' don't you understand?"

"We got to talk."

"No, we *don't* have to talk." She felt rage rising up again in her chest. "We don't have anything to say to each other."

What was he doing here? She had only seen him one time, talked to him for a few minutes on her front porch. Then he had so inserted himself into her affairs that he was a part of everything that came after.

He was the reason she was still here, still alive and not in some quiet place of dark oblivion that she had longed for every moment of every day since *soon* had become a meaningless word. It was his fault. He'd shown up at her door with that painting…

The painting.

"You know what, you're right, we *do* have to talk …

correction, I have something to say to you. Or rather to give to you."

She turned away from the door and went to the china cabinet on the wall next to the window. She bent down and felt around, found the edge of the painting and dragged it out into the light.

Why had she kept it? She could have thrown it away, destroyed it, burned it up. Why was it still here?

She didn't know the answers to those questions, blamed the omission on the jumble in her brain, which in truth had been clearing more every day, and couldn't reasonably be used as an excuse for much of anything anymore.

The truth still in the husk was that she had not gotten rid of the painting because she was still in some state of denial about its very existence. She'd shoved it out of sight the moment she saw it the day she walked back into this house and into life from that fuzzy time in the hospital which had left her mind in the state of disarray she had to get ordered before she could begin to plan suicide.

And part of the ordering of that thought process was to deal with this painting and with the old man on her porch who had shown up out of nowhere. Well, she'd dispatch him right back to nowhere.

As she lifted the painting off the floor, she noticed details about it she had not attended to before. She had been so mesmerized by the face — her face or the face of her doppel-ganger image — in the portrait that she hadn't examined any other facet of it. Now, she saw the battered frame and it registered with her. The flaking paint, the old canvas.

The old man had said his mother had painted it. His *mother.* That had seemed so outrageously ridiculous she had dismissed it out of hand at the time. But now it was clear to her that the painting was, indeed, old. Maybe not old enough for his mother to have painted it, but old. It was not something some artist had created a couple of months ago.

So where had the old man gotten the painting? And why … yeah, a much better question. Why had he gotten it, from whatever source, and hauled it over here the night she was…?

He'd told her not to do it, not to shoot herself. Had known what she was planning because of the image of her dead in that painting.

That was crazy. It couldn't possibly be.

The mosquito bite. *The mosquito bite!*

Nope, she absolutely was not going *there*.

Then the anger returned in such a flood it washed away all questions and all implications. She didn't give a rip in Aunt Annie's corset why he had brought the painting to her house, why he had gotten it who knew where, why he seemed determined to insert himself into her life whether she liked it or not.

What difference did it make?

What she wanted now — with a white-hot, laser focus — was only one thing: to get rid of the painting, the old man, his friend … even the adorable dog. To evict them from her life and her world and never see any of them again. Ever.

In the grip of that clarifying rage, she marched to the door, flung the screen open so abruptly the old man had to leap back to avoid being whacked in the face with it. She threw the painting out onto the porch where it landed on a corner and split apart, the old frame buckling under the force of the impact, the ancient canvas ripping down the side, the whole of it crumpling in a heap beside the wicker rocking chair.

"This is not *mine*," she shouted, not caring that she sounded more or less unhinged. "It does *not* belong to me. It is yours and I want you to get it off my porch, off my property, out of my yard. Take it, take yourselves, *take your dog* and get out of here and never — do you hear me, I said *never* — bother me again."

The old man started to speak but she was on a roll now

and had no intention of letting him interrupt her.

"Because if you don't, if you *ever* bother me again, if you ever get within a hundred yards of me again, I will have you arrested. I have already filed for a restraining order against you."

That was a lie, of course, but the moment the words leapt out of her mouth she realized she was an idiot for not having done so and she determined to remedy that omission as soon as she got the old man off her porch. She would go to the courthouse, to the too-nice-to-be-real sheriff and tell him that the old man and his friend were stalking her, harassing her, and she wanted a judge to tell them to leave her alone.

She made a show of looking at the watch on her wrist.

"You have exactly thirty seconds to turn around, get off my porch and off my property, or I swear by everything I hold dear in this world I will see you" — she glared at the other man whose name she couldn't remember — *"both of you* behind bars!"

She stood there trembling, waiting for the two of them to scramble away, dragging the adorable dog behind them.

Instead, the old man said to the dog, "Sparky, sit."

The dog sat.

Then the old man smiled, actually smiled, and held out to her a piece of paper. When she didn't take it from his hand, he held it up for her to see.

"Recognize this, do you?"

It was … looked like a survey, like that idiot survey the nurse had insisted she fill out the morning before she was released from the hospital. Yes, that's what it was. There was the frowny face she'd drawn on it, the barest minimum of disapproval she dared to display.

Where did he get…? Why…?

Wordlessly, he turned the piece of paper over. On the back of the survey form were pencil marks, some kind of sketch.

"You drew this." He shook the paper to indicate the marks

on the back of the form. "You don't likely remember drawing it because you wasn't thinking about it at the time."

Somehow, the old man had a way of sucker-punching her, coming at her with such an unexpected blow she was always off balance. She fought to maintain her focus, but found it slipping away.

"And not only was you not thinking about it when you drew it, but you drew it with your left hand."

"That's absurd. I'm right-handed."

Don't do it. Don't let him draw you in.

"So was my mama."

Oh, boy, here we go again. The his-mother-the-artist song and dance.

She discovered to her dismay that his latest jab and parry had muddied her resolve. The rage that had carried her along in a full-frontal assault had ebbed, leaving behind confusion and a vague sense of unease that felt like a cold stone in her belly.

Neither confusion nor unease carried sufficient force to propel the old man off the porch. She sensed he knew that because he seemed to soften.

"I don't mean you no harm, I swear I don't. What's going on here … it's a mystery to me, same as it is to you."

She looked at him, suddenly emotionally exhausted.

"You're crazy."

"No ma'am, I am not. But it's not gonna be long before you start to b'lieve *you* are unless you hear me out."

She was done. Finished. No longer had the energy to resist.

"Fine. Talk. Say your piece. Babble out whatever lunacy has infected your mind. If I listen, if I hear you out, will you leave? Will you promise to leave then and not come back?"

"Before I go, I need you to do more than listen. I need you to—" He exchanged a glance with the big man behind him who had not yet spoken a single word. "I need you to paint me a picture."

Chapter Thirteen

THE WOMAN with a small bandage on her right temple seated on the chair across from him seemed so frail, looked so delicate and fragile the slightest breeze might blow her away.

After T.J.'d met her on the porch that afternoon painting a kidney or a liver or whatever it was, he had described Jessie Cunningham, aka Bailey Donahue, told Dobbs she was "sad, sunken and sick." And that'd been *before* she put a bullet in her brain. A bullet that was still here — or so Sheriff McGreggor had told them, said it could move at any moment and kill her.

And yet here he and T.J. were about to upset her, might even cause her so much distress it'd dislodge the bullet and complete the task she had set out to do when she put the Smith & Wesson revolver to her temple and pulled the trigger.

Maybe the two of them ought to tip their hats to her, tell her to have a nice day, have a nice life, turn and walk away. If they did what they'd come here to do, it might be that in trying to save her life, they would kill her.

He and T.J. had talked about that … and talked about that … and talked about that. *Wore the subject out.*

In the end, they'd both decided — well, mostly he had decided and T.J. had gone along — that the alternative to telling her was worse. They both knew what was going to happen to her, both saw what she couldn't — her future looming like a black tsunami rising out of the ocean, poised to come crashing down and destroy her. *That* would surely kill her. Like it had killed T.J.'s mother.

T.J. hadn't been able to help his mother, Dobbs had argued passionately for half the morning, but he *could* help this woman. He — *they* — could reassure her that even though none of them understood what was happening, she was *not* going crazy, was not a witch, as T.J.'s mother had come to believe she was.

He'd talked T.J. into reaching out to try to stop the suicide his mother had predicted, and now they had a responsibility to this woman they'd saved to see this through to the end with her. Wherever the end might be.

Dobbs had said all that to T.J. Multiple times. T.J.'d finally agreed, or said he did to shut Dobbs up. Either way, it amounted to the same thing: they had to explain to Bailey Donahue what had already happened and what was about to happen. And since Dobbs had been the one who'd shoved that boat out into the water, T.J.'d handed him the oar and said he had to take the first turn rowing.

He squared his shoulders and was about to launch into the spiel he'd put together in his head. Before he could get started, she lifted her hand in a gesture that seemed to take in everything and nothing.

"Why?" she said, then let her hand drop uselessly into her lap.

That was the first thing she'd said since she'd pushed open the screen door and allowed him, T.J. and Sparks to enter. They had left the painting on the porch where she'd thrown it, didn't need it anymore to convince her that there was something going on here that was unexplainable.

In the beat of silence that followed her question, Sparky worked his magic. Hopping down off the couch where he'd been curled up beside T.J., he padded over to Bailey, put his head up next to her leg and began to nudge his nose under her hand, urging her to pet him. She obliged, absently stroking the top of the dog's head, which was all the invitation Sparky needed to hop up into the chair beside her, plop down and lay his whole head in her lap. She relaxed into the motion of stroking his fur.

Sometimes, Dobbs believed T.J.'s dog was smarter than any human, and right now he was certain the animal's unfailingly accurate intuition had guided him to do the one thing, the only possible thing in the universe that would get Bailey Donahue to relax and be willing to hear what he and T.J. had to say.

Dobbs consciously resisted the urge to clear his throat, like an orator in front of a crowd.

"You don't know T.J., but if you asked around about him in Kavanaugh County, you'd learn quick that he's as respected and admired as any human being for two hundred miles in every direction." T.J. made to shush him, but Dobbs waved him off. "I tell you that so you know that what he's about to tell you, what the two of us are about to tell you, is as real as any one of those medals, a handful of them, the Marine Corps pinned on his chest." He could tell T.J. *really* wanted to shut him up then. "The ones he keeps locked up in a metal box in his garage and pretends for all the world they don't exist."

Dobbs gestured with his chin toward the open front door.

"That picture out on your porch, T.J.'s mama painted it when he and I were eleven years old. It was the last one she ever painted, but it was no different from the others, the ones she painted and then burned. I didn't even know T.J.'d kept her last painting until he came home from walking Sparky more than a week ago and said he'd found the woman in the painting. That he'd met you here on the porch that afternoon. The fact that we're having this conversation right now is a wonder to T.J. and me. His mama painted pictures of lots of people after she fell and hit her head, but she didn't sit down and talk to any of them about it. She *couldn't* because all those people were dead."

He saw T.J.'s eyes shift from engaged and present to that thousand-yard stare he got, and Dobbs knew he was remembering.

~

WHEN DOBBS GOT to the part about how T.J.'s mama couldn't tell anybody about the images she painted, T.J.'s memory served up to him unbidden images from the one and only time she ever did.

THE SOUND of the back door banging shut jars T.J. from sleep. Pa's home. He's been gone for three days, helping the Wimset brothers get their small tobacco crop to the tobacco auction in Fairmont.

Pa is drunk, of course. Likely spent every dime the Wimsets paid him buying round after round of cheap whiskey at Taffy's Tavern. But he doesn't hear his father collide with furniture as he staggers across the kitchen to his bedroom door, doesn't hear the big man call out, his speech slurred, "Eulalie, where you at? Ain't you gone welcome your man home with a big kiss?" Or her scurrying feet and whispered words, telling him he's gonna wake T.J. and the other children which, of course, he already has. Soothing him, cajoling him to keep him in his jovial frame of mind. He needs to be kept cheerful at all costs because Samuel Hamilton's mood could turn dark in an eye blink, could go from surly to mean and violent between one breath and the next. And that was a bad thing. A really bad thing.

"Eulalie," his father calls out into the dark house. "Come here to me, woman."

T.J. feels ice form in his veins. He has heard that tone of voice before and it is as dangerous as the rattle of a coiled rattlesnake.

Pa sounds cold sober.

T.J. scoots out of bed, turning to Luke, the oldest of the "littles," the younger brothers who sleep with him.

"Shhhh. You and Jacob stay in bed. Don't get up, neither one of you. No matter what you hear, stay in bed. You understand me?"

He can see the moon shining on their two faces, eyes wide, fearful, as they nod.

Then T.J. crawls across the loft floor and peers over the edge into the single large room below it where light now flows out from the lantern his mother has carried in from the bedroom.

"I'm right here, Sam," she says, hurrying to put the lantern on the table. Pa hasn't moved from the doorway. Looms in the shadows there.

"You want some cold buttermilk? I got—"

Pa takes two large strides toward her and slaps her, backhands her with such force that she literally flies through the air from the blow, collides with one of the kitchen chairs and crumples in a heap on the floor.

She says nothing, just looks up at him with doleful eyes, her split lip pouring blood down her chin. T.J. clenches his hands into fists at his sides.

He once tried to stand up to his father when he was beating his mother. Rushed into the room and dived at the man in a flying tackle that his father shook off like he was a pesky deer fly that had landed on his hand.

"You leave her alone," he had cried at the big man, scrambling to his feet and placing himself between his father and his mother, who was on her knees on the floor where his father had knocked her.

"No, T.J.!" she'd cried and reached out to him. He'd turned to look at her and never saw the blow coming. He woke up some time later, the side of his face on fire, his right eye swollen shut and a cut above his left eye where he had been knocked into the cabinet door.

His mama had made him swear he would never do that again. He reaches up now and feels the scar above his eye, grits his teeth and remains silent.

His father steps to where his mother is lying on her side on the floor, grabs her hair and pulls her upright into a kneeling position. Then he leans close and spits words into her face.

"You almost got me hung," he growls, then calls her all manner of foul names, words T.J. has never heard come out of the mouth of any other human being except his father.

"What … what are you talking about, Sam?" His mother's voice is small, the words slightly garbled. The blow must have knocked some of her teeth loose.

"I'm talkin' 'bout you going to the sheriff with that story about a little white girl getting strangled," he says. And he slaps her full across the face, but holds onto her hair so she doesn't fall, just snaps her head to the side. "You wanna tell me what that was about?" He slaps her again. Blood flies out of her nose and splatters on the plank flooring.

"Answer me!" he demands and draws his hand back to strike her again. She cringes away, and he lets go of her hair and she drops in a heap on the floor.

He straightens up and begins to unfasten the leather belt at his waist.

"I'd be locked up tight in a cell right now, thanks to you." He pulls the belt free, raises it high above his head and brings it down hard across her shoulders. She screams, curls in a ball, with her hands over her head. He then hits her after every accusation.

"I'd be sitting there in the dark while a mob of white men with torches come down the street to the jail."

Whap!

"They'd a'drug me out of that cell and hauled me off to that big oak tree out back of the courthouse!"

Whap!

"They'd a put a rope 'round my neck and strung me up — right then and there. Ain't no jury trial for a nigger kills a white girl."

He hits her twice, whap, whap!

T.J. cringes from every blow, feeling each one not on his back where his mother feels them but on his soul.

His father is breathing hard, either from the effort or from the rage that so contorts his features T.J. can barely recognize him.

His father kicks his mother hard on the hip, then again in the side.

"The only reason I ain't dead right now is 'cause I had a alibi, the only alibi a black man could give that a white man'd believe. I was in

jail *when that little girl went missing! Got into a fight in a bar in Fairmont Friday night and they didn't cut me loose until this morning."*

Pa reaches down and grabs T.J.'s mother by the upper arm and hauls her to her feet. She staggers, but he shakes her hard and yells, "Stand up!" and she remains upright.

He puts his face in hers, inches from her nose and demands in a voice filled with pent-up menace.

"Why'd you do that? Why'd you tell the sheriff you knowed some little white girl was gonna get killed? How could you know a thing like that when didn't nobody know it except the ones found her body? The sheriff figured you knew 'cause you seen me do it. *And when he found out it couldn't a'been me, he'd a'come out here and hauled* you *off to jail — if the little girl's neighbors hadn't seen that white man with a red beard comin' out of the woods right after she went missing. He confessed — that's the only reason you ain't in jail right now about to get lynched your own self."*

He shoves her away from him, slams her against the wall, but she remains standing.

Then his voice gets soft, as full of venom as a water moccasin.

"Now you tell me straight, Eulalie. Tell me how you knew."

"I seen it…" his mother says. The words are hard to understand spoken through her mangled mouth, her broken nose clogged with blood. "…Here." She points to the chifforobe in the corner of the room. Her paints are stored there, the canvases shoved between it and the wall.

Mama staggers to the piece of furniture, pulls a canvas from behind it and turns it toward the light. It is the painting T.J. had seen on her easel in the shed when he found her writhing in the dirt, clawing at her throat as if she were being strangled.

Pa looks like he's been kicked in the belly when he sees the painting. He tries to speak, but can't seem to find the air to form words.

"Where'd you get that?" he finally gasps.

Mama says nothing, only looks down at her feet.

"I asked you a question, woman!" Pa roars. "Where'd you get that?"

"I … I painted it."

"You painted *it?" It is preposterous. Mama only does black-and-*

white sketches with just enough color to make them realistic — a red bow in a little girl's hair or a little boy in a blue shirt — humorous drawings of little white kids where they look so adorable their mamas and daddies is willing to pay Mama good money for her work. There is no way she could possibly have created the portrait she holds in her hand.

T.J. wouldn't have believed it either if he hadn't seen her lying in the dirt in front of it, the paint still wet and a look of horror on her face.

Suddenly, Pa staggers backward, holding his finger out at her, shaking it, his voice quaking with an equal mixture of rage and fear.

"You're a witch! Dear holy God in heaven, you're a witch! Only way you coulda done that was … black magic!"

Then he thunders across the room and yanks the painting out of Mama's hands, he slams it into the edge of the table, ripping the canvas and breaking the wooden struts. He hammers it on the table and the floor, again and again until there is nothing left but broken sticks and tattered pieces of canvas. He throws the last piece across the room and turns to face Mama.

T.J. believes he is going to kill her. He has never seen so murderous a look on anyone's face as he sees now on his father's. But he doesn't move toward her, just looks at her in rage and hatred … and terror.

"You hear me good, woman. You listen up with all your whole self. Don't you never, never paint nothing like this ever again. Do you hear me? If you do—" He crosses the room in two giant strides and grabs Mama around the throat. He lifts her with one hand on her neck and slams her into the wall, then holds her there, choking, her feet dangling above the floor.

"If you ever do black magic again … I will kill you. I will drag you out into the backyard, tie you to the clothesline pole, pour gasoline on you and strike a match … witches should be burned at the stake."

T.J. SHOOK HIS HEAD, a physical gesture to clear out the mental images in his brain. He had spent his whole life avoiding memories of that time, had so walled off the horror it was almost like it didn't exist, them things didn't really happen. But the moment he got a good look at the three moles on Bailey Donahue's neck, the memories come back to him in a flood, a storm-swollen creek, the water roaring downstream, washing away everything in its path.

Now, them memories was as crisp and real as rememberin' the Egg McMuffin he'd had for breakfast this morning. And it 'peared they was gonna stay right where they was, in the front of his mind, right alongside the new ones he was collecting that was just as bad.

Chapter Fourteen

MAYBE IT WAS the head wound. Yes, that was surely part of it. The fact that she had recently suffered a brain injury as traumatic as she had ought to be enough to explain all manner of strange phenomena.

But as she listened to the two earnest old men in her living room tell her a fantastic story that they obviously believed, she felt an otherworldliness, like she had stepped through the looking glass into Wonderland, or had stepped onto the train on Platform Nine and Three Quarters at King's Cross Station and been whisked off to Hogwarts.

At some point during the telling of their tale, she had stopped being angry at them. How could she stay mad at two pathetic old men who had shared some kind of collective fantasy or delusion their whole lives?

They were to be pitied, not reviled. She felt sorry for them.

As the one called Dobbs talked, she caught T.J. studying her. Even as she grasped that the two men must suffer from some form of mental illness, she was also forced to admit how totally sane they seemed. More than sane. Astute. Their minds quick and sharp.

"That didn't take long," T.J. said, when Dobbs had paused in the telling of a story about a time when they were children that they'd debated whether or not they should warn the mill workers that there was going to be an accident there.

"What didn't take long?" she asked.

"Didn't take long for you to decide to tell yourself that we're crazy." He cocked his head to the side. "You have to tell yourself that 'cause any other explanation puts you in the same coop as the two looney roosters sitting here cluckin' in your living room."

She was too tired, too emotionally exhausted to play cat and mouse.

"Let's say I have been careful to leave a trail of bread-crumbs so I can find my way back to the wardrobe."

"What stories you been telling yourself about my mama's painting of you? You decided I painted it? Maybe Dobbs here did? No, wait, I know. I found it in a yard sale and realized that it looked like you — though I hadn't never met you — and decided to haul it over here to show you in the pouring rain because … oh, I don't know … I was bored watching reruns of CSI?"

"I don't have an explanation. But just because I don't have an explanation doesn't mean that your explanation is reality."

She was done. This was getting nowhere and her head had begun thudding, the solemn bong, bong of a gong in some Himalayan temple.

"When did it happen?" T.J. asked.

"When did what happen?"

"When did you paint a picture with a window in it … that you don't remember painting?"

Bailey's heart began to pound, the gong in her head keeping rhythm with the beats.

"That, my dear, was a shot in the dark," Dobbs observed.

"But if you's plannin' to begin life anew as a professional poker player, I'd advise you not to quit your day job."

"What you don't understand is that it doesn't matter *when* you believe us," the man named Dobbs said. His voice was deep and melodious. "You can do it today, or tomorrow or a week from Thursday. But you *will* eventually believe us. You don't have any choice because you'll prove it to yourself."

"And what makes you think I plan to be alive next Thursday?"

"Let's just say I don't think you got a plan, an active plan *not* to be alive," T.J. replied.

She merely looked at him.

"I don't think you want to live, but I also don't think you got no current, pressing *need* to be dead, neither. My read is that whatever it was drove you to pull the trigger on that revolver isn't driving you quite so hard no more."

Bailey got to her feet, not exactly knocking Sparky out onto the floor, but making him scramble.

"Game over. You said if I'd listen to you, hear you out, you would leave me alone, you'd go away and not come back. I've kept my end of the bargain. It's time you kept yours."

"Actually, the bargain was that you would listen to what we had to say … *and* paint me a picture."

All the accumulated goodwill and pity the two men had banked as they told their story vanished in an instant. Bailey felt anger rise up with a taste of bile in the back of her throat. She was objective enough to see that her emotions had slipped their moorings, that ever since she and the ceiling tile had become homies, she had lost significant control over how she felt and what she said.

She could see it, but she didn't care. No, more than that. She was glad.

"Fine! Done. *You got it.* You want a painting? I will give you a painting!" She fixed the two of them with a laser-focused stare. *"And then you will leave and never come back!"*

She turned on her heel and headed toward her studio.

"Come on."

She flung open the studio door and marched across the room to the canvas … the one that contained the window … the one she…

No, not going there. The origin of the painting was not up for discussion. Just paint something on it. Anything. A pituitary gland. A gallbladder. Anything. Throw paint up on it, smear it around and bada boom, bada bing, the two old men would finally be out of her house, her life and her world — forever.

Extending out beneath the canvas was a tray affixed to the front of the easel. A pallet with gobs of paint on it lay on the tray beside a cup with half a dozen brushes. Bailey didn't even pick up the pallet, just grabbed a brush out of the cup, shoved it into a blob of dark blue paint and touched it to the canvas.

THE WORLD IS BLACK, cold and dark all around. Bailey can't breathe.

Water. She's in black water. She can't swim!

It's so dark, she can see nothing. She's drowning!

She has totally lost her sense of direction, doesn't know which way is up or how to get "up." It feels like she's tumbling over and over but she doesn't know how to stop, how to right herself.

Her head suddenly pops above the surface and images form in a blur before her — there's water in her eyes, it stings and she's squinting, can't see. She fights the water, but doesn't know how to keep from going back under again. Keeping your head above the water has something to do with kicking your feet, doesn't it? It's almost impossible to kick with shoes on, though. She tries, one shoe slips off, but the other weighs her down.

Voices. People shouting, crying out, screaming. Other people in the water. Someone's hand brushes her cheek.

"Mommy!" she cries, or tries to, but when she opens her mouth it fills with foul-tasting water and she begins to strangle.

Bright sparkling lights. An explosion.

She reaches out, grasping at empty air, tries to grab something, anything.

Her fingers curl around a piece of wood, it's attached to ... it's the arm of a chair, a heavy wooden Adirondack chair tumbling in the water. She holds on, tries to use it to pull herself up ... but it's slick and it slips out of her grasp and tumbles over on top of her, pushing her head back under the water again.

She can't see, doesn't know which way is up.

Mommy! Momeeeee! But there is no air to cry out.

Bursting the surface again, gasping for air, flashes of colorful light.

Back under. Darkness. Cold. She's holding her breath, fighting the water, wanting to scream. She can hear nothing now, see and feel only water around with hunks of things, pieces of ... things bump into her ... she doesn't know what. They whack her face, she grabs for them.

Up. Up. She has to get up, get air.

She's desperate to expel the breath she's holding. The pain in her lungs sears her chest, aching, throbbing, the pressure building and building—

She can't hold her breath anymore.

It whooshes out of her in a rush of bubbles she ought to be able to see in front of her face but she can't.

The pressure to hold her breath, keep it from bursting out of her was not nearly as fierce as the urgent, frantic need to breathe air back into lungs now empty.

It is more powerful than she is. She can't control it, has to gasp, has to breathe back in.

No, it's water, she can't. Can't. Ca—

Reflexively, she sucks in ... not air. Water. Water rushes into her mouth and nose, burning.

It hurts. She can't ... there's no...

Thoughts are gone.

She's...

Nothing.

RAYMOND DOBSON HAD HEARD descriptions of the phenomenon he was witnessing. Even though they had been whispered to him in urgent tones more years ago than he had fingers and toes to count, he could recall every detail.

But all T.J.'s accounts of what his mother had looked like when she painted had done nothing to prepare Dobbs for the reality of watching the process. It flat-out couldn't be, the way the woman with the black hair was applying paint to the canvas, almost flinging the paint onto the surface. Nobody could do that, paint tiny, intricate details like that. *Nobody could paint with both hands at the same time — two different parts of the picture!*

Dobbs was ashamed to admit now that there had been times all those years ago when he hadn't believed everything T.J. told him. He had never said as much to T.J., of course, would never have let on that he wondered sometimes if T.J. was either making it up or was in some way lost in his own fantasy. Now, he could see that not only had T.J. *not* exaggerated, his descriptions had fallen way short of reality. Hadn't captured how foreign, otherworldly and impossible — how flat-out *wrong* this looked.

Of course, Dobbs had often seen the finished paintings, sneaked terrified into the shed with T.J. to gawk at a still-wet horror. But seeing the process of creating them was an entirely different, more intense kind of horror. Watching the painting take on form and shape planted an elemental fear in his belly he hadn't felt since the days when a trembling T.J. would meet him in the woods, saying nothing, so frightened and upset it took him awhile before he could get his voice under control to speak. Dobbs had always been patient and kind, knowing his friend had seen something that would put the fear of God in a grown man, and when it'd first started, T.J.'d been only eight years old.

They would sit together in silence, sometimes dangling their toes in the cool creek water, sometimes sitting on the log at the top of Big Bear Mountain, looking out over the fields and woods below. Sometimes just standing silent in the trees, staring at the shed behind T.J.'s shack where T.J. said his mother was inside painting a picture, with both hands flying over the canvas and her eyes squeezed tight shut.

T.J. stood beside Dobbs now, saying nothing, his eyes fixed in rabid attention on the young woman in loose jeans and a Betty Boop t-shirt, standing in front of a three-foot-square canvas, making an image in the window she'd been compelled to paint — when? Long enough ago that the paint appeared to be dry.

Dobbs had immediately noticed the lone painting already on the easel when they'd walked into her art studio, the child-ishly inaccurate, out-of-proportion table and bowl of fruit in front of the way-too-big-for-the-painting window in the background. The scene stole all the air from his lungs.

He supposed that until that moment some part of him had clung to an irrational hope that T.J. was wrong about Bailey. Just because this woman had sketched a window — Dobbs still thought it looked more like a Cracker Jack box than a window — with her left hand, didn't mean she was destined to become the next Eulalie Hamilton. It didn't mean that the mystery horror of their childhood, the terrible magic of fifty years ago, had returned.

He'd been able to entertain that notion until he'd seen the canvas on the easel with the window already drawn there, the blank window. Then he knew. She had done what T.J. had said she'd do, what T.J. said his mama had done. She'd started painting pictures with blank windows in them. Was compelled to paint them. And one day, she began to fill the windows with an image.

The worst one Dobbs had ever seen was the one that showed the mill workers crushed by falling lumber, their insides squashed out of them.

Though T.J. had witnessed it, this was Dobbs's maiden

voyage down this river of impossible, and he marveled at it, knowing that he was watching an act that was not of this world. He was standing in the presence of the *supernatural* and that understanding instantly pebbled his skin with gooseflesh.

She had started with the one brush, had picked it up in her right hand, had glared at him and T.J. as if daring them to point out that she was standing in front of a canvas that already had a window painted on it.

The pallet in the tray in front of the easel had had gobs of paint on it, different colors, reds and blues and greens, white and burnt umber. In some places the paints had been swirled together to form other colors. But the paint was fresh, not dried out. She must have used that pallet recently. Dobbs knew nothing about paint, but surely you couldn't leave gobs of it sitting out for long or it would dry. Which meant she had been painting with that pallet … when? This morning before they got here?

She had dipped the brush into the blob of blue paint and touched the tip of the brush to the blank space in the window on the canvas. It was like watching a man grab a high-voltage electric wire — she instantly froze, every muscle rigid. As she slowly relaxed, she moved the brush downward, drew a line. She stopped then, like she didn't know what came next.

Then, she leaned her head back, tilted her face upward so she was looking at the ceiling instead of the painting — if her eyes had been open. Dobbs knew then that Bailey Donahue had left the building.

The hand that held the brush began to move over the canvas, smearing blue across the surface. She lifted the brush and dipped it into a gob of black paint, mixing the blue on the brush into the black, then returned the brush to the canvas, to the *exact spot* where she had left off.

Had her eyes closed the whole time.

Dobbs may have burped out some kind of sound then, surprise, shock, he didn't know, because T.J. glanced at him.

The hand moved faster and faster.

Then she picked up another brush with her left hand, touched it to the pallet, and began to paint with that brush on a different part of the window.

Dobbs felt suddenly weak and lightheaded, and nausea's greasy fingers clutched his belly. But he stood firm, watching as an image began to form in the window. With incredible speed, features began to appear.

First a foot, down at the bottom of the picture, painted with her right hand. A foot clad in a pink sneaker. A child's foot. Then the leg up from the foot. It was dirty, mud-splattered. The other foot formed next to it, but this foot had no shoe, only a sock so dirty you couldn't tell what color it had been.

Dobbs looked up then and saw what her right hand was painting at the top of the picture.

The image of a child began to form there. Wet, filthy, slathered in mud with pieces of twigs and sticks stuck to her. She was lying on her back in wet goo, splayed out, the right leg from the knee down at an impossible angle. Legs didn't bend that way. It had to be broken. As the image began to appear clear enough to identify, Bailey painted faster and faster, the brushes flying across the canvas so fast that paint splattered on her hands and the floor.

Her face was no longer serene, blank, eyes closed. Expressions crossed her face, she opened her mouth as if she were trying to speak, closed it again. She began to pant, to gasp. She shook her head, and her legs began to tremble so violently it was amazing she was able to stand. And still she painted, flawlessly, creating the image of a filthy child, lying injured in the mud.

She began to cry out, muffled, grunts coming from her throat, her face becoming a mask of terror, gasping, shaking her head.

Dobbs thought of the bullet in her brain. If it moved the

least little bit, it could kill her, paralyze her, rob her of sight or hearing, thought and memories. Now, she thrashed her head from side to side, crying out without making any noise, clearly terrified.

Dobbs was afraid for her, for what she might do to herself. How could she whip her head around like that without… When her head snapped back at an angle that looked like her neck had broken, Dobbs couldn't stand it anymore. He stepped forward and put his hand on her shoulder.

"Miss Donahue, Bailey, you can't—"

She froze the second he touched her. Her right hand had completed creating the image of muddy, wet hair in a tangle of sticks and debris and it was moving down onto the forehead, beginning to paint the face below the wet hair. But she froze in place at his touch, shook all over as if in the grip of a grand mal seizure.

"No," T.J. shouted, "don't touch her. Don't interrupt…"

But it was too late. The paintbrush dropped out of her right hand to the floor, splattering cream-colored paint. Then the left brush dropped. She stood frozen in front of the canvas. Not moving, not blinking, not breathing.

Then she folded up like a marionette and fell, boneless and limp.

T.J. was faster than Dobbs, stepped forward and caught her by the shoulders and eased her gently to the floor so her head wouldn't bang on the hardwood.

She was breathing fast. But no other part of her moved.

Dobbs looked at her pale face, immobile now where it had been contorted with emotion only seconds before. And he was certain that the expressionless look was one she would wear for the rest of her life, that she would never wake up, that the piece of metal in her brain had been torn loose by her frantic shaking and had moved.

Bailey was gone. Not dead, but gone. She would never wake up. Whoever had been Bailey Donahue, the woman whose body had been seized by some supernatural force, was no more.

Then her eyes fluttered, opened, closed again. Opened a second time and stayed open. They focused, registered recognition, traveled from T.J.'s face above hers to his and back to T.J.'s. She started to cry.

Chapter Fifteen

DARKNESS. Black. Nothing. Dead.

Then Bailey gasped, sucked in a lungful of air.

Air!

The cold was gone, the darkness was melting away into the normal dark of closed eyes, rather than the infinite dark of death. She blinked. Light, then dark again.

She opened her eyes and looked at...

Faces, one black, one white, looked down at her.

Why was she forever opening her eyes to faces looking down at her?

She glanced up past the faces, but her old friend the ceiling tile was nowhere to be found.

Jumbled thoughts began to untangle themselves.

"Bailey, you alright now? Can you talk to me?"

Sensation was returning all over. She lay on the floor, could feel the chill of the hardwood.

Why was she on the floor with these two — T.J. Hamilton and Raymond Dob—?

She gasped, not merely to get air into her lungs this time, cried out, a small squeak of a scream but it was all she could manage, then she began to scramble upright, trying to sit up.

"Now, why don't you lie where you're at for—?"

She shoved T.J.'s restraining hands aside and sat up. Then she pulled her knees up to her chin, wrapped her arms around her legs and sat there like that, breathing hard. Crying. Was she crying? Yes, she was crying.

She looked at T.J. who was down on one knee beside her, his hand on her shoulder.

"I was … I…"

How could she explain it?

"You seen something, didn't you, missy?"

"Yes, yes! I saw—"

"You more than seen it, though. You experienced it. You *lived* it."

Bailey was grateful that he was tagging words onto what she was trying to say because her own thoughts and emotions were so tangled up with impossible images, and horrible sensations, that she could make no sense of it.

"I was … *drowning!*" She gasped out the last word, the memory of water, cold black water, filling her lungs so visceral she clutched her chest, feeling again the agony.

T.J. stood, reached his hand down to her.

"Can you stand?"

She obediently took his hand and let him pull her to her feet. She was wobbly, unbalanced, but the other man — *Dobbs,* his name was *Dobbs* — was instantly at her side, steadying her.

T.J. turned her toward the door and walked her out through it and she went along gentle and pliable as a lamb. He took her into the living room and eased her down on the sofa. He sat beside her, and the little dog, the adorable little dog, hopped up into her lap and snuggled close. She was grateful for his warm presence, and she buried her face in his soft fur, trying to shake loose from the … what, hallucination?

She had been drowning.

"I thought I was…"

"You *was*. You was living something that was happenin' to somebody else. You was living what you was paintin'."

She looked toward the doorway leading into the studio and started to rise, but T.J. held her gently where she was.

"'Fore you go look at that painting, you'd best sit here a bit, get your breath."

He looked up at Dobbs.

"Why don't you go see if you can find a soft drink — you got soda pops, don't you?" She smiled at the reference.

"Yes, in the cabinet, cans. Just Diet Pepsi."

Dobbs lumbered off toward the kitchen and T.J. took her hands in his.

"What just happened to you, I seen it before. This ain't my first rodeo. I seen it happen to my mama when I was a little boy. We done told you the pictures she painted, but I hadn't got around yet to the part about what happened to her when she was paintin' 'em."

Bailey shook her head, so terribly confused. She had wandered out the back door of the wardrobe this time, right into Hogwarts, Oz and Wonderland put together. Into the Shire. Correction, into *Mordor*. She wasn't sure right now what was real and what was not.

"I suppose it's something like a hallucination, though I ain't never had a hallucination. But that's when you see and feel and taste, and experience something that ain't really happenin' to you."

"I was drowning." She sounded like a parrot. "I was … there was water and I couldn't get my breath and I kept going under and then … then I couldn't get back up and I … I…"

She began to tremble and he let go of one of her hands and slipped his arm around her shoulders, patting her comfortingly.

"What happened to me? Why? What *is* all this?"

"I wish I knew."

Dobbs returned then with a glass full of ice, popped the tab on a Diet Pepsi and poured it foaming into the glass.

"I didn't never expect to see anything like what just happened ever again. The last time I seen it was when I's eleven years old. I didn't watch her paint the picture of you, but I seen her paintin' the one before that, a painting of…"

His voice trailed off and he fell silent.

"There was a fire," Dobbs told her, taking a seat in the wingback chair across from the two of them on the couch. "It started at night. They think it was where creosote in the chimney seeped out through the cracks in the bricks, and when it got hot, it started a fire in the wall."

He stopped, looked at T.J., then finished simply. "A mama, daddy and three little kids."

T.J.'s voice sounded haunted when he continued. "They said the five of them died of smoke inhalation, that they's dead before the fire ever got to 'em. But that ain't the way of it. They burned up. Mama painted the fire. And she … burned, too."

Bailey pushed the memory of the sensation of drowning aside and tried to order her thoughts, tried to be rational and reasonable. She grabbed hold of her emotions, the terror and panic of a few minutes before still lingering like mist above a creek. She sat up straight, looked with a frank, direct stare into the eyes of the old man who had brought total chaos into her world at a time when all she asked of life was smooth waters and a dark, quiet peace.

"So you're telling me that your mother painted pictures of … things, events, people she couldn't see, didn't know about, that hadn't even happened yet, that she painted that portrait of me forty … fifty—?"

"Almost sixty years ago, in 1958."

"…*Sixty* years before I sat in that kitchen," she gestured with her chin toward it, "and put a bullet in my brain?"

"She started painting after she fell and hit her head. It was the end of June, the week before the fourth of July." Dobbs straightened as if he'd thought of something.

"And that is a portrait of me, I mean it *is* me — down to the moles on my neck and the mosquito bite on my forehead."

"Mosquito bite?" T.J. asked.

"I guess you didn't notice, but I did. There's a pink spot on the picture that matches the mosquito bite I got..." She reached up and felt around above her right eye. "It's gone now, but I was sitting at the kitchen table ... with the gun in my hand when I heard a mosquito buzzing around. I swatted it. And a minute later — no, it couldn't even have been that long — I heard your knock."

She took a shaky breath.

"And *that's* impossible. But it's also right there." She pointed to the front door, beyond which the broken painting lay on the porch. "You can see it, touch it, hold it in your hand. It's *real.*"

She shook her head in a last-ditch effort at denial. "This is crazy. It can't be!" She looked from one to the other of the men sitting in her parlor. Things like this didn't happen to ordinary people like her. This was from superhero comics and fantasy novels and.... It couldn't be. It flat out could *not* be.

But it was.

She took a deep breath.

"Why *me*? What does your mother's portrait have to do with what happened in there with me and that painting..." She looked toward the doorway into the studio, then got unsteadily to her feet and started toward it.

"I want to see that painting."

T.J. stood to block her way.

"You not gone like what you see and you still pale as a just-laid egg. With that bullet ... why don't you sit—"

"Let's get this out of the way right now, okay?" She pointed to the small bandage covering a fingertip-sized wound on her temple. "This bullet in my head, I have no intention of making it the hall monitor of my whole life, deciding what I can do and what I can't do, when and where. I could hiccup and drop dead. I could just as likely survive going over Niagara Falls in a barrel." She looked deep into eyes so brown you couldn't make out the pupils. "It's no secret that life doesn't matter to me. More than a week ago I turned toward the audience, took my final bow and stepped off the stage. Permanently, or so I thought. But even if my life were precious to me — no, *especially* if my life were precious to me — I wouldn't sign over the property and hand the keys to fear and timidity. We clear?"

She saw a look come into his eyes she hadn't seen before. It wasn't pity. Maybe it was respect.

He nodded and moved aside and she went into the studio, then walked in something like a trance to the still-wet painting, stepping in splatters of paint on the floor.

A child, a little girl in a wet sundress, lay sprawled on her back in a puddle of muddy water, her long braids so matted with mud and sticks you couldn't even tell the color, her arms and legs slathered with the same mud and lumps of nameless goo. Her right leg was crooked, must have been broken. Her face was … missing, nothing was painted there, only blank canvas.

T.J. must have seen her looking at the empty space.

"Dobbs, he … you was crying out and he was worried you was gonna … so he touched your shoulder, like to wake you up just as your brushes was starting on her face."

"Brush-*es*? Plural?"

"Uh huh." Dobbs nodded. "In both hands."

T.J. looked hard at the painting, examined it.

"This little girl drowned alright, but ain't no way it was in a swimming pool. Look at all the mess in her hair and on her clothes. She musta drowned in the lake."

"Maybe she was out fishing with her daddy and fell out of the boat," Dobbs said.

"Or might be she was on the shore playin' and fell in."

"She didn't drown alone," Bailey said, and T.J.'s eyes shifted from examining the painting to examining her face. "There were other people there, I could hear … the little girl could hear the cries of other people in the water, people crying for help. And there was some kind of explosion, I could see, I mean *she* could see—"

T.J. stopped her. "You was seeing out her eyes, so you saw it, too. An explosion — what kind of explosion?"

"I couldn't tell anything about it. I saw the bright lights, heard the boom sound. And there was stuff in the water, big pieces of, I don't know what, it was so dark, but pieces of broken things, debris."

"So something blew up, a boat maybe, and sank, and pieces of it were in the water?" Dobbs asked.

"Maybe. She was…" She glanced at T.J. and started over. "*I* was so scared. I couldn't swim, didn't even know how to kick my feet to get my head above the water." Bailey put her hands on her upper arms and gripped, hugging herself. "I tried to cry out for help but I got strangled."

She described the tumbling sensation and her fingers slipping on the arm of the Adirondack chair.

"I was holding my breath, but my chest hurt and I couldn't."

T.J. touched her hand. She realized she was squeezing her upper arms hard enough to leave bruises.

"It ain't real. It's happening in your head like it was real, and it was reality to the little girl here, but you're fine, you're here and it's dry and there's air. Come on, now, walk it back some."

She sank down into one of two armchairs in the studio, rejects from a yard sale somewhere, sometime, and put her head in her hands.

"What is this? *What's happening to me?*"

"I done told you, I don't know, didn't know sixty years ago

and don't know now. All's I do know is that little drowned girl … she ain't drowned *yet*. She's still alive now. Not for long, though. She's gonna drown, die, and apparently some other folks is gonna die along with her." He paused.

"Unless…"

"T.J." Dobbs only said his name. But the look he gave him was probably a whole paragraph of communication in T.J./Dobbs-speak. "You sure you want to go there?"

"Unless what?" But Bailey knew what.

"We saved your life, and until that happened, we didn't know if … We thought maybe once his mama painted something, it was going to happen, destined to happen *no matter what.*"

"But you *didn't* save me. I *did* pull the trigger. The only thing that saved me is the fact that the bullet didn't do what it was supposed to do. I'm not alive because you interfered. I'd be just as much alive, would be sitting right here, right now if you hadn't shown up on my doorstep that night and tried to talk me out of it."

"You b'lieve that, do ya?"

She merely looked at him.

"You think seeing that picture of yourself with a hole in your head didn't change nothing? You sure about that? You sure you didn't hesitate, pull back at the last second?"

He let the words hang out there in the air between them. Bailey couldn't speak.

"Sheriff McGreggor told me the doctors said the angle of the bullet wasn't straight in. If it had been, it would have tore through the center of your brain and you'd be dead."

It'd be nice if Dr. Villa and No Name Doctor had imparted that significant piece of information to *her*. And maybe they had. She did, after all, ignore almost everything they said to her.

"The bullet entered at a slant, a pretty severe upward angle, and lodged next to your skull. Couldn't a'done that unless you tilted the gun barrel, like at the last second you was pullin' away."

Bailey shook her head in total confusion. *Had* she changed her mind at the last instant, the last millisecond? And if she had, was it the painting that'd caused her hesitation?

She had absolutely no idea, and with a certainty she could attach to few things in her life right now, she understood that she would *never* know. Retrograde amnesia had permanently erased that information.

"So you think…" Bailey edged out there onto the fragile ice again, farther this time, so close to the bottomless abyss in her mind, the dark ditch of lunacy, that she could feel the cold wind from it blowing on her face. "You think this little girl hasn't drowned yet, and that maybe she doesn't have to drown? Is *that* what you're saying?"

It *was* what he was saying, but T.J. backpedaled from it, pulled away from the enormity of the possibility. Like Bailey'd pulled away from the bullet.

"I don't know what I'm saying." T.J. got up and began to pace. "I come here today to warn you about what I knew was gonna happen to you, that's all, so you wouldn't think you was crazy … or a witch." He gestured toward the wet painting on the easel. "I didn't know there was gonna be, that you was gonna paint—"

"Well, you knew I was going to paint *something* besides butterflies and cancerous tumors! What were you expecting? When I did what you knew I was going to do, painted…" She didn't finish the sentence, just gestured toward the wet canvas. "What were you planning to do about it?"

"I didn't have no plan," T.J. shot back.

"Yes, you did." Dobbs's melodious voice was quiet. "We both did. We never talked about it, but we both did."

He said nothing more, merely looked at T.J. Finally, T.J. let out a breath.

"I don't know how many of these paintings my mama

done after she fell and hit her head, before she hung herself from a barn rafter three years later."

Bailey might have gasped. She couldn't tell. She was so riveted on his every word she was barely aware of anything else.

"And she *lived* what she painted, just like you did. And once she'd painted something, she … I don't know, it was like she was connected to the people she painted in some way. I think maybe she seen or felt or heard things they did, sometimes, until … whatever she'd painted, actually happened."

He stopped pacing, stood in front of Bailey. She looked up into his earnest face and a terrible foreboding came over her, an understanding that beyond his words was a world she never dreamed existed, one far beyond where the wild things were. She thought of what Brice had said when he brought her home, how he'd left Kavanaugh County and traveled to Away From Here, a place on the other side of the spot on ancient maps where it said, "Beyond here be dragons." Beyond T.J.'s words was an unexplored world, a universe that likely contained horrors bigger and nastier than dragons.

"I think what drove my mama to hang herself wasn't just that she'd come by this incredible ability she didn't want, didn't understand, that terrified her — an ability my father told her was witchcraft. I think what put her over the edge was the fact that she *knew* these people was gonna die, knew *how* they was gonna die, sometimes even *when* they was gonna die, and she never lifted a finger to help them. I think that ate a hole in her soul."

"And this little girl…" Bailey didn't look at the portrait but deep into T.J.'s luminous eyes. "She's going to drown unless … You think *we* have to warn her, don't you? You think we have to save her."

"I think we got to try."

Dobbs's deep voice spoke into the silence that followed.

"It isn't just her, either. You said there were other people, an explosion. Must be one of those big boats out on the lake. Something blew up and it sank and all the people on it were thrown into the water to drown. This little girl did. Sounds like other people did, too. It's more than one life. More than one little girl."

an explosion... be one of those... ... on earth take
... any blow up and it ... and ... ... happens it too
without ... the ... ... This ... out and ... the
other people ... ... more sign one ... ... one
... ...

Chapter Sixteen

BAILEY PUT on a pot of coffee for T.J. and Dobbs. She was still nursing the Diet Pepsi in a glass with almost-melted ice cubes. Then they wandered with their cups and saucers back into the studio instead of sitting at the kitchen table. They had been drawn there. The magnetism of the incredible painting on the easel was a powerful thing.

Approaching it as tentatively as if it were a rattlesnake about to bite, Bailey stood in front of it, looking at the little girl lying on her back in the puddle, drawn not just to the content of the portrait but to the design and execution of it. It was an incredibly intense piece of art. Not just that it was a dead child, but the immediacy of it, the detail that Bailey couldn't believe had been painted in — what? She looked at the clock on the wall.

"Are you telling me I painted this in less than half an hour?"

"You were flying," Dobbs said.

Bailey had been painting her whole life. She had never had any illusions about her level of talent, was very sober about it, in fact. She was a solid B art student and would never rise above that level. She believed what the writer Stephen

King said about writing applied to art as well. He said that hard work and practice could make a mediocre writer into a good writer. But no amount of work could change a good writer into a great one. The bridge that separated good from great was talent.

But Bailey didn't care that she'd never be a great artist. She believed she painted well enough to earn a living at it — though she'd been wrong about that part — and that was enough because she painted for the pure joy of it. She had done crayon drawings as a child, using bright, primary colors, only a handful out of the whole box of sixty-four. Which now represented for her the disorder of the thoughts in her brain. But they were gradually sorting themselves out, going back into the box where they'd been before. There was still a mess, but not what it was when she and the ceiling tile became BFFs.

In all the years she had painted, in all the hundreds of pictures she had done in that period of time, including the years as an art major at Tulane University, she had never created anything with the exceptional excellence of this work of art. And that's what it was, just as the picture T.J.'s mother had painted of her was.

She froze, then turned and went out to the porch and picked up the painting she had tossed out at them that T.J. said his mother had painted before Bailey was born. The strut on one side was broken, the canvas torn, but she picked it up carefully, took it into the house, into the studio and set it on an easel, then she moved the easel to stand next to the one with fresh paint, the piece of art she had created in less than half an hour of furious painting only a few minutes earlier.

T.J. saw it immediately.

"They's the same, ain't they?"

"What's the same?" Dobbs asked.

"The style, the brushstrokes, the … it's called a 'signature' in the art world and takes into account different visual elements in the work that—" She looked at the blank faces of the two men and gave up. "If I had the right equipment — infrared spectroscopy, gas chromatography, that kind of thing, I think I could *prove* it. But right now, all I can give you is an educated opinion. If I were an art critic called in to authenticate these paintings, I would say unequivocally that *the same person painted them both.*"

That was a conversation stopper.

"How can that be?" Dobbs said.

"How would I know?" Bailey realized she'd snapped at him and patted his shoulder. "I don't understand any of it."

She stepped closer, reached out trembling fingers to the blank spot on the canvas where the little girl's face—

THE INSTANT she touches the canvas, she is drowning again, fighting the water, desperate to come up for air. Her head lifts for an instant out of the water and she utters a wordless cry, a scream of panic and desperation, coughing. She sputters, cries out—

SHE WAS BACK in the studio, a wailing scream that ended in *"Heeeeellp!"* exploding from her throat as Dobbs steadied her, his big hands on her shoulders.

"What's going on here?" demanded a voice from behind her.

All three of them jumped in surprise and turned to find Kavanaugh County Sheriff Brice McGreggor standing in the doorway of the studio with his gun drawn, held out in front of him in a two-handed grip.

BRICE MCGREGGOR PULLED his patrol car to a stop at the curb in front of the Watford House. He didn't pull into the driveway because there were already two cars there. One of them belonged to Bailey Donahue, the other one was, unless he was mistaken, the old Ford pickup T.J. Hamilton drove.

He got out of the car and approached the house, and as he did, he wondered at the connection between T.J. Hamilton and the woman who had tried to kill herself in this house. T.J. had come to him, asked him questions about the case while she was still in the hospital. He'd told the old man everything he wanted to know, and accepted on the face of it that T.J. was just curious to find out what had happened to the woman he met one afternoon who tried to blow her own brains out that same night.

Still, T.J.'s interest was … odd, itched in that particular spot in a police officer's mind where cop-gut instinct resided.

And while he was considering the grumblings of his gut instinct — or maybe just hunger since he'd only had a Starbucks coffee and a roll for breakfast — he forced himself to face square-on that his own interest in the case didn't pass the sniff test, either. He'd not kept his emotions in a tight-fisted grip where Bailey Donahue was concerned because she'd been safe, Sleeping Beauty, a woman he'd allowed himself to care about precisely because it could never go anywhere. But she'd broken the rules of Fairy Tale-dom, had opened her eyes sans a prince's kiss, and now Brice had to shove the genie back into the bottle — mixing those fairy tales again. Bailey would have to be relegated to a place among all the rest of humanity's women. Beyond the yellow-and-black barricade tape: Police Line Do Not Cross.

He stepped up onto the porch and noticed a scrap of canvas lying beside the screen door. He picked it up and thought it might be a piece of the painting he had shown the art teacher at the high school. Apparently, Miss Donahue had decided she didn't like the picture. No surprise there. Who *would* like a picture of themselves dead? She must have destroyed it.

Through the screen door, he watched Sparky bound across the room, tail wagging, to greet him. That *was* T.J. Hamilton's pickup in the driveway. He smiled at Sparky, who sat expectantly on the other side of the screen, as he drew his hand back to knock. Then he heard a scream, a piercing, terrified wail from inside the house, and a woman's voice cried out, "Help!"

Sparky turned and raced out of the room barking and Brice was inside the house in seconds, gun drawn. He cleared the living room with one broad sweep, edged carefully down the hallway behind the dog — that had abruptly stopped barking — and stepped to the open doorway of a room where three people stood looking at a painting on an easel. Beside it was the not-totally-destroyed painting of Bailey on a second easel.

"What's going on here?" he demanded, even as he recognized the three people, who were turning toward him in apprehension.

The sheriff instantly pointed the gun at the floor, then holstered it.

"I heard a scream," he said. "A cry for help." He looked at Bailey. "Was it you?"

She looked confused, glanced at T.J. as if to ask him what she should say, which was definitely odd.

"I did. Yes. I was painting a picture…" She gestured to the one on the easel. "And I … was feeling what … I felt like I was drowning." She sat down heavily in the chair next to the easel. "I'm sorry, I'm … my mind is a very scary place right now." Then she almost smiled. "I'd advise against going anywhere near it. Beyond this point be dragons."

Brice stepped to the painting on the easel. The paint was still wet, as if it had just been applied. It was a painting of a little girl lying on her back in a puddle — the child had no face, but everything about her posture made clear what her face would have revealed. She was dead.

He looked from that picture to the one beside it. It was the picture he'd thought Bailey had destroyed. It was damaged; one of the struts was broken and a piece of canvas was missing, the one he'd picked up off the porch. He looked from the picture of the child to the portrait of Bailey and back to the little girl. He didn't know art, but the style of both pictures was strikingly similar.

"So … you *did* paint the self-portrait?" he said, then realized an explanation was in order. "I saw it here the night of the 911 call." He saw no reason to explain further, to tell them he'd had the picture examined by the high school art teacher.

"No, actually, I didn't. I only painted that one." She indicated the drowned-child picture.

"But it looks like the same person painted both of them," he said.

"Maybe the same person did," Dobbs said.

They all turned to face him.

"And that means?" the sheriff asked, totally confused.

"Nothing," Dobbs said. "I was just thinking about … never mind."

"You do realize, don't you, that none of you is making any sense?"

T.J. looked at him with tired eyes.

"You don't know all the facts, son. I guess it's time you did."

WHEN T.J. WAS FINISHED with his tale, Brice didn't know whether to wind his watch or take third base.

He had never heard anything as strange and fanciful as this. Strange he could handle, but fanciful … not so much. If Brice McGreggor was anything, he was grounded in reality. He didn't read fiction, saw no point in it. It was make-believe. Movies and television shows fell into the same category, entertaining but useless. Even before his life circumstance had locked his future in chains, imprisoned him in a lifestyle as devoid of expectations as he could make it, he was a practical, pragmatic man. Sensible. But this…?

It was so far the other side of sensible UPS didn't even deliver there.

There was nobody in his life for whom Brice had more respect than he did T.J. Hamilton. He was a fellow Marine, and not just any Marine, a decorated war hero. Brice could not for the life of him come up with any reason the man would make up such a tale. A tale backed up by Dobbs. Brice was one of only a handful of people in the county who knew Raymond Dobson was way more than the "good ole boy" folks saw, that he'd become a millionaire before he was thirty and had retired to live modestly in his hometown. Why would a man like that invent such a fantasy? And then there was the evidence in front of him, the painting the art teacher had told him was more than half a century old. The rest of it, though, the tale of pictures T.J.'s mother painted without looking at them, that depicted events that hadn't happened yet…

He struggled to order his thoughts, forced himself to think sequentially, the linear logic of a law enforcement officer. He let the whole story lie, left it where it was, in all its fanciful ambiguity and took the next sequential step, the one he'd have taken if he had believed every word T.J. Hamilton said.

If it were true, then…

"Your mother painted this picture of Bailey sixty years ago, before Bailey was even born. What makes you think this picture of the little drowned girl isn't a picture of some other child who isn't even born yet?" That was a logical, reasonable question, applied to a circumstance that was neither. "If these are portraits of what hasn't happened yet, maybe this won't happen for twenty years, forty years, fifty."

"This here little girl is alive right now. And she's going to be dead in less than a week unless we can figure out who she is and come up with a way to keep whatever boat she's on from blowing up."

"And you know that because…?"

T.J. pointed to the top of the little girl's hand. Her arm was lying across her body with her hand on her chest, palm down, almost like she was pledging allegiance to the flag.

"Look at that mark."

There was a smudge on the top of her hand, but the sheriff had paid it no mind because her whole body was covered in mud and debris. Now, he leaned close and examined the smudge and realized it wasn't a smudge, it was a shape, like a tattoo.

"You know what that is?" T.J. asked, and Brice figured it out as the old man was speaking. He hadn't recognized it at first because of the angle of the hand; he was looking at it upside down. "It's some kind of stamp, some—"

"It's an admission stamp to that carnival that sets up in the parking lot of the Piggly Wiggly," Dobbs said.

"The one that comes every year with the *rigged* games." T.J. amended, then cast a baleful eye at Brice, who didn't bother to point out that he and his officers had patrolled the carnival every night since it opened, and could find nothing rigged about the games. What they found instead was that it was indeed a whole lot harder to toss a ring around the neck of a milk bottle than it appeared to be.

True, the design of some of the games caused optical illusions, making the targets seem bigger or smaller, closer or farther away than they actually were. But Brice had long ago done the math, figuring out how much the carneys paid for prizes and how much they charged for attempts to win them. Every prepubescent boy and jacked-up-on-steroids badass wannabe was so determined to impress the hottie on his arm that he'd spend ten, fifteen, twenty dollars to secure for her a stuffed animal filled with sawdust in some sweatshop in a Third World country that would begin to leak said sawdust out of the seams before she got it home and would likely come completely apart in less than a week.

The carneys paid a dime, a quarter tops, for each of the prizes, then charged patrons three-tries-for-a-dollar to try to win them. They didn't have to rig the games to make money.

"That's the ink stamp they put on kids when their parents pay their admission."

Brice leaned forward and squinted. "These things are dated, using the kind of indelible ink that won't wash out for several days."

"With kids who don't wash their hands very often, might last longer than that." Dobbs said.

Brice tilted his head to the side, trying to get a better angle on the smudge. "I can see 'Jul' and '15' here, but I can't make out anything else." He looked at Bailey. "What was the date you intended to paint?"

She looked as if he'd asked where she kept her third eye.

"I didn't *intend* to paint anything at all."

Dobbs pulled out cheaters, parked them on his nose and looked at the blob on the back of the child's hand. "I can't make out the date, either, with the mud smeared on her hand. But it has to be July something, 2015. Since the carnival closes up on July 4, that's a four-day window."

"Today's July 2, which means sometime in the next forty-eight hours, this little girl and a whole lot of other people are going to drown in Whispering Mountain Lake," Bailey said. "Unless we can figure out who she is and stop it … somehow."

Brice studied the three earnest people. Every one of them believed that unless they acted, did something, a little girl and maybe others would die.

They all believed it. *Including Bailey.*

Maybe the three of them were operating on the strength of some grand group delusion. Or maybe everyone in the room had been dragged unwilling through a door into The Twilight Zone. Brice had no idea which. But one thing he did know for certain — as long as Bailey believed it, as long as she thought the life of a little child was in her hands, she wouldn't try to finish the job she'd started when she put a gun to her temple and pulled the trigger.

This craziness or whatever it was had given Bailey a reason not to kill herself. Which meant that whether or not there really was an endangered child out there somewhere didn't matter. As long as Bailey believed there was, she would be saved from her own death wish.

At that moment, Brice McGreggor set aside his own belief system, and when he did, he felt a great burden lift off his shoulders. He didn't have to decide right now whether or not he believed what the three other people in the room obviously believed. There was for certain a life at stake — *Bailey's*. And to keep her safe, all he had to do was play along.

Chapter Seventeen

BAILEY WATCHED the play of emotions across the face of the sheriff and felt a pang of sympathy. The poor man. If she were in his place, she wouldn't have believed a word the three of them said. The story was totally preposterous and the three of them must look — what was it that old man next door used to say? — crazier than a soup sandwich.

She wouldn't believe it herself if she hadn't lived it. And even then … some part of the Essential Bailey wanted to keep arguing the case before the High Court of Common Sense. Things like this — painting the future? Living somebody else's death? That was ridiculous. Things like that didn't happen to real people! She and T.J. and Dobbs were real people, normal people, ordinary people. Maybe it was all a dream and she'd wake up tomorrow morning — No! She wouldn't go there again. For months after she'd crawled through the mud to escape the rats under a dumpster, she'd told herself that the whole nightmare had been just that, a nightmare, that she'd wake up with Aaron beside her and Bethany sound asleep in the nursery. Well, she hadn't. It hadn't been a dream. It had been real. This was real, too. She really had drowned with a faceless little girl who existed only in wet paint on her canvas. She might not want to believe it, but she had no choice.

The sheriff did have a choice, though. He had to *decide* to believe, and when he finally stopped studying their faces and spoke, she appreciated his honesty.

"I'm not going to pretend that I'm buying what you're selling." he said. Then he cast a glance at T.J. "Not that I could get away with lying to you, T.J."

She didn't know anything about the tall, thin man who had shown up in a thunderstorm with a sixty-year-old painting and a dripping dog. But she could tell that the sheriff held the man in high regard. And the sheriff didn't strike her as a man who handed out his approval, respect — no, *admiration* — like he was throwing feed to chickens.

"But if there is even the possibility that someone's life is in danger here, then I have to act 'as if.' So…" He spread his hands, fingers splayed in a gesture of submission. "So let's figure this out."

She hadn't expected him to cave in so easily, thought it would take way more convincing than he'd been given. T.J. appeared to be equally skeptical. Clearly, the sheriff was humoring them. But what if he was? If he was willing to help them, what difference did it make why?

She watched the big man step effortlessly into police officer mode, then noticed as he began to speak that T.J. seemed to be on the same page, asked questions in the same manner. It occurred to her then that maybe T.J. had once been a police officer, too.

"Okay, Bailey," the sheriff said. "You say you … saw, felt, experienced, whatever, this little girl drowning. I need to know everything you can remember about it."

Goody. She'd been expending considerable effort *not* to go back there. Even remembering the panic, the choking, the terror was a horrible experience.

"I just saw/felt this little girl drown." She hoped he wouldn't ask for anything more specific than that.

"You say she was not alone. How do you know that?"

"I couldn't see, but I could hear other people, other voices crying out for help, other people … drowning."

"Why couldn't you see?" T.J. asked. "Was it night?"

"Yes, the sky was dark. I could see the lights of the explosion on it."

"Explosion?" the sheriff asked.

So Bailey described what she'd seen a second time. The sheriff withdrew a small notebook from his pocket and jotted down notes in it.

"An Adirondack chair on the boat — that tells us something we can use," he said. "There's an organization of local craftspeople, the Kavanaugh County Co-op, that sells handmade items — Adirondack chairs, tables, small pieces of furniture — to the tourists in the parking lot of Joe's Hole Marina. If there was an Adirondack chair on the boat that little girl was on, there's a good chance it came from that booth. Only the big boats — like houseboats, or a pontoon, maybe — have decks big enough to put those chairs on."

"Wouldn't be a pontoon," Dobbs put in. "There's nothing to a pontoon but the pontoons, the deck, some metal railing and a canopy. Even if there were something on one to blow up, like a propane tank maybe, there's nothing of the boat to make the kind of debris she saw in the water."

"We're talking about a houseboat, then," the sheriff said. "Not even a yacht — the yachts have seats built in, bench seats, captain's chairs on swivels, that kind of thing. The furniture below the decks would be custom made. You don't put an Adirondack chair below decks. That's a chair to relax in to get some sun."

"That's progress, then," T.J. said.

"Narrows down the field … some. I'll make a call to the

state water patrol boys, get the registration numbers on the houseboats."

"How many boats are we talking about?" Bailey asked. "How big is this lake?"

When the three men looked at her in surprise, she realized they must have believed she was like the tourists who cruised the streets of the make-believe town, that she'd come because of the lake, when in truth, she had barely noticed it when she drove into town.

She was on thin ice here. She had revealed nothing of her past to these men. At least, not on purpose. She had let her real name slip and now both T.J. — which meant, by extension, Dobbs — and the sheriff knew what it was. But that was all they knew — she hoped. They didn't know why she had come here. Most everybody else who moved here came because of the lake, and since she knew nothing about it she couldn't palm herself off as merely one of the throng of "everybody elses."

The best lie always had an element of truth in it.

"When I decided to move here, I wasn't interested in sunbathing or fishing. I had already decided to … so I was more or less oblivious to my surroundings. Tell me about Whispering Mountain."

As the sheriff spoke, Bailey readjusted her understanding of what they were up against. *Twenty-five thousand acres of water!* She couldn't even fathom how big that was. *Six hundred miles of shoreline.*

"And then there's the Nautilus Casino." T.J. made a humph in his throat that in one sound conveyed his opinion of the establishment. "The super whiz-bang grand opening is set for the Fourth of July, but couldn't a'been the casino that blew up. It would be way below crass for Mr. W. Maxwell Crenshaw the third to put something as pedestrian as Adirondack chairs on that floating money pit. Wouldn't fit in with the undersea theme of the place anyway."

"There's a small fleet of support craft." The sheriff's tone of voice mirrored T.J.'s assessment of the enterprise, and the man who owned it. "But the yachts that ferry customers out to the casino aren't Adirondack-chair kinds of crafts either."

He must have noticed the confusion on Bailey's face. "The casino isn't on the shore of the lake, it's *in the lake* — to get around the casino gambling laws in West Virginia. The lake is federal property, and Crenshaw greased enough palms in the right halls of power to get a permit to put his money-sucking machine in a spot where gaming laws don't apply."

"How many boats are there on the lake that might have those chairs on the decks?" she asked.

"Hundreds of them."

Bailey felt like she'd been kicked in the belly. She'd had no idea there could possibly be that many.

"*Hundreds?* How will we ever figure out which ones have chairs?" One conundrum added to the next. "Once we figure out which have chairs, how do we figure out which ones of those also have a little girl with braids as a passenger?" And to the next, gaining speed on the downhill slide. "And once we figure that out, how do we … stop it? How do we prevent the explosion?" Bailey's heart sank and she had to stifle a sob. "We can't. There's no way we—"

"You don't know that," the sheriff said. "We don't know anything yet. We take this one step at a time. We need to take a look at the houseboats — the ones we can find, anyway — see which ones have chairs on the decks. Go from there."

The sheriff was as dubious about their chances of success as she was. But he appeared to be no less determined. She *knew* the little girl was going to drown. Knew it, felt it, lived it. He had experienced none of that. But he was a policeman, had the whole to-protect-and-to-serve motto on the door of his cruiser, maybe stamped in his underwear and very likely tattooed on his soul.

After the sheriff left, Dobbs and T.J. started for T.J.'s truck, but Sparky had not yet gotten his fill of Bailey's affection. He turned at the door and jumped up on her, wagging his tail and generally being adorable. Bailey stooped to pet him and T.J. stopped and waited.

"You might as well give up," he said. "No matter how long you pet him, he'll always want more. Sparky the Wonder Dog has an infinite, inexhaustible need for human affection."

There was something odd about that statement and at first Bailey couldn't quite put her finger on what it was. Suddenly, she knew.

"Wait a minute. You don't sound like … What happened to your accent?"

A smile took over his face.

"It went away." He made fluttering motions with his hands to indicate flight and Dobbs did an eyeroll and grinned.

"I wondered if you'd notice. You don't miss much, do you?"

Was this some kind of test?

"It was *phony*? You mean that hillbilly—?"

"West Virginians are *not* hillbillies," he corrected. "You need to remember that if you are ever to live in harmony among us. We're mountaineers."

"So that mountaineer accent was just an act?"

"No, it was real. This part is the act." He drew in a breath. "I left Possum Run Hollow when I was eighteen years old to join the Marines. I didn't come back home to live for forty years." He looked at her earnestly. "As long as I was the country bumpkin whose accent sounded like he just fell off a hay truck, I would stay a Marine grunt forever."

He paused and shook his head.

"Do you have any idea how hard it is to get rid of a dialect? Think: *My Fair Lady*." Then he feigned a reasonably passable Henry Higgins accent. "'It's aaaow and gwaaan that keep her in her place, not her wretched clothes and dirty face.'"

Bailey was speechless.

"It took me the better part of five years. On my own, listening hard, practicing pronunciations in a toilet stall after lights-out. But I managed. Once I sounded like everybody else I…"

He let the rest of it go.

She wanted to ask him about his military career, the medals he'd won that had earned him a lifetime of respect from fellow Marines. But she suspected that if she did, he'd slam the personal-life door shut in her face. From the look on his face when Dobbs brought it up earlier, it was *not* a subject he would be willing to talk about.

Besides, those conversations had a way of backfiring on you: *I've told you about my past, now you tell me about yours.*

"Every minute of every day for four decades, I was speaking a foreign language. It wasn't natural, native; it was always uncomfortable, like walking around with sand in my shoes. When I came back to the chicken house to roost, I relaxed, took off my shoes and settled into a pair of old, comfy linguistic slippers that 'didn't pinch my toes nowhere a'tall.'"

"You mean you went back to—?"

"Is that so strange? If you lived in Spain speaking Spanish for forty years, would you keep right on speaking it when you got back home?" He grinned. "Still, once you're fluent in a language, it may fade some with disuse, but you can usually summon the right words in a pinch."

"You are a complicated man, Thomas Jefferson Alexander Hamilton."

"I 'spect I am, *Miss Donahue*. I 'spect I am."

He turned and walked out to the truck with Sparky following obediently behind.

Bailey stood on the porch until they drove out of sight down the street. *Miss Donahue.* He remembered she'd introduced herself as Jessie Cunningham. She'd hoped it had slipped his mind. She sighed and closed the front door. Now that she knew T.J. better she realized that wasn't going to happen. She suspected there wasn't much of anything that slipped that man's mind.

BAILEY AWOKE to the smell of fresh coffee and frying bacon. She lay for a moment in her bed, eyes closed, savoring the aroma, smiling at the image of Aaron slipping out from under the warm sheets, tiptoeing into the kitchen, easing the cabinet door open — because the one that housed the frying pan was in desperate need of a large dose of WD-40 — and...

Her eyes popped open. Dawn light filtered in between the lacy yellow curtains through the leaves of the black walnut tree outside her window. There was no Aaron. No squeaky cabinet door. She was lying alone in a bed in an enormous old house in a small town in West Virginia. Aaron was dead. Bethany was ... gone.

Like it always did, those twin thoughts knocked the breath out of her.

Those people who said time heals all wounds — they were full of crap. Time only blunted the pain, that's all. So the agony didn't slice you open with a filleting knife but hacked at your soul with a rusty Boy Scout hatchet.

She breathed back in the breath that'd been knocked out of her. And smelled bacon and coffee.

If Aaron hadn't ... who was cooking? The smells were overpowering, making her mouth water before fear nausea began to work its greasy fingers through her.

Who...?

She got carefully out of bed, quiet, slipped into her house-shoes and crept down the darkened hallway to the kitchen. Her heart stumbled through a flurry of irregular beats as she pushed gently on the door to open it. The kitchen was empty.

No one stood at the stove, turning crisp pieces of bacon frying noisily in a pan. The room was dark. The coffee pot sat unused and silent on the cabinet next to the refrigerator.

Still, she smelled it!

It was crazy, but the aroma was undeniable. She closed her eyes and breathed deeply. Standing silent in the kitchen, concentrating, she listened with her whole body, taut, like a bow string with the arrow ready to fly. And she could ... almost ... hear voices. Murmurs. Conversations in another room in the house.

She left the kitchen and slowly toured the house. Room after room was empty and dark. But not silent. In all of them, she could hear the murmurs — like passing down the hallway in a hotel and hearing a group of people talking and laughing in one of the rooms.

The aroma began to diminish, as it would if you'd made breakfast and then eaten it. She wandered the rooms of the house as the sun rose and lit them in rosy dawn light, heard the murmuring soften until it was gone altogether. Eventually, the smells were gone, too.

Traumatic brain injury?

Mental illness?

Incipient dementia?

She had avoided the studio in her tour of the house, had closed the door behind her when she had followed the three men out of it the day before and had not opened it since. Now, she stood outside the closed door, but still she couldn't open it.

What she had smelled, what she had heard ... it had the authenticity, the stamp of "this is real" to it that the cold water and the terror and the straining lungs had had yesterday, when she had painted the dying child as she lived with her death.

The smell of coffee and bacon. The voices not quite heard. They both had something to do with the painting in that room. She didn't know how she knew that, but she did, was as sure of it as she was of anything in this world turned upside down, where nothing was what it seemed and everything was much more than it appeared.

She resolutely turned from the closed studio door and went to the kitchen, filled a teapot and put it on the stove. She had no stomach for coffee this morning. While it heated, she went into her bedroom and dressed, and was sitting at the table, her second cup of tea half drunk, toast left uneaten but for the initial bite, when her cellphone rang.

"Bailey, it's Brice McGreggor," said the voice when she answered.

Not *Sheriff* McGreggor. Brice.

"Good morning."

"I have some information from the West Virginia State Water Patrol. They've given me a list of all the houseboat registrations for Whispering Mountain. That includes the two marinas here, Joe's Hole and Baker's Junction, and the three at Westbrook, Tucker's Landing and Blackfoot. I already called T.J., and he said he and Dobbs would check the three small ones. How about I pick you up in say, half an hour, and we'll head down to the two outside Shadow Rock."

"Works for me. I'll see you then."

Good, she would see him alone. She hadn't had a chance to speak to him about … he had called her Ms. Cunningham. He had clearly called her by her right name as a test, which she had successfully flunked. So now, he knew. But knew what, exactly? She had to find out.

What could a determined police officer find out, ferret out about the fictitious Bailey Donahue and the real Jessie Cunningham? Supposedly, her new identity was foolproof, had a real paper trail, a backstory that would stand up to the closest scrutiny. But scrutiny by whom? It was one thing to convince the guy at the hardware store she was who she said she was, and more importantly, that she wasn't somebody else.

But a cop? Could a cop dig past the phony records to the truth?

And what if he could? What if the sheriff had dug out her real identity?

Maybe she should just tell him about it.

No! Every alarm bell in her being went off with a screech more piercing than a smoke detector.

No, she could not tell him. She couldn't tell anybody! No matter how innocuous, how innocent it might seem.

Bethany's life depended upon her mother's death.

Bailey wasn't willing to risk that for anything!

So she would find out what he knew and go from there. She'd take his advice: one step at a time. Find out what he knew and then produce a respectable display of smoke and mirrors to keep him from figuring out what her fake identity actually meant.

Chapter Eighteen

DOBBS HAD GIVEN up years ago trying to understand what happened to T.J.'s mother when they were kids, what power had seized the skinny little woman, had coursed through her at will, using her as a vehicle to bring the future back into the past and display it in a painting. Dobbs had let the conundrum go decades ago because there wasn't an explanation and never would be one.

But standing in Bailey's studio in the Watford House yesterday, looking at the two paintings side by side on the easels had put an itch in his mind he couldn't find a way to scratch. Why were those paintings so alike? Though the subjects of the pictures were entirely different, why did they look like they had both been painted by the same person?

And he had started to wonder … maybe they had been.

He pulled into the parking lot of the Arbor Dell Retirement Village that afternoon with a borrowed dog and a dozen roses. T.J. had gotten Sparky all spiffed up for the occasion, brushed his fur so he looked like a stuffed teddy bear — a ball of fluff with eyes, ears, a wagging tail and a personality that melted hearts everywhere he went.

And one of those hearts belonged to Miss Annabelle Lee,

the undisputed authority on all things Kavanaugh County. She knew the history in minute detail back to the first settlers who rode down the Allegheny River to Pittsburgh and poled up the Monongahela to settle in the West Virginia mountains in the early 1800s. She had lost the use of her legs in a traffic accident, but at ninety-three every single synapse she ever had was still firing nicely, thank you very much.

Dobbs had built something approaching a friendship with her when he'd brought Sparky to visit his dog-loving uncle who had lived down the hall from Miss Annabelle until his death.

"You put that lilac spray stuff on Sparky today, didn't you," she growled when the little dog hopped up onto her bed. "You know he hates it. You should be ashamed of yourself."

"And a good day to you, too, Miss Annabelle. Yes, I'm doing fine. Thanks for asking."

Sitting up in a "bed jacket" made of fine yellow silk with lace all around the collar, she gave Dobbs a baleful look.

"What do you want?"

"Want? I—"

"The Raymond Dobsons of this world don't bring flowers to old ladies unless there's something in it for them. I don't care how much money you made out there in the world that you think nobody knows about — don't try to unload a pile of horse hockey on me. What did you come here for?"

"Busted." He didn't have to fake the sheepish look. "I was wondering what you could tell me about the Watford House," he said, laying the flowers on the dresser and his cards on the table.

"And you're interested the Watford House because…?"

"T.J. Hamilton's mother worked there as a maid when he was a little boy. Did you know that?"

"And that has caused a burning curiosity in your soul about the building half a century later. You think I believe that?"

"There's a young woman renting it now. Her name is Bailey Donahue. She's the one curious about the place, but she didn't want to bother you, a stranger and all."

"Wise choice on her part."

"I don't want to bother you either. If you don't know—"

"Of course I *know*. Don't be ridiculous, Raymond. Sit down."

And for the next hour, the old woman told Dobbs way more than anybody would care to know about the building and its occupants. He suffered through the last forty-five minutes in silence, hearing the escapades of the people who'd occupied the house during the seventies and eighties. He'd found out everything he needed to know when she'd described the original owners, and told him a story he'd heard in bits and pieces all his life — the strange tale of Sophia Watford.

"The house was built by Alexander Foster Watford, of the Charleston Watfords, a family who made a fortune around the turn of the century in textile manufacturing. Alexander was a young man bitten by wanderlust who traveled all over the world — to places *nobody* went in the 1890s! And to his family's great dismay, he brought home a bride from one of his trips."

Miss Annabelle pursed her lips.

"I was always quite curious about her and did some digging. But there aren't any records that have much to say about the woman. I was able to find some old letters Alexander's sisters wrote to their cousins in Atlanta in the archives of the historical society, but I don't know how much of what they said is to be believed. It's quite strange, you know."

"Strange how?"

"It's not clear exactly where Alexander met her, what her nationality was. But she was quite lovely, exotic … and mysterious. One letter described her as," — Miss Annabelle then quoted verbatim from a letter she'd read once probably thirty years ago — "a stunning beauty with hair as black as the coal buried under the mountains, alabaster skin, pouty red lips and eyes the color of sapphires."

"When one woman describes another woman in those terms, there's always a but."

"True. And the 'but' was that Sophia did *not* fit in well with Charleston society." She made a humph sound in her throat. "Big surprise, that. She wasn't cut from exactly the same pattern and cloth as they were, so, of course, they didn't accept her. It wasn't long before rumors began to circulate about her, that she was," — big pause — "a *gypsy*." She made another dismissive sound. "In 1893 … Alexander might as well have brought home a pigmy cannibal."

Sophia had accompanied Alexander to a black-tie event at the governor's mansion and something happened there, Miss Annabelle mused. Sophia did something, or people thought and said she did. It was hushed up immediately, but after that she was an outcast, not acceptable in polite society regardless of her husband's money.

"That's probably why he built a lake house for her in Shadow Rock, a town so small she'd have been at the top of the societal food chain even if she had been a pigmy cannibal. The house was complete in the summer of 1895 and Sophia planned an elegant party to christen the structure. But a couple of weeks before the grand ball, Sophia was found on the kitchen floor beside an overturned chair, dead. It was assumed, but never established, that she had climbed onto the chair to get some crystal out of a high cabinet, fell off and hit her head."

Miss Annabelle actually sighed.

"Alexander was devastated, immediately sold the house and moved back to Charleston. It's had half a dozen owners since then, but it remains 'the Watford House.'"

Dobbs practically had to pry Sparky out of Miss Annabelle's arms to escape her rambling narrative long after he'd found out what he'd come to learn. He'd made his last question casual.

"Is it possible … was Sophia Watford an artist?"

"Why, yes. Now that you mention it, I believe she was."

❧

THE JOE'S HOLE Marina was shaped like a wagon wheel. It stretched out into the clear waters of Whispering Mountain Lake at the bottom of the rise like a city on the water with streets, intersections and a center island for shopping. No, not so much like a city as like a gigantic mobile home park, which in essence was what it was, only the "mobile homes" there had no wheels, just huge inboard/outboard motors to transport them to any spot on the twenty-five-thousand-acre lake, with all the amenities of home taken along for the ride.

Shaped like mobile homes, the houseboats were parked one each to slips that branched out from the spokes of the wheel, at the center of which was a grocery store/restaurant, a bait shop, and a general store. Without leaving the lake, you could buy a can of live crickets, a bikini, sunscreen, a gallon of milk and floaties for the little ones.

Each houseboat slip had four-foot-wide walkways on both sides separating it from the slip next door. Some of the houseboats were so large they barely fit between the walkways, huge double-deckers with two full floors of living area and huge decks fore, aft and on top of the craft. Most had slides, winding down from the sundecks on the top of the boat to the water. Most also had smaller crafts, ski boats or jet skis tied up behind them.

Out beyond the marina itself were row upon row of boats of all sizes, tied up to lines in the water attached to buoys. Apparently, that was the low-rent district, since access to them required using one of the marina's small-boat ferries. A sign announced ferry service to and from line boats cost five dollars each way.

"I had no idea…" was all Bailey could summon the wherewithal to say when she saw how massive it was.

"This is the biggest marina and Shadow Rock is the major resort area servicing the lake. There's a taxi service to and from an airport that can accommodate Lear Jets or you can rent a car there. You're standing at Ground Zero of the tourist trade on the lake. Access to the other marinas is by small, two-lane roads. The two that T.J. and Dobbs are checking are about half this size.

"At even half this size … how many houseboats are there here?"

The sheriff looked down at a sheaf of papers in his hand, ran his finger down to the bottom.

"About two hundred."

"And any one of them could … talk about looking for a needle in a haystack."

"No, that part comes later, after we've checked out the ones that are here at the dock."

She didn't ask what he meant by that. She was already overwhelmed.

The sheriff had picked her up in his cruiser, dressed in a summer uniform — brown, short-sleeved shirt and starched, cuffed pants. She was sure you could have sliced bread with the crease in them. But he did forgo the hat and she was glad of that. No amount of self-confidence could grant dignity to the ridiculous flat-brimmed hat, and without it, he had a bit of a boyish quality she found easier to be with than his official side.

He must have seen her eyeing his uniform.

"The West Virginia Water Patrol officers get to wear shorts, but the Shadow Rock City Council, in its infinite wisdom, has chosen to require me and my deputies to remain in full uniform anytime we're on duty." He gave her a rueful smile. "So let it be written, so let it be done."

She almost mentioned to him the strange phenomena of smelling bacon and coffee that morning, and the voices. But she couldn't bring herself to do it. *Hearing voices in your head, are you? Reeeeally…?*

He parked the cruiser in the no-parking zone in the parking lot near the stairs-and-ramp combination that serviced the marina, calling it "payback for the long pants."

The marina below them dozed in the morning sun.

Leading down to the dock, whose height varied according to the fluctuating water level of the lake, was an elaborate system of switchback ramps — for tourists carrying supplies down to the lake on the wheeled carts provided for that purpose — and stairs with frequent landings for those not similarly loaded down with gear.

In a large area near the top of the steps, local merchants had set up booths where they sold everything from life jackets and slalom skis, to handmade earrings and Amish chocolate. There was a festive, holiday atmosphere to the place even now, on a weekday morning. Little kids stood in line to have their faces painted and Bailey even spotted a woman with an easel set up, doing caricatures for five dollars each.

She shivered at the sight.

There were Adirondack chairs for sale in two different booths, hand made from wood sawn and milled in the nearby mountains.

Kavanaugh County's economy was based on tourism. The variety of activities advertised and the quantity of junk for sale testified to that here at the marina. They had passed a "lawn chair theatre" on their way down the winding road to the marina, reminiscent of the drive-in movie theaters of the fifties and sixties, where couples sat in cars munching popcorn and hot dogs — or making out in the back seat — as they watched a movie on a huge screen with the sound provided by metal speakers with extension cords that sat on a pole between the cars. The lawn chair theatre featured nothing more than the screen and a grassy area in front of it. Bailey didn't know where the sound came from, probably from some kind of app you could put on your phone.

At the bottom of the steps, they stood center stage in the phalanx of shops that occupied the area where the wheel of long boat docks connected. Bailey watched the beehive of activity as watercraft of every size and shape maneuvered into the slots on the side of the dock beside the gas pumps.

"How much gas can a houseboat hold?" Bailey asked, pointing to the young man in a Joe's Hole Marina shirt pumping liquid from one of the seven pumps into a boat with a sign on the front proclaiming it to be "Mama's Mink Coat."

"Varies. Average is one-hundred-fifty gallons."

He nodded, picking up her thought. "Yeah, that much fuel could create quite an explosion. Not to mention that most houseboats also have propane tanks to power stoves and grills and the generators that make electricity."

He must have seen her wince.

"Hey, it's not like they're floating bombs. They're no more likely to blow up than the engine on a car."

"But one of them is going to," she said under her breath and shivered at the thought. The sheriff didn't appear to hear.

"Boats don't get very good mileage — eight or nine miles to the gallon. Charlie Turner makes a killing, charging twenty-five cents a gallon more than gas stations in Shadow Rock. But when you're the only game in town…"

He shaded his eyes from the glare off the water and got down to business.

"You take the three docks on this side, I'll take the three on that side. All the slips are numbered. Use the list app on your phone and jot down the number of any empty slip, and the name of any boat where you see Adirondack chairs."

Bailey headed down the planked dock between the double rows of houseboats. They were all named.

Clocked Out. Aboat Time. Mama's Happy. Best of Boat Worlds. Seas The Day. Shaken Not Stirred. Lazy Days. Gloria Ann. Dream Boat.

It hadn't been evident from the top of the hill, but at least half the slips were indeed empty, which meant the boat and its occupants were out there, tied up somewhere on the huge lake.

Bailey found only six boats with Adirondack chairs on their decks. Three of those were closed up, not like whoever owned them had left for a while, but like whoever owned them was out of town.

Of the other three, two had children aboard. The sheriff had told her not to say anything when she found boats with chairs, that he would handle that part. Right now, they were on a seek-and-find mission. But when Bailey came to the first of the chaired boats and saw a little girl come gliding down the slide from the sundeck on top to splash into the lake, she stood there frozen, her heart in her throat. The life-jacketed child never even went under water when she hit the lake, just slid out across the water a few feet, then turned around and came paddling back to the boat. Could this be the little girl?

Memories flooded into Bailey's mind of the terror the child had felt, the horror of dark and panic and—

"Can I help you?"

Bailey turned toward the voice and realized that she had stopped right in front of the gangway to the boat, blocking the path of a woman carrying two bags of groceries.

"Oh no, I'm sorry, I didn't mean to stand in your way."

The woman eyed her suspiciously, and Bailey realized she'd watched Bailey gazing in rapt attention at the little girl.

"We're thinking about getting a slide for our boat," she blurted out. "I was watching your little girl. The straight slides shoot you farther out into the water than this one."

The woman bought it. Friendliness and openness were hallmarks of the summer lake culture.

"We thought about a straight slide," she said as she passed Bailey and stepped onto the deck of the boat. "But we decided we'd rather start out with a curved one. Abby's only five and I would just as soon she not hit the water so hard."

Bailey smiled and moved on, forcing herself not to stand there staring at the little girl, who had clambered back up the ladder to the boat, up the stairs to the top deck, and was preparing to go back down the slide. Her hair wasn't in braids, but it was shoulder length, maybe long enough for braids hanging down … no, probably not. It wasn't this little girl.

Bailey looked up and down the dock at boats and empty boat slips. The sheriff had said that this part wasn't the needle-in-a-haystack part. If it wasn't, what was?

Chapter Nineteen

HALF AN HOUR LATER, Bailey rendezvoused with the sheriff in front of the general store. He had found four boats with chairs. Two of them had no children aboard, at least right now they didn't. That didn't mean there'd be no children tonight, or tomorrow or whenever the houseboat blew up. The other two boats were still closed up and there were more than two dozen empty houseboat slips.

She had found only a couple of houseboats with chairs that also had children, but she had listed the numbers of eighteen empty boat slips.

"The only way to find out if there are chairs on those boats is to find the boats…" Brice made a sweeping gesture that encompassed all the lake they could see, "…somewhere out there, tied up in a cove, having a cookout on the shore, maybe dropped anchor off a rocky bluff for fishing."

He said the sheriff's department had a boat, but it was currently in the shop.

"One of my deputies, Raleigh Hamilton Fletcher the third — you'll meet him one of these days — didn't remove the covers on the water intake valves when he launched the boat last week. Started it up — and with no water coolant, he blew

195

the engine. The boat won't be available until the middle of next month."

"And that's it? No way to check the rest of these boats until way past too late? Are you okay with that?"

She hadn't realized until she started speaking that she was angry. The anger was an amorphous thing and she couldn't quite put her finger on the source. It was part fear, of course. As soon as she saw the water, her mind filled with images from the — what had it been? What should she call it? The vision? Was that what it was? But it was more a ... *connection*. With or without a name, the twinning of her awareness to that of a drowning child had been among the most horrifying experiences of her life. Piled on top of her ever-growing list of those that began one night in the rain on the way to the airport.

No, not going there. Absolutely not going there!

Whispering Mountain Lake was so much more vast than she'd ever dreamed and a little girl was going to drown in it unless Bailey found her first.

But she realized that part of her anger was the fact that her sense of urgency was not matched by the sheriff's. He was cooperating and she supposed, under the circumstances, she should be grateful for that and let it go. But he wasn't consumed by it as she was, and his lack of desperation, his unwillingness to match her emotional commitment, flat-out pissed her off.

"What would you like for me to do, Bailey?" He was trying to be conciliatory. She hated being "managed."

"I didn't know you needed an amateur to tell you how to do your job." She grew even more angry when the insult did not appear to offend him. "I don't know what you ought to do. But I know what *I'm* going to do. I'm going to look for those houseboats. You're welcome to join me."

She'd worn a bathing suit under her clothes, just in case. Reaching into her pocket, she pulled out a yellow elastic hair band with a small plastic minion on it, the kind little girls wore, and used it to tie her hair back in a ponytail. Then she turned on her heel and headed to the far end of the dock where a big man with a florid face and a straw hat stood beneath a sign that said "Jet Ski Rental."

When the sheriff figured out where she was going and what she obviously had in mind, he caught up to her in two long strides.

"You know how to drive a jet ski, do you?" he asked.

"I can ride a motorcycle," she lied. It had been a moped, but that was close enough. "How hard can it be? And the worst that can happen is I'll fall off. Can't skin your knee on water and I'll wear a life jacket."

He took her by the arm.

"Can we talk about this?"

"It's not up for negotiation. I'm going looking for chairs. There's nothing left to discuss."

"Think this through, Bailey. Riding a jet ski on rough water … the pounding…" He gestured toward the small bandage on her temple, visible now with her hair in a ponytail. "It's not safe."

"Safe? You really don't get what's going on here, do you, Sheriff McGreggor? *Nothing* is safe for me in my 'condition.' I've already made this speech to T.J. and Dobbs, so I'll give you the CliffsNotes. I could put on a hat that's too tight and drop dead. No precaution on my part will make any difference, so I have decided not to take precautions. It'll be what it'll be. End of discussion."

She paused, and looked him as directly in the eye as she could, given that he was more than a foot taller than she was. "I mean it. This is the end, the forever end of this discussion."

"Okay, then. *We're* going looking for houseboats." He held up both hands before she could protest. "I can't let you go flying off on your own. You'd be lost as soon as you got out of sight of the marina. Give me a few minutes, and I'll be your guide dog."

Bailey browsed the general store's gift shop until the sheriff returned out of uniform, dressed in a sheriff's department t-shirt, shorts and sandals. Did he carry a change of clothes in his cruiser? Apparently, he did. She tried not to let him see how glad she was that he'd opted to accompany her. She was all hat and no cattle here. In truth, she had no idea how to operate the machines that didn't look to her at all like riding a moped. Bailey wasn't a particularly adventurous sort. She didn't go rock climbing or spelunking as some of her college friends did. She was definitely not a risk-taker.

At least, the Essential Bailey hadn't been a risk-taker. The Bailey who now occupied the body with a bullet in the brain didn't have quite the same attitude. She couldn't pinpoint what exactly had changed, but something had. Maybe a near-death experience did that to everyone. Or maybe the fact that she lived only seconds away from certain death took the edge off risk. Stepping into the shower was risky for her now. There weren't levels of risk anymore when tripping on a banana peel could be fatal.

And there was something very freeing about that. Freeing and frightening in equal parts. But the fear was a manageable thing.

The man with the florid face and the straw hat gave her simple instructions. He placed a lanyard around her wrist that attached to a switch on the jet ski. It was, appropriately, she thought, called a *kill* switch. If she fell off, the switch would turn off the ski's motor.

"You get thrown, you won't have to swim fast enough to catch it." He laughed as if he hadn't said the same thing already to two dozen people today.

"Thrown?" Bailey asked.

"Oh, it don't buck like a bronco, if that's what you're thinking. Be careful going across boat wakes, though. If you don't hit them right, you'll fly right up in the air, ski and all."

"Goody."

She left her clothes, shoes and purse in the locker provided, then boarded the red jet ski. The sheriff took the blue one. He didn't bother with the lessons — apparently this wasn't his first rodeo — and they set out across the "Idle Zone." Boats were required to idle their motors inside the buoys that encircled the marina, so they didn't throw up huge wakes that would bang the tied-up boats into the dock.

Once out past the buoys, the sheriff called out to her and she slowly pulled up beside him. He held up his cellphone incased in plastic. "Floats and waterproof. We'll keep a list of what we turn up." Then he slipped the phone into the small compartment in front of the bench seat of the watercraft.

"One more thing…"

She waited.

"This 'Sheriff McGreggor' label has got to go. The name's Brice Creighton Drummond McGreggor. In my mother's world, only really important people had three first names, and she wanted to make sure I didn't forget my Scottish roots, particularly since they added a "g" to McGreggor at Ellis Island so that set us apart from our cousins in the old country." He paused. "Brice is Gaelic for 'spotted,' by the way." He held out his arm and nodded toward the freckles. "Busted."

Then he turned on the throttle and headed across the lake. Bailey took a deep breath, swallowed hard, cranked the throttle on her jet ski and followed.

It became quickly clear that the sheriff had been absolutely right. Left to her own devices, she'd have been lost in minutes. The shoreline looked the same everywhere — trees, rocks, hills. How anybody could keep track of where they were using that as a guide seemed a feat of some kind of magic.

Brice set out due north of the marina and it looked like he was heading into a solid wall of rocks and scrub trees. But as they drew closer, Bailey saw the opening, the cove that cut into the side of the shore and she followed the sheriff into it. As soon as he passed through the mouth of the cove he cut his speed to an idle. Bailey did the same, and saw why when they rounded the first bend. The water in the cove, not buffeted by the wind on the lake or the wakes of hundreds of boats, was as smooth and flat as a still pond. All manner of boats were tied up at various places down the length of it with lines running out and looping around a tree or rock on shore. Children played in the shallow waters. Adults floated in inflatable lounge chairs, complete with drink holders. Ski boats dragged huge inner tubes loaded with small children slowly up and down the cove, the children squealing in delight as if theirs was as exciting a ride as the tubers on the lake where waves sent them sometimes five feet into the air.

They followed the cove around bend after bend as it narrowed and became too shallow to safely use a jet ski, which was propelled by sucking water up through an opening in the bottom and pumping it forcefully out the back. Mud, sticks and debris would stop one dead. They turned around and headed back toward where the cove opened on the lake. They'd passed two houseboats. Neither had an Adirondack chair on the deck.

Back out on the open lake, the sheriff — *Brice!* — took off toward the next cove. Bailey hit the throttle on the jet ski, and it leapt to life under her as her ponytail whipped out behind her. The wind and spray in her face were exhilarating, the sun on her skin warm, and she found a smile sitting in the folds of her face that actually felt like it belonged there. She hated to admit it to herself, felt in some strange sense she was betraying Bethany. And Aaron, too. But the truth was inescapable. In this moment, this frozen piece of time, Jessie Cunningham, aka Bailey Donahue, was glad to be alive.

As the day wore on, the sun dragged the temperature higher and higher. Bailey squinted up at puffy clouds that seemed to be frying in the pan of the bright blue sky, and soon yearned for sunglasses. The glare on the water had produced a headache that had joined forces with the constant throbbing in her right temple. That pain had diminished in intensity daily since she left the hospital, but the pounding of the jet skis over boat wakes turned up the volume on it, too, and the combined effect gave the impression that a fissure had opened in her forehead and was slowly spreading around the top of her head. At some point, when the ends of the fissure met in the back, the top of her skull would fly off.

After a couple of hours of searching, during which they turned up half a dozen houseboats, but none with Adirondack chairs, the sheriff angled into a cove that had a small dock at the far end. It was a recreation area with a sandy beach populated by a herd of children and sunbathers, plus tie-offs for boats, a dock with gasoline pumps, and a general store/restaurant combination where she and Brice wolfed down hot dogs and French fries in a booth with plastic seats and a table with a red-and-white-checkered vinyl tablecloth.

Bailey had purchased a pair of sunglasses and some sunscreen from the store, and sat dabbing it too late on her tender sunburned nose as Brice finished the last of his turquoise coconut Slurpee.

Her headache had eased off as soon as there was unmoving land under her, settled back into the ache that had become her constant companion, might well be her new best friend for the rest of her life, replacing in her affections the hospital ceiling tile. She popped two extra-strength aspirins and washed them down with Slurpee and settled back against the padded back of the booth. There was a pleasant buzzing in her head that had nothing to do with injury and everything to do with sun, heat and fatigue.

"Tired?" Brice asked.

"A little." She sat up straighter. "But I'm good."

"Oscar bothering you?"

"Oscar?"

He smiled and indicated the bandage on her temple. "I

figure that anything as important in your life as something that could kill you ought to have a name, don't you think?"

"Actually, I never gave it much thought."

"There's no sense wasting a good name on it, though, right? My drill instructor in boot camp at Camp Lejeune when I joined the Marines was Sergeant Oscar P. Tillman. He was…" He paused and his smile grew bigger. "I am unable to describe the man accurately without using words not acceptable in polite conversation."

"Oscar. Works for me. And no, Oscar hasn't thrown a real tantrum in quite a while. All that bouncing, that'd give you a headache even if you didn't have a bullet in your skull."

"The sun, though. You've got some color in your cheeks. It's … you look good."

He sat smiling at her across the table, his own face sun-bronzed rather than sun-burned. His caramel-colored eyes, almost amber in this light, were kind. She was drawn to that kindness. There was something profoundly *safe* about Brice McGreggor, something that had nothing to do with the fact that he was a cop. As a man, as a human being, he was safe. And it'd been a long, long time since Bailey had felt that kind of "safe" with anyone.

The moment could have been awkward, but wasn't for reasons Bailey couldn't explain. The big man leaned across the table toward her and transitioned out of it smoothly.

"I'm not even going to bother urging you to go back to the marina and wait for me there, but you should, you know. It doesn't take two—" He spotted her rising response and held up his hands. "Fine, fine. We'll both go." Then he did look serious. "But you are beginning to realize, aren't you, how" — he didn't say hopeless, but that's what he wanted to say — "difficult this is? If we could freeze every boat on this lake where it is, stop time so we could go from one to the next, check them off a list, then maybe. But it's possible that the houseboat we're looking for was on the other side of the lake all morning and right after we pulled out of Coyote Cove, they pulled in. We're going from one moving target to another."

Resolve stiffened Bailey's backbone. She felt her jaw clench. No matter how compassionate, how dedicatedly professional Brice was, he did not have the "fire in his belly" for this chase that she did. She couldn't reasonably blame him for that. It was a huge stretch that he'd even been willing to entertain the possibility that there was a child out there somewhere who'd die if they didn't find her. But the fact that his passion didn't match hers, totally irrational though it was, pissed her off — *again.*

"I get it." Her voice was cold. "We were doomed before we even started this search. But I plan to keep on looking anyway." She got to her feet and headed toward the screen door of the little restaurant, pulling Brice along in her wake.

The remainder of the afternoon ground down through pleasantly tiring to exhausting, and then grueling. The wind picked up, decorating the surface of the lake with a delicate lace of white-capped chop that made simply traveling across water un-churned by boat wakes a bouncing, *bam, bam, bam* proposition. The fissure in her skull opened up again and began traveling down both sides of her head toward the back. Every time they crossed the three-foot swells created by the wake of some yacht or racing ski boat, she suspected the top of her head was held in place by her scalp alone. For the first time since they set out that morning, she genuinely considered the possibility that the next wake, the next swell, the next stretch of choppy water would be the last straw, would finally dislodge the piece of metal in her brain.

Would the world then just go black? Would she even know when it happened? Would Brice look back and see her jet ski idling, race back to find her bobbing in her life jacket, literally "dead in the water"?

A small icicle of apprehension began to spread a chill through her veins.

The fear itself scared her to death. It indicated the presence of something new and very different in her world.

The only reason she could possibly dread/fear dropping instantly dead was because she no longer *yearned* to be dead. It could only mean that she had turned some kind of emotional corner. Somewhere between her passionate desire to save this child from the horrible death she had experienced with her, and making ... okay, admit it, *friends* — T.J., Dobbs and ... yes, Brice — there had been a shift in the tectonic plates in her psyche. There were people in her life who mattered now. People she cared about and who cared about her. That was a sensation, a sense of family she hadn't felt since the day she saw Aaron's shoe lying in the street in the rain.

She had not connected on any level with another human being in almost a year and a half. That lack of connection was what had tipped her over the edge into the black whirlpool circling the drain, spiraling down into utter despair. That lack of connection had put the Smith & Wesson revolver in her hand, had helped her pull the trigger.

But she wasn't alone anymore. She hadn't planned it, didn't do anything to orchestrate it, didn't even actually *want* it, but it had happened whether she wanted it or not. And though it was too strange, too *bizarre* to possibly understand, she felt the strongest connection of all to the little girl in the cold, dark water, crying for her mother, holding her breath until it burst out of her throat. She was knit together with that child in an impossible relationship that transcended the bounds of normal humanity.

And that connection created an urgent, desperate need to keep the child alive, darkly ironic given that her own death had been the price she'd paid for Bethany's safety. The water's relentless pounding hammered a nail of truth into her soul: Bailey didn't want to die anymore.

Chapter Twenty

THE SUN HAD ALREADY PASSED behind the mountain to the west of Whispering Mountain Lake, casting its long, dark shadow out across the water, when Bailey and Brice turned in their jet skis at Joe's Hole Marina and she walked on wobbly legs up the switchback staircase to the parking lot.

She was exhausted, in mind, body and spirit. It was a good thing Brice was the one keeping track because she had lost count hours ago of how many houseboats they'd located. The number was irrelevant. They hadn't found the one they were looking for and it was the only one that mattered. She had no idea how many T.J. and Dobbs had been able to locate. But there couldn't be many. They could only have checked out the ones parked at the marinas they searched. The two old men had not likely climbed aboard jet skis and searched the coves, nooks and crannies of the huge lake that offered untold hidey-holes where a houseboat could tie up and its occupants enjoy their own private pond of still water.

She waited at the top of the steps while Brice changed back into his uniform in the restaurant bathroom. A few feet from the top of the steps, the vendors with booths were boxing up their wares, clearing off the display tables for the night.

She wandered over to the booth featuring a "Kavanaugh County Craftsman's Association" sign where handmade deck furniture of all kinds, including Adirondack chairs, were on display for sale. The drowning child of her vision had bumped into a chair like these in the water, had reached out to grab it, but she couldn't hold onto it. Instead of saving her, the big chair had tumbled over on top of her and knocked her underwater. Bailey reached out to the nearest chair to run her fingers over the smooth surface that'd been too slick for the little girl—

The instant her fingers came in contact with the chair's wood the world went black and she fell into another reality.

SHE BLINKS her eyes and instead of the chair and the parking lot and the sunset behind a mountaintop, she sees a little girl's hand, reaching out. An adult takes the hand and presses something down on top of it. When he lifts the stamp, her skin is marked with wet ink in the shape of a roaring lion's head. The initials WBTC are on the top of the circle surrounding the lion's head. Beneath it is the date: July 3, 2015.

Bailey can smell popcorn and something else sweet — cotton candy. And she can hear voices and music. A calliope. Children laughing.

I'm bigger now! I'm tall enough.

The little girl's thoughts become Bailey's thoughts.

The child remembers the line on the fence beside the Mad Walrus ride. You have to be tall enough for the top of your head to reach that line, or they won't let you ride.

Bailey hears the little girl say, "…wanna ride the Mad Walrus. I'm big enough this year. Mama said when I was tall—"

Then the world vanishes.

BAILEY FELT Brice's hand on her shoulder, gasped, heard his voice but it seemed to come from a great distance.

"…All right? Bailey, answer me. Bailey!"

"She's there. She's there right now. At the carnival. I *saw!*"

Bailey looked up into Brice's face in such fanatic desperation she knew it sounded like she'd come completely unhinged.

"Who's at the carnival?"

"The little girl, the little drowned girl."

Bailey realized then she was gripping the Adirondack chair with all her strength. She let go, stepped back and looked at it. There was a tag attached to the arm she wasn't clinging to. The tag read: "Sold."

She brushed past a totally confused Brice and ran to the man who was loading the contents of the booth into the back of a cargo van.

"That chair" — she pointed to the one Brice stood beside — "the tag says 'sold.' Who bought it?"

The man gave her the look her desperation and near hysteria deserved.

"Ma'am, if you want a chair, we got lots of others, but we're closed right now."

"I don't want to buy a chair. I want to know about *that* chair." She started to take him by the arm and drag him to the chair, but Brice appeared before she had the man totally spooked.

"You're Dan Ragland, aren't you?" Brice held out his hand. "From up near Turkey Neck Hollow?"

"That's me, Sheriff McGreggor." The man shook his hand. "How can I help you?"

Brice nodded toward Bailey. "She's with me. We're working on a case. What can you tell me about that chair?" He pointed to the one that Bailey had touched.

"I can tell you it's sold. And I can tell you the man who bought it was crazier'n an outhouse rat."

The man set the small table he was holding into the back of the van and went to the chair, looked at the tag.

"Yep, this is the one. We got to paint it blue."

Brice let silence urge the man to provide more information.

"My brother Joe was the one sold it to him, I's helping another customer. Heard him ask the guy, 'Why blue?' and the guy sneered and got all sarcastic like, said he already had a red one and a white one and tomorrow bein' the Fourth of July — he wanted to be patriotic."

Ragland shook his head.

"What Joe was tryin' to explain to the mo-ron was that this here chair's already got a finish on it." He pointed to the shiny surface of the wood. "You can't paint a chair's already got a finish. So I tried to help out, told the guy I could get him an unfinished chair and paint it any color he wanted, but he exploded like a shook-up Coca-Cola on a hot day. Said he wanted *that* chair, said he'd sat in every one we had here and that there chair was the most comfortable one of the lot." The man shook his head again. "Sheriff, every one of these chairs is the same, made from the same pattern. Ain't one no more comfortable than the next but wasn't no way to convince that jackass of nothing."

Ragland leaned close to the sheriff and spoke in a conspiratorial tone. "You ask me, if you's to do a blood test on that dude, you'd find every chemical known to man — including Ty-D-Bol. Eyes was wild, scary-like, pupils half the size of BBs. He was on crystal meth or I'm my own grandpa."

"Who was he? *What was his name?*" Bailey demanded, unable to stand quiet and let Brice do the talking. The man looked at Brice as if to ask if he really had to answer her question.

"Would you mind looking?"

Ragland sighed, went around to the cab of the van and retrieved a cash box off the front seat. He dug around in it, looked at receipts, compared one to the tag on the chair and finally said, "Here's the receipt."

He handed the receipt that had the same number on it as

the tag on the chair. The name on the receipt was totally inde-cipherable.

"Can you read that name?" Brice asked.

The man shrugged. "No, but it wasn't like I was gonna ask a guy who was that fried to spell it for me! It don't matter. He's got a copy of the receipt."

"So you don't know who this is?" Bailey asked, only barely managing to keep her voice from breaking.

"Like I said, I don't need to know his name. He gives me his copy of the receipt, I give him the chair."

"Was there a little girl with him?" Bailey asked. "With long hair, braids?"

"Mighta been. I didn't notice." He looked at Brice. "You need anything else? I gotta get this stuff loaded up, drop this chair by Seth Cosgrove's so he can paint it blue before tomor-row. Paint ain't gonna stick on that finish, but…"

"Thanks, Dan. You've been very helpful."

Brice turned and pulled Bailey along beside him. She had the presence of mind not to speak until they were out of earshot from the man loading furniture into the van.

"That chair, it's connected to … I don't know how to explain it, but when I touched it, I…" She paused, took a deep breath, knew her babbling wasn't winning her any sanity points with the sheriff. "I think she, the little girl in the portrait, must have touched this chair," she heard herself say and knew it for absolute truth the moment it came out her mouth, though she could have given no rational reason it should be so. "Think about it. The guy comes here to buy a chair, brings his family — wife, kids maybe. He was trying out the chairs, sitting in all of them. They probably did, too. The little girl sat in this chair. She must have because that chair connected me to her."

"*Connected* you?"

"It was like when she was drowning. I could see what she saw, see out her eyes."

She watched the sheriff struggle to keep his face neutral, knew for certain then he didn't really believe any of this, was just humoring her, T.J. and Dobbs. Fine! So long as he kept humoring them she didn't give a rat's ass what he believed.

"What did you see?" he asked.

"The carnival. She was at the carnival … *is* at the carnival, *right now*. She reached out her hand and the man stamped it with the stamp we saw. The smudge is the head of a lion with the letters WBTC—"

"Wasuski Brothers Traveling Carnival."

"And the date is July 3, 2015. *Today!*"

"So you're saying that chair was purchased by the little girl's father, the little girl we're looking for?"

"Yes, but—"

The sheriff turned and went back to the man loading the furniture into the van, reached into his shirt pocket and pulled out a card.

"This is my number, personal cell is on the back." Brice handed the card to the man. "When the guy comes back for that chair, I want you to call me. If you lose my card, dial 911 and give the dispatcher a message."

"I knew there was something wrong with that guy! What'd he do? What's he wanted for?"

"No, no, it's nothing like that. He's not in any trouble, but it's a matter of life or death that I find him and talk to him. Do *not* give him the chair until you talk to me."

"Then you best be on a short leash, Sheriff. I'll call you when he shows up, but I ain't gonna cross him. He wants the chair, he gets the chair. There wasn't nobody home in them eyes. That there was a man destined to electrocute himself on the great bug-light of life, if you know what I mean."

The sheriff returned to Bailey's side. "When the man shows up to pick up the chair, we'll—"

"No!" Bailey felt desperation clogging her throat, making it hard for her to breathe and form words. "It could be too late by then. Didn't you hear him? He said the guy had *two other chairs* already. We can't wait for him to come pick up this one. The guy's a druggie. Dangerous. What if the boat explodes *tonight*? The chair the little girl bumped into in the water could have been one of the other two chairs."

"The guy didn't actually have two other chairs, he was just being sar—"

"She could drown, she could die before they ever come back for the chair."

Brice stood looking at her, helpless.

Suddenly her face lit up. "She's at the carnival *right now!* She has to be. You said it opened every night at five o'clock. That stamp had today's date, she had to have gotten it in the past half hour or so. She's there, a little girl with braids. How many kids can that be?"

"Hundreds maybe. And how will you know which—?"

"I'll know! If I touch her, I'll … connect. I'm sure of it."

"And all you can tell me about her is that she's got braids?"

"No, that's not all." Bailey turned and started running toward the cruiser parked in the No Parking area near the head of the steps. "She wants to ride the Mad Walrus!"

BRICE HAD SPENT the day trying to keep his face from revealing his emotions. He had kept his skepticism, which was roughly the size of North Dakota, strictly in check. He had spent the evening after he had left Bailey, T.J., Dobbs and the two paintings sitting side by side on easels in her studio trying to figure out what he actually believed about the insanity he'd gone crashing into with his gun drawn that afternoon. He had narrowed the possibilities down to roughly half a dozen.

One: T.J. Hamilton and Raymond Dobson had, for reasons unfathomable, perpetuated some grand hoax on the unsuspecting Bailey Donahue, who, as far as the sheriff could determine, had met neither of the men until the day she put a bullet in her skull.

Two: T.J. and Dobbs were totally sincere, genuinely believed that his mother had painted a portrait of a dead Bailey Donahue more than a quarter of a century before she was born. They were sincere, but crazy.

Three: T.J. and Dobbs were *not* crazy. They were telling the truth. His mother *had* painted the portrait, had indeed painted lots of other portraits of people and events unseen, that had not yet occurred in real time, and they had tried to prevent Bailey's suicide when T.J. had recognized Bailey's face in the painting.

Four: Bailey Donahue had so damaged her brain with the bullet still lodged there that she had lost her grip on reality and believed she had somehow connected to a dead child — no, to a *live* child who would shortly be dead unless they could find her and keep her and a whole host of other unspecified people from drowning.

Five: All of the above.

Six: Something else entirely.

The story was absolutely too preposterous to be believed. But the evidence, backed up by the paintings themselves and by the characters of the people involved, testified to a reality that defied possibility.

Brice didn't have anywhere in his mind to put a thing like that. Oh, he didn't believe the universe operated with the precision of a pocket watch. You could sentence yourself to an all-expenses-paid stay at Club Mad by insisting *everything* in life made logical, rational sense, that it followed a this-because-that logic. Occasionally, you had to accept the unexplainable. And Brice was down with that. But this was so far on the other side of unexplainable you couldn't have found it on Google Earth.

So what *did* Brice believe? He believed … that he didn't have to decide that right now. One thing above the fog of screwy-ness here was clear. As a law enforcement officer, he had a sworn duty to protect his constituents, including Bailey Donahue. Though the methods were unorthodox, he believed he really was keeping her alive.

But he could tell Bailey wanted, *expected*, way more than that. She saw no gray areas here. She had grabbed hold of the quest of saving the life of a mysterious child with every ounce of her being and you didn't need a doctorate in psychology to figure out the connections her brain had made between this child and some other child somewhere in Bailey's past life. It wasn't hard to understand the motivation of a woman desperate to save the life of some unknown and possibly/probably fictional child as a surrogate for a little one she had lost. That kind of fanaticism knew no boundaries, accepted no limitations and required an equal level of fervency from everyone involved.

He'd done his best to keep pace with her passion, but as he raced down the highway from the marina toward town, lights flashing, siren screaming, he was certain she was again going to crash head-first into reality. The number of houseboats on Whispering Mountain Lake paled in comparison to the number of children who'd be at this carnival, all shapes and sizes, running here and there in the excited abandon of children at a carnival, and the likelihood that the two of them would be able to locate a single little girl among all the others, a faceless child whose lone identifiable characteristic was braids…

What if her mother'd put her hair in a ponytail tonight? Or pigtails? Or let it hang down straight? There was no face to identify.

The sheriff killed the lights and siren several blocks away from the parking lot where the carnival had set up. There was not a NO Parking area he could commandeer here, and no way to get close to the area you could see in the distance lit with colored lights. People walked down the middle of the streets, having parked along the adjacent side streets, and even lights and a siren wouldn't likely have parted the sea of humanity. He got as close as he could, then parked in the red zone in front of a fire hydrant.

Bailey leapt out of the front seat as soon as he pulled the cruiser to the curb and hurried through the throng of humanity toward the lighted archway that proclaimed Wasuski Brothers Traveling Carnival. She started off into the crowd once they passed beneath the archway but Brice grabbed her arm.

"Don't make me bust you for gate crashing." He pointed to a booth where a demure line of people waited patiently to hand the lone attendant their money. "That's where you pay for admission."

"But—"

"Which means that's the man you saw stamp the little girl's hand, right?"

She lit up, and would have marched up to the man and launched into an impromptu interrogation if Brice hadn't told her firmly, "I'll handle this."

Now in uniform, the crowd allowed him and Bailey through and the sheriff tipped his hat to the man taking admission money. The man looked up at him with tired, bloodshot eyes and Brice knew his questions would be useless, but he asked them anyway.

"Have you been here all night taking admission?"

"Yeah. Listen, we got all the city permits. You need to see Ralph in that trailer—"

"I'm looking for a little girl. About so high." Brice held out his hand to indicate a child somewhere between five and ten years old. "Braids. You seen her?"

"You're joking, right?" The man offered a mirthless smile that revealed teeth so broken and rotted it looked like he had a mouthful of half-chewed Oreos. "You know how many kids come through here every night? You think I remember every one of them?"

"I'm not asking if you remember all of them. I'm asking if you remember one little girl with braids."

The man sighed. "No, I don't remember any little girls with braids — satisfied?" He used his chin to indicate the long line of parents and children awaiting admission. "You got any more questions?"

"Thank you for your time." Brice stepped out of the way.

Bailey looked around, frantic, trying to get a look at every kid in sight. The place was packed, children ran here and there in small groups or walked along with their parents. Hundreds of them. They rode the rides, flew around and around on the Tilt-A-Whirl, sat atop the horses on the merry-go-round, stood at booths trying to win stuffed animals, or waited to buy popcorn, cotton candy, caramel apples, snow cones, corn dogs and funnel cakes. Even if they'd had a full description of the child, maybe even if they'd had a photograph, their chances of culling her out of the herd were next to nothing.

Bailey must have come to the same conclusion because her shoulders slumped.

"Let's go take a look at the Mad Walrus," Brice suggested, and they made their way through the crowd to the green-and-blue contraption decorated with sea creatures that featured spinning cups.

Bailey searched the faces in the crowd, but Brice could tell she had accepted the impossibility of their task.

"I'm sorry," he said.

"The clock has started ticking."

"Clock?"

"The stamp on the little girl's hand. She got it tonight. That ink will last — what? Two days, three, and swimming every day, probably less."

She suddenly looked worn out, totally spent. "Tomorrow's

the Fourth. Think about it — people setting off firecrackers, drunk maybe, on drugs, or merely inexperienced and careless. Sounds like a recipe for an explosion to me."

She let out a long, frustrated breath. "Let's go. I'm tired, sunburned and my skull feels like it's attached to my head with roofing nails. I suspect tomorrow's likely to be a big day."

She turned and headed slowly back to the front gate and Brice followed.

Chapter Twenty-One

BAILEY LEANED her head back against the head rest in the sheriff's cruiser and closed her eyes. With them open, her vision was pulsing to the rhythm of the thud, thud, thudding pain in her temple and that was making her dizzy. She was … go on, admit it — she was *weak*. Hadn't counted on that, but found that she didn't have the strength she expected. Well, what did she want? She did, after all, have the business end of a .22 shell lodged inside her skull.

The sheriff got into the cruiser and shut the door. She didn't open her eyes. He didn't start the motor.

"Bailey, I know how badly you want to find this little girl. I wish I could do more to help."

"Thanks." She hoped he would take the hint and not continue to talk. He did, put the key in the ignition, started the engine and pulled away from the curb, driving slowly to make his way upstream through the fish swimming downstream toward the carnival they were leaving.

The sound of the calliope slowly faded.

And then she heard singing. The voice soft. She couldn't make it out at first.

Almost Heaven. West Virginia. Blue Ridge Mountains, Shenandoah River.

John Denver.

Life is old there, older than the trees. Younger than the mountains, blowing like a breeze.

She began to sing along.

"Take me home, country roads, to the place I belong."

She had never been a fan of country music, but John Denver was one of the golden oldies she had grown up listening to. She loved all his music, and she relaxed back into the seat and breathed deep.

"West Virginia, mountain mama, take me home, country roads."

The music was so soft it was hard to hear. Without opening her eyes, she said, "Would you mind turning it up a little?"

"Turning what up?"

"The radio."

"There's no radio in this cruiser, at least not that kind."

It took her a moment to process that, because she could still hear the music.

"Then where's the music coming from?"

"I hate to sound like a ventriloquist dummy, but what music?"

"John Denver. *Country Roads.* Don't you hear it?"

"No."

She opened her eyes and looked around.

"You don't hear music." But it wasn't a question this time. He answered anyway.

"No"

"I do."

He said nothing.

She concentrated, could hear the second verse of the song, then something in the background. She strained to hear it.

"Bailey…?"

"This morning, I woke up to the smell of bacon frying and fresh coffee. Only there were no elves in my kitchen making me breakfast. I went into the kitchen, sniffed, and the smell was still so strong my mouth watered. And I could hear voices but couldn't make out what they were saying. I went from one room to another, but it was always like the voices had just moved out of that room into the next."

She paused, and when she continued there were equal parts awe and certainty in her voice.

"I am … connected to this little girl, somehow. Sounds wacky, but no wackier than all the rest of this. On some level, in some way, I have been hooked into this little girl's consciousness and sometimes I can … be in her world, smell her smells, hear what she hears."

"Do you hear voices now?"

She was quiet, listening.

"Yes, children's voices. Chattering, the kind of white noise you hear in a school hallway. Laughter."

He said nothing else. She listened. The song concluded. The voices faded.

Without opening her eyes, she asked, "You think I'm crazy, don't you?"

He deftly side-stepped the question.

"I think you're having an auditory hallucination, hearing sounds that are not really present in the real world."

"Hallucination? Well, that's crazy, don't you think?"

"Right now, I don't know what to think."

She opened her eyes and sat up. Might as well get to it, there wasn't likely to be an opportunity to broach the subject smoothly and effortlessly. She just walked to the edge of the cliff and jumped off.

"You called me 'Miss Cunningham' the other day. Why?"

He looked surprised but got control of it quickly.

"Because that's what you told T.J. your name was."

"My name is Bailey Donahue. Says so on my driver's license, car registration, credit cards … library card, or at least it will if I ever get a library card.

"Then why'd you tell T.J. it was Jessie Cunningham?"

There it was. Simple, direct question. She could tell him the truth, fess up. And after all, why not? He was a police officer, for crying out loud. If she couldn't trust a cop, who…? Truth was, nobody was safe … not even a county sheriff in West Virginia.

"Cunningham was my maiden name," she lied. "I was recently divorced and I took back my maiden name. I mean, I intend to take back my maiden name, haven't gotten the paperwork done on it yet."

She ignored the Jessie/Bailey discrepancy and gratefully, so did he.

"Yeah, why bother going to court to change your name when you don't plan to be alive to use the new one?"

"I don't want to talk about that," she snapped. Then added in a soft but firm voice, "Not the suicide … not *any* of it. The only thing you and I have to discuss is a little girl we have to find."

They both fell silent. When he pulled up in front of her house, she immediately opened the door to get out, but he reached out and took her arm.

"I didn't mean to pry. I won't push you. You are who you say you are and your past is none of my business. You don't owe me any explanations."

She looked at him.

"Well, you do owe *me* something."

"And what is that?"

"My gun back."

He reached past her and opened the glove box and took out her revolver. He dug around in the bottom of the glove box for the cartridges, then held both out to her.

She took the gun, and cupped her hand for him to pour the cartridges into it.

"You'll call me tomorrow, when the guy picks up the chair?"

"I'll call. Just know that holidays in a resort community are … it gets crazy. But I promise I'll call."

"I have to be there, see the little girl, make sure she's the right … and then…"

"And then I'll take it from there. One step at a time, remember."

She nodded, then spoke quieter, "And tonight, if anything … bad … happens tonight—?"

"If I find out anything at all, I'll let you know."

Bailey got out of the car and walked wordlessly into the house.

SHERIFF MCGREGGOR STOOD in the shade of a huge sycamore tree watching an emergency medical technician bandage the hand of a twelve-year-old boy, while a West Virginia State Police trooper tried to calm his nearly hysterical mother. He turned to the trooper's partner.

"I just love holidays," he said, "particularly ones where untrained amateurs and children entertain themselves with explosive devices … said no police officer ever!"

"Copy that!" said the trooper.

"My first call this morning was to the Fantastic Bob's fireworks stand on Route 19 where someone — I'm betting idiot teenager and I suspect I can put my finger on exactly which idiot — thought it would be fun to light a packet of Black Cats and throw it through an open window. It's a miracle the whole place didn't go off like a bottle rocket."

The trooper gave the sheriff a knowing look.

"I had three reports before noon today about kids riding

bikes down the streets in Fairmont tossing lighted firecrackers into any car with a window rolled down."

The radio mic on the sheriff's shoulder beeped.

"Sheriff McGreggor, this is dispatch. I have a 911 call from a Daniel Ragland, who said you wanted him to notify you about a subject who came to pick up a chair."

The sheriff started back to his cruiser, keying the microphone to speak into it.

"I'm on the other side of Lankford. It'll take me fifteen or twenty minutes to get to the marina. Any other unit closer?"

"Ten-four. Unit two is ten-seven on Ridge Road at the Esso Station."

Ten-seven meant out of service. Fletch loved barbecue, and the food truck that parked in front of the station had the best in town.

"Dispatch unit two, then, tell him to hold the subject until I get there."

"Ten-four."

The sheriff got behind the wheel of his cruiser and set off toward the marina, down winding roads that meandered through the mountains and hollows in no particular hurry to take anybody anywhere. He turned on his lights and siren. Ragland had said the dude who wanted the blue chair was belligerent. The sooner Brice got there and talked him off the ledge, the sooner...

Yeah, the sooner *what?* He had put off Bailey with the one-step-at-a-time mantra, but now that the Michelin Radial was about to make contact with the asphalt he had to admit to himself and pretty soon to her, that he had no idea what he was going to do next. Say they found the right guy and he actually did lead them to the mythical little girl, however reluctantly. What was Brice supposed to say?

Uh, my friend here painted a picture of...
I have it on good authority that...

Sir, your houseboat is going to blow up tonight, and I know that because…

Brice had no legal authority to impound the guy's boat to prevent him from taking it out on the lake, though he might be able to push the envelope and get the water patrol to inspect the craft, maybe find the source of whatever it was that was about to explode.

But if they found nothing, then what? He'd have to stand on the dock while the guy, other passengers — *and that little girl!* — sailed away.

And Bailey would go crackers if she found the little girl, *connected* to her — whatever *that* meant, and then had to watch her ride out of the marina to what Bailey believed was her certain death.

He reached into his pocket and took out his cellphone, punched Bailey's number. She answered on the first ring.

"I just got a call that the guy is at the marina right now to pick up the chair. I've sent a deputy to detain him until I get there."

"Thank God!" she cried, with such fervor he could hear tears in her voice. "I had nightmares all night. I kept jerking awake, thinking I heard an explosion. I bet I've paced a hundred miles this morning. I'll leave right now for the marina."

"Bailey, wait. You do realize, don't you, that when we find the little girl, *if* we find the little girl, I have no legal—"

"You'll think of something."

She hung up.

～

BAILEY HAD BEEN UP, dressed and pacing before the first streaks of dawn lit the morning sky. True dawn didn't come here the way it did in other places. The eastern horizon was on the other side of the mountains, so "dawn" was watching the black velvet sky — so full of bright stars you could gather them like plucking blackberries off a bush — begin to turn some shade of dark gray. Then the light just grew. The beautiful colors of sunrise, blue, pink and gold, weren't visible here and she missed that, missed watching dawn take over the day.

She had finally gotten out of bed when the lighted numbers on her bedside clock proclaimed 3:30. She was only occupying space there, anyway, not actually sleeping. The nightmares had washed over her as soon as she shut her eyes.

She saw the boat, sparkling with light in an empty nothingness of black lake joined to a starless black sky with no horizon. The boat was still in the water, floating motionless in darkness and Bailey was racing toward it on a jet ski. When she got within sight, she saw the little girl alone on the top deck of the boat, which was lit up as bright as a baseball field for a night game. She was sitting in a blue Adirondack chair and when she saw Bailey coming toward her on the jet ski she raised her hand to wave.

Suddenly, the black world burst into bright light like a lightning bolt had ripped a hole in the fabric of darkness. The boat exploded with a mighty roar, blew apart into thousands of chunks of flaming debris with such force that pieces struck Bailey in the face. She let off the throttle and the jet ski idled to a stop as burning debris rained down out of the sky into the water all around her. There was no chair, no little girl, just a fireball on the water. While she watched, the boat turned up on one end, like the movie version of the Titanic, and sank down into the black water.

Bailey had jerked awake at the sound of the explosion, but the dream continued to play out in her head even after she woke. After the first nightmare, she'd gotten up, gone to the kitchen and fixed a cup of hot chocolate. Chocolate had caffeine and probably wasn't the liquid most conducive to sleeping, but it was what she'd wanted. She'd tried to go back to sleep a couple of times after that, but each time she felt herself drifting off, the world would explode around her in bright light and flames and she would jerk awake, shaking.

When she finally got up, she dressed in denim shorts and a Pittsburgh Pirates t-shirt. She had loved playing sports in school but watching others play never interested her. Aaron had been a die-hard Pirates, Steelers and Penguins fan and had purchased t-shirts, hats, jackets, sweatshirts — black-and-gold everything for her anyway. Even bought a "terrible towel," the kind fans twirled in the stands during Steelers' games. She always felt close to Aaron now when she wore them.

After brewing a cup of strong black coffee, she'd headed out toward the porch, passed the closed door to the studio. She had closed that door behind her when the three men had left. And when this was over, when they'd found the little girl — *and saved her* — Bailey had plans for those paintings. She would take them both, the one T.J.'s mother had painted and her own, out into the backyard, pour gasoline on them and set them on fire. She would watch them burn to ash. And she would never, *never again* paint another picture with a window in it.

She set the steaming cup of coffee down on the small table at the end of the couch, went to the chifforobe, opened the top drawer and took out the blanket. She lifted it to her face, closed her eyes and rubbed the soft fabric against her cheek, then she took the blanket and the coffee out to the front porch and sat in the swing, moving slowly back and forth, listening to the comforting squawk of the protesting chain against the S hooks in the ceiling.

Back and forth.

Back and forth.

She smoothed the blanket out in her lap, looked at the little yellow creatures on it and smiled. She could smile, now — well, most of the time she could smile — looking at them.

When she'd first purchased the blanket, she'd cried every time she touched it.

Now, she smoothed down its soft surface and used it to conjure up Bethany's face. Bethany had had a minion blanket just like this one. Aaron had purchased it and brought it to the hospital and they'd wrapped Bethany in it to bring her home. As she grew, it became her blankie. She couldn't go to sleep without it clutched in her tiny fingers, sucking on an edge of it like some children sucked their thumbs.

This blanket was all of Bethany that Bailey had. She'd been sitting in that windowless room when it had first struck her that she didn't have a single photograph of Aaron or Bethany.

THE ROOM LOOKS for all the world like every interrogation room in every stupid cop show she's ever watched. The table where the suspect sits, waiting. The two-way mirror on the wall that conceals the detectives who are sizing him up, deciding who will be good cop and who will be bad cop, figuring out how to break him.

There is no two-way mirror in this room. No cop show. No drama. Reality.

How she had come to be here in this room is such a blur that even when she concentrates hard she can't make out but a couple of clear images.

The field of tall weeds in the rain, running away from the rats under the dumpster.

Aaron's body.

He's dead.

She shakes her head in denial but there's no denying it. How long has it been? Hours? Days? Years? They had been on their way to the airport. A flight to Freeport in the Bahamas. A taxi to the cruise ship. Then five days aboard, dining in the best restaurants, lounging in comfortable deck chairs in the sun, drinking fine wine … and at night, making beautiful love while the smell of salt air filled the room from an open porthole.

That had been the plan. That had been the dream. Gone. Gone as soon as they'd stopped to pick up a woman standing out in a downpour. If they hadn't picked her up — Bailey didn't even know her name, had not even had the time to ask. If they hadn't picked up No Name Woman, they'd have gotten on the interstate to the airport instead of taking the back route that wound through the industrial park to the homeless shelter. They wouldn't have been on Baxter Street. Wouldn't have seen.

The door opens and two men and a woman enter and sit down at the table with her.

"I am so sorry we had to bring you here, not a very comfortable place. But it is safe."

"Safe from what?"

The three of them exchange a look.

"You're very fortunate that the black-and-white that picked you up brought you directly here, didn't take you in through central booking, but came directly to me," says the tall man with a bulbous nose and sad, hound-dog eyes.

She remembers flagging down the police car, staggering out into the middle of the street so he would have to stop for her or run her down. She didn't think at the time how she must have seemed. Soaked to the skin, her clothes muddy and torn, her arms scratched and bleeding.

How had her arms gotten scratched? Something to do with ... rats under the dumpster?

The policeman had thought she was drunk, on drugs, was taking her to the police station when she started babbling about what had happened. He had called in on his radio then, written down some information, and then taken Bailey around to the back of a building, a police station maybe, she didn't know. She was met there by what seemed like a crowd of people, who herded her inside and closed the door behind her.

Her memories are blank after that.

There was a shower somewhere. She'd stood under the hot water with a woman, a nurse or a policewoman, holding onto her arm so she wouldn't collapse.

She'd dressed. Prisoner's clothes, an orange jumpsuit. With a tender grimace of apology on her face, the woman had told her it was all they had, like she'd be offended.

She remembers her arms being bandaged.

Someone had toweled her hair dry. Someone else had brought her coffee. But she couldn't hold the cup, her hands were shaking so badly that coffee splashed everywhere. Into her lap, staining the clean orange jumpsuit. The woman, the same one who had held onto her arm while she showered, helped her hold the cup to her lips and drink. It had been scalding, burned her mouth and her throat going down.

Nothing again. A black hole in her memories.

Then here, in this room, looking down at her bandaged arms.

She wiggles her toes and glances down at the floor. She's wearing shoes, those disposable slippers that the plumber wears so he won't track mud into your house and soil your new carpet when he comes to fix your clogged sink.

Aaron's shoe had come off. When the man had dragged Aaron's body across the wet pavement, his shoe…

She wants to cry. It's an urgent need in her, feels the way it feels when you're so nauseous you want to throw up, have to throw up, try to throw up, know that the pain in your gut will only go away when you vomit it up and out of your body. But you can't.

She can't cry either.

She wants to see Aaron's face! Bethany's face! She looks around, frantic. Where's her purse, her phone? She has pictures of…

She'd dropped her phone after she called 911. Aaron and Bethany are gone. Even their images are gone.

WHEN BAILEY HAD FIRST REALIZED in that windowless room that she didn't have a single photograph of Aaron or Bethany, she'd believed she would see Bethany soon.

Right, *soon.*

After a couple of months, she had gone in search of a minion blanket like the one Bethany slept with. She searched store after store. It couldn't be merely similar. It had to be identical. And she'd finally found one in Babies R Us, bought it, took it home and held it to her breast as she sobbed. Every time she looked at it in those first few months, she'd cried. Now it hurt, it *hurt* ... there was an aching need in her chest that almost stole her breath whenever she stroked the soft yellow minions. But it felt like a connection, too, to the little girl who had just celebrated her third birthday ... without her mother.

And now, Bailey was "connected" in some strange, supernatural, totally nutty way to another little girl, more powerfully even than her connection to Bethany. She couldn't feel what Bethany felt, couldn't hear what she heard, smell what she smelled, hear her thoughts and look out at the world through her eyes. So in that way, she was more connected to the little girl who might die, might drown tonight or tomorrow night or ... than she was to Bethany.

She couldn't let that little girl die! In some bizarre way, it would be like letting Bethany die. If she could just *find* her! She could make a difference in the life of that little girl and in some way she was unwilling to pick at and examine, that made the loss of Bethany a little easier to bear.

She paced back and forth in the living room, unable to form any intent to do anything, unable to think of anything but the little girl and the blue chair and the belligerent man, when her cellphone rang and Sheriff McGreggor told her that the man was at the marina to pick up the chair. She grabbed her car keys, raced out to her car and peeled rubber out of her driveway. The little girl was only minutes away! Bailey felt a hope well up in her chest she hadn't felt in a long time.

She had turned off onto Joe's Hole Marina Road when she heard the first wail, a mournful sound behind her, coming up fast. It was joined by a symphony of sirens that curdled the air with their cries. In less than a minute, the first sheriff's department cruiser blew past her as if she were standing still. Others followed, one after the other, sheriff's department and

West Virginia State Police cruisers with lights flashing and sirens screaming. And an ambulance, a big boxy truck followed by a Kavanaugh County Rescue Squad truck in its wake.

The hope that had welled up in Bailey's chest was replaced by sick dread, a cold hard stone deep in her belly.

Chapter Twenty-Two

BAILEY PULLED her car off to the side of the road and got out when she saw the road ahead blocked by a West Virginia State Police cruiser turned crossways. The trooper was directing drivers to pull into the driveway of a house about fifty yards away to turn around, was not allowing anybody through.

Bailey approached the trooper, who held up his hand before she had a chance to speak.

"I'm sorry ma'am, you'll have to turn around. This road is blocked."

"What's going on?" she asked.

"There is a police emergency," he said dismissively. "You need to move your car. You can't leave it parked on the side of the road."

"But I'm supposed to be there, supposed to go to the marina."

"Nobody's going to the marina right now except police and emergency personnel. You need to move your car."

Bailey felt a flash of desperation. Had the boat blown up? Is that what happened? But that made no sense. The explosion had happened at night, not in the daylight. It had been dark, and she saw the bright lights of the explosion glowing against the night sky. And besides, she had the sense, irrational as it seemed, that she'd have known if the boat had blown up. That she would have felt something. She was connected to that child and she would have felt something if the child had … died.

"Please, I'm supposed to be here. Sheriff McGreggor called me and told me to come. Call him. You can do that, can't you, radio him or something? Tell him Bailey Donahue is here."

The trooper looked at her and she was certain he was going to tell her no, send her away, but instead he stepped aside, waved another trooper to take his place directing traffic while he used the microphone attached to the shoulder of his uniform. She couldn't hear what he said, but after a brief conversation, he approached her.

"The sheriff said to let you through. But you're to stay on *this* side of the police line, do you understand? There's a yellow tape across the parking lot. Don't cross it. The sheriff said he'd meet you there."

Bailey hurried up the hill and around the bend. Below her, the parking lot stretched out in a flat area above the marina. It was a zoo. There must have been a dozen law enforcement officers there, and a crowd of onlookers, people from the marina and the houseboats were herded behind the piece of yellow tape. She saw paramedics slam shut the back door of an ambulance, rush around to the front and leap in. Then the ambulance pulled back, turned and came roaring up the hill toward her, siren screeching, lights flashing. She stepped to the side of the road and watched it pass, crest the hill and heard the siren wailing as it raced down the back side of the hill and away.

The booths were set up as they had been the day before, but they were deserted, the operators forced back behind the police tape, which she could now see outlined an area around the first booth, the one for the Kavanaugh County Craftsman's Association where the day before she had stood with the sheriff as the owner loaded up Adirondack chairs into the back of a van.

She spotted the sheriff striding toward her as she approached the tape. He wordlessly lifted it for her to duck under, then turned back toward the booth. The man before her was not the kind, affable man who had spent an afternoon on a jet ski searching the lake for a little girl he didn't really believe existed. He was a lawman, all business.

"What hap—?"

"The man who came back for the chair — name's Derrick Osbourne — he shot my deputy."

Bailey gasped and her hand flew to her mouth.

"Shot...? Is he ... all right?"

"Stable." He paused, and she could see the next words came hard from his throat. "He was gut shot, a wound in the abdomen right below his vest. That's ... *bad.*"

"But why?"

"Osbourne's wanted." The sheriff's words were clipped. "One of the bystanders got his license number when he hauled butt out of here and I got the registration. The vehicle's registered to a Derrick Neal Osbourne, twenty-eight, from Akron. Outstanding warrant in Cincinnati for assault, broke a guy's jaw in a bar fight. When he saw Fletch, he must have figured out that Ragland was stalling him until the police arrived." He looked at her full in the face for the first time and she could see the anguish in his eyes.

"He just pulled out a gun and fired. Fletch had no warning, never had a chance."

He looked away from her then.

"Ragland said the guy looked even more juiced up than he had when he bought the chair. Scared him so bad he acted like he was going to his van to unload the chair, got in the back and climbed through to the front door, jumped out and ran, left the guy standing there waiting."

She didn't need all the details, but she could see the sheriff needed to talk so she stood there, heartsick.

"He's a meth head, probably hasn't slept since he and his buddies got down here to the lake three days ago, been partying nonstop."

"He and his *buddies?*"

He looked back at her.

"Osbourne's uncle owns a houseboat here, and the uncle's on a cruise with his family so Osbourne rounded up some buddies and busted into the houseboat. They've been tied up in a cove for the past couple of days, partying hard, but came back to the dock yesterday for gas and supplies."

He unconsciously adjusted his sunglasses on his nose. She'd noticed the gesture the day before. It was something he did when he was focused hard on something.

"The crazy junkie destroyed an Adirondack chair just for fun — nothing left but little pieces, they said — so Osbourne came up here to replace it so the uncle wouldn't know. That's why it had to be blue."

Bailey felt a hole in her belly. "Then…"

"There's no little girl, only his two buddies, both with outstanding warrants." Brice pointed with his chin and she turned to see two men in handcuffs being escorted by state troopers to their cruisers.

She was stunned, speechless.

"But the chair…"

"I don't know what to tell you, Bailey, but there is no little girl involved in any way with that houseboat." One of the deputies looked his way. "I have to go now. Every law enforcement officer in West Virginia, Ohio, Kentucky, Pennsylvania and Virginia is looking for this guy. He shot a police officer, he's on meth, armed and in the wind. That's the picture they put beside the word 'desperate' in the dictionary."

He paused for a moment, a tender expression briefly softening his hard features.

"I'm sorry, Bailey."

Then he turned and headed back into the pandemonium.

Bailey stood where she was, ignoring the hum of activity around her, trying to make sense of what had just happened. The sheriff's deputy had been shot.

She gasped. Was that *her* fault? Was it her fault the man might *die?*"

And she couldn't help thinking that if Brice had been the officer who approached the meth head, he would have been in that ambulance with a bullet in his belly.

She wandered toward the booth where the owner had only unloaded a couple of chairs and tables before running for his life. Thoughts chased themselves around in her mind so fast she couldn't grab hold of any one of them long enough to think it.

No little girl.

The words echoed like a gong on some mountainside in Tibet.

It made no sense at all. She stopped next to the van, looked in the open back doors and saw the chair, the now-blue chair. She reached out a finger in a might-be-wet-paint gesture and touched it.

Bailey's vision goes black, no light, *the total darkness of someone sightless since birth — even though she has her eyes open, she knows she does, she can reach up her hand and touch her face and feel her eyelids.*

Then other eyes open in front of hers. It's like she'd been looking out through binoculars with the lens cap on and someone removed it.

Now there is a scene in front of her, but it is not the parking lot where she is leaned up against the back of a van, reaching inside it to touch the arm of an Adirondack chair with still-wet blue paint.

What she sees is a room somewhere. It doesn't have the sense of immediacy that she'd felt when the little girl was at the carnival, a sense of "this is happening right now!" It feels more like the vision she had when she painted the child, a sense that this is reality, alright. It will happen, but it hasn't happened yet.

When the lens cap comes off, she sees a child in a highchair. It's a little boy, looks to be about eighteen months old, with fat cheeks, rust-colored hair and eyes as pale blue as a baby blanket. He is wearing a bib smeared with something orange, creamed carrots maybe. And when Bailey sees a hand reach toward him with a spoonful of food, she grasps the perspective. She is looking out through the eyes of the person holding the spoon out to the baby. She is looking out through the little girl's eyes at the world she sees.

The little girl holds the spoon toward the baby's mouth and he turns his head to the side and pushes the spoon away, spilling its contents on the highchair tray.

He used to be so easy to feed, the little girl thinks. It was fun, like he was a life-sized doll. But he's gotten cranky lately and she doesn't like feeding him anymore.

"Stop that, Jakey," the little girl says. "This is carrots. They're gooooood!" She smacks her lips but the baby is not impressed.

Bailey hears background noise behind the little girl, conversation, though she only catches bits and pieces of what is said.

"...a piece of chocolate pie when it's cooled off..."

"...got the last chicken leg..."

"...have to eat all of it?"

The little girl scoops another spoonful of carrots out of the baby food jar and starts toward the baby's mouth with it.

"Come on Jakey, be a good boy and eat. Mommy says we can't go out until you eat your supper."

Thunder rumbles in the distance, and at the sound, the little girl takes the baby's hand and holds it so he can't push the spoon away while she shoves the food at his face. He opens his mouth, takes the food, then spits it back out.

"Stop that!"

She can't sound mad. If she sounds mad at him, he'll tune up and cry and then he'll never finish eating. And the longer the baby takes to eat, the longer she has to sit here before she can go out back to watch.

"Just two more bites and you'll be all done," she cajoles him sweetly,
From behind her, a voice says, "I'm finished, Mom. Can I go now?"
Another voice chimes in, "Me, too. See, my plate's clean."
"Okay, skat."
The little girl hears the sound of chairs pushing back, running feet,
and the stretching of the spring on a screen door.
"Don't let the door sl—"
Bam, the door slams.
The little girl looks over her shoulder and sees a woman standing in
front of the open door of a refrigerator, setting something inside. She's
blonde, hair in a ponytail, wearing a blue tank top and cutoff shorts. Her
left arm is covered in a tattoo from her wrist to her shoulder — red and
white flowers on a vine with green leaves. The little girl turns back and
hurriedly eats the bite of baby food she was shoving at the baby. Scrapes
the last bite out of the jar and eats it, too.
"Jakey's finished, Mommy," she says, and begins pulling the tray out
and unfastening the strap around the baby.
There is a knock at the front door and her mother turns, closes the
refrigerator door and starts out of the room to answer it. The little girl
reaches to pick up the baby.
"You take him out to watch," her mother says. "I'll be along
directly."
It probably hasn't even started yet. She hasn't missed a single one.
The little girl pulls the child up into her arms and the scene fades.

THE BLACKNESS RETURNED to Bailey's eyes and another reality formed around her, the sounds of the milling crowd behind the police line, the heat of the sun on her skin, the faint smell of fish that wafted up from the marina.

She opened her eyes and the parking lot scene downloaded into her brain.

Trembling violently, her legs felt so weak she had to sit down on the back bumper of the van or she might have collapsed.

She had connected to the little girl through that chair. But how? *There was no little girl on that houseboat!*

It took close to three hours for police to clear the scene and Bailey sat on the top step of the marina, staring out at the lake the whole time. Then she got into her car and drove. Just drove. The lake had six hundred miles of shoreline and she wandered around a considerable bit of it in the hours that followed.

She thought of the little rock-polishing machine she'd gotten for her tenth birthday. Put rocks and water in it and the tumbler would roll the rocks around until they were smooth. There wasn't a thought in her head about the little girl with braids that had a rough edge on it anywhere. She'd rolled all of them around in her head until they were flat and glossy.

Her mind hauled out denial and shook the dust off it. Couldn't be happening. Preposterous. She was a normal human being, after all, and ordinary people like Bailey Donahue didn't — except she wasn't Bailey Donahue. She was Jessie Cunningham, and ordinary people like Jessie Cunningham didn't live a secret life with a fake identity, arms aching to hold a daughter who would die if Bailey so much as looked into her face. *That* didn't happen to ordinary people, either. Normal people didn't wind up in the Witness Protection Program.

And certainly normal, ordinary people didn't paint portraits of events that hadn't happened yet and see out other people's eyes. But Bailey had — *for real* — and pretending it wasn't happening changed nothing. There was a little girl out there somewhere, alive right now, who wouldn't be alive much longer unless...

Bailey had only one card left to play. The issue was — *could* she play it?

She called T.J. He answered on the third ring.

"Can you come to my house right now? Meet me in a few minutes?"

"Done."

~

T.J. SAT in the swing on Bailey's porch with Sparky curled up beside him. She pulled into the driveway and as soon as she got out of the car, the dog leapt off the swing and dashed to her, jumped up on her begging to be petted. She stopped, got down on one knee and ruffled the animal's soft fur. When she lifted her eyes to T.J.'s, he could see hurt, pain and confusion in them so stark, it was like looking into an Alaskan winter.

He got to his feet, but she waved him back into the swing, climbed the porch steps and sat down herself in the rocker across from it. Sparky proceeded to hop immediately into her lap and her hands caressed the little dog absentmindedly as she spoke.

"Where you been?"

She told him what happened, her voice almost devoid of emotion.

"*Shot* him? Shot Fletch?"

"You know him?"

"Everybody knows Fletch. He gone be alright?"

"Brice didn't know."

Brice, huh? Not Sheriff McGreggor. Okay.

"But that's not all of it, not the whole story. I touched the chair, the blue chair, and I … saw out the little girl's eyes."

"What'd you see?"

"Nothing useful. She was feeding a baby in a highchair. It didn't tell me anything about where she was or when it happened. At least when I saw her get her hand stamped at the carnival, it provided a place and time. But T.J., *why?* Why did that chair connect me to her when she wasn't on that Osbourne guy's houseboat? Was it just because it's an Adirondack chair? Would I be connected to her by just any Adirondack chair? It doesn't have to be one she touched? Is that it?"

T.J. shook his head. "They's not much about any of this I understand. When I's little, I used to see Mama acting strange. Like maybe she was hearing or seeing something I couldn't. But she never told me what she seen and I never asked." He stood. "I want to look at them two paintings again."

He saw her flinch at the mere mention of them.

"And then I got something I want to tell you."

She got slowly to her feet, swayed a little.

"You had anything to eat today?" he asked.

She looked puzzled. "Eat?"

"Yeah, eat. You know, food. Chewing. Swallowing, that kind of thing. You done that before, ain't you?"

"I don't know if … no … coffee this morning is all."

T.J. shook his head.

"Never knowed a *man* in my life could just 'forget' to eat, but women…" He reached into his pocket and drew out his cellphone. "I'd offer to whip us up something but my cookin's so bad the flies done took up a collection to get the hole in my screen door patched."

No reaction at all. He punched a favorites number and Dobbs answered.

"I'm at Bailey's house and we's starving. Why don't you swing by Delgados and bring us some supper, an extra-large pizza?" He stopped, looked at Bailey. "You like anchovies?"

She stared at him like he was speaking Mandarin Chinese.

"Hold the anchovies."

To Bailey again, "How about—?" He stopped. Wouldn't do no good to ask. "Put some extra cheese on it, and bacon. Everybody likes bacon."

He paused and listened.

"Yeah, put olives on it if you want … whatever you want. And get a big one. No, make it two large."

Best to get two large. If he was hungry enough, Dobbs could chew through a pizza like a woodchipper through a log.

He hung up and indicated the door. Bailey rose and

walked into the house, downcast as somebody on the way to the gallows.

He went before her down the hallway to the studio, stepped inside and turned on the lights, not that he needed to. The two windows with north light funneled light into the room. Even at almost seven o'clock in the evening, there was still plenty of sun.

He went to stand in front of the two paintings, side by side on easels in the middle of the room, and Bailey reluctantly followed.

"Dobbs had his self a nice long talk yesterday with Miss Annabelle Lee. She lives in Arbor Dell Retirement Village. She's ninety-three years old, sharp as a switchblade and mean as a serial killer with a sinus infection. She taught history here in Kavanaugh County for forty years. Dobbs asked her about the Watford House."

When he was finished telling her Dobbs's story, he took a deep breath and jumped off the bridge into darkness.

"That first night when I come here, I told you I knew this house, that my mama was a maid here when I was a little boy in the 1950s. She was helping the Whittakers get ready for a Fourth of July party and fell, hit her head, and that's when it all started."

T.J. watched Bailey's reaction as he continued.

"I knew about that Watford woman, just wasn't sure when. The details is what I needed from Annabelle. Now, think about this … in the summer of 1895, Sophia Watford fell and hit her head…"

He turned and pointed out the door of the studio.

"And she *died in that kitchen*. Sixty years later, in the summer of 1955, mama fell and hit her head *in that kitchen* … but she didn't die. She was unconscious and when she woke up, she was different, compelled to paint portraits she didn't want to paint — the last one of you with a bullet hole in your right temple. Exactly sixty years after that – this summer, 2015 —

you shot yourself in the head *in that kitchen* and when you woke up, you were different, too. Different the same way my mama was."

He paused, could see Bailey's wheels turning around in her head, dots connecting of their own accord.

"Maybe the same person *did* paint both those paintings." He paused. "And maybe the artist was Sophia Watford."

Bailey's face was totally blank, like she had walked away from her body and had gone somewhere else entirely. When he saw her countenance return, there was a kind of recognition in her eyes.

"You're saying you think Sophia Watford's … what? *Ghost?* … painted both these pictures?"

"As God is my witness I ain't sure what it is I'm saying. Ghost? Spirit? Presence? Essence? Life force? I don't know what. And maybe none of this means anything at all. Maybe it's all a coincidence. Maybe Sophia Watford don't have nothing to do with nothing. But…"

Bailey stepped over to one of the two wingback chairs and sat down heavily.

She smiled a little half smile.

"Do you hear it?" she asked.

"Hear what?"

"Na-na, Na-na; Na-na, Na-na." She hummed the theme from *The Twilight Zone.*

Then she burped out a bleat of laughter that sounded semi-hysterical and he watched her swallow back the emotion that'd produced it. She sat still, getting herself under control before she spoke.

"I don't know if it's the ghost of Sophia Watford or the ghosts of Jimmy Hoffa, Elvis Presley and Elias Howe and his sewing machine. I don't have any idea what *force* paints these pictures." She paused for a beat. "But does it really matter, T.J.? Does it matter how it's happening? It's a reality we can see and feel and hold in our hands."

She rose and went to stand beside the picture of herself his mother had painted. He could see she judiciously avoided the painting of the little girl. "The only thing that matters is that you and I know, we *know* that this little girl" — she pointed, but didn't touch — "is going to drown unless we can figure out who she is and do something to prevent it."

He nodded but said nothing.

When she spoke again, her voice was quiet.

"It took me all day to drag myself around to the obvious, inescapable conclusion. To screw myself up to it."

"And that is?"

The haunted look in her eyes broke his heart.

"I have to finish it, the painting. I have to paint her face."

Chapter Twenty-Three

BAILEY DIDN'T WAIT for T.J. to agree with her, didn't put the matter up for discussion so perhaps the two of them could come to a joint, reasoned decision. She had to paint the little girl's face. Period.

Some part of her had known that from the beginning. As she stood on the marina, looking at the hundreds of houseboats there, it was clear then. There was only one way they could be certain they had found the right boat, the right child. The child had to have a face.

It was just that she knew what would happen as soon as she touched a brush to the canvas. The little girl would drown all over again. And Bailey would drown with her.

T.J. knew that, too.

"Hold up a minute, missy. You—"

"Know what's going to happen? Yes. We both do."

She walked to the other side of the room, selected a clean pallet and began to squeeze out gobs of black and white paint onto it.

"And you're up for that?"

She could hear the concern in his voice and it touched her

more deeply than she wanted him to see. So she said nothing, just continued to prepare the paint.

"That bullet in your head and all, are you sure?"

She laughed, not a big laugh but genuine.

"Oscar, you mean?" He looked blank. "Brice named it, the bullet. Have you ever ridden a jet ski?" She could see T.J. had no idea where she was going with such a non sequitur.

"I have not and don't never intend to. I've ridden contraptions a lot more dangerous than that, though." He didn't elaborate. "But I ain't got nothing to prove no more."

"I can't speak to the danger part, but I am here to tell you that the pounding I took on that thing yesterday—"

"You rode a jet ski yesterday?

"Brice and I both did, went out looking in the coves, trying to find houseboats with Adirondack chairs."

She smiled a real smile. Yeah, it had been jolting, bumpy. But it had also been fun.

"If that ride didn't knock Oscar loose, I don't think standing here with a paintbrush in my hand and…"

She stopped. Her breath suddenly stuck in her throat.

"Not just standin' here … standin' here *and drowning,*" he finished for her. "You never know what it might take to knock that thing cockeyed."

She turned to him. "We've already had this discussion, remember? It is what it is."

Then she stepped around him and stood in front of the incomplete portrait of the dead child. It was time to give that child a face. She laid the pallet in the tray on the front of the easel, resolutely dipped the brush into a gob of white paint, quickly lifted it to the canvas before the tattered fabric of her courage could unravel and touched the brush to the canvas.

SHE IS FILLED with a terror that totally consumes her. The pain in her chest — it feels like it might explode, spew her heart out into the darkness.

She has to breathe.

Dark, so dark.

The water is cold. She opens her eyes, tries to see, but her eyes sting and she reflexively squeezes them shut again, pawing at the water, struggling upward.

Her face breaks the surface and she gasps in a lungful of air, gets water along with it. It tastes nasty, smells like—

She begins to cough, strangled, kicking her feet frantically to stay upright. She forces her eyes open, burning, and sees colored lights. Something bumps into her and she grabs at it, catches it, holds on. It's big, a chair. She grasps with all her strength, tries to pull herself up out of the water and onto it. But it is slick and she can't keep her grip.

The chair slides out of her grasp, turns in the water and comes down on top of her.

She goes under again, cold, struggling, pushing at the chair, trying to push it out of the way, but the effort shoves her farther underwater. And her lungs are screaming, the strangling cough reflex grips her throat.

Can't … can't let the air out, can't…

But the air explodes out of her burning lungs and she involuntarily gasps — not air. Water.

It hurts! It hurts so bad. Black water flows into her mouth, burning in her nose.

No!

Hel—

Nothing. All light is gone. She is gone. She is dead.

BAILEY FELT SOMETHING, a hand on her shoulder.

A voice echoed down through time and space from another universe, too faint to hear.

Then louder, in her ear.

"Bailey. Bailey, come on back now, hear?"

Her eyes snapped open to see the black water and—

No black water. Sunlight. So bright she squinted, not like

she did with the stinging water in her eyes. She gasped in a great lungful of air. Then another. Panting.

T.J. was beside her, his hand on her shoulder.

Why she didn't fall to the floor was … how was she standing here when she drowned? Died!

Her not-stinging eyes focused on the canvas in front of her. Shock knocked the brush*es* out of *both hands* to the floor.

The little girl had a face. She was a beautiful child, her features small and perfect, a button nose and full lips. Her eyes were closed, so there was no way to tell the color, but if Bailey'd had to guess, she'd have said blue. Though her face was smeared with the black mud that covered the rest of her body, her forehead had a small clean spot from her hairline down about two inches, far enough to reveal the spray of red freckles on her forehead, and her hair color. The gooey black braids were actually red.

Bailey heard a knock at the front door, followed by Dobbs's voice.

"I've got pizza. Who's hungry?"

She heard the door open and close, heard his lumbering steps cross the living room and go into the kitchen. But she didn't turn, stood transfixed, staring at the face of the little girl who would be dead soon unless…

"Take a picture," T.J. said and pulled his cellphone from his pants pocket, lifted it and began snapping photos of the still-wet canvas, moving around a bit to get slightly different angles. "We'll need these to show people."

Bailey stepped to the table where she had set her phone, reached for it and was surprised to see that her hands were shaking. She took several photos, too, showing the frame sitting on an easel, and then the painting itself. She even stepped close and captured a shot of nothing but the little girl's face. It was a haunting picture. The child's eyes closed, mud on her cheeks and smeared across her mouth, her braided hair tangled with black mud and pieces of debris.

"Pizza's on the table," said Dobbs as he came into the room through the door behind them. "I got extra cheese on—"

He stopped in mid-sentence but Bailey paid him no mind, studying the lines of the perfect little face, awed by so many things at once, emotions and thoughts flitting around like moths around the back porch light at night.

She was awed at the perfection of the painting. Every detail was just right, the whole much bigger than the sum of its parts, a captivating — no, *spellbinding* — portrait that would stop anyone in his tracks. The art itself, merely on the face of it, was the work of a spectacular talent.

And, of course, that talent was *not* Bailey's. Which, of course, begged the question — if not Bailey's, then *whose*?

Sophia Watford's?

The mysterious beauty from some strange land who had to have possessed an artistic skill level second to none, a woman brought here to escape … what? What had happened at the governor's mansion that night? What was she running from to this house? To that kitchen, where she died?

But was Sophia Watford actually dead at all? Was some part of her, some force, some—?

Nope, couldn't go there. Talk about crossing the line with the warning: *beyond here be dragons!*

Bailey was willing to admit only so much. She did not of her own free will or with her own level of skill, paint that portrait. Who did paint it, to what end — not for her to say.

As Bailey stared at the face in wet paint perfection before her, she yearned to connect with the child. Oh, not as she had in death, in dying with the child in the cold dark waters of Whispering Mountain Lake. But to connect to the living child, the person who this minute still breathed, wrinkled what was surely a freckled nose at her baby brother, Jakey, making faces, cajoling him to take that last bite of carrots so they could go outside to…

To something. To what? What was she rushing outside onto the back deck of the houseboat for?

It then occurred to Bailey, what fancy houseboat with a name like Mama's Mink Coat or My First Million — with a supped-up ski boat and jet skis in tow, and a thirty-foot sundeck on top for sunbathing — *had a screen door?* With a squeaky hinge?

…the sound of running feet, and the stretching of the spring on a screen door.

"Don't let the door sl—"

Bam, the door slams.

Houseboats had sliding glass doors that led from the interiors out to the decks on the front and the back, with screens, sure. Sliding screens.

"…Take these pictures and show them around," T.J. was saying, "so we can figure out who this little girl is, get her name and—"

"I know her name," Dobbs said.

She and T.J. turned from the painting to gawk at Dobbs, who had come into the room earlier and stood silently behind them.

"That's Macy Cosgrove, Seth Cosgrove's little girl. I saw her with him yesterday in the check-out line at Piggly Wiggly, gave her a piece of bubblegum and told her I'd teach her how to blow a bubble if her daddy'd let me. And Seth laughed."

"'You ain't gonna be blowing no bubbles, are you, sugar?' he said, and she gave me a great big smile and I saw why not — she didn't have any front teeth. That's Macy Cosgrove. I'm sure of it."

The statement sucked all the oxygen out of the room and Bailey was suddenly almost as breathless as she'd been when she was drowning with … *Macy Cosgrove!*

T.J. wasn't ready to give it up yet.

"That can't be right. The Cosgroves live up in Turkey Neck Hollow. Ain't no way Seth and his family would be out cruising around on the lake in a houseboat! Shoot, he's a laid-off coal miner, part-time carpenter, got three or four kids. They don't have that kind of money."

"That's Macy Cosgrove," Dobbs said, but T.J. talked over him.

"If she ain't on a boat in the lake, how'd she fall in and drown? Tell me that! And she did drown, didn't she, Bailey?"

Bailey could only nod her head, had no words or voice for speech.

"And how'd all them other people Bailey heard screamin' drown?"

T.J. had started to pace in front of the two portraits of dead people side by side on easels, seemed angry but he wasn't, only keyed up and frustrated. Clearly, he was trying to make it all fit in his head and it wouldn't.

"I bet the Cosgroves ain't never even been out on the lake. Maybe on the shore fishing, but not in water deep enough to drown in. And ain't no other body of water bigger'n a bathtub anywhere near their house 'cept that wastewater impound at the top of the holler. And that sludge lake ain't 'xactly a tour bus destination," he turned to Bailey, "for folks who want to jet around on them motor skis, maybe decide they want to take a dip in black sludge to cool off!"

There was a beat of silence after T.J.'s bluster, before Dobbs dropped the next words like pebbles into a pond that sent ripples off in all directions.

"You wouldn't have to go swimming in that sludge lake to drown in that water. Not if the water came looking for you. Not if it came after you, came roaring down the mountainside and washed you away."

T.J. STOPPED IN MID-PACE, literally froze as he was about to lift his foot off the floor. Dobbs's words was bouncing around in his head, echoing, multiplying and fracturing.

His mind wanted to back up from it.

"That ain't possible."

"Why not? It's no more improbable than some houseboat blowing up out on the lake."

"What are you two talking about? What's a coal sludge lake?"

"A lake formed by a strip mine," Dobbs said.

That was the simple answer. Then Dobbs told Bailey how strip mine canker sores had first infected the West Virginia landscape before World War I and the blight had spread like smallpox in the decades that followed.

"The coal companies done the math — it don't take hardly no manpower a'tall to rip the tops off mountains, which makes it a whole lot cheaper than paying miners to dig the coal out."

The environmental ramifications were enormous, of course.

"Strip-mined coal's gotta be washed, and when you do it leaves behind an acidic sludge that'd just about eat a hole in boot leather."

"That water has to go somewhere. Most coal companies bulldoze all the coal waste, it's called slurry or 'gob,' across a hollow to dam up one end of it and then release the black sludge water behind it."

"The coal companies don't got to draw up engineering designs for a dam like that 'cause technically what they built wasn't no dam. Just a gob pile. Wasn't no lake, neither. Just an 'impoundment.'"

"That's how they danced around federal regulations about the structure and safety of dams. There are a handful of state regulations regarding impoundment dams, but a lot of palms were greased in Charleston when those were drawn up."

"You're saying one of those dams might be damaged or defective and cause a flood?" Bailey said.

"If the whole damn let go, it wouldn't be just a *flood*. It'd be a wall of water roaring down that hollow." Dobbs looked at T.J. "Water — how high?"

"Shoot, with that much water, thirty, forty feet."

"Black, oily sludge water. The force of it … it would be like pointing a high-pressure water hose at the ground."

"I seen where a run-off dam busted, wasn't nothing like big as this one, but it took out the whole streambed below for half a mile, like a bulldozer had scraped off everything down to bare rock, then poured motor oil on it."

Bailey had been standing, but she sat down then on the arm of one of the wingback chairs.

"How many people live in Turkey Neck Hollow?" she asked.

T.J. wasn't sure. "A dozen, maybe more. There's four or five houses, strung out all down the hollow. It's an old coal camp, a small one."

"And a coal camp is…?"

"The housing coal companies built for their miners. They created strings of small communities clustered up and down just about every creek in West Virginia."

"Shoot, they's maybe a hundred-twenty coal camps in the Pocahontas Coal Field alone with five, maybe eight hundred people living in each one. And that's just one coal field. You ever been up in the mountains?"

Bailey shook her head.

"They're so steep there usually isn't enough room in the hollows between them for more than a creek and a road. But anywhere there was enough space to put a house, the coal companies built one. A couple here, a couple there."

"The coal companies got hold of them miners and run they whole lives." T.J. scowled. "They wasn't nothing but white slaves, Irish and Welsh mostly."

"I haven't been in Turkey Neck Hollow in years, but whether there's one house there now or fifty, if that dam lets go, they'll all wash away. There's nowhere for the water to go but down that creek bed, no place for it to spread out until the meadow that's a mile and a half downstream."

"And I don't know if they's people living in all the houses that are there — them houses was shacks when they were built, out of the cheapest material. Unless a man worked on 'em, fixed the roofs, shored 'em up, eventually they'd fall apart. They's hundreds of falling-down houses up in these mountains."

As T.J. listened to his own description, the sickening possibilities began to sink in and it was so horrifying he backed up from it, like yanking his hand off a hot stove.

"Whoa, whoa!" He quoted back to him what Dobbs had said about the painting of Bailey. "Let's pull this buggy back up to the barn and start over. We got to reason this out."

"Okay, let's say it's *not* a houseboat," Bailey said. "Let's say it's a flood like you're describing. That explains some things."

"What things?" T.J. asked.

She pointed to the painting of the little girl, to her smeared dress and legs. "Most mud is brown. That's black. I didn't think about it at the time, and the water stung her eyes. She opened them underwater and it *burned*. When she came up out of the water she was squinting and couldn't see, like she'd gotten something more in her eyes than lake water."

Bailey got to her feet, didn't pace like T.J. had done, but couldn't keep still either, walked to the paintings, to the window, along the rows of shelves and back to the paintings.

"And the chair!" She grabbed T.J.'s arm. "She couldn't hold onto the chair *because it was slick*. It wasn't just wet, it was slick, almost *slimy*."

"About that chair — if she wasn't at the lake, why'd you connect with her when you touched that chair?"

But T.J. answered his own question as soon as the words left his mouth.

"Seth Cosgrove builds Adirondack chairs." His voice was soft, full of wonder. "That's why Bailey connected with the little girl when she touched the chair. The little girl *had* touched the chair … Macy Cosgrove had touched that chair while her father was building it."

All three fell silent then, the enormity of what they were saying so sobering they had nothing left to say.

Bailey picked up her cellphone from the table where she'd placed it after she used it to take pictures of the painting. "We have to call the sheriff."

"And tell him what?" T.J. asked.

"Tell him the little girl's not on a houseboat, that we were wrong, that there's going to be a flood—"

"And he's going to believe what you's saying because…?"

Bailey sagged. "He won't believe us. If I were him, I wouldn't believe us either."

"But don't we have to try?" That was Dobbs. T.J. would have bet his pension that's what he'd say. "Without the sheriff, how can you evacuate the hollow?"

Bailey lifted the phone and punched a number. T.J. didn't fail to note that it was on her "favorites" list.

Chapter Twenty-Four

BRICE MCGREGGOR SAT ALONE NOW in his office in the sheriff's department, which occupied most of the first floor of the Kavanaugh County Courthouse. It had become the de facto command center for the massive manhunt the sheriff's department and the West Virginia State Police were conducting for Derrick Osbourne, the whack-job who had shot Fletch. Brice was in charge of the search. He had shoved the paperwork, the forms and files and reports to process, into a cardboard box so he could spread out a map of the county on his desk. Earlier in the afternoon, he and deputies Owen Smith, Jason O'Loughlin and Tom Hennessy had been pouring over it, pointing out things to four West Virginia State Police troopers jammed between his desk and the walls.

"We've set up roadblocks here, here, here and here," Deputy Smith had said, pointing to red stick pins on the map in the lower right-hand corner, another two higher up the right side, and a fourth at the very top of the map on a dotted line indicating the road was not paved.

"If he's still in here," Brice had indicated the whole width of the county, "we've got Osbourne bottled up. As far as I can tell, he's not local. Maybe we missed something, but right now

I can't establish any ties to anybody in the county other than the uncle who owns the houseboat on the lake. So he's in the wind in a place he's not familiar with. If he's just looking for somewhere to hole up, he could stop anywhere, stash his van in the woods. Or in a barn or behind a chicken house, and if that's the case, whoever has him as a guest isn't entertaining him willingly."

The department had been a beehive of activity all afternoon. Osbourne's description and a description of the van and the plate number had gone out over the local radio station and was being rebroadcast every half hour. The county also boasted its own small local-access television station — WWML for Whispering Mountain Lake — and activities there were ninety percent of its programming. Admittedly, few people watched it, but the fugitive's picture was there to alert any who chanced to turn it on.

Officers had been fielding calls and investigating sightings for hours, but for the moment it was quiet and the stillness gave Brice time to think, to consider all that had happened since he'd answered the first call of the day at Fantastic Bob's Fireworks on Route 19. He felt a flash of guilt, but shoved it resolutely aside. Maybe he ought to feel guilty, maybe Fletch's gunshot wound was his fault for involving him in the wild goose chase to find a little girl and an Adirondack chair on a houseboat. If he should feel guilty about that, he would. Just not right now.

His cellphone buzzed in his pocket. Caller ID identified Bailey Donahue. He almost sent it to voicemail, but she wouldn't call him, certainly not *now*, unless she had a good reason.

"Bailey, what's up? Is something wrong?"

There was a pause.

"Okay, this is going to sound ... please, hear me out."

And she told him the story. As he listened to her description of painting the little girl's face, of drowning again with her, he felt himself being sucked back into the drama.

"What we figured out about the painting — we were wrong. Dobbs says the little girl is Macy Cosgrove, Seth Cosgrove's daughter."

Then he listened to her explanation of the conclusion she, T.J. and Dobbs had reached about the fate of the little girl. She wasn't going to drown in the lake. She was going to drown in a flood, when the dam at the top of the hollow let go.

Brice did *not* have time for this.

"Bailey ... *Bailey!* Listen to me." He interrupted the flood of words coming from the woman he had been so intent on keeping alive that he had set Fletch up to get shot for her.

That wasn't fair. Fletch's shooting might or might not be his own fault, but it certainly wasn't hers. Still, enough was enough.

"Bailey, I can't talk about this right now."

"But you have to evacuate—"

"No. I don't have to evacuate anybody. There is nothing wrong with the dam on the sludge impoundment in Turkey Neck Hollow. Are you listening to me?" His tone had become stern but he couldn't help it. "The dam has passed inspections by the Mine Safety and Health—"

"Brice, please..."

He felt the anger drain out of him, but he was still done with this conversation.

"You want me to evacuate the hollow? Go up there and warn those people to run for the hills, that if they don't they're going to drown, that the dam is about to bust? So tell me — *when* is it going to blow?"

There was silence on the other end of the phone.

"I can't evacuate unless there's *imminent danger.* Is the danger imminent? Is it, Bailey? Is it?"

More silence.

"I have to go now." He ended the call. Then he sat back for a moment, listening to the dispatcher down the hall confirm the description for a neighboring county sheriff's department.

"...Is a white male, approximately thirty years old, six feet, a hundred and seventy pounds. He was last seen wearing a black t-shirt, jeans and carrying a blue backpack..."

He shook his head, the words "armed and dangerous, approach with caution" ringing in his ears.

Fletch had had no such warning. And now Fletch was fighting for his life.

~

BAILEY PUT the phone back down on the table.

"Sounded like that went well," T.J. said.

"He says the dam is safe."

"If he thinks it's safe because it's been inspected, then he's not thinking about who was doing the inspecting and who *owns* the inspectors," Dobbs said.

Bailey didn't get the reference.

"W. Maxwell Crenshaw." T.J. said the name like it tasted bad in his mouth. "He owns the Nautilus Casino that's opening with all the hoopla today. Also owns Crenshaw Coal Company. You prob'ly seen the C3 logo around town, a big yellow C with the number three stamped on top of it."

Bailey hadn't, but nodded as if she had so as not to interrupt him.

"He also owns one out of every two legislators in Charleston, the governor, maybe a supreme court justice or two—"

"And the pope," put in Dobbs.

"Brice said he couldn't evacuate that hollow — even if he'd believed me and I'm sure he didn't — because he could not establish 'imminent danger.' And he's right. We may know where, and even who. But we don't know *when*."

"Soon. The stamp ain't gonna stay on that little girl's hand for long."

"We have to figure out when," Dobbs said.

"How?" Bailey asked.

"I don't know——" T.J.'s head snapped up and he turned to her. "You told me you had another one of them encounters with that little girl when you touched that chair, right?"

"Yes, I did."

"But you didn't tell me much of nothin' about it."

"There wasn't much to tell." She thought back, remembered the blackness that came into her head, opening her eyes in a new reality.

"I was in a room. It was a kitchen with a screen door that had a squeaky spring."

"That narrows it down." Then T.J. dropped the sarcasm. "Think on it, see what else you can remember."

"All I saw was a baby in a highchair."

"Now, that ain't *all* you seen, was it?"

"Yes, it is. That's all I saw."

"What color was the bib the baby was wearing?"

"I don't know." She thought about it for a moment. "It was blue, and it was smeared with orange. Macy was feeding the baby carrots."

"See, you did see mor'n you think you did. What else did you see?"

Now T.J. sounded like a cop. Brice had mentioned to her that T.J. had been a Chicago police officer and that had sounded farfetched at the time. It didn't now.

"Nothing else."

T.J. gave her a look sharp enough to fillet a fish. She closed her eyes and concentrated hard, calling the scene back to mind, scrutinizing every detail of what she saw out Macy Cosgrove's eyes.

"The baby has blue eyes, and freckles on his nose, not much hair, but I can see a fuzz on his head and it's red. Like his big sister's. The highchair back is colored in some floral fabric, plastic, and it's torn on the right corner and the tear has been repaired with duct tape."

Now that she was concentrating hard, she did notice details. Not important ones, though, details that would tell them when the events were happening. But the scene had more clarity than before.

"The little girl is mad at the baby for taking so long because she wants to go outside and she can't until he's finished eating."

"Why does she want to go outside?"

"I thought she meant on the back deck of the boat, but she was talking about the backyard. There's something out there she wants to see. To watch."

"What?"

"I don't know."

"Tell me more about the kitchen."

"The countertop behind the highchair has a turquoise Formica top, I think. There's spilled flour on the countertop, and an overturned half cup measure with a little bit of milk dripping out."

"Fried chicken," Dobbs said.

He looked from one to the other when they turned to stare at him. "She made fried chicken for supper. Mrs. Cosgrove. Her name's Hattie, I think. She'd put some milk and a couple of eggs in a bowl, stirred it up and dipped the chicken pieces in it before rolling them in flour."

"What else?" T.J. said.

"Nothing else." Bailey was frustrated, but she continued to describe the useless details she could see through the little girl's eyes. "There's a toaster on the cabinet, pushed back because where the flour's spilled is probably were it's set and there's no flour on it. It's shiny and clean. And beside that is the open flour canister and—"

Bailey stopped. In her head, her eyes jerked back to the

toaster. The surface was metal, shined up so clean you could see your face in it. The toaster was facing the wall across from the highchair. Bailey could see a window reflected on its surface, but it was a dark hole. It was night outside. Then she saw a sudden flash of color — red. Then another, blue.

"Colors," Bailey said, excited. "The toaster is facing a window and reflecting smeared flashes of red and blue ... lights of some kind."

"Maybe the lights on the top of a police car on the road outside—"

There were green flashes, too. "No, not a police car ... some other kind of flashing light."

"Ain't no flashing light."

Bailey looked at T.J. and his face was at once wondering and frightened. His eyes were open wide and she had time to think that if he were a cartoon, there would be a lightbulb lit up right now over his head.

"Fireworks. Them lights is *fireworks*."

"The fireworks display on the lake!" Dobbs said.

"It wasn't the lights of a houseboat exploding that little girl seen when she was drowning. It was *fireworks*. And what she heard — it was the sound of the dam lettin' go."

"Or the boom of the cannons," Dobbs said.

"What cannons?" Bailey turned bewildered from one to the other.

"Every year, Crenshaw pays for a massive Fourth of July fireworks display on the lake to entertain the tourists. Shoots rockets so high the lights are visible for miles. Even folks in the mountains can see it. They bring in howitzers from American Legion posts as far away as Gilbertville and Rutherford, a dozen of them, maybe more, and fire off a round from all of them at the same time. It's *deafening*. That starts the show."

"When? What time?"

"As soon as it's dark enough."

"Last year, it started at eighteen minutes after nine o'clock.

The boom jarred the 'larm clock off the table beside my bed, knocked the battery out."

"That's our when. Tonight."

Bailey's breath caught in her throat. "How far is it to Turkey Neck Hollow?"

"It ain't about distance, it's about time. On them roads — least half an hour."

Dobbs choked.

"Okay, probably more'n that."

Bailey looked at her watch. "It's almost eight o'clock now!" Her hands shook when she reached for her cellphone to call the sheriff back.

"You gone tell him you know when the dam's gone blow 'cause you looked out through somebody else's eyes and seen a reflection of flashing lights in a toaster? Think that'll work, do you?"

She put the cellphone down again. She'd already lost one little girl…

THE MAN SITTING across the table from her is talking and she ought to pay attention to what he's saying, but she can't.

She had listened before, in another room, somewhere else, or here in this room. She doesn't know. She had talked, too, poured out words. Once she got started, the torrent of words swelled up in her chest and gushed out so fast and furious she could barely get her breath. She told the men seated there … one was the guy across from her now. Or maybe not. And the woman. The woman from the shower was here.

She'd told them what had happened, what she'd seen. About running through the rain, all of it. No, not all of it. She didn't tell them about the baby. There weren't any words to use to tell such a thing. If she had opened her mouth and tried, she'd have found nothing but broken pieces of glass, rusty can lids and razorblades on her tongue instead of words.

The man is speaking again; she should listen. She tries.

"…Mikhailov."

"What?"

"I said his name is Sergei Wassily Mikhailov."

"Whose name is Sergio Mik-Whatever?"

The three people at the table exchange a glance.

"Stop looking at each other like that, like you think I'm simple-minded, like I'm crazy or something."

"We know you're not crazy. Your story checks out. We found a shoe, a Rockport, in the street. And—"

"Story? My story!"

Heat rushes into Bailey's cheeks and her tenuous control on her emotions slips out of her grasp.

"Like maybe I made the whole thing up — is that it? Concocted an interesting tale to tell as a bedtime story to my little girl?"

Little girl. Bethany.

Bailey had not once, not since … since … the sound of a firecracker … thought about Bethany. Now images of the child flood into her consciousness so fast and rich her eyes fill with sudden tears. Bethany, sweet precious, alive Bethany.

She has lost her Daddy. A sob starts in the back of Bailey's throat but she swallows it. Aaron is gone. But Bethany is alive.

She starts to rise.

"I want to see my little girl."

"You need to sit down, Mrs. Cunningham, and listen to us."

"Why? Am I under arrest? Did I break the law?" She sticks out her arms, the ones with bandages from the dumpster … and the rats. "Here, cuff me. Lock me up or let me go. I want to see Bethany."

"Mrs. Cunningham, if you see your daughter, you are putting her life in danger."

It's like he has kicked her hard in the belly and she sinks back into the chair.

"Her life in danger? What do you mean?"

"That's what we've been trying to explain to you."

The woman speaks then, the woman from the shower.

"You've lived a nightmare, a horror none of us can even begin to imagine." She shoots glances at the two men and their faces match hers in either real or feigned sympathy. "I know it's hard for you to concentrate, to understand what we're saying. But you have to listen. Your life is in danger. So is the life of your daughter ... your whole family."

"What are you talking about?"

Bailey's heart begins to hammer, beats so hard and fast she can see the movement, or thinks she can, in the fabric of the orange jumpsuit that has coffee stains down the front.

"If you'll be patient and listen, I'll explain it to you," the man says, and this time Bailey listens.

"The man you described is Sergei Wassily Mikhailov. He is a Russian mafia boss, one of the most powerful men in the organization, maybe the most powerful of all. It's hard to know, we don't have good informants ... anymore."

They look at each other again and this time it doesn't seem to have anything to do with Jessie.

"Informants?"

She knows she sounds like a parrot, but she can't seem to do anything but burp out single words.

"We have a mole placed in the organization. Had a mole. He was discovered and ... killed."

"So the man is some kind of mafia boss? What does that have to do with anything?"

Again, the shared look. If they do that again, Bailey will scream.

The third speaks now for the first time. He's short, square. Dressed as he is in a dark blue suit, he looks like a mailbox.

"What the two of you saw, that's why your husband had to die. And you, too. Sergei could leave no witnesses."

It begins to sink in, a little.

"So this Sergei ... he wants to kill me now?"

There is no fear in the question because she's so wrung out she doesn't have any emotion left in her body to be afraid.

"No. He doesn't want to kill you because he thinks you're already dead."

Nothing about that makes any sense.

"*Apparently, they didn't see you. When your husband called out to you to run, the homeless woman ran away. They thought she was you.*"

Soaking wet, hair drenched, the woman didn't look like a derelict. She could have been anybody.

"*So they put her body and the body of your husband into the car and then set off the gas tank. The bodies were burned beyond recognition. No medical examiner could determine that the cause of death was gunshot wounds.*"

"*They thought that woman was me? But who was she?*"

"*We don't know. We've been trying to find out, but the homeless community doesn't exactly keep census records of its residents. We've done a little asking around, but so far we haven't turned up a name.*"

"*And Mrs. Cunningham, that's the good news for you. As long as she remains anonymous, she can … be you.*"

"*Be me?*" The parrot speaks two words this time.

"*Sergei thinks he killed you both. He heard your husband call out to you, telling you to run, so he knows you were there, that you saw. And he thinks you died there, too, end of story. He needs to continue to think that. He needs to believe that you're dead.*"

Confusion begins to well back up inside Bailey, clouding her thinking. Images swirl around and around in front of her and she feels dizzy. They see her lurch in her chair and the woman is instantly beside her with her arm around Bailey's shoulders.

The others are talking but Bailey isn't tuned in to it, tries but can't, like when you hear a song on the radio through static and you really want to listen to it, want to sing along, but when you turn the dial you can't get the station clearly. The static gets louder or softer, but the music stays in the background, drowned out by the other noise.

She catches words, phrases.

"…spend the night…"

"…safe house…"

"…sedative…"

The woman gets close to her face and speaks to her, and her words rise up through the static.

"*We'll talk about this later, when you're up to it.*"

And then the static comes back and Bailey gives in to it and it all melts away, all the images and sounds. The whump. The firecracker. Aaron's shoe in the street. Everything. She lets her head fill with delicious mind-numbing white noise that erases the world.

BAILEY HAD PUT a gun to her temple and pulled the trigger because she yearned for that white noise again. Wanted it to fill her forever. That had been the only thing that mattered to her … until she painted the portrait of a little girl slathered in black mud. Until she *died* with that little girl.

"I will not let Macy Cosgrove drown!" She ground the words out through clenched teeth, the steel of determination in her voice.

"That's it, then," Dobbs said, getting to his feet.

T.J. rose, too. "Let's go get them people, that little girl, out of that hollow."

How? Bailey wondered as the three of them hurried to Dobbs's Jeep. Maybe she spoke or maybe T.J. just read her face.

"We'll think of something," he said.

Chapter Twenty-Five

BAILEY WATCHED the world fly past the windows of Dobbs's Jeep. Even as big as it was, it felt crowded with the big man taking up so much of the front seat. She sat in the seat behind, looking out at a world unlike any she had ever seen.

The steep, tree-lined Blue Ridge Mountains rose up around her like the walls of a Medieval castle, their lush green set against a perfect blue sky dotted with cotton-candy clouds that floated like hot air balloons tethered to the mountain tops.

The resort town of Shadow Rock on the lakeshore was all she had seen of West Virginia, had been driven there in the night by two taciturn federal marshals she had never met. Why did they always show up to move her in the middle of the night? She sometimes had the sense that the federal marshals liked the cloak-and-dagger quality of their lives, like they played to it, were the stars of their own movies.

She'd done as she had done in the past, packed up what she could carry with her, then selected furniture and the necessities of a new home out of a catalogue — from a used furniture place, of course, because showing up with all-new furniture would raise the eyebrows of the neighbors, and if there was anything Bailey had learned to do in the past year and a half was to make sure all eyebrows with which she came in contact remained resolutely down.

Oh, she knew there were mountains in West Virginia, the same way you know there's an ocean on the other side of California. But knowing there's an ocean, and standing on the shore as the surf crashes against the rocks were two entirely different things.

This world of mountains and hollows was as staggering in its grandeur as any ocean.

As they followed the winding roads, they seemed to be traveling through time as well as space, back to another era, another century. Certainly into another culture Bailey had only read about. They passed houses that looked ready to collapse from the weight of the sunlight on the roof, and other neat ones, one-story shoeboxes out of red brick, with flowers lining the walk to the drive and lawns so manicured they might have been cut with cuticle scissors.

The sign out front of the Four Square Full Gospel Pentecostal Church proclaimed "Stop, drop and roll won't work in Hell!" Trailer houses clung to the mountainsides as precariously as the nests of mud-dobbers to rocky cliffs, alone or in small flocks, affixed with round, white satellite-dish stickpins. She remembered T.J. remarking that the satellite dish was the unofficial state flower of West Virginia.

The road hugged the creek that spilled in a white cascade back the way they'd come. The mountains grew taller, and the sides of the valley rose so sharply on either side in some places there was room only for the creek, the road and the railroad tracks.

They passed through coal camps — a dozen houses, maybe half of them occupied, or a scattering of half a dozen all fallen into disrepair, with sagging roofs, weedy yards, broken porch railings. People lived in some of those. And it seemed they came upon an elephant's graveyard of cars around every bend in the serpentine road, carcasses, propped up on blocks in the front yard beside pieces of unidentifiable machinery, wires going every which way, looking like the autopsy of a robot.

She couldn't seem to draw in a full breath, only little sips of air, could feel her gut tie in such a knot it'd take a boy scout a week to get it straight. She knew her blood pressure must be soaring,

Blood pressure. No. Not now. *Oscar.* Not now. *Please God, just give me enough time to find Macy Cosgrove.* Then her fear turned to anger. *You owe me, okay! You already took one little girl away from me.*

"It won't be long now, only a couple of miles," T.J. told her. They had gotten stuck behind several slow-moving cars, and with no place to pass, merely had to poke along behind them until the vehicles turned into a driveway or onto another road. Obviously, T.J. and Dobbs were used to the snail's pace of travel in the mountains and took that into account when they told her how long the trip would take. Surely they did.

Bailey found herself winding tighter and tighter every time they pulled up behind a pickup that appeared to be held together with duct tape and Bondo, traveling fifteen miles an hour, probably as fast as it could go without coming apart.

Instead of following the latest road snail they'd gotten stuck behind, Dobbs took a sudden left turn and headed up a dirt road, a washboard of holes and rocks.

The sign next to the road had no words, only a logo. The letter C with a 3 stamped on top of it.

"Figured we ought to take a look at the dam, don't you think?"

They jolted up the side of the mountain on a road so torn apart by huge pieces of mining equipment it would have been utterly impassible in anything other than a four-wheel-drive vehicle like Dobbs's Jeep.

Suddenly, they were on the bare top of the mountain, and

from here could see the ugly gash of wasteland there that the coal company had left behind after they'd sucked out all the coal. They'd also left behind the water used in the strip-mining process. A lake of it twice the size of a football field spread out at the end of the road.

Bailey leapt out of the truck and went to stand at the edge of the water. It looked like viscous tar or used motor oil. The stagnant stink off the oily black liquid was almost overpowering — dead water, a chemical odor like sulfur and something else, something un-nameable. No wonder it had stung Macy's eyes!

T.J. and Dobbs left Bailey on the lakeshore and walked to the dam. Coarse coal mining refuse, rocks, soil, anything and everything that'd been lopped off the top of the mountain had been bulldozed into the valley where it narrowed at the top of the hollow to create a dam, with no more intent or fore-thought than a kid stacking up rocks to divert a creek. It was no engineering marvel, that was for sure. But for all that, it did look stable. There was no water leaking out of it anywhere. It looked like Brice had said it would look … just fine.

"Now what?" Dobbs said.

Even to Bailey, it seemed ludicrous to rush down into the coal camp in the valley at the base of this mountain, crying disaster, urging everyone to run, to get to high ground.

They'd sound like Chicken Little.

"I say we stick to the original plan," T.J. said.

The others turned to face him.

"If we're wrong, we gone look like idiots. Won't be the first time … well, not for Dobbs, anyway."

"What if we missed something about the date or the time?" Bailey said. "We go crying wolf now, when the real flood comes, nobody'll listen."

"That's the worm in the apple, then, ain't it? Do we believe this dam is going to let go and flood that hollow, wash away all them houses, drown all them people, including Macy

Cosgrove? Or not? Do we believe it's gonna happen *today*" — he looked at his watch — "in something like fifteen minutes?"

He paused, then continued quietly. "Bottom line, do we believe the painting?"

There was silence.

"My mama wasn't never wrong. All them paintings, all them years. Not one time."

Bailey closed her eyes. The "vision" of drowning was so horrifying that she always did everything she could to banish the images. But now she opened the doors, invited them in and they rolled over her in a flood of backwater.

She *had* drowned, in the dark, hearing the cries of other people who were drowning with her.

She opened her eyes.

"It's going to happen now, tonight. We have to get those people out. Convince them somehow that we're not crazy."

She unconsciously touched the small bandage on her temple, then pulled off the yellow minion hair band holding her hair in a ponytail. It broke and she tossed it aside, fluffing her hair out so it covered up the wound.

T.J. put his hand on Bailey's arm. "You do know you could drown *for real* this time."

She looked deep into his chocolate-drop eyes. "Save Oscar the trouble of killing me."

As they pulled back onto the paved road and turned down the hollow, Bailey glanced back over her shoulder. A black van came around a curve beyond the road leading up to the dam. It seemed to slow down as it approached the turnoff, but then it was blocked from view and she looked resolutely forward.

"SHERIFF, we just got in some more information about Osbourne."

Brice looked up to see Deputy Tom Hennessy standing in

the doorway.

"The Lexington PD had an outstanding warrant for him, too. I just forwarded it to you. Don't know why it didn't show up in our system until now, but it didn't."

"For what?"

"Terroristic threatening."

"Who'd he threaten?"

"He was pulling weeds in the tall cotton. Went after Maxwell Crenshaw."

"Crenshaw?" Brice barked out a sardonic laugh. "Had some sense of moral turpitude about gambling, did he?" Crenshaw owned two riverboat casinos on the Ohio River between Kentucky and Indiana as well as the Nautilus.

"That wasn't the bone he had to pick with Crenshaw."

"Why, then?"

"It's about 3C. Apparently, this dude's a miner and got laid off."

"Get in line."

"Yeah, and then his brother got injured in a 3C mine in Eastern Kentucky — roof collapse, random rockfall, nobody's fault, put him in a wheelchair, though. Says here the family sued the coal company, came up snake eyes, or if they got some kind of piddly settlement the lawyers ate it.

"He blames *the owner of the coal company* for that?"

"Hey, half the country blamed George Bush for global warming. This Osbourne guy was stalking Crenshaw, caught him hanging around Crenshaw's horse farm outside Lexington. Made some pretty vicious threats, beyond your basic 'I'll-get-you' variety. Serious enough Crenshaw swore out a warrant."

The deputy turned to leave, then stopped, considering.

"You know, it might be Osbourne was out on that houseboat to do more than par-tay with his homies. Maybe he was going to dock it at the Nautilus and try to blow the casino out of the water during today's grand opening."

"Why would you think a thing like that? There weren't any explosives on the houseboat."

"Maybe he took them with him. I mean, anybody who can blow up an Adirondack chair without taking out the rest of the hillside knows his way around a stick of dynamite."

"*Blow up* an Adirondack chair? His buddies said he 'destroyed' it just for fun, nothing left but little pieces. You're saying he *blew it up*?"

"Yes, sir. That's what his friends told the state police before they lawyered up and stopped answering questions."

The deputy left the room. Brice sat where he was, processing this piece of information that'd somehow slipped through the cracks. Maybe the chair was — what? A practice shot? Maybe it wasn't farfetched to believe the guy'd been planning to blow up the casino, and when he saw Fletch, the paranoid meth head thought the deputy was onto him. Made more sense than shooting a cop over assault and terroristic threatening charges any lawyer could plead down to misdemeanors.

Witnesses said he'd had a backpack with him, looked big and heavy. Explosives, maybe?

The sheriff's eyes traveled to the piece of paper where he'd been doodling when he was on the phone to Bailey, curls and squares, shaded in. Simple shapes. Beside them were a couple of words he'd written down without thinking, sifted out of his mind with the flow of conversation.

He stared at one of the words, written in bold black strokes.

Bomb.

Bailey hadn't said anything about a bomb.

The other form on the paper had floated up into his consciousness out of … nowhere. Now he sat looking at the dark black letters.

It was capitalized letter C with a 3 stamped on top of it.

Crenshaw Coal Company owned the strip mine at the top

of Turkey Neck Hollow. There was a 3C logo on the sign on the road leading up to the wastewater lake the mine had created.

He picked up his phone and punched in Bailey's number. The call went directly to voicemail. That meant either she had turned the phone off or she was up in the mountains where there was no cell coverage. He tried T.J. Then Dobbs. Voicemail.

Brice got up and started for the door. Found himself running.

"Sheriff—?" said Hennessy as Brice pushed past him in the hallway.

"Gotta check something out," he said and raced out to his cruiser.

THE COAL CAMP in Turkey Neck Hollow looked just like the others they'd driven through on the way here. A collection of houses in varying states of disrepair on both sides of the road in an area probably half a mile long where the valley widened enough to build them. Some were occupied, others abandoned. The houses on the right side of the road backed up against a mountainside cliff face, a rock wall several hundred feet tall with the creek meandering along the base. On the left, a rocky hillside dotted with trees angled down to the valley floor. It was steep, but climbable. In desperation, it was climbable.

Dobbs screeched to a stop in front of the first of the occupied houses. It was on the left side of the road.

"This is where the Cosgroves live," he said.

It was clear the house hadn't been built as a coal camp house, though it was in the same state of decrepitude as the ones that had been. It was a two-story clapboard shoebox with a tin roof, chimneys on both ends and a shingle roof out over the front porch. Two windows above the porch looked out like dark eyes on the road. The sagging porch roof was held up by five pillars that connected to a railing around the porch, the missing spindles there as evident as missing teeth.

Bailey thought about Macy Cosgrove's missing front teeth.

The yard wasn't full of weeds, but the grass needed mowing. There was a gravel driveway that led to an unattached building that appeared to be in better shape than the house. It was certainly of newer, sturdier construction. Maybe a garage, or maybe it was Seth Cosgrove's woodworking shop. The untidy grass was littered with kids' plastic riding toys in various states of disrepair. A tricycle was missing one back wheel, a bike had all its wheels but the tires were flat. There were two Adirondack chairs on the porch.

For all its dilapidation, the house didn't look uncared for, though. Only well used, worn out, not neglected. It had a kind of aliveness to it that was part a product of the yellow light streaming out into the dusk from every window on the first floor of the house and part a product of the music, Carrie Underwood wailing "Somethin' Bad."

Bailey leapt out of the back seat of the Jeep into the road, slamming the door behind her. She paused for a heartbeat, her eyes on T.J. He held her look for a moment, then he and Dobbs roared off toward the other houses.

Panic rose up in her chest as she looked at the mountains that sandwiched this narrow part of the valley. Behind the house was a hillside, not a rock wall. How high would they have to climb up it to be safe? Bailey had no idea, only knew that she had only minutes to convince them to try.

She raced up onto the porch. The front door of the house was open and as Bailey looked in through the screen, the world cranked down into slow motion. She could see through the living room into the kitchen. A woman there was standing in front of an open refrigerator door. She was dressed in a blue tank top and cutoff shorts. A full sleeve tattoo covered her left arm all the way to the shoulder, a vine with green leaves and red and white flowers curled around it. Bailey felt her own arm leave her voluntary control and her fist came up and knocked on the door.

The woman closed the refrigerator door. Behind the woman, Bailey could see a little girl with red braids lift a toddler out of a highchair — a toddler with a blue bib, maybe smeared with orange, with carrots — and start across the kitchen.

"You take him out to watch," the woman said to the little girl as she turned toward the door and Bailey. "I'll be along directly."

The world returned to normal speed and Bailey craned around the approaching woman to see the little girl but she had disappeared from sight.

"Yes?" the woman said, then turned, her blonde ponytail swishing, to see what Bailey was looking at behind her. When she turned back, the beginning of a confused look morphed instead toward hostile.

"Can I hep you with somethin'?" Her voice was hard.

Bailey stopped craning around trying to see behind her and looked into the woman's eyes. They were a startling shade of light blue.

Then she opened her mouth to speak, but nothing came out. Not a word.

She hadn't been able to speak that other night, either, couldn't make a sound. It had been the homeless woman who'd screamed.

Bailey teetered on the edge of the abyss of memory, all the horror of the night Aaron had died lurking in the gray mists below, the ground beneath her feet crumbling. If she fell off into those memories, they would overwhelm her, steal her strength and she would never be able to do what she'd come here to do -- save the little girl in braids whose drowning death Bailey had shared.

Chapter Twenty-Six

THE SHERIFF HAD KILLED his siren several miles back, but kept the light bar on the top of the cruiser flashing, warning the chronically slow mountain drivers to find somewhere — *anywhere!* — to pull over so he could pass. The handful of cars, pickups and trucks he came upon had obliged and he made it to Turkey Neck Hollow in record time.

He careened around the last curve before the road spread out straight for a quarter of a mile and the valley widened slightly. The creek was on the right side and a dirt road, a pot-holed, rock-strewn dirt track on the left led up the mountainside to the dam. It was marked with a small sign that had no words, only a logo: a C with a 3 stamped on top.

A black Ford van was pulled to the side of the road next to the track. The sheriff didn't have to look at the license plate to confirm that the vehicle was the one he was looking for.

Brice was momentarily drained of will, felt an immense weariness, as if all his internal organs had been turned into boulders, weighing him down. He recognized the feeling. Images beat with fluttering moth wings on the back side of his eyeballs.

A little boy still strapped into his car seat, not a scratch on him anywhere but he is clearly dead.

A floater hooked by a fisherman and dragged out of whatever had snagged it on the bottom, how the stench hit him fifty yards out.

He knew the *please-God-**no**!* feeling would pass. But for a second or two after the lightning bolt struck, it was totally debilitating. Every time.

One heartbeat. Two.

He keyed his microphone.

"Base, this is unit one. Dispatch immediate backup! Repeat, immediate backup to County Road 1720 in Turkey Neck Hollow, five miles east of the Route 11 intersection. Subject's van is parked beside the road that leads up to the C3 impound dam."

He didn't even hesitate before he continued.

"Dispatch units three, five and nine and the closest state police units to the coal camp at the bottom of the hollow to evacuate residents. Subject has some kind of explosive device and intends to blow up the dam — repeat, *blow up the dam*."

He'd requested backup because that was protocol, but he knew he was on the hook for the whole thing here. One reason mountaineers were so independent, looked after their own, was because they were so isolated that traditional help was useless. He'd once heard an old miner joke that it didn't do any good to call the sheriff's department when there was trouble "'cause by the time they show up, the dead bodies is already be so stiff you gotta break their legs to get 'em into the hearse."

The closest unit was probably number three, West Virginia State Police Trooper Virgil Furgeson, who was working a roadblock on Route 11. It'd take him fifteen minutes to get here with full lights and siren and the sheriff knew whatever was going to happen here this day would be long over by then.

He also knew that the units he had dispatched to evacuate the residents would not arrive in time either. He refused to admit it even to himself, but he did not believe this was going to end well. He might be able to find Osbourne — arrest him. Or kill him. But he had no illusions about the likelihood that he'd be able to accomplish that task before it was too late. He had seen the painting of Macy Cosgrove in Bailey's studio.

Finally, his mind snapped into place beside Bailey's, Dobbs's and T.J.'s, a magnet pulled instantly into position. He knew now what he believed about the strange paintings, T.J.'s story and Bailey's visions. They were all absolutely true. Incomprehensible. Absurdly, ridiculously impossible. But true. He'd been trying for too long to jam reality into the shape of his own personal belief system and it flat out didn't fit. Reality was that there would be a flood here today, despite his very best efforts to prevent it.

A little girl named Macy Cosgrove and a lot of other people were going to drown, *unless…*

The dispatcher was still confirming receipt of his message when he slid his cruiser to a stop beside the black van like a slalom skier sliding sideways at the bottom of a hill. He leapt out of the car, unlocking his seatbelt with one hand while he grabbed his M4 rifle with the other.

Protocol decreed that he wait for backup. Not a chance.

"I'm going up to the dam after the subject," he said into his shoulder mic.

Leaving his door open so Osbourne wouldn't hear it slam, Brice took off at a dead run up the road to the dam.

T.J. LOOKED out the back window of the truck as they drove away from Bailey, leaving her in the dirt on the side of the road in front of the house where Seth Cosgrove and his wife and children lived, where *Macy Cosgrove lived.* Then they turned a corner and she was gone and Dobbs was pulling to a grinding stop in front of a house that had an unfamiliar name on the mailbox. Hendrix. It was obviously occupied because the yard was littered with chickens, pecking in the grassless dirt in search of whatever it was pecking chickens pecked for. There were pigs in a pen on the far side of the house and their aroma wafted out into the front yard in a red tide.

On the other side of the road was a vacant tumble-down shack with the door hanging open on one hinge and the roof collapsed on the far side. A gigantic oak tree that had to be a century old took up almost the whole front yard, must have been fifteen feet around and seventy feet tall, with a gnarled, textured trunk and low limbs perfect for little-boy climbing, if any had lived there when the families of miners had waited in the shack while the menfolk "went down" to pull the coal out of the guts of the mountain.

T.J. reached over the seats to the gun rack on the back window of Dobbs's truck, lifted the shotgun down off it and grabbed a handful of shells out of the basket on the side of the rack.

"What are you planning on doing with that? Order them up the mountainside at gunpoint?"

T.J. didn't reply, merely hopped down out of the truck, shoved the shells in his pocket and headed across the road toward the house. Truth was, he didn't know what he intended to do with the shotgun. Taking it was one of those things a man just did and then figured out the why of it later on. Dobbs left a tail of dust hanging in the air as he gunned the Jeep and sped down the road to search for more occupied houses.

The house T.J. approached was a coal camp house but a second story had been added, and not expertly. The wood didn't fit together properly at the seams so the inevitable leaks that had sprung up over the years had been patched with old, unpainted barn wood that had turned gray with age.

The house had a side addition, too, that was as tall as the two stories it was attached to. It appeared to be held upright by the brick chimney on the end where birds now perched on the top. A wide porch was affixed to the front door, literally added on, with its own roof, held up with four posts that formed the corners of the porch railing. The spindles were missing in spots, but it appeared sturdy. What didn't appear sturdy were the three porch steps that sagged like a sway-backed mare. T.J. kept to the outside edges where the steps were attached to the frame as he climbed, thinking as he did so that if his was enough weight to break through the wood, there couldn't be anyone inside older than the age of twelve.

He had his fist drawn back to knock when the door beyond the screen swung open.

"What you want?" asked the man inside.

He was small, with gray hair and a bony frame under the t-shirt and overalls he wore. His lower lip was swollen with a plug of snuff, his teeth dark from it, and he sported a beard as wild and wooly as those twins in the cough drop commercials.

Or ZZ Top.

"My name's T.J.—"

"I know who you are."

"Do I know you?" T.J. tried to place the face, mentally removing the beard, adding fifty pounds.

"Don't know if you know me or not, but I know you, know who you are, anyway. I used to work in the lumber yard in Fairmont. You's with your friend — Hobbs or something — when he was loading up a truck to build a fence a few years back."

Then it came to T.J.

"Harlan Bolyard. Your brother Mitchell was the mailman—"

"You want to talk about my brother, go bother him. Like I said, what chew want?"

T.J. looked around the man into the house.

"Your family home?"

"The wife and little bit's here. The boys is out catting

around somewhere, stirrin' up trouble likely. You gonna tell me why you're here?"

"Got bad news and worse news." He tried to keep his voice level, keep the tension and fear out of it. "You and your wife and child have got to get out, right now. You ain't got time to grab nothing to take with you. You got to turn and run, uphill, to high ground. The dam's about to blow!"

"The dam?" The man acted like he didn't even know what the word meant. "You're crazy. There ain't nothing wrong with that dam."

"You don't think so? You seen it *lately*?"

"Last week, as a matter of fact. That dam's fine."

So much for bluffing.

"You think I'd come here and tell you to run for you life for no reason?"

"I don't know why you come here, what it is you really want. But I ain't goin' nowhere."

Bolyard went to close the door in T.J.'s face but T.J. lifted the shotgun and he hesitated.

"I ain't here to hurt nobody. I'm here to save your darned fool neck." He could hear the scared in his voice and didn't try to hide it. "We ain't got time to stand around jawing. You got to run!"

"What, you gonna *shoot me* if I don't?"

He stared at T.J. belligerently.

Definitely not a man who could be bluffed.

"No, I ain't gonna shoot you."

"Then get off my por—"

"But I will shoot your chickens."

T.J. turned and pointed the shotgun at the nearest chicken pecking in the dirt in front of the porch. He pulled the trigger and the bird exploded in a bloody mass of buckshot, feathers and bones, emitting a small squawk before it disintegrated.

~

Dobbs drove past three houses — shacks — that clearly were unoccupied after he let T.J. out in front of the house with Hendrix on the mailbox. Then he ground to a stop in front of the last house on the stretch of road before the valley widened about a hundred yards farther down, and the creek flowed out across a large meadow. The road curved around the right edge of the meadow, hugging the mountainside, leaving no room for houses. And there were no houses in the meadow, either. If there had been, they'd flood when the sludge water hit them, but wouldn't likely wash away because the water would spread out in the unrestricted area. The monster would lose its force, spend itself filling the meadow with black goo.

But this house would take a hammer blow from the raging flood waters. Even a strong structure wouldn't be able to withstand the force that would be unleashed against it, but a coal camp house like this … splinters. Even though it was farther from the source of the flood than where he'd left Bailey and T.J., the house would offer no protection to whoever was inside when it collapsed.

In truth, the house wasn't strictly a coal camp house. It was a modification of the original design and one more artfully executed than the house where he'd left T.J. The original structure stood pretty much as built — shoebox shaped, tin roof, porch sticking out like a Groucho nose off the front of the building. But an almost identical structure had been built right beside it on the same piece of property and a covered breezeway stretched out across the space between the two with doors into the buildings on each end.

It appeared that the second structure was occupied and the first not, but he'd have to check to make sure. The structure on the right had curtains on the windows and there was a clothesline stretching between the posts that held up the porch roof with clothing on it. A sheet, pants in a couple of different sizes and socks and underwear.

Dobbs hurried as fast as his ever-increasing bulk would

allow across the weedy front yard and up the steps to the first house, the one he thought unoccupied. He banged hard on the door, waited, banged again. When he banged a third time, no one answered in that house, but an elderly man stepped out onto the porch of the other house, looked at him and called out, "Don't nobody live there. Who you looking for?"

Dobbs plastered his best imitation of a smile on his face then, and called back, "Then this here, sir, is your lucky day."

T.J. Hamilton had once described Dobbs as "a man whose still waters run deep … with sharks cruising around on the bottom."

Growing up in a bigoted world, the best friend of a black kid, had given Dobbs an appreciation for the contradictions in life as well as a skill he used often. Take a single true fact, "I'm late because I was out fishing, Ma…" with generalizations that skirted around the edges of that truth, "…with some guys…" and then chuck the truth altogether when he had to and put the best possible face he could on an outright lie: "…and Charlie Phillips stole my pole — that's why I don't have any fish."

Dobbs cleared his throat, swallowed once, hard, and put that long-honed skill to work, with the slightest bit of added pressure being that if he couldn't pull this off, he and some other folks were minutes away from drowning.

He lumbered back down the steps, crossed the yard and joined the man standing on the porch. A woman had come to stand behind him in the shadows. She appeared to have almost no hair. Sick, chemotherapy perhaps. But probably not. She had a certain look, her features thick and heavy, that was not as uncommon among mountain folk as some wanted to believe. For all the disclaimers about how mountaineers had been disrespected for years for inbreeding, the plain truth was that there had been, was now and at least for the foreseeable future would continue to be too much marrying among people too closely related to each other. It was unavoidable. If you were born, grew up and died within thirty miles of where your parents and grandparents had done the same, the gene pool was, of necessity, limited.

Dobbs was out of breath by the time he made it up to stand in front of the man who had stepped back into his house but kept the screen door pushed open in front of him. Without missing a beat, Dobbs reached into the hip pocket of his overalls, pulled out his wallet and extracted from it a crisp one-hundred-dollar bill.

"How'd you like to make yourself a hundred dollars?" he asked.

The man was small and wiry, wearing no t-shirt under his overalls. His arms were scrawny, with boney nobs at the elbows and shoulders like the joints on an action figure doll that a kid could pose in different positions. Bald, except for a bathtub ring of gray hair above his ears, he wore wire-rimmed glasses, and now, up close, Dobbs could see the concave lips that indicated there was not a single tooth left in his mouth.

But when he opened it to speak, Dobbs saw he'd been wrong. There were two. One on the upper right side, blackened and crooked, another on the bottom on the left. That tooth stood like a lone tombstone, straight and tall and perfectly white.

A couple of different looks played across the man's face as he stared at the hundred-dollar bill Dobbs held by the corner, the way you'd hold a dead mouse by the tail.

One was greed. The other was suspicion.

Suspicion won the tug-of-war.

"Who are you and what do you want?" he demanded.

Dobbs ignored the question and continued with the spiel he had constructed in his head in the handful of seconds he'd had to concoct it after he dropped T.J. in front of the previous house. T.J. was maybe going to use intimidation, a threat to get the people to run for their lives. Bailey would likely use charm. Dobbs wasn't cut out to be good at either one. But he did have that hundred-dollar bill.

"It's your lucky day because those people ain't home, which means you get to be the last person I offer this money to," he said, affecting a totally authentic West Virginia dialect. "It ain't no joke, ain't no trick. I'm serious as a heart attack. This here one-hundred-dollar bill is yours — and I get to make fifty dollars for giving it to you — and all you got to do to earn it is run up the hillside behind your house."

The man pulled back into his house and started closing the door in Dobbs's face.

"You ain't draggin' a full string of fish!"

"Okay, then, I'll give you my fifty, too, 'cause if I can't get everybody in this holler to cooperate I don't get no bonus. Just hear me out."

The man didn't look any less suspicious, but upping the ante turned up the force of the greed in his eyes. One hundred and fifty dollars was a lot of money to a man like this. He hoped the man wouldn't demand to see the fifty-dollar bill as well, because all Dobbs had left in his wallet was a twenty, a ten and a couple of ones.

"Some flatlander from the University of Kentucky come knocking on my door a couple of days ago and said he was doing a survey for the U.S. Bureau of Mines. He give me some cock-and-bull story 'bout why they wanted to know. But 'neers ain't stupid as them folks think we are and I know what he was *really* after. Them folks is covering their butts. They may *say* they're gonna put warning sirens in all these hollers 'cause they care about the safety of the folks who live down hollow from a strip-mine impoundment." He made a disdainful sound in his throat. "Riiiiight. You and me both know they figure sirens is cheaper than the lawsuits they'd get slapped with if somethin' happens to one of them dams." He looked up the street toward the top of the hollow and his heart began to beat faster. He was taking entirely too long with this. Any second now … any second…

"But I was glad to take the fool's money!" Dobbs reached into his front pocket and pulled out Uncle Hurl's pocket watch. "He give me this stopwatch, said he'd give me fifty dollars for every survey I completed and a two-hundred-dollar bonus if I got everybody in the holler to cooperate in the test."

He had the guy's whole attention now. He had not stopped looking at the $100 bill since Dobbs took it out of his wallet.

"What test?"

"All's you got to do is run up the side of the mountain." He indicated it with his chin. "Fast as you can. And I got to use this here stopwatch to time how long it takes you to get up a hundred feet."

The man started to close the door again.

"Yore crazy."

Dobbs wanted to push, offer something else. But he was good at reading people, so he took a chance.

Letting out an elaborate sigh, he dropped the watch back into the front pocket of his pants and reached for his wallet to return the hundred-dollar bill.

"Suit yourself. You just cost yourself a hundred and fifty dollars and me two hundred." He gestured back up the road. "You're the only man on this road didn't need the money. Seth Cosgrove's family made it out of the house and up the hill in thirty-seven seconds flat, and he's got them little kids and a baby. He made $175, $100 for participating and a $25 bonus for every child under the age of seven." Dobbs paused for a beat. "Maybe he'll use some of it to buy a case of beer and you can help him celebrate."

It took every bit of strength Dobbs had to turn around and start slowly back down the porch steps.

Chapter Twenty-Seven

KAVANAUGH COUNTY SHERIFF BRICE MCGREGGOR ran as fast as he could up the rutted dirt road, leapt the potholes and circled several rocks as big as washing machines. He held his rifle in the low-ready position — snug against his shoulder with the barrel pointed at the ground. As he approached the flattened top of the mountain, he slowed. Moved from cover to cover. Behind a big rock. Shielded by a mound of fossilized coal sludge that had been returned to its original solid state by time and the sun. But there was no cover at the top. It was flat and featureless.

As he climbed, he saw tire tracks in the soft dirt. A Jeep. Raymond Dobson drove a Jeep. But so did every third mountaineer in Kavanaugh County. It meant nothing, and even if it did mean something, he couldn't think about that and the ramifications of it right now.

Peering out from behind the last large rock, he could see nothing but an expanse of flat dirt. But he was on the level of the lake. The dam itself sloped down in front of the lake with rocks piled up on the steep incline that led to the hollow below. He couldn't see anyone on that incline without coming out into the open. And as soon as he did, he'd be a target.

He stepped out from behind the rock. Standing tall the better to see over the lip of the dam. He lifted the rifle barrel, cocked his head to the side to look through the sight, a small optic with a four-power magnification, the kind used by the military. He'd only taken a couple of steps when he heard a voice from the other side of the dam, someone down on the face of it. The someone was laughing.

"How'd you do that?" The sheriff advanced in the direction of the voice, rifle ready. "How'd you find me?"

As he approached the dam, a man came into view, standing on a rock about twenty feet below the top of the dam, halfway across. Just standing there, his hands hanging loose at his sides. A single piece of duct tape was wrapped around one of them, all the way around the back of the hand and the palm.

The description given to law enforcement agencies in three states had been accurate. The man was six feet, 170 pounds, wearing a black t-shirt and jeans. The t-shirt had a white skull emblazoned on the on the front. His face was all sharp angles, hard enough to break up concrete.

As he got nearer, Brice could see a blue nylon backpack on a nearby rock. It was unzipped and flat, appeared to be empty. In a single sweeping glance, Brice put it together. Some of the rocks near the flat backpack were dark on one side. Damp from the dirt that had been beneath them *before they'd been moved.* The man had shoved the rocks aside, digging to make a hole for...

"Get your hands in the air and lock your fingers behind your head," Brice called out as he continued walking slowly toward the man.

"Think you can stop me, do you?"

"Do it now."

"And if I don't? What are you going to do, shoot me?"

"Derrick Osbourne, you are under arrest for attempted murder of a police officer." Unless Fletch hadn't made it out of surgery. Then, the charge would be murder. As he spoke, the sheriff continued to move closer, closing the distance between them. If he had to shoot, he couldn't miss, and the man was still too far away. "You have the right to remain silent. If you give up—"

"Put a sock in it. I know what my rights are."

"I told you to—"

"You *don't* want to shoot me, Sheriff. I swear, you surely do not want to do that."

He held out his hand then and slowly turned it over. Taped to his palm was a small device that looked like a garage door opener.

"I squeeze and the whole dam goes up. Might take the whole top of the mountain with it, so if I's you, I'd get back a ways."

~

The voice of the woman with the startling blue eyes — Hattie, Dobbs had said her name was Hattie — brought Bailey back to the now, but the feeling in her gut changed little. It was a lead ball of fear and dread and she felt as powerless to do anything about it now as she had been eighteen months ago.

But it wasn't over yet. Macy Cosgrove was still alive, not flying backward dead onto a wet street. She was right here now, breathing, and Bailey still had a chance to save her.

"…Asked you what it is you want."

"I want … My name is Bailey Donahue and what I'm about to tell you is going to be hard to believe." She took a deep breath. "That dam at the top of the hollow is about to fail, to collapse, and if you and your family don't get out of here right now, that water is going to come roaring down the valley … and you're going to drown. Macy is going to drown. And Jakey, too. All of you."

The whole speech had come out of a piece, a torrent of words no less powerful and violent than the flood that any minute was going to wash the world away. But even as she spoke, Bailey could see disbelief, then hostile suspicion growing on the woman's face.

"How do you know my Macy?"

Bailey had no answer for her. Well, she did have an answer, but if she gave it the woman would take her for an even greater raving lunatic than she already did.

"I'm … I'm a friend of Raymond Dobson's … Dobbs. He knows your husband, Seth, saw him the other day in the checkout line at Piggly Wiggly."

The woman wasn't buying.

"I don't know nobody named Dobbs. How do you know my children? Macy and Jakey. What did you say your name was again?" The woman had been either consciously or subconsciously backing up from Bailey as she spoke. She turned then and cried out, "Seth! Seth, come here. There's—" Bailey didn't hear the rest when the woman disappeared into the next room.

Bailey turned and raced across the porch, down the steps and around the side of the house toward the backyard. That's where the kids would be, that's where Macy would be, out in the yard looking up at the fireworks in the sky.

Just as she was about to clear the corner of the house, she saw Seth turn toward the back door and hurry back into the house. Out at the far end of the backyard, next to the woods and the hillside, stood three stair-stepped children. Two little boys and a little girl. A little girl with braids hanging down her back. In the dusk of early evening, it was impossible to tell the color. But Bailey knew they were red. The girl was the smallest, maybe six or seven. Even so, she had a chubby baby on her hip and was pointing up into the night sky.

Operating on pure instinct, Bailey raced across the backyard toward the children. She stopped short of bowling into them. Stood for a moment, then said softly, "Macy..."

The little girl turned and looked up at her, the wash of light from the house illuminating her face, the familiar face, perfect in every detail, the image on the canvas in her living room. Except this little girl's eyes were open. Even in the dim light, Bailey could see they were the same pale blue as her mother's.

"Do I know you?" the little girl asked, and cocked her head to the side quizzically.

"No.... *Yes!* Yes, you know me!" Bailey touched the child's shoulder with a trembling hand.

"Hey, you, get away from them kids!" It was a man's voice, angry. Bailey looked back toward the house. Seth was coming out the back door, his wife along the side of the house, obviously searching for Bailey when they couldn't find her on the front porch.

Bailey looked back at Macy, who was smiling up at her, displaying a blank space in her mouth where her front teeth had not yet grown.

"I ... *do* know you..." There was wonder in Macy's voice, as if she had recognized an old friend.

Bailey snatched the baby out of the little girl's arms and the surprised infant burst into frightened tears, holding his chubby arms out to his sister and wiggling to get free.

"Come with me!" Bailey told Macy. "*Now!*"

Macy's mother screamed when Bailey turned and raced up the hillside with the baby. And with Macy right beside her.

"*Put him down!*" Seth Cosgrove roared and came barreling across the yard after her.

"Macy, stop!" cried his wife, only a step or two behind him. "Maaaaaacy!"

The boys looked from their parents toward the stranger carrying off their baby brother and little sister, and then took off after her.

Up the mountainside Bailey went, holding tight to the screaming, wiggling baby in her arms. Macy never left her side, ignoring the cries of her parents and brothers behind her. Bailey ran faster than she ever dreamed she could run, in a steep climb with a baby—

~

HARLAN BOLYARD JUMPED BACK from T.J. in shock and alarm.

"What the—?"

"Want me to shoot another one?"

"You're *crazy*. What'd you come here for, shooting my chickens like that?"

T.J. took aim at another chicken and fired the second barrel, sending chicken feathers and guts to splatter on the wall of the house.

A woman appeared beside Bolyard along with a little girl, maybe ten or eleven.

"What's he doin'?" the woman asked. Then she saw the pieces of the dead chickens in the yard, and gave voice to way more squawking than the birds had done when T.J.'d shot them. "Who is this man and why's he shooting our chickens?"

T.J. flipped the catch on the shotgun with his thumb, cracked it open, tilted the tip of the barrel up to drop out the spent rounds, then reached into his pocket for two shells, popped one down into each barrel and snapped it shut.

"Do something, Harlan," she wailed. "Make him stop!"

"Mrs. Bolyard" — T.J. tried not to grind his teeth in impatience — "you gotta get out of here. I told your husband the dam's about to blow."

"Are you serious?" wailed the woman.

"Do I *look* serious? Ain't nothing I can do to force you to leave, but if you don't go right this second — *run* — across your backyard and up the hill behind the house, as God is my witness I will kill every chicken in this yard!"

He turned the rifle on another chicken.

"Alright, alright," said the man, his hands up, palms out, placating. He had begun to be alarmed by T.J.'s tone, by his determination, maybe had finally decided it'd be a good idea for him to listen.

"Come on, Mildred."

The man, his wife and the little girl stepped out onto the porch and the woman rushed down the front steps, oblivious to the frailty of the wood that looked like it was ready to buckle under her considerable girth.

That's when T.J. heard laughter. He turned toward the abandoned shack across the road and saw two teenage boys leaning against the porch railing beneath the half-collapsed roof. They were laughing hysterically.

"OSBOURNE, I won't tell you again. Get your hands in the air."

"Are you serious?" The edge of menace and incipient rage in his voice was sharp enough to cut stale bread. He mimicked the sheriff's voice, "*Get your hands in the air!* Right. I done everything I done and now I'm gonna roll over like an old dog and give up? Hold out my wrists and say 'cuff me' and let you lead me away to spend the rest of my life behind bars?"

"Behind bars is better than six feet under."

"*Says who?*" The man laughed again. Not like before, though. Not a cynical, resigned, looks-like-you-caught-me laugh. This laugh was high-pitched and maniacal, the laugh of a man strung out on crystal meth, wound as tight as a guitar string. He'd gone from something resembling normal to crazier than a nuclear waste dump rat between one heartbeat and the next. There had seemed to be someone home at first. Now, it was clear that Derrick Osbourne had left the building.

"You think dying scares me? Do ya? Huh? I ain't scared of

nuthin'. I built me this bomb that coulda blown me apart at any minute, but I done it. Done it 'cause somebody's gotta pay." He might have been looking at Brice as he spoke. It was hard to tell. Then he turned his head away and smiled, as if he were watching a scene Brice couldn't see.

"That boy can run faster'n a baby rabbit. Would ya look at that. Whoo-ee doggies! Give him the ball and can't nobody catch him!" He paused and the animation left his face.

He did look at Brice then, made eye contact. "His busted legs never did heal back right — was all twisted up. Doctor said they couldn't fix something that'd been smashed bad as that, said the bone looked like ground glass."

His voice lowered to a growl. "Mr. W. Maxwell Crenshaw the third's gonna pay for that!"

"How does blowing up this dam make Crenshaw pay?"

Brice continued to edge closer.

"It wasn't my first choice, I'll grant, but people gonna die either way, and it'll be his fault just like my brother in a wheel-chair is his fault. He don't care 'bout the people livin' below his dam no more'n he cares 'bout the men workin' in his dog-hole mines." A dog-hole mine was just what the name implied — a mine no safer than a hole dug by a dog. "He don't care what happens to other people so long as he makes a buck. Well, I'll show him."

The tortured logic was no logic at all, merely the mental gymnastics of a man as high as he intended to blow the dam.

Osbourne realized how close Brice had gotten while he was talking and he cried out, "Stop right there! Come one step closer and … kaboom!"

The sheriff stopped advancing. He still wasn't as close as he'd like. He could certainly land a lethal body shot or a simple headshot from this range, but he had to hit the T-zone for an instant kill. The T-zone was an area about an inch wide that stretches across the eyebrow ridge and the bridge of the nose. Though a shot anywhere in the head would be fatal, only a shot to the T-zone would sever the medulla, the lower base of the brainstem, preventing brain signals from reaching the rest of the body. Instant death, not so much as the twitch of a finger to push a button.

Even with a T-zone shot, Osbourne's body might fall on the detonator and set off the charge, but there was nothing Brice could do about that.

As if Osbourne were reading his thoughts, he cried, "Shoot it out of my hand!" He bleated out a peal of high-pitched laughter. "Go on, try." He waved his arm around to provide a moving target. "The Lone Ranger coulda done it. Course, I just got to *barely touch it* and…"

"Do you honestly think you're going to get away with this?"

"What makes you think I plan to get away with anything? I'd give my life five times over to make Crenshaw pay."

That was it, then. Osbourne didn't intend to come out of it alive. Brice had to take the shot — now, before the man's wild arm-waving set off the device. He had stopped with his feet spread wide for stability. Now, he steadied his hands, drew in a breath…

"There ain't but one way to get me to put down this deto-nator." Brice released the pressure he had begun to apply to the trigger.

"And that is?"

"I want Maxwell Crenshaw here. You bring him in one of his fancy helicopters to this very mountaintop. Park him right here in front of—" He gestured emphatically.

And then the world was all roaring sound.

~

"Wait!" the woman who'd been standing behind the man called out to Dobbs as he started down the porch steps. "We'll take your money!"

"Now, Marjorie, this fella—"

"Shut your mouth, Rupert," she told him. To Dobbs, she said, "Now, what is it we got to do, again?"

Dobbs whirled back around.

"You got to drop what you're doing right now and run fast as you can up the mountain," he said, breathless, yanking his not-a-stopwatch back out of his pocket and flipping the catch so the lid popped up. "Just like if you'd heard a siren. Everybody in the whole house. Can't stop to grab nothing, you got to run." He pretended to push a button on the watch. "Starting *right now!*"

The woman never hesitated. She turned instantly around and bolted back through her house. The man gave Dobbs a look of mistrust, then turned, too, and headed out behind her.

Dobbs took the front steps of the porch two at a time and ran faster than he thought possible around the house to the backyard. He heard the screech of the spring on the screen door pull taut before he made it all the way around the house. Saw the woman moving as fast as she could, her best approximation of a sprint, across the backyard toward the woods as he cleared the building, with the man only a few steps behind her. The screen door they'd pushed open banged shut. The sound caught his attention and he glanced toward the house.

An old woman in a wheelchair was sitting on the back porch.

Chapter Twenty-Eight

THERE WAS a sudden rumbling roar and then T.J. didn't have to urge the Bolyards to run. They took off toward the hillside like their pants were on fire. At the sound of the boom, the two teenage boys stopped laughing and looked fearfully up toward the top of the hollow.

One of the boys was white, the other black. But that's where the resemblance to himself and Dobbs ended. The white kid was tall, almost as skinny as T.J., all long arms and legs, moving like a marionette in the hands of a drunk puppeteer. The other kid was as round and black as a dung beetle. Both looked to be sixteen-ish.

What were they doing in an abandoned shack in danger of imminent collapse? Duh. Something they didn't want their parents to see them doing.

They stood frozen, riveted to the spot, no doubt with slower reflexes than might otherwise have been the case. If T.J. turned and bolted up the mountainside behind the Bolyard house right this instant, *he* had a chance of making it. The boys? Not so much. They had more ground to cover — across the front yard of the shack, around the enormous tree, across the road and the front and back yards of the Bolyards. They also lacked something much more important — the presence of mind to try.

There was only one possible way for them to escape.

Dropping the shotgun in the dirt, T.J. dashed across the road toward them.

"Ditch that joint and climb!" he cried, and leapt up onto the picnic table below the lowest limb of the gigantic tree, grabbed the first of the handholds worn into it by generations of climbing children and started up it. *"Climb!"*

The second grumbling roar was not as loud as the first, not as dramatic, but far more intimidating. It was the scraping rock-against-rock collapse of the dam, which must now have had a hole in it that was, judging from the ferocity of the first explosion, roughly the size of Panama.

T.J. scrambled up the tree trunk as fast as he could, not looking back to see if the boys had followed. They would come with him or they wouldn't. He'd done everything he could.

He heard a sound behind him then and suddenly the white kid was beside him, scaling the tree like a squirrel. Then he was gone, up higher on the trunk, and the black kid took his place, and promptly passed T.J. like he was standing still. Clearly, this wasn't the first time these boys had climbed this tree.

In the gloom, T.J. couldn't see the handholds they'd used. He stuck his foot into an indentation, but it was too shallow and when he put his weight on it, the slick sole of the shoe slipped out and he almost lost his balance and fell. He had no idea how high up the tree they'd have to get to keep from being washed out of its limbs by the coming black water. He also didn't know if the tree itself would withstand the assault. It was huge, with roots that went down no telling how far. But it was also old and might not be strong enough.

Well, T.J. was old, too! And he was by golly strong enough to survive this flood and live to tell the tale. Then he heard the sound of oncoming rushing water, looked to his right, and knew he had not climbed high enough into the tree.

~

THE WORLD ERUPTED in a gigantic roar that shook the ground under their feet. The noise reverberating against the mountainsides, compounding and magnifying until it seemed directionless, coming from everywhere and nowhere at once. Still, all their heads turned in one direction — looking up the mountainside toward the top of the hollow.

"Run!" yelled Seth Cosgrove, grabbing the arm of his wife who'd been scrambling up the hillside behind him and yanking her forward. *"Run!"*

The Cosgroves' was the first house on the road, the closest to the dam. They had the least time of anyone to get out of the way of the flood. Now the whole family — Bailey in front with the baby and Macy, then the two boys, followed close by their parents — clawed their way frantically up the mountainside behind their house as a grumbling, grinding rumble followed on the heels of the roaring boom.

That rumble morphed into a horrifying freight-train roar that grew louder and louder until the whole world was nothing but sound, they breathed it and felt it, the rattling, grating, scraping sound of gravel in a blender.

Bailey strained upward. One more step. *One more.* A jagged rock outcrop the size of a car jutted out of the mountainside on her left. Shaped like the raised ridge in the middle of a turtle's shell, it continued in a broken line all the way from the bottom to the top of the mountain. The soil was thinner next to the rock and the fingers of her right hand that she was using to dig her way up the slope, clinging to the baby with her left, clawed at rock only a few inches under the surface, broke her nails and savaged her fingertips.

A gagging stench wafted in a wave in front of the growing

wall of sound, an invisible wind that stank of petroleum, chemicals and sulfur, as if hell had opened up a crack in the world right there in Turkey Neck Hollow and belched out its reek into the world.

Bailey looked to her left through a small space in the broken rock outcrop and saw it coming, a dark shadow against the dusky shades of evening, a black hole of nothingness that sucked the world into its gaping maw as it chewed its way down the mountainside.

That one glance told Bailey she had come too late, was not far enough up the mountainside to avoid being washed away. She'd tempted the gods when she tried to change a destiny already decreed, set down in vivid detail perhaps by the hand of Sophia Watford herself.

Macy Cosgrove would become the little girl in the painting. When the waters passed and the horrified rescue workers arrived, they would find her face-up in the muck, her hair a tangle of black goo, her hand, stamped with the carnival admission date "July 3," lying on her chest like she was saluting the flag.

And Bailey would drown with her, which was destined to be as well. It had been set down half a century ago that she would die with a bullet hole in her head and she had escaped. Now destiny would collect the debt it was owed.

In moments, she would feel the bite of cold, foul water, stinging her eyes, a shroud blotting out the night with a greater darkness. She would feel her lungs strain for breath, bursting out of her chest until she could stand it no more.

Then she would give in to her body's final yearning and breathe deeply.

She would suck in cold black death and be no more.

"Bethany," she whispered.

The image of Bethany flashed into her consciousness, filled up her whole mind. Just like it had done in that *safe house* somewhere, she never found out where, that place where she'd demanded they bring her Bethany. And they'd refused.

JESSIE SITS bolt upright in bed in the midnight dark, tangled in sweat-damp sheets. She's had the most horrible nightmare. Her heart is thudding, her vision blurring with each beat, so she can't seem to shed the gossamer skein of the dream, pull free from the web of it and return to the real world of her bedroom with Bethany asleep in her crib down the hall and Aaron beside her.

She feels for Aaron on the other side of the bed. The sheets are cold.

She cries out, must have cried out, because the room suddenly floods with light.

What room? Where is she? This isn't her bedroom. Where's Aaron?

And then a woman who looks vaguely familiar crosses the room to her and sits on the edge of the bed. Bailey remembers her then. She's the woman from the police station.

The room with the table and the three people.

It's real. It had happened. It wasn't a nightmare.

Bailey bursts into tears, gut-wrenching spasms of grief that wrack her whole body like seizures. The sobbing goes on and on until her chest hurts and the muscles refuse to make her chest move and her voice is gone. But still she cries, silently, tearlessly.

The woman holds her in her arms, rocks her back and forth, says nothing, just lets her cry.

When her eyes open again, she knows where she is. She knows what has happened. There is no disorientation now, only the horrible weight of understanding, the rock of cold lead so heavy in her belly the weight of it draws her whole body downward.

The woman is sitting in a chair on the other side of the room, has been watching her sleep. How had she slept? There's a bitter taste in her mouth and she recognizes it as some kind of sedative. She hates narcotics. They make her feel hungover the next day and that's how she feels now.

"Would you like a cup of coffee?"

"Yes, please."

"Cream and sugar?"

"No sugar, a bucket of cream."

She feels pain so intense in her belly that she looks down expecting to see a blade buried up to the hilt there. Aaron always gives the bucket-of-cream line when he orders coffee for her in a restaurant because waitresses never bring enough of those little thimble-sized containers.

Aaron.

Aaron, who is dead.

Later, seated around the kitchen table, a breakfast of McDonalds McMuffins uneaten on a paper towel in front of her, she listens to the same three people who had spoken to her the night before. But there is a fourth man with them who didn't speak until near the end. They introduce him as Bernard Jordan, an officer with the U.S. Marshals Service.

"Mrs. Cunningham, we spoke last night. Do you recall, we told you about—?"

"The Sergei guy, yes, I remember. You don't have to go back over it all."

The people at the table exchange a glance, but this time it's a relaxing gesture, tension gone, she has returned to the land of the sane and living and they can talk to her like a normal person.

"Just don't do that looking-at-each-other thing again, okay? I'm with you."

The woman at least has the decency to look chagrined.

"Let's get this over with. I want to go home and see my little girl. My baby."

"I'm afraid that won't be possible."

"Not possible!" She is flabbergasted. "You're the ones who're crazy. My baby needs her mother." She almost sobs and she would have sworn that there is not a tear left in her whole body to shed. "And I need her!"

She turns to the woman.

"She looks like her daddy. Just like Aaron. Has his eyes." An aching need to hold Bethany wells up in her chest so powerfully it takes her breath away. "I want my baby!"

The man who'd said "that won't be possible" takes his phone out of his pocket and places in on the table in front of him.

"*Remember I told you last night that we had … moles, informants in Mikhailov's organization? This is a recording one of them made when Mikhailov was grilling a new plebe in the organization.*"

He picks up the phone and touches the screen and a gravelly voice issues from the speaker. The English is heavily accented, but the words are mostly understandable.

"*Cross me and you die. A guarantee, I kill you.*" *The voice is emotionless, not as if he were making a horrible threat but like he's telling the speaker box in a drive-through window to super-size his fries. "Any two-bit hood can say that, yes? But does anybody else guarantee to kill those you love, too? No, they do not, but I, Sergei Wassily Mikhailov, make you that promise. You cross Sergei and you die.*" *He pauses and his voice grows softer, but there still is no threat in it, no emotion of any kind. "And your wife dies, your mother, your brothers and sisters, your children. I will find those you love and I will butcher them, one by one.*"

Bailey feels the voice slither into her ear like a poisonous serpent, coil through her head and down into her belly where a cold lump of fear begins to freeze everything it touches, ice spreading out inside her so fast she can hear the cracking sound it makes.

"*It could take a week, a month, a lifetime. A fall from a high window, yes? A hit-and-run driver. A car explosion. A gunshot from a dark alley. One by one, I will not leave breathing anyone you care about. Even after you are dead, you can look up through the fires of hell and watch me slice the throat of your baby son lying in his soiled diaper in your dead wife's arms. And then I lick his blood off the dagger.*"

Bailey is unprepared for the nausea. It rises up in the back of her throat so instantly that she only has time to turn her head before she begins to wretch, spewing out coffee and acidic bile all over the floor in the kitchen of the house that could have been anywhere. Anywhere at all.

She wretches until her stomach is empty, then continues to dry heave until she is breathless, tears running down her face.

The woman helps her to her feet and leads her to the bathroom, uses a cold washcloth to wash her face, clean her mouth.

When she returns to the kitchen, someone has cleaned up the mess, though the room still smells vaguely of vomit.

She sits back down where she had been seated and looks at the table. The cellphone filled with words of unfathomable horror is gone.

"Sergei Mikhailov is not human," says the other man at the table, not the one who had turned on the recording from his cellphone. "I'm serious, I really don't think there's a man in there anywhere. He is pure evil, has made his way in life by annihilating the competition and ruthlessly butchering anybody who stands in his way."

The woman speaks and her voice is hard-edged, not soothing.

"You have to understand what you're dealing with here, Mrs. Cunningham. His whole life is built on intimidation. He keeps the troops in line, and his enemies at bay, because they know he always … always keeps his promises."

"If he knew you were alive, he would kill you," says the man who had played the recording. "And eventually he would kill every member of your family, too."

The man from the federal marshal's office speaks.

"I work with the Witness Protection Program. It will be our job to keep you safe until we're ready for you to testify."

"Testify? You think I'm going to … you want me to testify?"

"There is only one way you and your family will ever be safe, and that's if we put a needle in Sergei Mikhailov's arm and turn on the poison. We still impose the death penalty in this state."

Then he continues to talk. Some portion of Bailey's brain records and processes what he says, about the absolute anonymity of the program, its record for keeping future witnesses safe. He talks about how she would receive a whole new identity, complete with all the paperwork to back it up, would be placed in a safe environment, would be protected.

She listens, but feels like she has somehow not quite caught up to what he's saying. Like his lips are moving, but his words don't sync up with them. There is some deeper, darker meaning she isn't getting.

And then she knows, but it's more than a sudden understanding. It's an urgent message lashing in red letters on an LED screen: BETHANY! BETHANY! BETHANY!

"My baby!" she cries. "When will you bring her to me?"

But she knows. Even as she asks the question she knows. She just has to hear the words out loud.

"Mrs. Cunningham, as far as anybody knows, you were killed in a terrible traffic accident with your husband. You can't let anybody in your family know you're alive. If you do, you're not merely putting your own life in danger. You're signing their death warrants, too."

She can't breathe.

The other man seems to think she needs further convincing.

"Mrs. Cunningham, if you get hit by a bus while you're in the Witness Protection Program, you will be buried anonymously. We will not tell your family. If Mikhailov found out that you'd been in hiding, waiting to testify against him, he'd keep his promise, and without your testimony, we couldn't lock him up to protect your family."

They say they'll be convening a super-secret grand jury. That it will issue sealed indictments against Mikhailov and the others. That's the first time they use the word "soon."

Soon.

The word bounces around like a pinball in her mind as she sits at the table in the kitchen of the anonymous house. She never does find out where that place was, had not been aware of her environment enough to notice or care when they picked her up in the nondescript blue Honda Accord and then set out on the road, driving day after day.

Final stop: Albuquerque.

Well, the first final stop. The second final stop is Omaha. The third...

She's never told the reasons why they suddenly uproot her without warning, federal marshals swooping down on her in the middle of the night and whisking her off into the darkness. They're always vague, non-committal. They'd felt some danger, some threat. Afraid she might have blown her cover, somehow. It is all very James Bond-esque.

But before they have a chance to serve the super-secret, hush-hush sealed indictment, Mikhailov slips out of the country and returns to Russia where there is no extradition treaty. After that, they lose track of him. He might have come back to the U.S. Might not. His son was never seen again after that night. Maybe his father turfed him off to some rehab program to dry him out, then to some foreign country for a new start. Maybe he simply killed him. Nobody knew.

After a while, after the weeks blend into months that blend into years, Bailey's life becomes a ship adrift on a still sea. No land in sight. No wind to fill her sails. No current to bear her along. Just there. Motionless. Waiting for "soon."

BAILEY UNDERSTOOD that soon would *never* come now, that she'd never hold her own baby girl in her arms again, cradle her tiny body as she now cradled the squirming baby boy. She fell forward onto the slope on her elbows, shielding baby Jake, wondering how it would feel different to drown for real this time, but in her own body. She felt a small hand grab hers. She grasped it tight, and the little girl snuggled close. *Macy* snuggled close. The roar struck then, a rumble that ate her breath, a sound assaulting all her senses at once, disorienting and dizzying in its magnitude.

The sound left no space in her head for memories, for thoughts of any kind. It consumed her.

DOBBS DIDN'T EVEN BREAK stride when he saw the old lady in the wheelchair. He merely changed direction, calling out as he ran.

"I said *everybody* in the house!"

The man slowed, looked back toward Dobbs. The woman kept running.

The back porch was nothing but a slab of three-inch concrete that stretched out in a fifteen-foot square in front of the back door. Dobbs stepped up on it in one stride, grabbed the wheelchair handles and shoved the chair and the woman in it off into the dirt.

The old woman's back was bent so badly in a dowager's

hump that she had to lift her chin to see anything but her gnarled hands in her lap. She cried out when Dobbs leapt up onto the porch and ran at her. When he started shoving her, she grabbed hold of the arms of her chair with fingers so bent and twisted with arthritis they looked useless. But she held firm.

The chair made it about twenty feet on hard packed dirt behind the concrete slab, but when the wheels hit the tangle of weeds beyond it, the chair bogged down and refused to roll.

"You don't get paid unless you take everybody!" Dobbs called out.

Perhaps it was the act of running itself, or maybe the intensity of Dobbs's manner, but something had ignited a sense of urgency in the others that was beyond their desire for the hundred-dollar bill they had seen and the fifty they hadn't. The woman kept running, shooing the girl ahead of her, and had made it to the bottom of the incline and started to climb. The man stopped, turned around and ran back to Dobbs.

"Come on, Ma." He took her hands and pulled her to a standing position in front of the chair.

There was a sudden boom, the roar of a thousand MGM lions, from the top of the hollow. The boom resounded down the mountains in a continuous, rumbling cry.

The man's head jerked up toward the top of the hollow at the sound, then his wide, terrified eyes locked with Dobbs's. He started to pull his mother toward the hillside, but Dobbs knew there was no time for that. He leaned over and picked up the old woman — hoped he didn't hurt her! — and slung her over his shoulder in a fireman carry and lumbered as fast as he could across the weedy yard.

He imagined he could hear a growing rumble behind him as he started up the incline and realized that even leaning over, he was too top heavy and off balance to climb.

"Drag her!" the man cried, and pulled his mother off Dobbs's shoulder to the ground. Taking one of her arms, he started pulling her up the hillside. Dobbs grabbed her other arm and hauled her upward. The hillside was covered in fallen leaves, slick to climb, but a surface over which the two of them could drag a body. Dobbs dug his big feet into the soft leaves, leaned forward and shoved his free hand into the dirt, hauling up the weight between him and the other man as fast as they could.

Chapter Twenty-Nine

BRICE WAS FLUNG off his feet by the explosion, flew backward as if he had been slapped by an invisible hand. The roar ate into his head, the sound rebounding inside his skull, echoing and reverberating.

He hit the dirt on his back and slid another ten feet. The full force of the blast had been directed outward from the bottom center of the dam, or he'd have been killed. Now, he lay on his back watching huge boulders take flight, rocket up into the sky, up and up, until the energy propelling them was expended. Then the debris seemed to pause in the air, hang suspended there for a heartbeat before it began to drop back to the earth in a rain of rocks and dirt and chunks of coal.

The rain fell on Brice where he lay stunned, pummeling him. He'd have been crushed if any of the bigger rocks had landed on him. As it was, he was merely cut and bruised by the flying debris. The world was strangely silent after the blast, but for the ringing in Brice's ears and the thudding and splashing of the rocks crashing back to earth. The universe held its breath for a second. Two. Three.

He sat up, unable yet to get to his feet, looking at what only moments before had been a solid bulldozed wall of rock, dirt and coal refuse. Now, the wall had a gigantic rip in the middle, through which thick black water had begun to flow. He watched, still in shock, as the water's flow began to rip out more rock along its edges, dislodging huge hunks, the hole growing ever wider and wider in both directions.

Then it let go. With a grinding rock-on-rock rumble, the whole dam collapsed and a wave of black water rushed forward and dived off into the hollow. The sound it made as it fell was not a peaceful waterfall sound but a grumbling roar as it ate away everything in its path.

The people in the hollow … how many? He didn't know.

The painting of a little girl drowned in black mud. Macy Cosgrove. It was exactly as Bailey had painted it.

Bailey.

He started to stagger to his feet, but the roaring in his ears was disorienting and he lost his balance, sat back down hard on the ground. That's when he saw it, an object lying in the dirt near him. He reached out and picked it up, a broken yellow hair band with a small plastic minion on it, the one he'd seen Bailey use to pull her hair back into a ponytail that day at the lake. The day they had flown out across clear water together, feeling the wind and spray in their faces.

He turned the hair band over and over in his hand, as if expecting the piece of yellow plastic to use minion-magic to call forth its owner and Bailey would materialize right there in front of him.

But she wasn't here at the top of the hollow. She was down there, where the black water was rushing out to eat up the world. She, T.J. and Dobbs had come up here to the dam — he'd seen the Jeep tracks — and then had decided to evacuate the hollow all by themselves. There was no way he could know that to be true, but he was absolutely certain.

What he did *not* know was if they had made it in time. He leapt to his feet then, staggered, regained his balance and stood for a moment as the black water poured through the breech and down into the hollow. He snatched up his gun and holstered it, turned and ran for all he was worth back down the impossible road to his cruiser.

He keyed the microphone on his shoulder as he ran, blurted out, breathless and staccato.

"Subject is down," he said. "Repeat, down…"

He leapt over a rock and landed precariously on the rubble below, lost his footing, fell on his side and slid across the gravel, ripping his uniform and scraping the skin off his whole upper arm, shoulder to elbow. He never even stopped moving, just used the fall's momentum to execute a roll that catapulted him back onto his feet.

"The dam on the impound lake…" Running slower now. He'd be no good to anybody with a broken ankle. "…Osbourne blew it up." He took a breath. "Copy?" He un-keyed the microphone.

"Copy," came a voice from the mic. "Subject is down. What about the dam?"

The sheriff arrived at his cruiser and leapt behind the wheel.

"It exploded. The dam's *gone!* The whole lake washed down the hollow." The water was mostly gone by now, had emptied the basin as he ran down the hillside. "Dispatch all available rescue and emergency personnel to…"

It didn't even have a name. The collection of houses that might be home to half a dozen residents or fifty, was anonymous — as nameless as every other coal camp in the mountains. He knew the Cosgroves lived there. Seth and his wife, two boys, he thought, and a baby. And Macy. That's who Bailey had come here to save.

Bailey, T.J. and Dobbs were down there.

"…The coal camp down the hollow from the dam."

He slammed the car into gear and peeled out down the highway.

"Do you copy?"

Bailey felt a spray of cold water douse her, like she'd walked through a door where somebody'd arranged a bucket of water above the jamb as a joke so when they pulled on the string, the whole bucketful would splash down on your head. This was more than a bucketful. She was instantly drenched from head to foot with the spray, lay shivering in the mud as the water poured down on her.

Water that smelled of chemicals, sticky water, splashed down all around her, a spraying waterfall of it. But it was coming down from above her instead of a wave of it washing her away into its depths. It took a moment for her to process that and then she understood. She hadn't climbed above the high-water mark of the wave of black death plummeting down the hollow. Its top edge had struck the rock outcrop to her left and was splashing up and over it — above Bailey's head.

But it was also squirting through the small broken place in the ridge Bailey had looked through with the pressure of a firehose and the force of that blast was slowly shoving Bailey sideways away from the rock, scooting her, and she had nothing to grab to hold herself in place and no hand to grab with. She had to remain on her elbows to shield the wiggling baby beneath her, and Macy's small hand clutched her right hand in an iron grip. Shoved sideways across the slick mud, she would eventually be pushed out of the lee side of the protective rock, would be struck by a hammer blow of the water splashing over it, and washed away.

Macy was on that side of her. She squeezed the child's hand as tight as she could, knowing that no matter how tightly she clutched the little fingers, when the water struck the child, the force of it would yank her out of Bailey's grasp and away. Then the sideways movement stopped. Macy had been shoved into a small tree, a sapling, and she had grabbed it, had wrapped her arm around it.

The intensity of the roar continued, on and on. Then slowly, it diminished. The firehose pressure abated. She and Macy were suddenly drenched with water, a hammering waterfall of it that pinned them to the ground, and threatened to suck them downward with its flow. They might have been washed away then if Macy hadn't clung so tenaciously to the tree. But the waterfall pressure lasted only a short time. With every passing second there was less water. And then none at all fell on them, though they could still hear the sound of it rushing by below them.

The sound dwindled, faded and then died away altogether.

Bailey lifted herself up off the baby. He lay slathered in black mud, head to foot, but he had stopped crying, had been shocked into silence. Then he looked at her, recognition registered in his eyes, and he sucked in a big lungful of air and began to wail.

It was perhaps the sweetest sound Bailey had ever heard.

"Jake! *Jakey!*" a woman's voice cried from below her. Bailey looked back over her shoulder to see four people huddled in a cleft of rock thirty feet back down the mountainside. Seth Cosgrove likely knew the side of that mountain like the creases in his hand, and had had the presence of mind to veer off and huddle with his wife and sons in a cleft of rock, carved out of the ridge of rock on Bailey's left, a small cave Bailey hadn't known was there when she passed it.

The woman scrambled up the slick mountainside, slipping and sliding, frantically clawing her way up until she reached Bailey, Macy and the baby. When she reached them, she stopped, her eyes devouring her children in awe, before she snatched the crying baby up into her arms and pulled Macy to her side. She was crying, but she probably didn't know it. Was babbling out unintelligible sounds as she rocked back and forth on her knees.

Then Seth and the two little boys were crouching in the mud beside them and their combined voices sang a song of joy and relief that didn't need the words they tagged onto the music. Bailey sat back and listened and watched and might even have been crying herself. She didn't know.

The light had failed altogether … sometime, Bailey wasn't aware of exactly when. It was a ballet of twilight here. The darkling shadow of the mountain lengthening, melting into evening. Sundown somewhere out there on the flatland was accompanied by the rising of a full moon over the peaks that changed the quality of light, shades of silver instead of dim gray, shadows receding back under the trees in a world aglow in a gossamer light that outlined everything, every shape and form with silver Magic Marker.

Macy's face glowed in that light like the face of a fairy. Or an angel. Her hair was drenched, but there was only a small smudge of black mud on one cheek. Bailey imagined she could see the freckles she knew decorated the child's face like a fine dusting of cinnamon, though there was not enough light to see them.

"Who are you?" Macy asked, her voice quiet and serious against the backdrop of excited chatter. "I know you — why?"

What was Bailey to say? Clearly, the little girl recognized her intuitively from a connection Bailey had no words to describe. So she didn't try, merely looked deeply into Macy's eyes, squeezed her hand and planted a gentle kiss on her forehead.

"You want to tell me what just happened here?" Seth Cosgrove demanded, and he wouldn't be dismissed with a hand squeeze and a kiss on the forehead. He had turned away from the family gushing in relief over the still-wailing Jakey, and sat in the mud in front of her, his look and body language impossible to read in the gloom. She had, after all, snatched his baby son and had run off with his little girl. Had, in some sense, kidnapped them right before his eyes. Of course, if she hadn't...

There was that.

But what was she supposed to say? *Well, you see, it's like this, Mr. Cosgrove. Seth. May I call you Seth? I paint gallbladders, duodenal ulcers, inflamed appendixes and the like, but the other day I picked up brushes in both hands, closed my eyes and painted a picture of your little girl dead, drowned. So naturally I came rushing up here with—*

T.J. and Dobbs.

She looked past Seth Cosgrove to the hollow behind and below him. Even in the moonglow the devastation was a stark black-and-white tableau. No, just black. Where there had been bushes, a backyard with a swing set and an old Johnboat leaned up against a tree, a clothesline with white sheets and a pair of coveralls, a garage, a woodworking shop, a house with a back porch, a road...

It was all gone. Erased. Painted over with a single black stroke. T.J.'s description was chillingly accurate, "like a bulldozer had scraped off everything down to bare rock, then poured motor oil on it." Everything below the rock outcrop on the hillside had been obliterated. On the other side of the hollow, right before it curved and the rest of the hollow was out of sight, something big lay wedged up against the rock wall there, jammed in somehow. It might have been the blue pickup truck Bailey had seen in the driveway of the Cosgroves' house when she raced up the sidewalk to the front door — how long ago? She looked at her wrist as if she actually expected to see the watch through the slather of mud.

Dobbs had a watch, the pocket watch with the flip catch he kept tethered to his belt and brought out now and then to look at — a watch that wouldn't tell him what time it was now, either.

She knew her mind was pinballing, maybe refusing to land on any one thought long enough to think it because thinking it made all this — the black slash of goo before her and the flood and T.J. and Dobbs and *everything* — *real.*

T.J. and Dobbs!

Ignoring Seth Cosgrove's question, without saying anything at all, in fact, not to anyone, not since she'd whispered Bethany in an anguished cry to the universe, Bailey leapt to her feet and started down the hillside, slipping and falling on the slick mud.

"Hey, wait just a minute here!" Seth Cosgrove called after her. "Where do you think you're going?"

She spoke then for the first time, called out over her shoulder as she reached the bottom of the incline.

"I have to find my friends!"

Yes, *friends.*

Chapter Thirty

T.J. FELT hands grab his wrists, saw one white, the other black, and he felt himself hauled upward, an elevator passing the second floor — sporting goods, casual apparel, children's clothes and toys — and rising higher.

"Jump, old man!" cried one of the boys.

He scrabbled with his feet, found footing on a solid limb. The water was almost on them when T.J. launched himself upward off the limb with the desperation-fueled velocity of Michael Jordan going up for a slam dunk. The boys grabbed his shirt, hauled him higher. A second later, foul-smelling black water splashed up on his shoes.

The whole tree shuddered and swayed from the initial hammer blow of the brunt of the flood. If the boys hadn't been holding onto him and to the tree with the strength of two strapping, scared-to-death teenagers, the three of them would have been knocked loose with the first blow. The thirty or so feet of tree trunk that was instantly under water stood firm, but the churning torrent took the higher, smaller limbs and shook them like a dog with a rag, whipping them back and forth as if in an intentional attempt to throw the tree's occupants into the water.

A large limb just below T.J. began to rip loose from the tree, its smaller limbs clawing at him as they dragged over his body. He heard one of the teenagers cry out a high, keening obscenity reminiscent of Butch Cassidy and the Sundance Kid and he joined his voice to the boy's and then all three of them were shouting, riding the bucking tree like a bronco.

The tree swayed and shook, reeled and pitched, hammered by the roaring water inches below T.J.'s feet.

And then it was over.

That fast.

The angle of the hollow down which the lake of goo plummeted was steep, the speed of the water incalculable. But there was a finite amount of water, and when it was gone, when the lakebed was empty in a minute, two — a lifetime — the water level fell, the speed lessened, the water drained away, minus the slurping sound of water draining out of a bathtub.

"You boys can let go now." T.J. was surprised that his voice was hoarse — had he yelled that loud for that long? — and trembly. "I got plans for these arms."

He looked up into their faces, hard to see now in the fading light, but residual terror still dwelt there in their huge, dark eyes. Of course, their eyes were also dilated for another reason altogether.

"You ain't gonna tell, are you, mister?" said the white kid. "That you caught us doing ... you know?"

Ahhh, to be young again, powering through life and circumstance with an unshakable belief in your own immortality. These two boys had come within a hair's breadth of a brutal death, and their biggest concern was getting caught smoking weed.

He made a zipping motion across his mouth.

"Lips are sealed. They can torture me, pull out my fingernails, make me eat my own eyeballs, but I'll never tell."

Their laughter warmed T.J. like Kentucky bourbon, going down smooth and strong. Painted on the black sky above the boys' heads, T.J. glimpsed through the leaves of the tree sudden splashes of color — red, blue and green, the twinkling explosions of fireworks.

~

THE WHOLE WORLD narrowed down into a stretch of leaf-covered dirt ahead and above him, the damp, mulch smell mingling with the stench of his own fear sweat.

Dobbs grabbed a sapling to his left, hauled himself and the old woman upward with it, praying it wouldn't break off in his hand because if it did, he would topple backward, and the rampaging elephant was almost on them.

He grunted, *pulled*, dug his feet in a step higher, *pulled*.

He could smell it now, the foul chemical stench, its roar eating up the shrieking of the woman above him on the hillside.

Pull.

Pull!

Another step.

One more.

A great cracking, crashing sound erupted to his left and below him as the front waters of the black monster crashed into the hillside trees. He heard them tumbling. He lurched, leapt upward and grabbed hold of the base of a juniper tree, about twelve inches across, wrapped his free arm around, hugged it. Held on.

The cold water slammed into his legs with such force it shoved him sideways, almost yanked free his grip on the old woman, tried to wrench her out of his grasp. But he held onto her skinny arm, looked down at her as the water swelled up around her, saw the terror in her eyes. Her son had made it a step higher and straddled the base of a sugar maple tree, and was leaning over and holding onto his mother's other arm with both hands.

She was screaming, but the roar of the flood carried the sound away. Or maybe she only had her mouth open and was trying to scream but nothing came out.

The rushing water scrubbed away the dirt beneath them, pulled at them with a strength Dobbs would never have thought possible, rose up briefly higher, past Dobbs's knees. The old woman was afloat in it, held in place only by the two men grasping her arms, clinging to trees. This far from the dam, at the far end of the hollow, the force of the flood water wasn't as fierce as it had been higher up. That was all that saved them.

Then the water level began to recede. The rushing water went slowly down past Dobbs's knees, depositing the top portion of the woman's body in the mud, but still carried her legs and feet sideways. He could hear the woman in the woods above them screaming, could see the old woman's mouth still open, but could still hear no sound from her above the rushing water. Maybe she'd screamed herself hoarse or maybe she'd had no air to scream at all.

Then the water was rushing past below Dobbs. The old woman lay slathered in black slime at an angle below him, the water flowing over her bare feet where it had carried her shoes away. He pulled on her arm and she slid easily up the slimy hillside, out of the water, then he leaned against the tree he'd been hugging, unwilling and unable to release his grip on it, though there was no longer any force trying to rip him free from it. He bowed his head against the bark, panting — maybe crying, he couldn't tell.

Then he lifted his head and looked out at the black water, bubbling and boiling past them, carrying debris — a piece of the roof of a house, trees, unrecognizable pieces of whatever, stretching across the narrow valley, making a pulsing lake where once there had been houses, trees and a road.

The water level fell remarkably fast, leaving black slime behind on broken-off tree stumps and muddy dirt. Dobbs looked for the house to emerge above the waters, the roof peeking out of the flow, though the water was low enough he should be able to see it by now. Then he realized there was no house to see. It was gone. The garage was gone. The old car in the driveway and the poverty-debris in the front yard — the washing machine or dryer or whatever it was, the old outhouse that'd leaned precariously out over the creek. Gone.

His Jeep. Gone.

As the raging flood diminished, the water now probably no more than three or four feet deep, it was clear that when it was done, when the fury had completely spent itself, there would be nothing left to mark its passing but a swath of black muck, a slash of slime on bare dirt from the top of the hollow all the way to the meadow, where the water was now spreading out to wash away the daisies and wildflowers, bury them in washed-away debris and coagulated goo that stunk of sulfur and chemicals and death.

The old woman below him spoke for the first time. Her voice wasn't hoarse, so perhaps she hadn't been screaming after all.

"Smell that? Some fool done burnt the beans. I swear, if idiots was quarters we could buy ourselves a waffle iron."

Dobbs realized he was still clutching her arm — a miracle he hadn't broken it and maybe he had. Surely, the woman had all manner of injuries he couldn't see and she couldn't yet feel. But she was alive. She'd survived.

"She's got the old-timers disease," her son said, and Dobbs let go of the woman's arm and turned to look at him. The man continued to hold his mother's other arm as he spoke. "She ain't got no idea what just happened."

"You keep talkin' 'bout me like I ain't here, boy, and I'm gonna snatch you bald-headed." She looked down at her body. "Don't you think you went a little overboard with the sunscreen?"

His wife approached then. Making her way down the hillside toward them with the girl behind her, she stopped short of the high-water mark of black mud that rose up on the hillside. She looked out over the lowering waters of the black lake that had taken from her everything she owned in the world.

The man spoke again, his face as solemn as hers.

"You owe me a hundred-and-fifty dollars," he told Dobbs.

Dobbs just looked at him.

He nodded toward the ebbing black waters and smiled, showing his one perfect white tooth and the crooked one above it. "But seein' as how you maybe lost the cash, I take plastic."

"Copy." The dispatcher maintained professional calm, but Brice could hear the wonder and horror in her voice. "Dispatch fire, rescue, all officers and emergency personnel to Turkey Neck Hollow."

Then the radio was silent. There was no sound but the screech of the tires on the road as he careened around corners *knowing he would meet no oncoming traffic.*

When he rounded the last bend, his headlights reflected nothing back to him. Illuminated nothing. The light reached out into the darkness and broke like foaming surf over ... nothing. There was only a black hole, a cave. But shiny black, motor-oil black.

His gasp pulled no air into his lungs.

No nightmare conjuring of imagination could have produced the absolute desolation that opened up in front of his cruiser. Everything ... *everything* was gone. Erased. Wiped out and carried away by an oily monster that slimed every surface it touched with black goo.

No living being could possibly have survived contact with the creature. It was an instrument of instant devastation and destruction. All the horsemen of the Apocalypse riding in wild abandon down the mountainside.

He might have made some kind of sound, a grunt perhaps, some verbal expending of the emotion that had tied his gut into a knot from the moment he picked up the minion hair band out of the dirt. He had it in his pocket.

Then his headlights illuminated movement.

Someone was running! Racing down — not the road, there was no road anymore — through the mud toward the far end of the hollow.

BAILEY STAGGERED off through mud so sticky it sucked her shoes off her feet in half a dozen steps. It didn't matter, she kept going barefoot, her heart in her throat. Now that she had been through it, survived it, she fully understood how little time there had been, how balanced on a knife's edge living and dying had been. One fall, one wasted second, one balking child or hesitant parent and…

The others could be somewhere in this mess, washed down the hollow with the goo, their bodies deposited in puddles as the flood spread out on the meadow at the end of the valley. The image of the painting of Macy Cosgrove flashed through her mind but she banished it instantly.

It had not happened.

Macy had survived. *She was alive,* up on a muddy hillside with her family. They had stopped the "what hadn't happened yet" from happening to her. Macy was safe.

But what about T.J. and Dobbs? They were old men, didn't move fast … though, now that she thought about it, she suspected T.J. could move as fast as somebody half his age. He was lithe and agile. Not Dobbs, though. He was big and clumsy and she was sure the best he could muster would be to lumber forward like a mastodon. And that wasn't fast enough.

The other houses, how many of them were occupied — two, three, half a dozen? What if they'd been unable to convince those people to leave? She had managed it by kidnapping two children and running off with them but T.J. and Dobbs wouldn't have had that option. How had they persuaded … there'd been *no time for talk!*

She struggled forward as fast as she could toward what used to be a road that led down the hollow toward the meadow.

Suddenly, twin sabers of bright light stabbed through the darkness, followed by red and blue alternating flashes of light, bouncing off the shiny black surfaces of mud-slathered everything. She turned toward them, up the road that led back the way she and the others had come, where a dirt track had snaked up the other side of the hill to the dam and sludge lake at the top of the mountain. The dam that wasn't there anymore, the lake that had now smeared its putrid ugliness over every surface for as far as the eye could see.

The saber lights drilled through the darkness, growing brighter and she stood staring, blinded so she had to squint and look away, as the white sheriff's department cruiser roared down what was left of the road, then slowed to a crawl and made its way out across the muddy black wasteland toward her.

Brice! One part of her mind produced a snarky *So he decided to come to the party after all*. But the whole rest of her rejoiced at the sight of him and raced toward the car.

He had stopped and was about to open his car door, but she cried out, "No! We have to find the others."

She ran around the front of the cruiser, grabbed the door handle but it slipped out of her muddy hand. A second try flung the door open and she slid into the seat beside him.

The look on his face. Maybe there was an artist somewhere talented enough to capture it, maybe the ghost of Sophia Watford herself, though you really didn't want *her* painting your portrait. Disbelief paired with wonder and relief. With a side order of pure, stunned surprise.

And a pinch of revulsion.

It occurred to her then what she must look like. *Smell* like. But none of that mattered now.

"T.J. and Dobbs — they're down the road. We have to find them."

The terror in her voice was apparently contagious, because he put his foot on the accelerator and threw mud out behind the back tires, let off then, realizing he was driving on a substance resembling gorilla snot, and proceeded with caution and care.

Caution and care were not what Bailey had in mind.

"Go on! Hurry. They might be—"

Might be what? In truth, there was no need at all for haste. No peril anymore from which they could be rescued. Either they had made it or they hadn't. They'd survived, or their bodies were lying in black goo in a meadow a mile down the valley.

They rounded a curve and Brice's headlights illuminated a tree on the right side of the road. It stood sentinel there on the stark landscape, black goo rising up on its trunk, the only thing that had not been washed away.

As they neared it, Bailey saw people climbing down out of the branches of the tree! Her eyes devoured one, then another — there he was!

T.J. had just let go of a low limb and dropped to the muddy earth, catching himself with a hand on the tree trunk when he slipped. She flung the door open and jumped out. He wiped his hand off on his pants and she realized he was clean just in time to abort her intended bear hug. But when she crossed into the headlights where he could see her, he grabbed her in a hug of his own.

"Dobbs," he said, and they both looked down the road into the darkness.

W‍ITH B‍AILEY in the front seat and T.J. in back, Brice headed slowly down the not-road toward where the hollow opened out into a meadow. Through the buzzing in his ears, he could hear the distant symphony of sirens he had summoned, their wailing growing louder by the moment.

There were no landmarks, nothing recognizable that granted special recognition. It was like driving down through the spout used to pour motor oil into your car. Everything in every direction was shiny black.

"Maybe wasn't nobody living in the houses down this way," T.J. said. "Or maybe he knocked and they wasn't nobody home, they was visiting family or went to a movie or something."

Maybe Dobbs had just kept driving, out around the bend where the creek and road hugged the side of the mountain and the hollow emptied into a meadow.

Maybe he was fine, just fine. Safe.

Brice saw him catch himself then, and he stopped launching maybes out into the air and fell silent.

No one else in the car spoke. They inched along with him operating the searchlight on the top of the cruiser, gliding it along the bottom of the mountainside, illuminating black lumps of unidentifiable nothing slimed with goo.

"There!" Bailey pointed, and Brice moved the beam forward slightly. Up above the black smear of the flood, *there were people in the woods!* They were beginning to make their way downward. Dobbs was unmistakable, a big man whose white t-shirt stuck out like a beacon above his blackened pants, trailing a small band of survivors behind him.

Brice didn't have to look at T.J. to see the smile on his face, could almost feel it, the warmth from it would have melted the frost off a windowpane. He was chuckling softly.

The sheriff drove around what was probably the foundation of a house, and toward the base of the incline.

The wailing of sirens was close now, screaming into the night. If not for Bailey's painting, they would have had the grisly task of digging more than a dozen bodies out of the goo.

Dobbs called out, "We'll need a stretcher here. Could be Granny's hurt, but she for sure can't walk even if she's not hurt."

T.J. and Bailey got out and joined Dobbs in the glare of the cruiser's headlights. The sirens were upon them now, and other lights were appearing at the bottom of the hollow, red and blue bubble-gum lights that reflected off the slick black walls of the hollow above.

The sheriff got out to direct the efforts of the would-be rescuers, heard Dobbs comment on how lovely Bailey looked tonight and he remembered. He fished in his pocket until he found it, then held out to her the broken minion hair band he'd found in the dirt above the dam.

"Maybe you could Super Glue it." She took it, but said nothing. Then he walked away, left the three of them there alone together, talking among themselves.

Chapter Thirty-One

T.J. WATCHED Bailey's efforts to guide Dobbs and the sheriff as they moved the heavy chifforobe first one direction and then another. Her face was flushed — August heat in an un-air-conditioned house, even one with fourteen-foot ceilings, would do that to you. Dobbs had offered to get her a couple of window units, but she'd told him she was fine.

And she looked fine. Better than T.J.'d ever seen her, though he understood the "Bailey Donahue" he saw before him was a shadow of someone else she had once been, someone happy. She never talked about her past and he never asked. But he seen her, the way she looked at Macy the day they'd had that celebration picnic in the park. It was a mother look if ever there was one. Yearning in it that'd break your heart.

But she never said, and he never asked.

Course, the look Macy's father had given Bailey that day was a father look, too — a father bear protectin' his cubs. All the rest had saluted the explanation Sheriff McGreggor had run up the flagpole the night of the flood. Lame as it was, T.J. gave the sheriff points for creativity. Brice had hauled out the same cock-and-bull story for Fletch, who'd been there to celebrate that day, too, looking thin and weak but getting around good. Brice had described how Bailey'd been at the dock when that Derrick Osbourne fella come in to gas up the houseboat the day he bought the chair, overheard him braggin' to his buddies about the "big bang" he was gonna make in Turkey Neck Hollow, talking crazy-like, about the itsy bitsy spider and how he'd 'wash the spider out.' She hadn't paid it no mind, of course, had just moved to Kavanaugh County and didn't even know where Turkey Neck Hollow was. But after Osbourne shot Fletch and run off, she'd mentioned the conversation to T.J. and Dobbs and they'd come up with the crazy notion Osbourne was gonna blow up the dam.

Fletch'd swallowed the tale. Of course, there were folks a whole lot quicker on the uptake than Fletch.

Seth Cosgrove had seen through it like it was cling wrap.

Guess you couldn't blame the man for takin' a dislike to Bailey. He'd watched her snatch up his baby son and run off with him, after all, and that'd put a bad taste in anybody's mouth. But it was her connection to Macy that'd really got under his skin. How'd she get his little girl to run away with her like she done? Questioning Macy only produced a smile and an enigmatic, "She was my friend." The fact that what Bailey done had saved the lives of his entire family had somehow got lost in the weeds in his head. He looked daggers at her whenever he seen her and the sheriff'd advised Bailey to give the man a wide berth.

Seth had pointedly looked the other way when T.J. waved at him in town this morning on his way to help with the chifforobe, which T.J.'d got out of moving by complaining he was too old, to which Dobbs had said they were the same age. And then he'd laid claim to a bad back, to which Dobbs burst out laughing. Then he'd said Dobbs and the sheriff was plenty and T.J.'d just get in the way. Dobbs had rolled his eyes then, give up and kept on shovin'.

T.J. didn't really mind helping, of course, just wiggled out of it to irritate Dobbs.

When they finally had it where Bailey wanted, the four adjourned to the kitchen where Bailey provided lemonade and chocolate chip cookies.

"They're homemade." She waved a chunk of cookie dough in a wrapper around like a baseball bat. "I cut them off this thing and cooked them. That makes them homemade."

There was laughter among them, soft as blossoms falling off a dogwood tree, no sharp edges nowhere. They'd done what they'd done and a dozen people was alive that would have died if he had "minded his own business," as Bailey had told him to do, back in Before. Yeah, his life'd been chopped in two again with an axe. Into Before, which seemed a lifetime ago instead of only a month, and After, which was whatever come next.

They didn't speak of it, though. To do so was to bring up the why of it all, the painting, and any time the conversation got into the same UPS Delivery Zone as that, Bailey paled and that haunted look come into her eyes that T.J. was so familiar with.

He'd seen it before.

Only once was the painting mentioned — the day of the flood, just before dawn when they'd brought Bailey home. They had all three waited for her to shower. T.J.'d carried out the clothes she'd been wearing and dumped them into the garbage barrel behind the house. Dobbs had sat on the porch swing — Bailey could hose the mud off it later — eating nuked-up pizza that had sat untouched on the kitchen counter after they went runnin' off to Turkey Neck Hollow.

Bailey had come downstairs, her hair still wet, and looked T.J. square in the eye.

"If it weren't for you, I would be dead right now and so would a dozen other people," she'd said. When he had lifted his hands to protest, she'd plowed right over him. "Thank you for giving me my life back." And she had hugged him hard and kissed him on the cheek.

Then she'd turned toward the closed door of her studio.

"When I get up tomorrow, I'm going to burn them both." She didn't have to tell them both what. She'd turned back and a steel thread of determination hardened her voice. "And I'm not *ever* going to paint anything like that again!"

Now, he watched Sparky work his magic, wagging his tail and looking pathetic so Bailey'd give him another dog biscuit out of the jar of them she kept for him on the counter.

She shooed them out after that and went back to "rearranging her furniture," saying the Watford House, when she got through with it, would be "restored to its former glory … except with Ikea furniture."

He walked down the steps with Dobbs and the sheriff. Dobbs had parked in the driveway the brand new, shiny, all-the-bells-and-whistles black Jeep he'd bought to replace the one that'd been washed away. He'd also replaced what the Turkey Neck Hollow "refugees" had lost in the flood, only they didn't know it. He'd set up a fund administered by the sheriff's department as an "anonymous benefactor" — swearing Brice to absolute secrecy — to pay for housing and the essentials to get the three displaced families back on their feet again.

The three men stopped beside Brice's cruiser at the curb.

"We got to stay nearby, all of us. Stick close." He looked at the sheriff, a man he didn't think needed any encouragement to stick close to Bailey. "They's things you don't know, Brice. About my mama."

"You said the picture of Bailey was the last thing she painted before she committed suicide, right?"

"They's more."

He looked at Dobbs, who nodded.

"I b'lieve my mama killed herself because of the picture of a fire she painted, a horrible house fire that killed a whole family. Three days later, she hung herself with a piece of extension cord from a barn rafter."

Dobbs put in, "And it was during those three days that she painted the picture of Bailey."

"Didn't you say she destroyed all the pictures she painted? Then why not that one?"

"I don't know. I know she always destroyed the pictures *after* whatever it was they'd predicted happened. Somebody would fall off a roof or get run over by a truck. Then after my daddy went to work at the mill the next day, she'd go out to the chicken house where she'd hid the painting, break it up into nothing but pieces of canvas and sticks of wood. She'd pour gasoline over the pile, and strike a match. She always stood there the whole time, 'til there wasn't no trace left of the painting."

"There were times, though, that his mama painted something awful and it seemed like nothing happened. We'd wait and wait, wondering. At first, we thought that not everything she painted came true."

"But when you seen my mama paint one of them things, you knew she lived it. That it really happened … somewhere."

"We finally decided that whatever she painted *did* happen, but not always where we knew about it. Possum Run Hollow in the fifties was about as isolated as the far side of the moon."

"Even when we didn't hear, Mama *knew.* In the same way Bailey 'connected' to Macy Cosgrove."

"You're saying if Bailey had done nothing, if she had ignored you … which any sane, rational person would have done, and Macy *had* drowned, then the connection would have broken?"

"Yep. Bailey might still be on the line but Macy'd hung up her end."

T.J. could see Brice connecting the dots.

"But your mother made no connection to Bailey, one way

or the other. She couldn't have because Bailey hadn't even been born."

"That fire Mama painted, that's why she killed herself. I thought so at the time and I still do. But as a kid, I didn't understand the *whole* why."

"We all knew the Monroe family. They had a brand-new baby, wasn't even a week old."

"Mama even held it, a sweet little baby girl."

"They were asleep when the fire started and the whole family died."

"Mama knew the when. There was charred Easter baskets in the painting. We seen them baskets sitting out on the porch when we passed by their house that afternoon."

"Knowing it was going to happen … and doing nothing." Dobbs shook his head. "How hard would *that* be to live with?"

"Wasn't just guilt. She lived it, *burned to death with those people* — and that was the final straw. She just wasn't able to go through that kind of thing time and time again."

T.J. took a deep breath and let it out slowly. He looked toward the house where Bailey was "returning the Watford House to its former glory."

"Now, I think it was something else, though, pushed her over the edge."

He was quiet for so long, Brice finally asked, "What else?"

"The only time my daddy ever knowed about the things Mama painted — that one time with the little girl who got strangled — he told Mama she was a witch. And she b'lieved him. What else was she s'posed to believe? She maybe went through third grade in school, lived her whole life two miles from where she was born. What other explanation was there?"

T.J.'d been staring out into space as he spoke but now he turned to Brice.

"When I say my mama changed after she started painting them pictures, I mean more than just being freaked out by livin' pieces of other people's lives. *She* changed. Everything 'bout her changed. She had this horrible power and *not a soul in her life to tell about it.* She couldn't share the burden of knowin' something awful was about to happen, not understandin' why she knew. She was isolated, afraid, ashamed and *alone.* I think *that's* what really killed her."

He stopped then and his face hardened.

"That, and…" T.J. stopped and took a breath. He *never* allowed himself to think about his father. His grandmother, who'd come from Nashville to look after the children, found their father passed out in the snow, froze to death the following winter. "The night my daddy found the painting that almost got him hung, he told Mama she was a witch. He also told her if he ever caught her painting another one of them pictures, he'd kill her … he would take her out into the backyard where we burned the garbage, where she burned untold numbers of canvasses he never knew nothin' 'bout … and he'd pour gasoline on her and burn her at the stake."

T.J. saw Brice stiffen at the mental image.

"I b'lieve my daddy meant ever word of that. My mama b'lieved it, too. And I think after she lived through the fire she painted, *lived it,* she … didn't want to die that way. And she just couldn't go on, not *all by herself.*"

He stopped and looked pointedly into the faces of the other two men standing by the cruiser.

"They's three *other* people in the world 'sides Bailey who know what she can do, believe she's not making somethin' up and ought to be hauled off to St. Somebody's Home for the Bewildered. Bailey *ain't* alone like Mama was, carryin' that awful burden by herself. That's why we got to stick close."

The sheriff understood, looked like he agreed, but couldn't see the kind of urgency in the situation that T.J. did.

"But you heard her when we brought her home. She said she was never going to paint another painting like that — ever. I wouldn't be surprised if she locked up her paints or threw them out."

NINIE HAMMON

"Then she'll just doodle a picture with a crayon on the back of a grocery sack," Dobbs said.

"Or take a piece of charred stick out of the fireplace and draw on the floor," T.J. said.

"You're saying she can't—"

"I'm saying she can't *not* paint."

Ice water started to inch down T.J.'s backbone. He could almost believe he heard the hollow sound of it drippin' from one vertebra to the next.

"*Something* … reaches out through Bailey's canvas. Same thing as usta reach out through my mama's. And it *messes* with stuff happenin' out here in the real world. That *something* — it's calling the shots. Bailey's just along for the ride — in one of them cheap, chewing-on-your-knees seats in the back of the bus."

THE END

The Series Continues...

A boy vanishes from a Shadow Rock school playground and Bailey offers to help. But when she attempts to paint a portrait of the missing boy, she paints a little girl instead. Who is the mysterious little girl? What's her connection to the boy? As more children disappear, Bailey races the clock to unravel a twisted web of lies before the children are lost forever.

Pick Up Your Copy of Red Web Today

A Note from the Author

Thank you for reading *Black Water*.

If you enjoyed this book please consider writing a review of it on your favorite bookseller's website so other readers might enjoy it too. Just a couple of sentences would mean a lot to me.

Thank you!
Ninie Hammon

About the Author

Ninie Hammon (rhymes with shiny, not skinny) grew up in Muleshoe, Texas, got a BA in English and theatre from Texas Tech University and snagged a job as a newspaper reporter. She didn't know a thing about journalism, but her editor said if she could write he could teach her the rest of it and if she couldn't write the rest of it didn't matter. She hung in there for a 25-year career as a journalist. As soon as she figured out that making up the facts was a whole lot more fun than reporting them, she turned to fiction and never looked back.

Ninie now writes suspense--every flavor except pistachio: psychological suspense, inspirational suspense, suspense thrillers, paranormal suspense, suspense mysteries.

In every book she keeps this promise to her Loyal Reader: "I will tell you a story in a distinctive voice you'll always recognize, about people as ordinary as you are--people who have been slammed by something they didn't sign on for, and now they must fight for their lives. Then smack in the middle of their everyday worlds, those people encounter the unexplainable--and it's always the game-changer."

Also By Ninie Hammon

Cornbread Mafia

Fire In The Hole

Blown' Up A Storm

Ridin' For A Fall

So Shall The Tree Grow

Nowhere, USA

The Jabberwock

Mad Dog

Trapped

The Hanging Judge

The Witch of Gideon

Blown Away

Nowhere People

Through The Canvas Series

Black Water

Red Web

Gold Promise

Blue Tears

The Taken Saga

The Taken

The Changed

The Hidden

The Saved

The Unexplainable Collection

Five Days in May

Black Sunshine

The Based on True Stories Collection

Home Grown

Sudan

When Butterflies Cry

The Knowing Series

The Knowing

The Deceiving

The Reckoning

The Fault

Stand-alone Psychological Thrillers

The Memory Closet

The Last Safe Place

www.ingramcontent.com/pod-product-compliance
Lightning Source LLC
Chambersburg PA
CBHW010527100726
47903CB00011B/2920